WIZARD

By Ken Warner

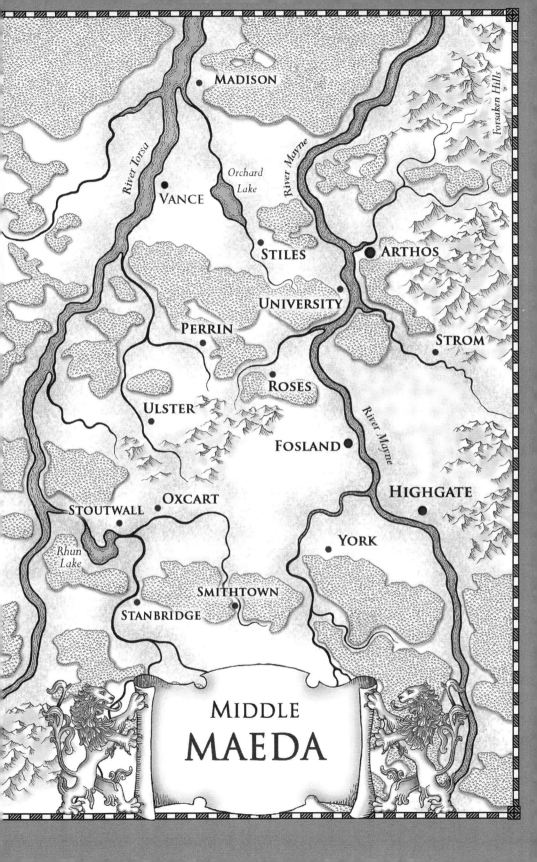

MADISON

River Torsa

VANCE

Orchard Lake

River Mayne

STILES

ARTHOS

Forsaken Hills

UNIVERSITY

PERRIN

STROM

ROSES

ULSTER

FOSLAND

River Mayne

OXCART

HIGHGATE

STOUTWALL

Rhun Lake

YORK

SMITHTOWN

STANBRIDGE

MIDDLE
MAEDA

CONTENTS

WIZARD

PROLOGUE

yron heard the trumpets and sat up straight, a jolt of fear wracking his body. Had he imagined that? No, now there were drumbeats, too.

He got to his feet, grabbed his staff, and ran into the corridor. Reaching the tower, he hurried up the steps, emerging on the roof. This location afforded him the best view of the land surrounding the castle. And there could be no mistaking what he saw below: an entire army marching toward them. Wearing Fosland's uniforms and flying its flag. Then he spotted the rider leading the troops and blanched. He'd recognize that witch's flaming red hair anywhere.

Byron had enjoyed his life as a court mage. Stanbridge was a small princedom, and its location held no strategic value; the prince was a peaceful man with no tyrannical impulses. But Byron knew that the quiet life he loved so much had just reached its end. Stanbridge had no standing army.

As one of the prince's top advisers, it was his solemn duty to evacuate the royal family from the castle in the face of imminent death. But he had a deeper responsibility to fulfill first—to the university and ultimately to the entire continent. Fosland didn't share a border with Stanbridge. So there was only one reason High Prince Henry would send an army here.

Byron had begged his prince to send the artifact to the university to be destroyed many times over the years, starting the day he'd been assigned here and learned of the object's existence. But the prince refused. Always. The artifact was a family heirloom, passed down for generations, and he wouldn't be the one to surrender it.

Thankfully, the prince had never asked Byron to use it. Not that the wizard would have had the first clue what to do with the thing. And luckily, the prince's ancestors and their mages had seen fit to hide it out of plain sight. But Byron was no fool; that was Nineve out there. It was only a matter of time before the witch would find the thing and take it to Henry.

There was only one thing Byron could do. He had to send a messenger to the university to warn the governors. Hopefully, they could dispatch someone to retrieve the artifact before it was too late.

CHAPTER ONE
AMBUSH

ira gazed down the road, back the way they'd come. It was nighttime, the twin crescent moons providing the only light. There was movement, but it was still far off, and she couldn't tell for sure who or what it was. But it sounded like a group of people on horseback moving quickly toward them. Her mount snorted nervously.

"We should get off the road and let them pass, my lady," said Oscar. He was one of the three soldiers her father had sent with her on this journey. The other two stood by him, staring into the distance, their expressions grim.

"Oh, for heaven's sake, would you *please* stop addressing me that way?"

Oscar had been a member of her father's guard for a couple of years now, but he'd been her closest friend for far longer than that.

"I'm afraid not, my lady," he replied with a grin. "We must observe protocol when we're on duty."

Heaving a sigh, she followed the men toward the trees. They positioned their horses to keep themselves between her and the road and drew their swords. Mira grasped her wand but kept it concealed beneath her cloak. Within minutes, she could see that about a dozen riders were approaching. As they came closer, she realized they were soldiers, but their colors and sigil were not those of the local princedom.

"Identify yourselves," one of the men demanded, separating from the others as they came to a halt. He took in her guards' weapons but did not draw his own.

"You first," said Oscar, his tone calm but confident. "You display Fosland's banner, but this is Oxcart unless our map is out of date."

The soldier grasped the handle of his sword but still didn't draw it. "I don't recognize your uniforms. You must be from somewhere faraway—what brings you to this area?"

"We are from Blacksand, in the northwest of Dorshire, where we serve the Lord Grisham of Graystone. Our business here is our own, but I assure you it doesn't concern you."

The soldier locked eyes with Mira for a moment and nodded. "We are seeking an outlaw who escaped from us in Stanbridge. His trail disappeared in Oxcart Town, but witnesses there told us they saw him fleeing this way up the road. Have you seen him?"

"We left the town ourselves just before sunset," Oscar told him. "But you are the first people we have encountered since then. I'm sorry we can't help you."

The soldier turned to look back at his comrades, and Mira gasped, noticing their wizard for the first time. The man was a giant mass of flesh with wild hair and a graying beard that hung to his waist. His staff looked more like a tree trunk than the slender rods most mages favored. For a moment, Mira felt a tingle down her spine and guessed that he must have cast some sort of spell, but the sensation stopped, and nothing else happened. He nodded, the motion barely perceptible, and turned to speak with one of the others.

"Very well," the soldier said to Oscar. "Keep an eye out for him; our prince has offered a reward for his safe return. But beware—he's sneaky and dangerous." He guided his horse back to the rest of the group, and they resumed their course to the north.

"Let's slacken our pace," Oscar suggested as they returned to the road. "I do not wish to encounter them again—Fosland's forces do not belong in Oxcart *or* Stanbridge. Their story about seeking an outlaw does not ring true."

"No, it certainly doesn't," Mira agreed. "Part of me feels like we should go back and warn the prince of their intrusion, but I think I'd prefer to keep going."

They'd been on the road for many weeks now, and based on the information her father's envoy had given them, they'd expected to find the wayfarers camped right outside of the town. But upon their arrival, a couple of locals told them that the troupe had moved on earlier that same day. Mira still hoped to catch up to them that night. The moons provided enough light for them to travel.

"Well, they didn't seem too interested in us," said Harry, one of the other guards.

"And a good thing that is—their mage had a sinister look about him," added Thomas, the third guard.

"An understatement," Mira told him. "That was Gunthar."

"I thought so," said Oscar, his expression dark. "But that's the first time I've seen him. Matches his description well enough."

"Never heard of him," said Harry. "Who is he?"

"One of High Prince Henry's mages," Oscar replied. "He's got a nasty reputation, that one."

"*High* Prince Henry?" asked Thomas. "What makes him a *high* prince?"

"He's annexed two neighboring princedoms," Oscar explained. "That's the title he's taken as a way of placing himself above the other princes. Rumor has it he's planning on conquering the rest of Maeda and restoring the old kingdom."

"Which could explain his presence here and in Stanbridge," Mira noted. "Perhaps the rumors are true. Although it would take more than twelve men to sack a princedom."

"And why is Gunthar so bad?" asked Harry. "He looked like a fat slob to me."

Thomas sniggered. "Aye, he did—I think I spotted a bit of mutton in his beard."

"He's a fat slob who was expelled from the university and arrested for raping and murdering three young witches," said Mira.

"He's Henry's attack dog," Oscar added. "Sends him in whenever he needs someone killed. Not much for brains, I'm told, but Henry doesn't pay him to think."

"I fear he did something when their soldier was talking to us," said Mira. "Some sort of magic—I could feel it, but I couldn't identify the spell."

"Let's hope he didn't realize that you're a mage," Oscar replied. "Henry's always looking to add to his stable."

Mira knew he was right and shivered slightly. The thought of Henry capturing her was terrifying; every holding on the continent had heard of him and the tyranny he inflicted upon his people. Most princes had two or three mages on staff, but Henry had assembled a small army of them. The university had issued an alert that he was abducting wizards and witches who crossed his lands. Mira had been glad that there would be no reason to enter his territory on this journey. But now, this encounter had her worried. She hoped they would reach their destination before running into the Foslanders again.

They continued for several minutes in silence. Mira's thoughts returned to the wayfarers and her imminent reunion with the troupe. In particular, she thought of Khaldun, and her heart skipped a beat. She'd dreamed about seeing him again since the day she left for her father's holding. But after so many years, she wondered if he'd even remember her. They were older, and he was certain to have lost interest in her long ago, especially in light of the wayfarer lifestyle. The promises they'd made seemed silly now—borne of the childish crushes they'd had for each other. Mira had been only twelve then, and Khaldun just a few months older.

Yet the butterflies in Mira's stomach persisted. She'd kept her feelings for Khaldun locked away in her heart, nurturing her hope that one day they'd meet again. Much to her father's chagrin, she'd brushed aside the flirtations of more appropriate and more local suitors. He'd hoped to arrange a mutually advantageous marriage for her to some other lord's heir, but Mira had refused to play along. The highborn life felt like a prison to her, and she yearned for the freedom of the wayfarers.

Suddenly Thomas made a gurgling sound, bringing his hands to his throat. Mira realized with a start that he had an arrow protruding from his neck. Blood was gushing out of the wound.

"Oscar!" Mira shouted as Thomas fell off his horse; the other two reined in their mounts.

But at that moment, five men stepped out of the trees—the mage, Gunthar, and four Foslander soldiers. One had an arrow nocked in his bow, pointing it at Harry; the others had their swords drawn. Oscar drew his sword as Mira dismounted and moved toward Thomas.

"Not another step," Gunthar ordered, his voice gravelly. He held his staff in front of him; Mira could feel the power of his spell wash over her. This time, she recognized it, but still, it did nothing. "As I suspected," he muttered.

"Our prince will hear of this outrage!" Oscar shouted, moving his mount to shield Mira from the archer. "Let us go if you wish to live!" Mira knew this was an empty threat but appreciated the effort.

Gunthar chuckled. "Where is it you're from again? Blackshit? Crapsand? Practically the other side of the world."

Another soldier emerged from the trees before Oscar could reply. "Sir, we've found the messenger."

"About time," Gunthar muttered. "You four, bind the girl. She's coming with us. Make sure you take her wand. Kill the boys."

Gunthar followed the new arrival into the forest. The archer shot Harry through the eye; his corpse toppled off his mount.

"No!" shouted Oscar. Then, urging his horse into motion, he swung his sword and decapitated the archer. But as the other three soldiers advanced on him, he took off down the road, leaving Mira with the men.

"Oscar!" she screamed, her heart hammering in her chest. But it was no use; he was gone. What the hell was he doing? Never did she think he'd abandon her like this. What was she supposed to do now? She thought about jumping back onto her horse and galloping off in the other direction, but one of the soldiers grabbed the dead man's bow and pointed an arrow at her.

"Not so fast, little lady," he said. Mira realized he was missing his front teeth. "You stay right there."

"What about the boy?" one of the other soldiers demanded.

"We'll get him later," the toothless man said. "It's this one Gunthar wants."

Mira grasped her wand inside her cloak. But the instrument was useless to her in this situation.

"Hand it over," the toothless soldier ordered. "No funny business, or I'll put this arrow in ya."

"Gunthar wants me alive."

"Oh, you'll live," he said with a leer. "But it's gonna be hard to think about your spells with this thing stickin' outta your leg, I reckon."

Mira pulled out her wand, holding it out to one of the soldiers. He snatched it from her and handed it to the toothless one while the remaining two pulled out some twine. One tied her wrists together while the other took care of her ankles. The toothless one kept the arrow on her the whole time. Once they'd finished binding her, they removed the pack from one of the horses, tossing it into the trees, and hoisted Mira over the animal's back in its place. Toothless climbed into the saddle in front of her, the other two mounted the remaining horses, and they headed up the road.

8

"Where are you taking me?" Mira demanded.

"Fosland eventually," Toothless replied. "But Gunthar likes to play with the pretty ones for a while before bringing them to His Highness." He giggled to himself.

Mira felt like she might vomit. She took a few deep breaths, trying to stave off a panic attack. Oscar had left her for dead; it was up to her to get out of this. She tried wriggling her hands free, but the twine was too tight; the only thing she accomplished was chafing her wrists against it.

Though she was pretty sure she could bend and twist her way off the horse, she didn't see what good it would do. She'd probably hurt herself landing on the packed dirt of the road, and then they'd just throw her back on the horse again. If they passed any other people, she could scream for help, but it was unlikely any locals would come to her aid against three armed soldiers. But maybe they'd run to the local lord to report the situation, and then *he* could send members of his guard to help.

Of course, it was the middle of the night, so they weren't likely to encounter many other people...

Suddenly, one of the soldiers screamed in pain and fell off his horse. When he hit the ground, Mira could see that he was bleeding from the head; a large, bloody rock had landed in the dirt next to him.

What the hell?

But a moment later, she spotted Oscar jumping out of a nearby tree. He charged the other soldier, driving his sword through his back. The man spewed blood from his mouth for a moment before toppling to the ground.

"Surrender!" Oscar shouted, brandishing his blade at the toothless soldier. "Leave the girl, and I'll let you go free!"

"Fuck yourself!" Toothless yelled, kicking his mount into a gallop. They flew down the road, Mira bouncing painfully on the animal's back; she felt sure she would fall off. The soldier glanced back and said, "Shit."

Mira looked behind them and saw that Oscar had mounted one of the other horses and was charging after them. She decided now was the time to act. Shifting her weight and twisting, she kicked out hard with both legs. It worked—she'd launched herself right off the horse. She hit the ground hard, feet first, before pitching over sideways and rolling several times in the dirt. Her right hip and shoulder hurt from the impact, but she didn't think she'd broken anything. Sitting up, she spotted the toothless soldier reining in the horse and turning around. Oscar pulled up next to her, jumping off his mount.

"My lady, are you hurt?" he asked.

"I'm fine—but look out!"

Toothless was charging toward them now, raising his sword for a mighty swing. Mira managed to roll herself away from the road. Looking back, she saw Oscar dart the other way, opposite the toothless soldier's sword hand. As the man flew past, Oscar stabbed him in the side. The toothless man screamed. His horse slowed to a trot, then stopped as Toothless fell from its back. Oscar ran toward him. The toothless man got to his feet, brandishing his sword in front of him. He swung at Oscar when he approached, but Oscar sidestepped, slicing the back of the man's knee on the way by. He fell to the dirt, dropping his sword and screaming again. Oscar moved in for the kill.

"You said you'd let me live if I freed the girl!"

"You didn't free me!" Mira shouted. "I jumped!"

Oscar stabbed the man in the chest. Mira heard his screams falter as Oscar ran over to her. He cut her bonds and helped her to her feet.

"We need to go, my lady. Can you ride?"

Mira nodded. "Yes, but he's got my wand."

Oscar went back to the man and removed her wand from his pocket. He returned it to her, and then they each mounted one of the horses and galloped down the road. After a few minutes, there had been no pursuit nor any sign of Gunthar and the rest of the soldiers, so they slowed to a trot to give the horses a break.

"I cannot believe you abandoned me like that!" Mira told Oscar. "Never have I been so terrified!"

"Apologies, my lady," he replied. "But it was the only way. The odds were stacked against me—it was three on one, with their mage close by. Only by putting some distance between us and getting off the road was I able to ambush them."

Mira sighed. "You're right, of course. I should have known you'd save me. Can we go back for the other two horses?"

Oscar shook his head. "I don't think so. We've lost the Foslanders for now, but we're not out of danger yet. We should try to find the nearest holding. They can protect us and get word of this incursion to the prince."

"No," Mira replied. "We should still try to find the wayfarers. Gunthar is no match for Nomad—we'll be safe with him."

Oscar nodded. "That would work. And it might be our only choice. Unfortunately, I don't recall where the next holding might be, and the map was in my pack."

"I can't believe they killed Thomas and Harry," said Mira, her eyes welling up with tears. She hadn't known them well before their journey, but they'd been her constant companions for the last several weeks.

"I know, my lady," Oscar agreed. "We will mourn them once we've reached safety."

"Oscar, for the love of the gods, would you *stop* with the 'my lady' bullshit? It's just the two of us now. Surely, you can call me by my name?"

"I'm sorry, my lady," he replied, but this time, he wasn't smiling.

Mira shook her head. They rode in silence for several minutes. But then she spotted a light through the trees up ahead.

"That must be the wayfarer camp," she said, pointing it out to Oscar.

He stared off into the woods for a moment. "Maybe," he said finally. "But there's too much light for campfires."

"Oh, no," said Mira, her heart jumping into her throat.

They pushed their horses to a gallop again. But as they drew closer to the source of the light, they slowed down again. Mira's jaw dropped; she was speechless. The wayfarer camp was in a clearing in the trees, dozens of different-colored tents, maybe a hundred feet from the road—but someone had torched several of them.

Suddenly, someone screamed. Mira spotted a woman running toward them, carrying something in her arms. As she drew closer, Mira realized it was a young child.

"Help me! They're trying to kill my son!"

The woman's clothing was ripped, and there was soot on her cheek. Her hair was flying all over the place, and her eyes were wide with terror. Mira looked down at her child. He was lying limp in her arms; he must have been four or five years old. And he was missing half his skull; his mother must have been in shock.

A little scream parted Mira's lips, and she covered her mouth with one hand, giving Oscar a pleading look.

"Those Foslanders must have done this," she said. "We have to help!"

Oscar was staring off toward the camp, his brow furrowed in concentration. He glanced at Mira, nodding quickly before setting off and drawing his sword. Mira dismounted and guided the woman into the forest. She instructed her to take cover behind the trunk of a fallen tree, then followed Oscar into the camp.

CHAPTER TWO
MASSACRE

haldun took a swig from his bottle. "This is good mead," he said, nodding appreciatively. He was sitting on the ground outside his tent, his back against a tree, staring up at the stars, his staff lying nearby. "Sweeter than your last batch."

"Aye," Arman replied, taking a drink. He was sitting back against an adjacent tree. "Still not as good as the brewer who taught me. But I'll take it."

Khaldun knew he should probably get some rest—Nomad had taken the first watch tonight, and he'd have to relieve him in a few hours. But he was restless. Mira would be arriving any day now, and she was all he could think about.

If he were honest with himself, he *hadn't* thought about her much for at least a couple of years. But the memories of their time together were still some of the fondest of his entire life. She'd been his first crush—and his first kiss. He could never have forgotten her entirely. But ever since word had arrived that she was returning to the wayfarers, he found he couldn't get his mind off of her.

What would she be like now? Would *she* remember *him*? How much would she have changed after living among highborn for so long? Mira had always been a little different from the other wayfarers. Her mother, Nareen, harbored high hopes for her daughter. She'd never let anyone forget that Mira's father was a lord. This had made it difficult for Mira to fit in with the other wayfarer children. Khaldun knew that had been tough on her. Chances were that she hadn't felt a sense of belonging with her father's people, either.

"No sign of her yet, then?" Arman said with a knowing look.

"Huh? Who?"

"Mira, who else? You've been pining after her for days now."

Khaldun let out a long sigh. "I haven't been *pining*. But you're right—she hasn't turned up yet."

Suddenly, there were noises in the forest. Branches cracking. Footsteps. Someone or something was running through the trees. Then there was a wail—it sounded human. Khaldun jumped to his feet, grabbing his staff and trying to see what had made all the noise, but couldn't make out anything in the moonlight.

"It's gone quiet again," Arman whispered a moment later. He was standing now, too. "Probably just a deer or something."

"I don't think so. It sounded like a man—might be those bandits again."

"This far north?" Arman asked skeptically. "We haven't seen them since before Oxcart."

Khaldun took a step toward the trees, but at that moment, a wall of fire erupted out there, and there was a scream. Khaldun could feel the spell's power from where he stood and had no doubt who'd cast it. He returned his staff to its place against the tent and retook his seat by the tree.

"Well, looks like Nomad took care of them… whoever they are," said Arman, sitting down and taking a drink from his bottle.

Khaldun sat back for a few minutes, listening to Arman recount the changes he'd made to his brewing technique to improve his mead. But he was alert now; he couldn't shake the feeling that something was wrong. Then he felt magic in the air—and it wasn't Nomad's this time. Getting to his feet, he grabbed his staff again, trying to sense where the spell had come from.

"What is it?" Arman asked nervously, joining Khaldun and gazing out at the forest.

All the torches in the camp went out at once, and Khaldun heard hoofbeats in the distance. Again, there was a scream—coming from inside the camp this time. Khaldun set off at a run, but before he'd gone more than two steps, a horse whinnied behind him, and Arman yelped. Wheeling around, he spotted the two riders. One had impaled Arman in the chest with his sword; the second was nearly on top of Khaldun.

With no time to cast a spell, he dove to the ground, rolling out of the way. Regaining his feet, he called earth and spoke the word of command as he held out his staff. The spell slammed into the rider, knocking him from his horse. He hit the ground with a grunt. The second rider sped off into the camp, and the riderless horse followed him.

Khaldun found Arman lying face down in the dirt. Dropping to his knees, he rolled him onto his back. He gasped when he saw the pool of blood he'd been lying in, and the wound in his friend's chest.

"Arman!"

But it was no use; his lifeless eyes stared up at the sky. Khaldun felt hot tears streaming down his cheeks, but there was no time to dwell on his loss—the fallen rider was on his feet again, stumbling toward him, brandishing his sword.

Khaldun stood up and called fire. Then, shouting the word of command, he pointed his staff at the soldier and incinerated him from the inside out. The man hit the ground again, wailing for a moment before the flames consumed his entire body.

There was another scream. Khaldun turned in time to see one of the tents burst into flames.

"No!" he shouted, running toward the blaze.

He heard cries coming from inside. Holding out his staff, he called fire—this time to extinguish rather than ignite. He spoke the word of command, and the flames sputtered out. Hurrying inside, he found four children cowering in the far corner behind an older woman. Once he'd made sure they were all right, he rushed out of the tent but stopped in his tracks at the sight before him. Three soldiers on horseback were riding among the tents using their torches to set them ablaze. Cries and screams erupted from inside them; most of their people would have been asleep at this hour, waking now to the flames.

"Hey!" Khaldun shouted, running toward the nearest soldier. The man wheeled his horse around, spotted Khaldun, and charged toward him. Khaldun called earth again, knocking the man from his horse.

But before he could put out the other fires, another soldier emerged from behind one of the tents, only feet away, and lunged toward him with his blade. Khaldun sidestepped, swinging his staff and smashing the man in the back of the head. He hit the ground and dropped his sword; as he scrambled to retrieve his blade, Khaldun called fire, igniting him from within.

Focusing on the three nearest tents, Khaldun called fire again, extinguishing the blazes. One of the riders spotted him and trotted toward him. At the same time, a girl of twelve or thirteen named Karina stepped out of one of the tents, only feet from the soldier. The man grabbed her under the arms and hoisted her onto his horse, right in front of him. Karina screamed.

"Let her go!" Khaldun shouted, holding out his staff and preparing a spell. But the soldier drew a knife and held it to Karina's throat; the girl went still. "Drop your staff, boy, or I'll slit her throat." Karina screamed again. "And you shut your damn mouth!"

"She's only a girl—whatever you people want, she can't help you get it. Set her free!"

"Maybe *she's* what we want, eh?" the man said with a grin. "Spoils of war. But there are plenty more where she came from, so drop the stick, or I'll cut her!"

The soldier had his blade pressed against her neck. Even if Khaldun incinerated him, he might kill her before he died; he couldn't risk it. So instead, he focused on the knife. This might burn the girl's neck, but she'd live. Summoning fire, he held out his staff and spoke the word of command. The knife grew red-hot in an instant; the soldier shouted in surprise, dropping the weapon. Khaldun called earth next; an invisible force slammed into the man's torso, throwing him from the horse. But at that moment, the horse reared, neighing loudly; Karina toppled off his back, and the animal ran into the night. Khaldun rushed to the girl's side, kneeling next to her; she was crying and shaking.

"Are you hurt?" he asked, taking one of her hands.

"N-no," she replied through her sobs. "I'm all right. Y-you saved me—I was so scared!"

"We're not out of danger yet," he told her. "Come on, let's get you to one of the caretakers."

Karina nodded. Khaldun helped her to her feet and guided her through the camp. But before they'd gone twenty yards, a ring of fire sprang up around them. The girl screamed; Khaldun could feel the heat of the spell and backed away from the flames. He extinguished them, revealing a giant mage on horseback standing nearby, flanked by two soldiers. Khaldun recognized him immediately: this was Gunthar, one of High Prince Henry's wizards.

"You must be the sorcerer's whelp," Gunthar said, holding his staff before him. "We can't find *him*, so you'll have to do. We're looking for a messenger who was last seen running for your camp. What have you done with him?"

"I don't know what you're talking about," Khaldun replied, although he thought about Nomad's spell work in the forest earlier and wondered if that had anything to do with this.

"Think harder, boy," Gunthar said, and suddenly a tongue of fire appeared on the ground, only a foot from Khaldun. He tried to cancel the spell, but the flame persisted; Gunthar's power far exceeded Khaldun's. "Things will go very badly for you and your people if you don't turn him over."

"I'm telling you I don't know anything about any messenger!" Khaldun yelled. He gathered all his strength, called earth, and held out his staff, shouting the word of command. His spell should have knocked the wizard from his horse but did nothing. He tried calling fire to ignite him from within, but again, nothing happened.

Gunthar gave a low chuckle. "You're nothing but a gadfly to me, boy. Now surrender that messenger!"

Khaldun grabbed Karina's hand. She looked up at him, fear in her eyes. "Run," he told her, leading her back the way they'd come. But suddenly, a wall of fire erupted before them, twenty feet high. Khaldun tried to cancel the spell, but nothing happened. Pulling up short, he turned toward Gunthar again. The wall of flame grew around them, enclosing them in a semi-circle.

"You're wasting my time," the wizard said. "Give me what I want, or I'll kill you and the little girl." The soldier on his left raised his bow, pointing an arrow at Khaldun. He knew a spell to make himself invisible and could escape using that, but then they'd kill Karina. Khaldun wracked his brain trying to think of a way out of this. He *didn't* know anything about a messenger, but even if he did, Gunthar would probably kill them anyway.

But an instant later, the flames disappeared. Gunthar cried out in surprise. Turning, Khaldun spotted a wayfarer woman standing behind them—the most beautiful woman he'd ever seen, yet she looked only vaguely familiar. She was staring at Gunthar and his soldiers, an expression of steely determination on her face, clutching a wand in her outstretched hand.

"Mira!" Khaldun blurted, needing a second to realize who this was.

Returning his gaze to Gunthar, he called earth, catching the giant wizard off guard and knocking his staff from his hands. Then, with his next incantation, he launched the man off his horse. He fired off two more spells in quick succession to unseat the two soldiers, then turned his attention to Karina and Mira.

"Let's get out of here before he recovers his staff!" said Mira.

Khaldun nodded. Holding Karina's hand, he hurried off toward the other side of the camp, Mira close behind. He found Aynoor, one of the caretakers, huddled with several other children outside the large community tent. A few of the men were with them, standing guard.

"Who are they?" Aynoor asked, taking Karina from him. "Why are they doing this?"

Khaldun shook his head. "They're Foslanders, but I don't know what they're doing here—we're still in Oxcart. They're looking for a messenger. Have any of you seen Nomad?"

"Not since dinner," Aynoor said, looking around at the men. They shook their heads.

"We've got to find him," Khaldun replied. "Come on," he added to Mira.

She nodded, and they set off through the camp.

"The timing of your arrival couldn't have been much better," he told her, stealing a glance as they ran. Mira had grown into a woman in her absence. She wore her long, dark hair in a braid, like the wayfarers, and her lips were fuller than he remembered. Catching his glance, she smiled but then averted her dark eyes. Her sly expression triggered so many memories he hadn't recalled in ages.

Mira told him what had happened on her way to the camp. Khaldun felt a familiar bond with her as she spoke as if their time apart had been erased.

"Where are your guards now?" he asked when she was done.

"Gunthar's men killed two of them. Oscar is here—he was pulling people out of a burning tent when I left him. Where the hell is Nomad?"

"I don't know," Khaldun replied, shaking his head. "But I think he might have found the man they're looking for. We'll see if he's with Badru."

Badru was the wayfarer leader; his tent was at the far end of the clearing. But they arrived to find it empty.

"Damn," said Khaldun, gazing back across the camp. A few more tents had gone up in flames; he could hear people screaming and shouting. "I can't believe Nomad would abandon us like this!"

"Something must have required his attention," Mira suggested. "Let's go put out some fires!"

They hurried back across the camp. Together, they managed to extinguish most of the burning tents, but the soldiers ignited more as they worked. But suddenly, some unseen force ripped Khaldun's staff out of his hand. He turned in time to see Mira's wand fly out of her grasp. A moment later, something lifted him off the ground, suspending him several feet in the air. The Foslander soldiers emerged from behind the surrounding tents, gathering around them with their swords drawn and driving Mira toward Khaldun.

Khaldun struggled against the spell, trying to free himself and return to the ground, but it was futile. Suddenly Gunthar appeared out of thin air in front of them, holding his staff in one hand, and Khaldun's staff and Mira's wand in the other.

"My patience has reached its end," he told them with a growl. "You can turn over the messenger now, or my men will burn your entire camp to the ground!"

But before Khaldun could reply, a deep voice boomed across the clearing.

"Do so, and you shall perish in your own fire."

Gunthar started, looking around in fear. The wand and both staves flew out of his hands and vanished; the soldiers' swords began to glow red, and they dropped them, yelping in pain. Khaldun felt Gunthar's spell dissolve, and he hit the ground. A hooded man appeared out of nowhere, standing between Khaldun and Gunthar.

"Nomad!" said Mira, relief in her voice.

The soldiers turned and ran; Nomad let them go. Gunthar tried to follow them, but Nomad held out one hand, his fingers splayed, and Gunthar rose a few feet into the air; his legs kept working as if he were still running. Finally, Nomad clenched his outstretched fist, and Gunthar turned in midair, coming face-to-face with the sorcerer but still hovering above the ground.

"If you hurt me, Henry will hunt you down," Gunthar told him, a look of terror on his face. "He'll send an army and—"

"Why have you attacked us?" Nomad demanded.

"You have the messenger. Hand him over, and we'll let you be."

"I'm afraid you are mistaken," Nomad replied. "A man from Stanbridge ran through the forest headed north, but he did not enter our camp. I questioned him and let him go on his way."

Gunthar's eyes narrowed, his expression skeptical. "And how did he respond to your *questioning*?"

"He told me he had urgent business with the university. I sensed no deception."

Gunthar seemed to consider his words for a moment. "In that case, release me, and I'll be on my way."

"We'll see," said Nomad, turning toward Khaldun and Mira. His skin was golden and metallic-looking, the irises of his eyes red. "Welcome home," he added to Mira with a smile. "You two should come with me."

Nomad led them farther into the camp, Gunthar floating along behind them. By the far edge of the clearing, Khaldun spotted a group of men striding toward them. It was the wayfarer leader, Badru, with three of the troupe elders. Badru had a dark complexion, like all the wayfarers, and wore his straight, dark hair in a long ponytail.

"Put him down," he said as he passed Nomad and approached Gunthar. The sorcerer returned the mage to the ground but used his powers to keep his arms pinned to his side. Badru drew a knife and held it to the wizard's throat. "You murdered six of our people tonight, including two children. Give me one reason why I should let you live."

Gunthar only glared at him, saying nothing.

"Say the word, and I will end him," said Nomad.

Badru kept the blade against the big man's flesh a moment longer, then said, "Bah. If we kill him, Henry will come after us with a vengeance." Gunthar grinned. "Let him go—but destroy his staff." Gunthar's expression turned into a scowl.

"He'll seek revenge for this," Nomad pointed out.

"Better him than Henry," Badru replied.

Nomad nodded. He held out one hand, and the wizard's staff materialized in his grip; after a moment, it burst into flames and turned to ash. Gunthar stood there staring at him, his eyes wide.

"Get out of our camp before I change my mind," Badru told him.

"You will pay for this," Gunthar told them with his gravelly voice before turning and waddling into the night.

Nomad held out both hands; Khaldun's staff appeared in one, Mira's wand in the other. He handed them their instruments.

"Follow him," Badru said to Khaldun once the mage had moved out of earshot. "Make sure he leaves the camp. Hurt him if he gives you any trouble—but keep him alive. You can take the watch once he's gone."

Khaldun nodded.

"You two, come with me," Badru added to Nomad and Mira. "It's time to interrogate this messenger."

Khaldun raised his eyebrows in surprise as he hurried after Gunthar. So they had the Foslanders' quarry in their possession after all? Maybe that was what had kept Nomad busy. He caught up to

Gunthar but kept his distance. Even without his powers, this one could still be treacherous; and he still had command of his soldiers. The mage glanced back at him over one shoulder but kept walking.

"That little slut's your sweetheart, then?"

"Mind your tongue, or I'll cut it out," said Khaldun.

"Try it and see what happens, boy."

Khaldun glowered at him but said nothing more.

"Where did you find her?" the wizard asked.

"We didn't *find* her. She grew up with our people."

Gunthar grunted. "Well, she ain't no normal mage. You get tired of her, take her to the high prince. He'd pay a nice reward for that one."

"What the hell are you talking about? Of course, she's a normal mage."

"Ask her about it. See what she says."

Khaldun walked in silence for a minute, trying to puzzle out what might be different about Mira, but could think of nothing.

"Anyway, that monster wouldn't give me a reward—he'd just enslave both of us."

Gunthar chuckled. "Aye, he probably would."

They found Gunthar's remaining men gathered by the side of the road. Khaldun kept his distance while the mage conferred with them for a minute before heading off. He made himself invisible and followed them for a couple of miles to make sure they weren't coming back, then returned to the camp.

CHAPTER THREE
THE MESSENGER

ira followed Nomad and Badru across the camp.

"Welcome home, Mira," said Badru. "I'm sorry for this ordeal you've had to endure. I trust the rest of your journey was uneventful?"

"Yes, quite. But we ran into Gunthar and his men before reaching the camp." She told them about the encounter.

"Well, Henry's got plenty of other mages, but we won't have to worry about Gunthar for a while," Nomad said when she was done.

"For a *while*?" asked Mira. "You destroyed his staff—he's powerless now, isn't he?"

"Yes, but Dredmort will undoubtedly provide him with a new one."

"But he'd be starting over again, wouldn't he?"

"There is a spell Dredmort can use to transfer Gunthar's power to his new wand or staff. It will take a few weeks to come to fruition, but he should regain his full strength."

Dredmort was Henry's chief mage. His name struck fear into the heart of any mage who had heard his story. Mira knew that only sorcerers possessed the power to imbue a physical object with magical properties, but as Fosland's chief mage, Dredmort was sure to have a supply of freshly fabricated wands and staves on hand.

"That's good to know," Mira observed. "I always thought losing my wand would mean the end of my magic."

They reached the far end of the camp. Nomad led them a little farther beyond, into an empty area of the clearing, then turned to face the camp. He waved his arm as Mira and Badru gathered behind him. Suddenly a tent popped into existence before them.

"I don't understand," said Mira. "We just walked through that space and there was nothing there—it wasn't merely invisible."

"Correct," Nomad replied. "I tucked it into oblivion to make sure Gunthar couldn't find it." Mira had never heard of such a spell before.

Nomad lifted the flap and held it open as Badru and Mira walked through, then followed them inside. A young man was sitting cross-legged on the ground; he looked up at them in surprise, his expression anxious until he spotted Nomad.

"May I introduce Roland of Stanbridge," said Nomad as the messenger got to his feet. "This is our leader, Badru, and the Lady Mira of Blacksand." The messenger bowed low.

"We have protected you from the Foslanders," said Badru, "at a great cost to our own people. Nomad's delay gave them time to infiltrate our camp and murder several of our people. Now what is this urgent message you carry? It had better be worth it."

"My apologies, my lord," said Roland, bowing again. "As I told your sorcerer earlier, Henry's army arrived in the dead of night. They sacked the castle and murdered Prince Edward and Princess Miriam."

"But Stanbridge does not share a border with Fosland," said Badru.

"No, my lord," Roland agreed.

"I am not a lord—you may call me Badru."

"Yes, sir," said the messenger.

"For what purpose did Henry attack?"

"The court mage, Byron, told me that Stanbridge harbors an ancient artifact that Henry's wizard, Dredmort, greatly desires."

"What kind of artifact?" asked Badru.

"I'm sorry, sir, I do not know. Byron said only that it would give Dredmort power that has not been seen in Anoria for centuries. He sent me to the university—he said their mages would be able to retrieve the artifact and prevent Henry from acquiring it."

"But Henry's army sacked the castle," said Nomad. "Surely it's already too late."

"No, sir," Roland replied. "Byron told me that the artifact is not kept in the castle. Henry's men were searching for it there, but they will not be able to find it."

"Then where is it?" asked Badru.

"I have no idea," said Roland. "Byron didn't tell me in case the Foslanders intercepted me. But he believed the mages at the university would know how to find it."

Badru took a deep breath, considering the situation for a moment. "Well, we have done what we can. We've thrown Henry's men off your trail, and destroyed Gunthar's staff. If you continue on your way, you should be able to make it to the university before the Foslanders can regroup."

"I do not believe they will give up this easily," said Nomad. "There are only so many routes to the university from here. Gunthar will get word to the army and they could have people watching the roads north."

"It's out of our hands," Badru insisted. "If he leaves now, he'll have a head start. It will take time for Gunthar to get a message to his people."

"Perhaps. But by the time he makes it to the university and they send someone to Stanbridge, it may be too late. Henry's people could find this artifact before that."

"What are you suggesting?" asked Badru.

"Khaldun and I could travel to Stanbridge and retrieve it."

"Out of the question," said Badru. "That would leave the troupe unprotected. We cannot take that risk—look what happened tonight.

Without you, we would be defenseless if the Foslanders were to return."

Nomad considered this for a moment. "We could take our people back to Oxcart. Petition the prince to extend his protection until Khaldun and I return."

Badru shook his head. "This artifact is not our problem—let the university take care of it. There is no reason for us to get involved."

"What do you think the artifact might be?" asked Mira.

"I'm not sure," said Nomad. "But consider the facts. Whatever it is, Henry wants it badly enough to dispatch an entire army to a princedom well beyond his borders. And Stanbridge's mage said it would give him power 'not seen in centuries.' That can mean only one thing."

Mira gasped. "Necromancy! Dredmort was expelled from the university for experimenting with it."

"My thought exactly," said Nomad. "Henry has already annexed two princedoms and it is believed he plans on conquering the rest of Maeda and restoring the old kingdom. If he accomplishes this, it will not be safe for us to travel anywhere within his borders."

Badru took a deep breath. "If you *do* go to Stanbridge, you'd have to get past Henry's army," he pointed out. "And at this point, you have *no idea* where they might have hidden the artifact. Do you plan on searching the entire princedom?"

Nomad thought about it for a moment. "Byron gave you no indication where the artifact might be?" he said to Roland.

Roland shook his head. "No, none."

"Yet he believed that mages from the university would be able to find it when Henry's men could not?" Badru said incredulously.

"I guess," Roland said with a shrug.

"Maybe the university already knows where it's hidden," Mira suggested. "They could have some record of it."

"Unlikely," Nomad replied, gazing pensively at the messenger. "The university's stance against necromancy has been unequivocal. They're the ones who eradicated its secrets all those years ago. If they had any record of an artifact like this, they would have sent someone to destroy it long ago. But I have another idea." He approached Roland, extending one hand toward his forehead.

"Wha-what are you doing?" the messenger stammered, backing away from the sorcerer. But suddenly his eyes rolled into his head and he went into a trance.

Nomad closed his eyes. The two of them stood very still for a minute. Finally, Roland came out of his stupor, and Nomad opened his eyes. "As I suspected. Byron implanted a message in his mind, concealed in a way that only a sorcerer would be able to detect."

"I'm sorry, what?" said Roland. "I assure you, he did no such thing—"

Suddenly a cloud of smoke formed in the air between Nomad and Roland. It grew and changed its shape and Mira realized it was turning into a castle. Out behind the structure a second, smaller cloud grew into the shape of a small pyramid.

"The artifact is there," Nomad told them, pointing to the pyramid. "About a thousand feet behind the castle."

Badru took a deep breath, letting it out with a frown. "I still don't like it." Nomad opened his mouth to reply, but Badru held up one hand to stop him. "Let me sleep on it and I'll give you an answer in the morning."

Nomad nodded.

"You are welcome to stay here tonight," Badru said to the messenger. "My people will bring you some bedding. You will have my decision tomorrow."

"Thank you, sir," said Roland, bowing low.

Mira left the tent with Nomad and Badru.

"Have you seen your mother yet?" Badru asked as they walked back into the camp.

"No, but I'll go to her now."

"That would be best—she must be worried sick about you after tonight's events."

"Yes, thank you."

Mira headed off to find Nareen's tent, but ran into Oscar on the way. He was bleeding from a gash in his cheek. "You're injured!"

"Only a shallow wound," he said, touching a finger to his face. "It looks worse than it is, I'll wager."

"All the same, you should see the healer and have him tend to it."

"As you wish, my lady."

Mira rolled her eyes, leading him off through the tents. The healer was quite busy with people injured in the attack; most had suffered burns. Mira told Oscar what she'd learned from Nomad and Badru.

"He should let Nomad retrieve the artifact," Oscar said when she was done. "They cannot risk Henry acquiring it—he could conquer the entire continent with that kind of power."

"Yes, well, we'll see," she replied with a sigh. "What have you been up to since we parted ways?"

"I helped bring some of the injured here once the Foslanders were defeated. But then I went to tend to the horses—the two we abandoned on the road wandered into camp. All four of them are with the wayfarers' animals, now."

"Some good news, at least," Mira said with a sigh. "We should recover Thomas and Harry's bodies in the morning."

"Aye," Oscar agreed. "We can give them a proper burial."

"The wayfarers burn their dead," Mira told him. "We could add them to the pyre."

Oscar nodded. Once the healer had treated his wound, they went to Nareen's tent. The woman was still awake, and hugged Mira when she walked in, crying tears of joy.

"I was so worried about you," she said. "They told me you got caught up in the fight with those Foslanders. You should have let the mages sort it out!"

"Mother, I *am* a mage!"

"You are a lady! You mustn't put yourself at risk like that!"

"She's right, my lady," Oscar agreed with a grin. "You should refrain from putting yourself in harm's way."

"Oh, shush," said Mira, pulling away from Nareen. "Mother, this is Oscar. He is a dear friend, and one of the guards father sent to look after me on the journey here."

"It's a pleasure to finally make your acquaintance, ma'am," Oscar said with a bow. "Mira has told me so much about you—"

Nareen pulled him into a hug. "Thank you for bringing my daughter to me safely."

"We should try to get some sleep," Mira suggested. "We'll need to rise at dawn, and not much of the night remains."

"Yes, my lady," said Oscar, heading out through the flaps.

"Where are you going?" said Mira.

"I'll sleep outside," Oscar told her.

"Nonsense—there's plenty of room for you in here."

"It would not be proper, my lady."

"Oscar, we're not in Blacksand anymore. My people have their own sense of propriety—trust me. It won't be comfortable on the bare ground. You can sleep in here with us—I insist."

Nareen nodded in agreement but Oscar refused. In the end, he agreed to take one of the bedrolls and set it up right outside of the entry.

Mira curled up inside and tried to go to sleep, but it was no use. She was restless and couldn't help reliving the night's events in her mind. The implications of Henry's incursion into Stanbridge were alarming. But more than anything else, she couldn't get her mind off of Khaldun. Her heart had skipped a beat when she'd first seen him rescuing that little girl, despite the impending danger. His dark eyes and long black hair were common among her people, as was his olive complexion. But there was a unique beauty about his face; something about his smile made her melt. She found that her feelings for him, long buried, were resurfacing stronger than ever.

Nareen started snoring, snapping Mira out of her reverie. She gave up on sleep. Getting to her feet, she crept out of the tent as quietly as possible. Oscar was lying still in his bedroll.

"Where are you going, my lady?"

"I can't sleep," she said with a start—she didn't think he was awake. "I'm just going for a walk."

"I'm afraid that's not wise," he replied with a frown. "The Foslanders could still be about. It would be safer to stay in your tent until daylight returns."

Mira sighed. "Don't worry, Oscar—I won't go far. I was thinking of visiting Khaldun—he's on patrol now."

"I'll escort you to him," he said, getting to his feet and strapping on his sword belt.

"Very well," she replied.

They set out across the camp.

"I ran into Nomad during the battle," Oscar told her. "First time I've ever met a sorcerer. I have to say, his appearance startled me at first."

"I've described him to you before."

"Aye, you did. But seeing him firsthand is another matter. Must be convenient being able to cast spells without a wand or staff."

"It's more than that, though," said Mira. "Sorcerers are much more powerful. Their body is a conduit for the magical force and their channels of power are open to the world around them."

"Hmm... if you say so," Oscar replied with a chuckle. "Can't say that I understand any of that stuff. I overheard one of the women saying that Khaldun lives with Nomad. Is he his father?"

"No, Khaldun's parents died from the plague when he was very young."

"Did the sorcerer adopt him, then?"

"Not in the way that you're thinking, no," said Mira. "He took him under his wing—he'd already been training Khaldun in magic when his parents died. But it's different with my people... they raise their offspring communally. And people don't usually get married; most have many different partners."

"Then how does anyone know who their father is? There must be a lot of bastards floating around."

"The concept of a 'bastard' is foreign to them, but it's not uncommon for a child never to know for sure which man is their father."

Oscar shook his head. "So... how do they decide who takes care of which child?"

"They look after all of the children collectively," Mira repeated with a shrug. "But there are certain women who are designated caretakers."

"Their ways seem very strange to me."

"Think of it like this. You grew up with your parents and your older sister—that was your family. For the wayfarers, the entire troupe is their family."

Oscar nodded slowly. "All right. I guess I can understand that. Your mother is different, though. You've always said she wanted you to marry a lord."

"Yes, Nareen is... unique. She fell in love with my father when the troupe passed through Blacksand and got it in her head that she was raising a highborn daughter."

"Ah," Oscar said with a nod. "So I'm guessing you weren't raised communally when you were young."

"No, that's for sure," Mira replied, rolling her eyes. "Nareen guarded her own maternal duties quite jealously."

They stopped at the edge of the camp and Mira looked both ways, trying to find any sign of Khaldun. But suddenly a voice said, "You're up late."

Turning, Mira spotted Khaldun materializing out of thin air; Oscar drew his sword, positioning himself between them. "Oscar, this is Khaldun," Mira said, placing a hand on Oscar's shoulder.

"Oh, forgive me," Oscar replied, sheathing his blade. "You startled me," he added, shaking Khaldun's hand.

"I can't blame you after the night we've had," Khaldun said with a nod.

The two of them looked at Mira expectantly; she suddenly felt very awkward. "I was hoping to speak to Khaldun privately," she said to Oscar.

"Of course, my lady," he replied. "I will wait nearby."

"No, Oscar—go back and get some sleep. I'll be safe with Khaldun."

"I would prefer to wait for you so I can escort you back when you're done."

"Don't worry, I'll see her back to her tent," Khaldun assured him.

Oscar looked from him to Mira; she nodded encouragingly. "Very well," he said finally, heading back the way they'd come.

"He's a little possessive, no?" Khaldun said, raising his eyebrows as they set out around the camp's perimeter.

"He takes his duty very seriously," Mira told him. "My father assigned him to guard me on the journey here, and I'm afraid he'll uphold that responsibility until his dying breath."

"Well, you're here now, won't he be heading back to Blacksand?"

"I'm not so sure that he will. That was the plan, of course, but after tonight… I don't know. He may be planning to stay. I'll have to talk to him."

"He's going to be in for a little culture shock," Khaldun said with a grin.

"Yes. We broached that topic on our way out here, in fact. But he'll get used to it if he stays. He was my closest friend for many years before entering my father's guard, so he's not entirely unfamiliar with our ways."

"Oh? And how close was he exactly?"

Mira gave him a look of mock surprise. "Is that a tone of jealousy I hear?"

"No, of course not," he said quickly, returning her gaze. "I was just… curious."

"Curious—yes, of course," she replied with a sly grin. "Well, we were only friends. Don't worry, I kept that promise we made each other," she added, feeling herself blush now.

"Oh—uh… yes. I'd almost forgotten…"

Mira felt her heart sink; part of her had hoped he'd saved himself for her, despite knowing how unrealistic that was.

"I'm sure you've had many lovers by now," she said quietly.

"Not *many*… but um… well, there have been a few."

Mira didn't reply; she felt tears welling up in her eyes. Though she felt stupid for it now, she *had* held onto a glimmer of hope that he might have kept his promise, too.

"Mira, I'm sorry… we were so young. We didn't know what we were doing. And after so many years… I lost hope that you'd ever come back."

Mira took a deep breath. "I never did. In the beginning, I *begged* my father to let me return. As I grew older, I could tell how much it upset him, so I stopped. But I held on to that desire in my heart, and I promised myself that as soon as I could, I would find a way back."

"I'm sorry…"

"Don't worry about it," she said. "You're right—we were only children then. The little girl in me is crushed, but the woman knows better."

They walked in silence for a minute.

"You know, I *did* hold onto that promise for a long time," Khaldun told her. "I missed you so much after you left. And for a few years, I kept thinking that you'd return and we would be married. But eventually I lost faith."

"Well, I can't really blame you," she said with a sigh. "The whole idea was Nareen's fault, if you think about it. How else would two wayfarer children have come up with such a notion?" Mira giggled.

"That's a good point," Khaldun agreed. "I never thought about that, but you're right. I've felt guilty about breaking that promise, but I should be blaming her!"

"I wouldn't go *that* far," she chided, poking him in the ribs. "She didn't hold a knife to your throat and force you to make love to some other girl."

"No, no—you've absolved me of my sins," he said, grabbing her arm and staring deep into her eyes. "There's no going back now."

Mira grabbed him and kissed him passionately. She didn't know what had come over her, but being with him now felt so familiar, as if they'd never been separated. Her feelings for him erupted, like a dam bursting in her heart.

"It's ironic in a way," Mira said pensively.

"What is?" he asked, kissing her again.

"Nareen brought me up to believe I'd love only one, but she never thought it would be *you*."

"She's still hoping you'll marry a lord?" he asked as they resumed their walk.

"Oh, of course. She wanted me to stay in Blacksand. And my father did try very hard to marry me off—he would have been more than happy to make my mother's dreams come true."

"Why did you return? Why now, I mean?"

"I'm of age finally; they can't stop me anymore. I always *wanted* to come back but they wouldn't allow it. Living inside those stone walls never felt right—I missed the freedom we have out here. I guess I'll always have a wayfarer heart."

"Well, I'm glad you're back," he said with a grin.

They walked in silence for a few more minutes.

"You acted very bravely tonight," Mira told him. "I can remember when we were little and your father used to help protect the troupe. You reminded me of him."

"People tell me that all the time," Khaldun said with a sigh, "but I don't remember my parents."

"Not at all?"

"Vague impressions, nothing more. I know my father was a mage, and I've heard stories about all the adventures he went on with Nomad, but only because others have told me about them."

"Huh. You know, your father taught me my first spell."

"He did? I don't recall hearing about this before."

"We were all eating dinner together, and I started playing with his wand. So Raja taught me a simple fire spell, and I was able to call a small flame. I started training with Nomad right after that."

"Wow," Khaldun replied. "I don't remember that. You know, Gunthar said something I didn't understand when I was escorting him out of the camp."

"What exactly?"

"He told me you're not a 'normal mage.' What did he mean by that?"

"Oh. Well, he's right. I can't do magic anymore—that is to say I can't call any of the forces. I can only cancel them."

Khaldun gave her a strange look. "But that's impossible. All mages can summon the forces—that's how magic works."

"Not for me, it doesn't. My power manifests itself in two ways: I can actively cancel other mages' spells, but also, whether I cancel it or not, magic has no effect on me."

Khaldun stopped in his tracks and shot her a quizzical look. "I don't follow."

"Spells don't work on me," she said with a shrug. "Try something."

"What? Like what?"

"I don't know—call earth. Try to knock me down."

"This is absurd—I'm not going to—"

"You won't hurt me; you can't actually. The spell won't do anything."

Khaldun stared at her doubtfully for a moment longer, then raised his staff, formed his spell and spoke the word of command. As she'd explained, the incantation did nothing. "I don't understand," he muttered, looking at his staff as if it were broken. "You didn't cancel the spell…"

"I don't have to. Try calling fire," Mira suggested.

"What? No—that could kill you."

Mira shook her head. "It couldn't. Trust me."

Khaldun raised his staff to cast a fire spell; once again, it had no effect. "This makes no sense," he said with a frown. "I saw you do magic during the battle."

"No, you saw me *cancel* magic. *That* I can do—quite well, if I do say so myself. Unlike normal mages, I don't need to know a spell to cancel it."

"*What*? But that's impossible…"

"It should be, but it's not. Watch—call an illusion."

Khaldun held out his staff, and cast a spell to create a cat lying on the ground nearby. Mira pointed her wand, called out an incantation, and the illusion vanished.

"See?"

"But that spell you used—that's for canceling fire, not illusions…"

"I know," Mira said with a shrug. "We discovered this by accident one day when I was training with my father's witch, Belinda. She didn't understand how or why it worked, but no matter what kind of cancellation spell I use, it neutralizes any magic it hits."

"This is astonishing," Khaldun said, shaking his head. "I can only cancel spells that I know myself—that's how it is for every other mage I've ever met. Well, normal mages, anyway—I know Nomad can neutralize magic he's never encountered before."

"Yes, Belinda told me that sorcerers can do that," Mira agreed.

"But when we were little, you were able to call the forces. You said yourself that you called a flame for my father, and I distinctly recall a training session with Nomad when you lit my shirt on fire."

Mira giggled. "Yeah, when we were about nine years old. But don't you remember how I lagged way behind you? I used to get so frustrated because you were learning more quickly than I was."

"Well, sure, but mages always learn at different rates—"

"No, this is something different. The limited spellcasting I acquired disappeared completely by the time I'd left for Blacksand. Belinda tried to teach me, but the only thing I could do anymore was counter spells."

"Did Nomad know about this?"

"Sure, but he said it was normal for mages to have peaks and valleys in their progress. And we were hitting puberty back then; that can upset anyone's magical development."

"True, but I've never heard of it eliminating it completely."

"But it didn't."

Khaldun nodded. "You should consider enrolling in the university. They may be able to help you develop this talent further."

"I can't. Belinda looked into it but they won't accept me because I'm half wayfarer."

"Ah," Khaldun replied knowingly. "The old prejudice. They allowed Nomad to attend once he'd transformed, so I thought perhaps they would make an exception for you, too."

"They *require* sorcerers to train there, but apparently that's the only way around the interdiction," Mira said with a sigh.

"Well, Gunthar did say that Henry would pay me a reward for bringing you to him. Now I know why."

"Yes," Mira agreed, shaking her head. "I've heard that he has a thing for collecting powerful and unique mages."

"How did Gunthar find out you're a mage? Did you cancel one of his spells?"

"No—I'm actually not sure, now that you mention it. He did something when we first encountered him but I couldn't identify the spell. But then later, he tried incinerating me. It had no effect, of course, but somehow it sounded like he hadn't expected it to work. But by then he knew I was a witch, and had his men confiscate my wand."

"Hmm," Khaldun wondered aloud. "Perhaps that first spell was something to detect magical ability. We'll have to ask Nomad about that."

They moved back into the clearing and Mira realized that dawn was upon them. "Time flies," she said with a smile.

Khaldun gazed at the sky. "You're right—we should get back to camp."

CHAPTER FOUR
CONVICTION

haldun escorted Mira back to her mother's tent. But when they arrived, they found Nareen berating Oscar.

"Mother, what's wrong?" asked Mira.

"There you are!" Nareen replied, turning to Mira. "What is wrong, you ask? I awoke to find you gone, with no explanation!"

"I tried to explain, my lady," Oscar told her abashedly.

"Oh, he told me that you'd gone off with this one," she said, indicating Khaldun. "But that's hardly safe after the attack—"

"Mother, I'm fine," Mira insisted, ducking inside the tent. Nareen followed her in.

Oscar looked pleadingly at Khaldun and sighed. "I fear I have failed in my duty."

"Nonsense," Khaldun told him with a reassuring grin. "Nareen has always been a little overprotective where her daughter is concerned. You did nothing wrong."

Oscar nodded and shrugged. "I've found a man with a cart. Could you let Lady Mira know that I'm going to fetch our fallen comrades?"

"Yes," Khaldun replied. "But it might have been better to do that last night. Animals may have gotten to them by now."

"Aye, perhaps. But I felt that protecting the living was more important than honoring the dead. The road should be safer now in broad daylight."

Khaldun nodded. "Will you bury them?"

"No, Lady Mira explained that your people burn their dead. We figured we would add our men to your pyre, if that's acceptable."

"I'll let them know; they'll be making the preparations by now."

"Very well. Oh, and Nomad was looking for you and Lady Mira— he said that Badru would like to see you both."

"Thank you," Khaldun said with a nod. Oscar headed off and Khaldun poked his head inside the tent. "I'm sorry, my lady," he said to Mira, interrupting Nareen's ongoing tirade, "but our honorable leader has requested the presence—"

"Oh, now don't *you* start!"

Khaldun grinned at her; Mira left the tent.

"I'm not done with you!" said Nareen, following her out.

"Later, Mother!" said Mira, following Khaldun across the camp.

"She does realize that you've come of age, right?"

"And you think that makes any difference to her? She wants me to go straight back to Blacksand."

"I guess that shouldn't be too surprising…"

They found Nomad and Badru outside the leader's tent, Nomad standing with his arms folded across his chest, his hood covering his head, and Badru drinking from a steaming mug of coffee.

"Good morning," Badru said with a nod. "I've reached my decision. We will break camp and return to Oxcart. But I will only allow the two of you to venture off to Stanbridge if Prince Bichon agrees to extend his protection to the troupe during your absence," he added to Nomad and Khaldun. "We will petition him when we arrive; I would like you to accompany us for that, Mira. The presence of a highborn lady in our midst may help sway him."

"Of course," Mira replied. "If I may, we should also report Henry's incursion to him. Gunthar marched through his territory with a dozen armed soldiers on a murderous rampage—he needs to know about that."

"Indeed," Nomad agreed. "He may already be aware of those events, but they should certainly help influence him to provide us with the aid we seek."

"Gunthar told us that they interviewed some people in Oxcart Town, so the prince may know that the Foslanders invaded his territory," Mira told them. "But we encountered no one else on the road once we'd left the town, so I doubt he knows about the murders."

"True. But I'm also sure he will have heard about the sacking of Stanbridge. There's a good chance Henry's entire army marched through the outskirts of Bichon's territory to get there. That alone should have him alarmed. Oxcart does not possess the resources to defeat Henry should it come to a pitched battle."

Badru nodded, taking another sip of his coffee. "I would like to ask him for an armed escort for the two of you as well," he said to Nomad and Khaldun.

"Forgive me, but that may not be wise," said Nomad. "If Henry's army has overrun Stanbridge, then stealth and secrecy will provide us with our best chance of success—and that will be best achieved if Khaldun and I proceed on our own."

Badru considered this for a moment. "Very well. How will the university feel about your taking part in this?"

"I will not be acting on their behalf so they will not object. The governors must maintain neutrality, but they place no such burden upon those of us who work in the field. As long as I do not claim to represent them, there should be no issue."

"Good. We will have to find a way to get this artifact to them, but we will address that when the time comes. I may be pointing out the obvious, but it would be for the best if nobody there realizes that you have so much as set foot in Stanbridge."

Nomad nodded. "Of course."

They waited in silence for a few moments—it seemed like Badru had something more to say. "It *shouldn't* fall to us to contain this threat. These princes and lords—they're the ones with the castles and the armies. Let them deal with this! I considered sending only a messenger to Bichon, alerting him to the presence and location of the artifact, and letting him decide what to do. But I don't trust him any more than I do Henry. The only difference is that Henry has already conquered a couple of neighbors. These highborn lords care only about power. Any one of them would seek to use this artifact to gain an advantage over the others."

"Which is precisely why we must intervene and make sure it finds its way to the university," Nomad pointed out. "Only there can we be sure that it will be destroyed."

"The highborn aren't *all* bad," said Mira. "Prince Edward didn't try to use this artifact, even in the face of Henry's army sacking his princedom."

"His mages may not have possessed the ability to use it," Nomad told her. "It may require necromantic spells that they simply don't know. A sorcerer would likely be able to access it regardless, but there are no sorcerers in Stanbridge."

"Yes, I'm sure Edward would have instructed his mages to use it if they could," Badru agreed. "No prince would hesitate to use any means at his disposal to hold onto power."

"How did he come to possess such a device in the first place?" asked Khaldun.

"It was probably a family heirloom," Nomad suggested. "It could have been passed down from father to son since the days prior to the ban on necromancy. The university's purge of such relics was pretty thorough, but it's a big continent. Some items are sure to have survived."

"Well, we've got work to do," said Badru. "We'll head out after the ceremony."

Khaldun escorted Mira back to her mother's tent, then went to check on the funeral pyre. Several of the men were erecting it out in the field beyond the camp, and the bodies of the dead wayfarers were lying nearby. Khaldun let them know that they'd need to wait for Oscar to return with the two guards. He still couldn't believe Arman was gone; they'd been friends since boyhood. Tears welled up in his eyes at the thought.

The pyre's construction was completed and they moved the bodies to the top. People began gathering for the ceremony. Mira arrived with her mother, and Khaldun spotted the mothers of the dead children gathered with a couple of the caregivers. Oscar arrived soon after, and helped load the guards' bodies onto the pyre.

Once the preparations were completed, Badru moved to the front of the crowd with Nomad and started the proceedings. He spoke the traditional words for the deceased wayfarers, giving their souls their proper sendoff to the stars.

Khaldun could hear the dead children's mothers sobbing as Badru spoke. He couldn't imagine the depth of their grief. What kind of monster would murder a child? None of these people deserved to die at the hands of the Foslanders—the wayfarers had not wronged them in any way. But the children had barely lived at all.

He wondered if they would have done the same thing if this had been some lord's holding instead of a wayfarer camp. The highborn held his people in the lowest possible regard—they were little more than animals to them. But he suspected these Foslanders would have committed these murders no matter who they were. Rumors of the atrocities they'd committed in conquering their neighboring princedoms would seem to confirm his suspicions.

After Badru was finished, he invited Mira to speak for her guards. Once she was done, Nomad turned to face the pyre. Casting back his hood, his long, black hair blowing in the breeze, he held his arms out to his sides and called fire.

The wayfarers sang their ancient funeral dirge as the bodies burned. Khaldun knew that Nomad would be adding power to the fire to speed up the process; the wayfarers did not care for long goodbyes. Once the flames had burned out, and the bodies had been reduced to ashes, those closest to the deceased came forward to say their last words to their loved ones. Finally, Nomad called air, releasing their ashes on the wind.

The troupe dispersed and Khaldun headed back to his tent to break camp. He'd spent his entire life among his people, always moving from one princedom to the next. They would typically spend a few weeks at each location, performing for the highborn and commoners alike. Their circus show included jugglers and clowns, trapeze and high-wire acts, as well as a stage magician. This process of breaking down their camp, relocating, and setting it up again was one Khaldun knew by rote. He couldn't hope to count the number of times he'd done it.

Once he'd finished, he brought his pack and Nomad's over to the paddock they'd erected for the animals. The troupe had a couple of dozen horses; Khaldun and Nomad each rode one, as did Badru, and each of the elders. They also had a dozen pack mules and carts they used to carry the communal supplies, such as the fencing for the paddock.

Khaldun strapped their packs to their two horses. Nomad showed up as he was finishing. The two of them headed out to the road where the troupe was beginning to arrive for their journey. Nomad typically rode point with Badru, while Khaldun served as rearguard. But Khaldun didn't need to take his position until they were ready to move out, so he went to find Mira. He ended up locating her by following the sound of Nareen's voice as she berated her daughter. They'd taken up position in the middle of the formation. Mira was on foot; she'd let Nareen ride her horse.

"Khaldun!" Mira said when she spotted him approaching. "Just the man I was looking for." Nareen glared at him; once again, his arrival had interrupted her.

"What can I do for you?" he asked, dismounting.

"There's something over here I wanted to ask you about," she said, heading toward the rear of the line. Khaldun followed her on foot, leading his horse by the reins. Once they'd moved out of earshot from Nareen, Mira took him by the arm and giggled. "I didn't actually need to talk to you—I just needed an excuse to get away from her for a little while."

"Ah, I see," he replied with a grin. "Well, I'm happy to oblige. What is she yelling at you about now?"

"The same thing since I got here. She wants me to pack up and go back to my father's holding."

They moved past the mules, and found Oscar at the back of the line.

"Are you taking rearguard with me today?" Khaldun asked him.

"He refuses to go home, so I've officially put him on loan to Badru," Mira told him with a grin.

"It is clear that my lady is not yet out of danger," said Oscar. "I would be remiss to abandon her."

"And now I have reassigned you to a more useful post."

"Aye, my lady does technically have that authority," Oscar said with a scowl.

"It was the only way I could get him to leave me alone," she told Khaldun. "He insisted on following me around like a lost puppy."

"Only doing my sworn duty, my lady."

"Well, I'm sure Badru is happy to have a real soldier along in light of recent events," Khaldun noted.

The rest of the line formed and the troupe moved out.

"I'd better get back to Nareen," Mira said with a sigh. "I'll catch up with you boys later." She blew Khaldun a kiss and departed at a run.

Khaldun caught Oscar staring after her with a wistful expression.

"I will miss her when I leave," said Oscar. "But she does seem much happier here."

"She told me she's wanted to return ever since she left but her parents wouldn't allow it."

"It's true. She used to argue with her father about that vehemently. But our lord wouldn't budge."

"That's unusual, though, isn't it?" asked Khaldun. "In my experience, lords who have fathered children on wayfarer women go to great lengths to hide the fact, much less accept them into their homes."

"Aye, but Dorian Grisham is not the usual lord," Oscar replied. "My understanding is that Nareen petitioned him to take Mira into his care from the very beginning. He always refused, as one would expect. But apparently the day after his father passed away and he inherited his holding, he sent word to Nareen that he would accept Mira as his daughter, and dispatched guards to bring her home."

Khaldun had never heard about this before. "Why would he do that?"

"Afraid I have no idea. He dotes on her, though, I can tell you that much. Judging solely by the way he treats her, no one would ever know she wasn't fully highborn."

"Yet I doubt your people judged her on that basis alone," said Khaldun. "She looks more wayfarer than she does highborn. Her skin tone and dark eyes must stand out like a sore thumb in your princedom."

"True," Oscar admitted with a shrug. "And don't get me wrong, she's had to deal with her share of prejudice. Many people look down on her for being a bastard, and doubly so for being a *wayfarer* bastard. Nevertheless, our prince raised no objection to Lord Grisham accepting her as his trueborn daughter. And it took some time, but the people of Graystone came to love her as one of their own. She's had no lack of suitors seeking her hand in marriage, either."

Khaldun felt an odd sensation in his stomach at these words, as if he'd missed a step going down a flight of stairs. "How many suitors, exactly?"

Oscar shot him a look and chuckled softly. "At least a dozen, but don't worry, she spurned every one of them. Even Lord Eldrick's son, Arthur. He stands to inherit the most powerful holding in Blacksand—Gemstone-by-the-Sea, they call it. The castle sits on a bluff overlooking Gemstone Harbor—it's the second largest port city in Dorshire, after Oldport. And the Eldricks are one of the richest families in the kingdom. Graystone's a decent holding, but it's no Gemstone. Any Grisham daughter would be lucky to land that one, never mind a wayfarer girl—not meaning any offense."

"None taken," Khaldun said with a frown.

"I told her she was crazy not to accept his offer. It wouldn't make her a princess, but it would be the next best thing."

"Then I don't understand," Khaldun replied. "Why did she reject him? Is he stupid or ugly or something?"

"No, nothing like that," Oscar said with a chuckle. "He's educated, and he's handsome enough, I reckon. But Mira was hellbent on returning to your troupe. Always was—she'd never consider any other possibility. I still remember the first day she came to Graystone. 'I'm Mira Grisham, and I'm a wayfarer,' was the way she introduced herself to me. 'I won't be here long; I'm going back to my people as soon as I can,' she said. And she never wavered from that conviction."

"Not even for Arthur Eldrick," Khaldun muttered. "Her father didn't try to force her into marriage?"

"Oh, he did everything he could to *convince* her. But I don't think there's a man alive who could *force* Mira Grisham into anything she didn't want to do herself."

"What about Lady Grisham? I can't imagine she was so accepting of a daughter her lord husband fathered on a wayfarer."

"They never met. Lady Rosalind Grisham passed away giving birth to their son, Devon, many years ago. He's a couple of years older than Mira."

"And Mira's father never remarried?"

"Nay. He's never seemed interested in looking for a new wife. Rosalind already gave him an heir; otherwise I'd imagine he might have. Don't rightly know, though."

Khaldun considered all of this for a few minutes. It was perplexing that Mira would turn down a life of luxury to return to the wandering life of the wayfarers.

"Did, uh… she ever mention me?" Khaldun asked.

"Only about a million times," Oscar said with a grin. Khaldun's heart soared. "Always said you were like a brother to her." Khaldun's heart came crashing back into his chest.

"A brother? Really? She never said anything about wanting to marry me?"

"*Marry* you?" Oscar repeated with a frown. "No, I don't recall her ever mentioning anything like that. But you never know with Mira. She's about the best friend I've ever had, but there's a part of her she keeps closed off from everyone else, even me."

"How do you mean?"

"Well, like I said, she was always hellbent on returning to the wayfarers. But she never could offer a good explanation for it. I mean, I could tell there was one, but she wouldn't share. 'Because that's where I belong,' she'd say. Or, 'Because that's who I am.' Not really a proper answer, you know?"

"Hmm. How about you? Mira's never taken a romantic interest?"

"In *me*?" said Oscar. "Aw, hell no. I mean, don't mistake my meaning—I'd marry her in a heartbeat if she'd have me. She's about the prettiest girl I've ever seen, and like I said, we've been close since the day she arrived at Graystone. But I've got nothing to give her. I'm a lowborn baker's son; don't own any property or anything. Hell, I'm lucky her father invited me to his guard. That's a higher station than anyone like me could rightfully hope for."

They rode in silence for quite a while after that; the conversation weighed heavily on Khaldun's mind. After his encounter with Mira the previous night, he strongly suspected *he* might be the reason she'd returned to the troupe after all. And now he felt more guilty than ever for forgetting about her so easily.

CHAPTER FIVE
PRINCE BICHON

he troupe continued south on the road all day. Khaldun couldn't stop thinking about Mira and what he'd learned about her time at Graystone. He wanted desperately to speak to her privately, but there was no opportunity. Mira dropped to the back of the line a couple of times, but Oscar was there with them. Khaldun could have accompanied her back up to her mother's position, but duty required him to keep his post at rearguard.

They approached Oxcart Town in the midafternoon. The castle was located at the south end of the village, but their entire line halted to its north. Khaldun rode away from the troupe to try and get a view of what was going on at the front, but couldn't see that far ahead.

"Wait here," he said to Oscar after a few more minutes. "I'm going to see what's going on."

Khaldun reined in his horse when he reached Mira.

"Why have we stopped?" she asked.

"I'm going to find out now."

"Take me with you," she said, moving to climb up behind him on his horse.

"Mira!" Nareen chided her from her mount. "By the stars in heaven, would you mind your place and let the leaders handle this, whatever it is?"

"I'll be right back, Mother," she replied as she took her position behind Khaldun, wrapping her arms around his torso.

They rode to the front of the line, and found Badru and Nomad standing by their mounts. Badru looked frustrated. Two soldiers wearing Oxcart's colors stood in the road barring their passage at the northern limits of the town. A crowd of locals had gathered behind them, gawking at the wayfarers.

"What's the trouble?" Khaldun asked.

"They won't allow us to pass," Nomad told him, indicating the soldiers. "There was a third one—he's gone to fetch their captain."

"We encountered no guards on our way through here," Mira commented.

Khaldun spotted two soldiers pushing their way through the crowd. The older one addressed Badru when they reached the front of the line. "You the leader?"

"I am. Badru's the name," he said, reaching out to shake his hand. The soldier ignored the gesture and Badru dropped his hand.

"We've closed our borders," he said, eyeing Nomad nervously. "You people should have passed out of our lands by now—why are you back here?"

"We need to speak to Prince Bichon—"

"Impossible. His Highness does not grant audiences to common rabble."

"A matter of the utmost urgency has come to our attention and we must alert your prince," Badru insisted.

"Let me know what it is and I will see if I can send a messenger."

"It is a sensitive matter," Nomad told him in his deep voice. "One that could impact the security of Oxcart and its neighbors."

The man regarded the sorcerer fearfully but shook his head. "I'll bring him a message myself. That's the best I can do."

"Sir, our people have learned the reason for Henry's invasion of Stanbridge," Mira told him. "He is seeking a weapon that has long been hidden there—one that he could use to conquer the entire kingdom."

The soldier considered her words for a moment. "What sort of weapon?"

"Forgive me, but we will trust this information with nobody but the prince."

"All right, there's a weapon in Stanbridge that Henry's going to use to against us. I'll let His Highness know. Now turn this horde around and be on your way." The soldier headed away, but Mira laughed out loud before he'd taken more than a few steps. He stopped short, rounding on her. "You laughing at me?"

"At your stupidity!" she said.

"Mira, please," said Badru, holding up both hands as if to say "Stop!"

"Excuse me?" the soldier demanded, moving toward her.

"If you go back to your prince and tell him that, don't you think he's going to want to know *what kind* of weapon it is? And its location? If he asks you any of that, and you don't have the answers, and then he finds out that you sent away the only people who do, how long do you think you'll keep your job?"

The soldier's eyes narrowed.

"Of course I'm guessing you have no intention of bringing this news to him. And then when Henry's army overruns the princedom, these other men here will remember this encounter. And what do you think Prince Bichon will do to you when he learns that you could have forestalled the invasion, but failed to do so?"

The man gazed at the other soldiers, but Khaldun noted that they averted their eyes.

"The lady has a point," Badru told him with a grin, patting him on the shoulder. "But have it your way. Let's go, everyone—time to turn around," he called out louder, turning to face the troupe.

"Hang on, now," said the soldier. "Let's not be hasty."

"Yes?" Badru replied, returning his attention to him.

"I don't have the authority to let your entire group pass any further. But I can escort a couple of you to the castle to take this news to the prince."

"That will do nicely," Badru told him with a grin. "Thank you. Khaldun and Mira, you're with me. Nomad, I want you to remain here and stand guard."

Nomad bowed.

"You'll need to clear the road, though," the solider added. "We can't have this blockage."

"Very well," Badru agreed.

Nomad rode down the line instructing their people to move to the side of the road. Badru mounted his horse, then he, Khaldun, and Mira followed the soldier through the growing crowd and into the village. The man stopped at a guard station to mount his horse, then led them down the road.

Within minutes, the castle loomed into view. They turned onto the lane leading to its entrance. They crossed the drawbridge over the moat and stopped at the gate, where the soldier spoke with the chief guard on duty. Khaldun could tell he was reluctant to let them pass, but allowed it in the end. They raised the gate, and the wayfarers followed the soldier into the courtyard.

For a prince's stronghold, the castle was smaller than most Khaldun had seen; he'd visited a few lesser holdings that were more impressive. But Oxcart was not a large princedom, and didn't have much strategic value.

They left their horses in the stables and followed the soldier to the keep. The guards at the entry nodded to him and opened the doors. Inside, the soldier led them to a small antechamber outside the main hall.

"The guardian at the gate sent a messenger to alert the prince to your arrival. It will be a few minutes."

The prince kept them waiting for what felt like hours. Badru grew steadily more impatient, imploring the soldier to send another messenger to investigate the cause of the delay, but he demurred.

"One does not rush a prince."

Khaldun began to wonder if they would be granted an audience at all, but finally the doors to the hall opened, and a servant ushered them inside. The soldier led them across the chamber. There were several large tables and dozens of chairs pushed up against the side walls—this room probably served as their dining hall. At the far end was one long table, behind which sat an older man with graying hair and a neatly trimmed goatee. Khaldun thought that this must be Prince Bichon. There was a man seated to his left, his hands resting on the wooden surface in front of him. Khaldun spotted a wand beneath his hands, and guessed that this must be the court wizard. A younger man and a woman sat to the prince's right; Khaldun didn't know who they might be. The soldier bowed when they reached them.

"Your Highness, forgive the interruption. But the wayfarers have returned, and their leader claims they have urgent information regarding a weapon hidden in Stanbridge. They say Henry could use it to conquer the entire kingdom, but insisted on brining this information to you themselves."

The prince raised one eyebrow. "Very well, you may leave us, Captain Westmore."

"Thank you, sir," the captain said, bowing again, then turning on his heel and striding back across the room. Khaldun watched as the servant followed him out, closing the doors behind him.

"Welcome to Oxcart. This is my son, Phillip, my adviser, Catherine, and my mage, Tristan," he told them. "Well, let's hear it," he added with an impatient tone. Prince Phillip sat up straighter, staring interestedly at Mira.

"Your Highness," Badru began. He told them about the messenger from Stanbridge, and the news that Henry had sacked the princedom and murdered the ruling family. "According to this messenger, Henry sent his army to retrieve an ancient artifact long kept hidden in the princedom. The messenger said it was something that could provide Henry's mage, Dredmort, with 'a power not seen in Anoria for centuries.' We believe he's talking about necromancy."

"I trained with Prince Edward's mage, Byron, at the university," said the prince's wizard. "I know him well. If such an artifact existed in Stanbridge, he would have taken it to the university to be destroyed."

Badru opened his mouth to reply, but the prince spoke first.

"Unlikely. It had probably been in his family for centuries. I very much doubt Edward would have allowed him to remove an heirloom like that from his possession. However, I find it strange that he wouldn't have ordered his mage to use it to overpower Henry's army."

"Your Highness, forgive me," said Tristan, "but Byron does not possess the skill. Neither do I for that matter. But communion with the dead is Dredmort's specialty—his experiments in that area are the reason the university expelled him. Long have there been rumors that he seeks to discover the long-lost secrets of necromancy."

"The messenger also told us that the artifact is hidden somewhere outside the castle, where Henry may be unable to find it. But we believe we know its location."

The prince thrummed his fingers on the tabletop for a moment. "I thank you for bringing us this dire news. But I'm afraid we do not possess the resources to do anything about this. We are a small princedom, and our army is no match for Henry's. News reached us that the Foslanders crossed our territory to reach Stanbridge in the dead of the night, and this incursion has outraged us. We have closed our borders and will do what we can to prevent them from violating our sovereignty again when they return to Fosland. But the truth is that if they march in force, we will be unable to stop them. We will have to hope that they do not find what they seek."

"Your Highness," said Badru, "we believe it would be best to remove the artifact from Stanbridge to ensure—"

"I will not risk sending my men into that territory—it would be suicide. Henry's forces would overpower them and undoubtedly torture the artifact's location out of them. No. Our best course is to secure our borders and hope that they cannot find this relic."

"Sir, we intend to send our sorcerer and his protégé into Stanbridge to recover the artifact," Badru told him. "But doing so would leave our troupe unprotected. We would petition Your Highness only to extend your protection to our people long enough for our mages to complete this task."

"Your Highness, this would be a wise course of action," said Bichon's wizard. "Nomad certainly possesses the skills necessary to slip past Henry's forces and retrieve the artifact undetected."

The prince considered this for a moment. "I will allow your troupe to remain on our land while your mages undertake this mission. That should be enough."

"We would ask simply that you station a few guards to keep watch—"

"I've told you that we do not have a large army. We are spread thin as it is protecting the border with Stanbridge. There is nobody to spare, but you are welcome to set up camp in the fields to the north of the town. Your people should be safe there."

"With all due respect, Your Highness, Gunthar and his band attacked my party on the road north of town, and murdered two of my guards," Mira told him. "You said yourself that you would be unable to stop Henry's army if they march in force, and that means the wayfarers could well suffer a similar fate."

"I'm sorry, but who are you?" the prince asked.

"Lady Mira Grisham of Blacksand. My father is Dorian Grisham, Lord of Graystone."

"You are very far from home, my lady," Bichon observed. "What brings you to our fair princedom?"

"I grew up with the wayfarers, and I was returning to them when Gunthar attacked."

"I apologize for your ordeal," the prince replied. "We did not learn of Gunthar's raid until the next morning."

"Your Highness," said Catherine, speaking for the first time, "perhaps we could allow them to camp on the grounds. The garrison stationed in town is already patrolling the castle exterior. It would not require any additional manpower to protect their troupe."

The prince nodded, considering her suggestion for a few moments. "I'll tell you what," he said finally. "We will extend our protection to your people for the duration of your mages' absence. In return, you will bring the artifact to me. I daresay that kind of power could be what we need to repel Henry's army."

"Your Highness, necromancy has been forbidden by the university for centuries," said Khaldun. "We need to bring the artifact to them to be destroyed."

"Unfortunately, I must agree," said Tristan. "I do not possess the knowledge to utilize such a device—"

"Have you ever seen it before?" the prince asked him. "Or examined it?"

"No, sir—"

"Do you have any experience with a similar item?"

"No, sir—"

"Well, then, how do you know that you would be unable to use it?" the prince asked, his eyebrows raised.

"We are talking about necromancy, Your Highness. I have no experience with *that*. Never have I learned the spells such a thing would require, nor even heard anyone else speak them."

"The wayfarers will bring the artifact here, and you will *try*, Tristan," the prince told him, patting him on the shoulder. "If you can get the thing to work, then we can use it against Henry's army. If not, then we will send a platoon to deliver it to the university."

"I thought you said you couldn't spare any men, Your Highness?" asked Mira.

"Mira!" said Badru.

"Not to stand guard over that horde," the prince told her. "But I agree that we must not allow this artifact to fall into Dredmort's hands."

"Nomad and I should be the ones to take it to the university," Khaldun said to Badru. "We should go there directly as soon as we retrieve it."

Badru ignored him. "We accept your offer, Your Highness. Our mages will retrieve the artifact and surrender it to you upon their return, in exchange for your protection while they are gone. After that, we will be on our way, and leave it to your best judgement what to do with the thing."

"What?!" said Mira, rounding on Badru.

"Sir—" said Khaldun.

"Enough! I have made up my mind."

The prince observed this exchange with his eyebrows raised. "Very well. You may have your people set up camp outside our castle walls. I would suggest that you instruct your mages to depart on their mission at first light."

"Thank you, Your Highness," said Badru, before bowing and turning to leave the hall. Mira and Khaldun each bowed as well, then followed him to the doors. "Not another word," he said to them once they'd reached the antechamber.

Captain Westmore had left, but another guard was waiting for them. He escorted them back to their horses, and then out of the castle and all the way back to the troupe. They found Nomad waiting for them; Badru explained the deal they had struck.

"Sir, I don't think we should have agreed to let him have the artifact!" Mira said when he was done. "What if he goes back on his word and refuses to bring it to the university?"

"Listen, I appreciate the help you've given us since your return. I doubt we would have been granted an audience with the prince if it weren't for you. But this arrangement is perfect. Nomad and Khaldun will retrieve this cursed object because they are the best equipped to do so. Beyond that, this should *not* be our responsibility! From what Nomad has told us, this Tristan won't be able to use the artifact—the man confirmed as much himself. As soon as the prince realizes it's useless to him, he will want it as far from his territory as possible! He knows Henry would burn his entire princedom to the ground to find the thing, and he wants to safeguard his people as badly as I want to protect ours. He's the one with the soldiers—so let *him* be the one to get it to the university!

"Now, that's it—the discussion is closed. We need to move everyone to the castle grounds and set up camp." With that, Badru dismounted and stormed off with Nomad, leaving Khaldun and Mira gaping in his wake.

"Well, the man has spoken," Khaldun said with a grin.

"He does have a point," Mira conceded. "The prince just has to discover for himself that the artifact will be worthless to him, and then he'll have a very strong motivation to be rid of it."

Khaldun brought Mira back to Nareen. She gave him a kiss on the cheek, then dismounted. Nareen started yelling at her the moment her feet hit the ground.

"Good luck," Khaldun told her before riding off to help get everyone organized.

It took a couple of hours, but the wayfarers reached the castle and set up camp. Nomad took the first watch, so Khaldun lay down in their tent to get some sleep. He'd have the second watch, and then they'd be setting out for Stanbridge at daybreak.

Exhausted as he was from not sleeping the previous night, Khaldun dozed off almost immediately. But after what had seemed like only minutes, he woke to the soft sounds of someone slipping inside the tent. Opening his eyes, he realized that it was Mira.

"Hey," he said, propping himself up on one elbow to get a better look at her. But she didn't reply; sliding into the bedroll next to him, she kissed him passionately.

Khaldun lay back, embracing her and returning the kiss. After a minute, he reached between her legs, but Mira gripped his wrist.

"I want to make love to you," he whispered.

"Not until we're married," she replied, kissing him again.

Khaldun pulled away. "You want to marry me?"

"I've thought about it now and then," she said with a smile.

"But you're not living among the highborn anymore. That's not our way."

"Well, it's *my* way."

"Didn't you say you missed the freedom of being a wayfarer?"

"I did. But freedom means I get to choose whom I love, and how I love them."

They kissed again for a minute.

"I heard that you thought of me as a brother, but that doesn't seem right somehow…"

"You've been talking to Oscar," she said, rolling her eyes. "I only *told* him that because I didn't want anyone to know about our promise. If my father found out that I was refusing all those suitors because I was planning to marry a wayfarer… he might have murdered me."

"I don't know, but from what Oscar said, I doubt it."

"Not literally, but he would have been extremely upset with me. He always thought I would grow out of my fantasy of returning to the troupe. I had to keep my feelings for you a secret."

They kissed again, but before long Khaldun's exhaustion overwhelmed him and he drifted off to sleep.

CHAPTER SIX
THE ARTIFACT

haldun… Khaldun, wake up!"

Khaldun opened his eyes. Nomad was shaking him by the shoulder; Mira was sound asleep in his arms. Judging by the amount of light outside, it must have been nearly dawn.

"I'm sorry—I overslept. Why didn't you come wake me earlier? You kept watch the entire night?"

"Don't worry, I don't require much sleep. But Nareen is on the prowl—she's looking for Mira and she's headed this way!"

"Oh!"

"I'll go distract her—hurry up and get Mira back to her tent!"

Nomad left. Khaldun brushed Mira's hair out of her face and kissed her. Mira moaned softly, kissing him back.

"You need to wake up—we have to get you back to your tent before Nareen gets here."

"What," she said groggily, opening her eyes and taking in her surroundings. "Oh, shit—it's morning?"

"Yes!" Khaldun said, getting to his feet, and holding out his hand to help her up.

"What happened—I figured Nomad would wake us up when his watch was over!"

"He let me sleep in. Come on!"

Khaldun grabbed his staff. Creeping outside, they spotted Nomad talking to Nareen nearby—Nomad had positioned himself to keep Nareen's back toward them. Khaldun led Mira quickly through the camp, both of them giggling quietly by the time they'd reached her tent.

"I'd better get out of here before Nareen gets back," said Khaldun.

Mira kissed him. "Yes, go—hurry. I'll come see you before you leave with Nomad."

Khaldun hurried off, but then made himself invisible and waited. Sure enough, Nareen returned only moments later.

"Again, I wake up to find you gone! Have you no care for your own safety?!"

"Mother, I only went to pee—please, calm down!"

Khaldun headed back to his own tent, chuckling softly as he made himself visible again. He found Nomad packing up their gear.

"Thanks for that," Khaldun said earnestly.

"Any time," Nomad replied with a grin. "I'm just glad I didn't interrupt anything."

Khaldun sighed. "I'm afraid there was nothing to interrupt."

"Oh?"

"Mira's saving herself for marriage."

Nomad nodded. "I can't say I'm surprised. She lived among the highborn for a long time."

Once they'd finished packing, they headed off to the paddock. Badru was waiting for them there, mug in hand.

"Remember, you two, your sole responsibility is to find this artifact and bring it here," he told them as they secured their packs on their horses' backs. "We do not want to engage with Henry's forces, no matter what. Nobody should see you."

"Understood," said Nomad.

"Khaldun?"

"Yes, no contact. I promise."

"Very well," said Badru, taking a sip of coffee. "Be safe and return as quickly as possible."

Khaldun was about to mount his horse when Mira came running over.

"Good luck," she said, embracing him and giving him a kiss. "Hurry back."

"I will," Khaldun told her.

Mira ran off again, and he knew she'd probably sneaked away when Nareen wasn't looking.

Khaldun climbed onto his horse and followed Nomad out of the camp and down the lane toward the road. When they reached the southern end of town, they ran into Captain Westmore at the guard station.

"Hoi! You two—hold on a minute," he called out, trotting over to them. Khaldun and Nomad reined in their horses. "Stay on the road until you reach the southern border. The captain there is expecting you. It won't be safe to cross into Stanbridge on the road, so you'll need to leave your horses with him and proceed on foot through the forest. He'll be able to tell you the best route to take to avoid Henry's army."

Nomad nodded. "Thank you."

"Safe journey," the captain said, heading back to the guard station.

Nomad and Khaldun proceeded down the road. The country here was hilly and wooded, but they did pass through a couple of small villages. It took only a few hours to reach the southern border. There was an army encampment in the field to the west and they'd set up barricades preventing easy passage up the road from Stanbridge.

"Halt!" shouted one of the soldiers as they approached the guard station. "What is your business here?" he demanded, but his eyes went wide when he got a look at Nomad. But before they could reply, another man came up behind him.

"It's all right, Stancil, we've been expecting them. I'm Captain Petra," he added to Nomad and Khaldun. "Stancil will look after your horses. If you'll come with me, I can introduce you to your guides."

"Our understanding was that we'd be proceeding on our own from here," Nomad told him as they dismounted.

"My orders come directly from the prince," Petra told them as they untied their packs from the horses. "My men know these woods like the backs of their hands. They'll get you within sight of Castle Stanbridge, then wait there for your return."

They followed him up to the barricade on foot, where a group of soldiers was gathered. Two of them approached when they spotted their captain.

"This is Stefan and Markus." The two soldiers nodded to Nomad and Khaldun. "Good hunting, gentlemen." The captain headed back to the guard station.

Nomad and Khaldun followed their guides off the road and into the forest to the east of the road. They picked up a narrow trail that wound its way through the hills.

"This path will take us to the old Stanbridge Trail," Stefan told them. "That used to be the primary route through the princedom back before they built the road."

They reached the trail a couple of hours later and headed south.

"Henry's army isn't watching this route?" Nomad asked.

"Not that we've seen so far, at least. Our scouts have reported that they've stationed platoons on the roads leading to Stanbridge Town, but have kept them close to the castle," Stefan replied. "They seem to be focused on defending their position there, and don't appear to be concerned with the rest of the princedom."

"That makes sense," Khaldun observed. "It's only the artifact they want. Occupying the territory would be difficult without controlling the neighboring areas. They're completely cut off from Fosland down here."

Nomad nodded. "For now."

An hour later, they came to a fork; Stefan led them to the right.

"Where does that lead?" Khaldun asked, indicating the other branch.

"That's the trail to Smithtown," Stefan replied.

Suddenly, Khaldun heard someone moaning up ahead. The soldiers drew their swords.

"Who's there?" Stefan called out. "Show yourself."

A man stepped out from behind a large tree, spotted the soldiers' weapons, and held his hands up in the air. "I'm unarmed. My name is Allister, former adviser to Prince Edward."

He was tall and spindly, and looked older; his light-brown hair hung to his shoulders. His face was smeared with blood and one pant leg was torn, revealing a wound in his thigh.

"What are you doing out here in the forest?" Stefan demanded, not lowering his sword.

"Henry's army sacked the castle and killed the prince and his family. I managed to escape, so I fled. But I might ask you the same thing—your colors are those of Oxcart… but you have a wizard and—oh, my, my—a sorcerer with you, who show no colors at all. Are the mages from the university, then? I had a feeling they might send someone to retrieve the artifact—"

"Our presence here is none of your business," Nomad told him.

"You witnessed the attack firsthand?" asked Stefan.

"I'm sorry to say that I did," Allister replied. "Oh, it was horrible— so much carnage. Blood everywhere. It all happened so fast… They murdered the entire royal family, as well as the prince's guard."

"How were you able to escape?" Stefan asked, his tone suspicious.

"Not without help. One of the castle guards guided me to the secret tunnel behind the library. They probably would have killed me, too, if it weren't for him."

"And where is he now?"

"Dead, I'd imagine," Allister said with a shrug. "He went back to fight after showing me to the tunnel. Poor lad…"

"The prince may wish to question this one," Stefan said to Markus. "Escort him back to camp and notify the captain."

Markus nodded.

"Oh, thank you," said Allister. "I was planning to seek asylum in Oxcart, but I'm quite sure I can find the way on my own."

Stefan shook his head. "It's not safe."

"All right, then," Allister said with a shrug. "Lead the way!"

Markus and the old man headed back toward Oxcart. Khaldun and Nomad pressed ahead with Stefan. A little before sunset, they began searching for somewhere to rest for the night. They found a clearing in the trees, and set up their camp as dusk gathered. Khaldun took care of the tent he would share with Nomad, while the soldier put his up nearby.

"Any progress with the invisibility spell?" Nomad asked Khaldun once he'd finished.

"It's consistent now, but only using it on myself. I haven't been able to make anyone else invisible yet."

"Let me see you try," said Nomad, moving back to the path. "We'll want to hide the entire camp tonight."

Khaldun nodded with a sigh. Clutching his staff, he called the magical force and spoke the word of command. Nomad chuckled.

"Well, I can't see *you* anymore. Try again but expand your focus. You've got to concentrate on the entire area you wish to affect with the spell."

Khaldun tried again, this time thinking about the entire camp, but Nomad shook his head. Three more times Khaldun worked the spell and on his final try managed to render Stefan and the tents invisible, too.

"So, you're telling me anyone going by on the trail wouldn't see us?" Stefan asked skeptically.

"Come and look for yourself," Nomad suggested.

Stefan got to his feet and moved over to the sorcerer, looking back toward Khaldun.

"I'll be damned," he said. "Just an empty clearing."

"The spell doesn't block sound," Khaldun told him. "So hopefully you don't snore too loud."

"I don't think so," Stefan replied with a chuckle.

"I'll block our noises," Nomad told him. "You can snore as much as you want."

They went without a fire—the smoke would have been visible once it had cleared Khaldun's spell. Instead, they sat on the ground, eating some of the dried meat and fruit they'd packed for the journey. Nomad told him he'd keep watch all night, so Stefan turned in early. Khaldun sat up with the sorcerer for a while longer.

"When we questioned the messenger from Stanbridge, and you showed us what the mage had hidden in his mind, you said that only a sorcerer could find that?" asked Khaldun. "If that's true, then how was the mage in Stanbridge able to leave such a message in the first place?"

"No, any mage could have uncovered the message if they'd already known it was there," Nomad told him. "*Detecting* it without foreknowledge of its existence requires a sorcerer. We can sense magic in a way that common mages cannot."

"But I can feel it when you cast spells," said Khaldun. "And I felt Gunthar doing magic in our camp before I saw him."

"Yes, and similarly, you would be able sense it if I were to tuck something into the void right now. But once the spell has been cast, you would not be able to detect the presence of whatever I had hidden."

"Ah. Would it have been the same for the messenger's tent, then? Any witch or wizard could have restored it from the void if they knew it was there?"

"Yes, that's correct. But only a sorcerer could have found it without already knowing about it. In fact, I suspect that is how they've hidden the artifact. If one of Henry's mages already knew its location, they surely would have found it by now. But I'll be able to detect the spell."

They sat in silence for a minute. Khaldun's thoughts turned to Mira. "Mira told me that she can't call any of the forces anymore—she can cancel magic, but she's lost the ability to cast spells of her own. Have you ever heard of that before?"

Nomad nodded. "It's extremely rare. I've never met anyone like that, but I've read about them. They're called magical nulls. I'm going to guess that spells don't work on her, either?"

"Yeah, that's right," Khaldun confirmed. "I tried calling fire on her, and it had no effect. I thought that only happened when a mage becomes very powerful?"

"Normally, that's true. Your spells would be unlikely to affect Dredmort, for example."

"Or you."

"Yes. But in the case of a null, the effect manifests much earlier and it's much stronger."

"She can also cancel spells that she doesn't know," Khaldun told him. "I created an illusion and she was able to eliminate it—but she did so using a fire spell."

"Cancellation works differently for her than it does for normal mages. When you cast a counter-spell, you are essentially unraveling the initial incantation. But Mira is projecting her null into the environment around her. It doesn't matter what spell she uses—it will neutralize any magic it hits."

"Mira told me that when they first encountered Gunthar, he cast some sort of spell, but she couldn't identify it. But after that, he seemed to suspect that she was a null—he tried incinerating her, and wasn't surprised when it didn't work. Why would he have expected her to be a null if they're so rare?"

"His first spell was probably meant to reveal any mages in her party," Nomad explained. "Battle mages typically use that when first encountering an enemy force to identify threats—it shows who's mundane and who's magical. But in Mira's case, the spell would not have had any effect at all, exposing her as a null."

"That explains it," Khaldun said with a nod.

"To the best of my knowledge, there have been only four other nulls since the university began keeping records," Nomad told him.

"But that was thousands of years ago, right?" Khaldun replied. "Mira's only the fifth one in all that time?"

"Indeed. The last one served a warlord in Kong. At the height of his power, he was able to cancel any magic cast across an entire battlefield."

"So, that's why Gunthar wanted to take her to Henry," Khaldun observed.

"Yes. With training, she could become quite powerful. I shudder to think what Henry might be able to achieve with her by his side."

Khaldun climbed into their tent a few minutes later to try and get some sleep. But he lay awake for a long time thinking about Mira's strange power. It was a good thing that Oscar had managed to free her from Gunthar's soldiers.

They rose at dawn, and after a quick breakfast, broke camp and continued on their path. The land grew steadily hillier as they drew closer to their destination. Finally, at midafternoon, they rounded a curve and found themselves standing at the top of the bluff overlooking Castle Stanbridge. There was a large encampment between their position and the building.

"This is as far as I'll go," Stefan told them. "I'll wait for you in that clearing we passed around that last bend. I can take your packs, if you'd like."

"Very well, thank you," said Nomad; he and Khaldun handed them over. "We'll continue a little farther now, but I think we'll wait until nightfall to complete the mission. Our passage might be noted if we were to try it in broad daylight—they'll have a clear view of the surrounding area from the ramparts."

"Won't we be invisible?" asked Khaldun.

"Yes but we'd kick up dirt and move the vegetation as we pass, and they could notice that."

Stefan nodded and headed back up the trail. Khaldun continued onward with Nomad. The trail moved back into the trees for a while, heading down and around to the east of the castle. They spotted a road up ahead, and it looked like the trail ended there—Khaldun guessed that it must be the road to Smithtown. But there was a platoon blocking the route, so they didn't go that far. Instead, they found a path leading toward the castle, and followed that to the tree line.

They were much closer to the building now than they had been on the bluff. Khaldun spotted a company of soldiers leading a group of twenty or so people out through the main gate. They directed them into the field to the east, and made them form a line. Khaldun noticed several archers nocking their bows and realized they were preparing to execute these people. He was about to turn away when he saw a woman with flaming red hair emerge from the castle. She was clad in skin-tight, black leather and carried a staff.

"That must be one of Henry's witches?"

"Yes," Nomad replied. "Her name is Nineve."

Nineve went to stand by the archers. Seconds later, they fired, shooting their arrows into their victims' chests. They fell to the ground and Khaldun could hear their screams. It took them three volleys to finish off all the people.

"What did they do to deserve that, I wonder?" said Khaldun.

"Wrong place at the wrong time," Nomad said with a shrug. "Come on. Let's get out of here. We'll stay out of sight until dark."

They moved farther into the trees and waited. Khaldun heard another set of screams a little before sunset, and knew they must have been executing more of the castle's inhabitants. Once it was fully dark, they set out, with only the twin moons to light their way. Nomad made them invisible, and they headed across the field, keeping their distance from both the castle and the soldiers camped outside.

Nomad stopped when they reached the rear of the grounds. Holding out one hand, he scanned the area. "There," he said, pointing. Khaldun could see nothing but empty land. "Let's go."

Nomad led them across the field. He slowed down several hundred feet later, holding out his hand again.

"There's a small building here," he told Khaldun. "As I suspected, someone has tucked it into oblivion. I'm going to make the area invisible before I bring it back."

Nomad focused for a moment, then waved his hand. A stone structure appeared out of nowhere with a faint popping sound. It reminded Khaldun of a religious temple—there were gargoyles perched on the corners. There were no windows, but in the center of the front wall was a heavy wooden door. Walking up to the building, Khaldun realized there was no door handle.

"How do we get inside?"

Nomad said nothing, but closed his eyes and held out one hand. The door opened slowly, creaking on its hinges. There was a rush of air and fog through the opening, and a chill ran down Khaldun's spine.

Peering inside, Khaldun could see that it was empty, except for a stone staircase leading into the ground that took up nearly the entire space. But staring down the steps, he could see nothing in the darkness. Holding out his staff, he called fire, projecting a beam of light into the passage. The stairs must have delved deep into the earth; his light did not reach the bottom.

"After you," Khaldun said nervously.

Nomad led the way. They climbed down for several minutes until finally Khaldun's staff illuminated the floor below. At the bottom, they found themselves inside a giant chamber. There were two rows of stone columns holding up the vaulted ceiling. Stained-glass murals were embedded in the walls—they looked like windows, except that there was nothing but earth beyond.

But the place was covered with dust and grime. It didn't look like anyone had set foot down here for centuries; it felt like a tomb.

Nomad moved up the aisle between the columns; Khaldun followed close behind. He sensed goosebumps forming on his skin. It felt like there was some other presence down here with them, lurking in the shadows, but he could see nothing.

"I don't like this place," Khaldun whispered.

"It does have an aura of death and decay," Nomad replied.

"Is there someone else here with us, behind a spell of invisibility, perhaps?"

Nomad extended one hand in a great arc, sweeping his arm around the chamber.

"Nobody else is here. No one alive, at least."

Khaldun shuddered.

At the far end of the chamber was an altar. In the middle of it, sitting on a velvet pillow, was a pyramid of black stone, intricate latticework on its faces. The base of the object was about the size of Khaldun's palm.

"The artifact, I presume?" said Khaldun, glancing warily around the chamber. He couldn't shake the sensation that there was someone else down here with them.

Nomad stepped up to the altar, holding one hand over the pyramid. "Yes, it must be," he said. "It is a portal to the spirit realm. I'm going to seal it before we remove it from here."

He closed his eyes, and Khaldun could sense him forming his spell; it was like a gentle wind blowing toward him, causing a tingling sensation along his skin. When he was done, Khaldun realized that he no longer felt that presence in the chamber with them.

"That… whatever that was can't get through the portal anymore?"

"No. It cannot be opened from the other side."

Nomad removed the pyramid from its pillow, holding it in his open hand for a moment. Then with a popping sound, it vanished.

"I've tucked it into the void," he explained to Khaldun.

"We're not taking it with us?" Khaldun asked.

"No, we are. Moving something into the void, one can tether it to its location, or to oneself. Whoever moved this structure into the void attached it to this spot. But the artifact will go where I go."

"So there wouldn't have been any way to remove the building from the void back at our camp?"

"No. It was anchored here, so it could not be accessed from anywhere else. I've tethered the artifact to my person, so it will travel with me wherever I go. But truthfully, I don't believe that kind of spell would be possible for something as large as a building. I certainly don't possess enough power."

"If *you* don't, then I doubt anyone does…"

"There are some who may," Nomad replied. "But let's get out of here."

CHAPTER SEVEN
UNWELCOME GUEST

haldun and Nomad hurried out of the chamber and back up the steps to the surface. Once outside, Nomad sealed the door, and pushed the structure back into the void. He made Khaldun and himself invisible, and removed the spell he'd cast hiding the surrounding area. Twenty minutes later, they reached Stefan's camp by the trail, high above the grounds.

"Were you successful?" he asked them.

"Yes," Nomad replied. "It's getting late, but we should put some more distance between us and the castle before we make camp."

They hoisted their packs onto their backs and set off up the trail. After about an hour had passed, they decided they'd gone far enough for the night. Khaldun set up their tent, then sat down with Nomad for a quick bite to eat. Stefan said goodnight and retired to his tent.

"Is there any chance Bichon's mage will be able to use the artifact?" Khaldun asked quietly.

Nomad met his gaze. "Hardly. The prince will force him to *try*, and knowing now what it is, I fear the results could be dire."

"We should refuse to turn it over," Khaldun suggested.

Nomad nodded. "I'll speak with Badru when we return."

"What about Dredmort? Could he use it to summon demons?" Khaldun asked.

"Perhaps," Nomad replied pensively. "But I'm not sure that he possesses the necessary power, either."

"He experimented with necromancy at the university, right?" asked Khaldun. "He might know the spells."

"True. But gaining control of a demon would require more than knowledge. Without sufficient power, it could allow the demon to control the mage instead of the other way around. But it's hard to know for sure; the university banned the practice of necromancy centuries ago. Knowledge of its workings has been lost. And since then, there has been only one true necromancer on the entire continent."

"Who?" Khaldun asked in surprise. "I didn't think there had been *any*."

"His name is Myrddin. He's the court mage in Spanbrook, a princedom far to the north in Dorshire, not too far from the sea. Nobody knows where he acquired the knowledge, though. He departed the university and entered service in Spanbrook as a sorcerer."

"His prince must be a warlord like Henry," said Khaldun. "I'm surprised I've never heard of him before."

"No, Prince Aldo is a man of peace. He's something of an isolationist, in fact. But the university sanctioned Myrddin ages ago, and he severed all ties with them."

"Well, what do you think Dredmort would do with the artifact if not control demons?"

"I have no idea," said Nomad. "Let's hope we never find out."

"Was that presence I felt beneath the building a demon?"

"Yes, I believe it was. Not a very strong one, though."

They sat quietly for a minute.

"Do you know how to control a demon?" Khaldun asked finally.

"No, although generally speaking, sorcerers do have an innate affinity with the spirit realm. Our channels of power are open to the world around us—that's why we're able to perform magic without any instrument. But it also makes us susceptible to demonic possession." He held up one hand, showing Khaldun the ring he always wore. "That's the reason for this. All sorcerers wear one; it hides us from demons."

"So you can't be possessed if you're wearing that?"

"No, I can, but it masks my presence from beings in the spirit world. Makes it nearly impossible for them to find me."

Khaldun didn't sleep well. He couldn't stop thinking about the demonic presence he'd felt in the underground chamber. If that one was weak, he shuddered to think what a stronger one would be like. He didn't ever want to find out.

They set out at first light and walked all day, but decided to cut their march a little short when a heavy rain moved through the area late in the afternoon. It was dry inside the tent, and Khaldun slept much better that night.

The next afternoon, they reached the border with Oxcart. Stefan bade them farewell at the guard station, and returned to the army camp. Khaldun and Nomad checked in with Captain Petra, retrieved their horses, and headed north. They reached the guard station outside of Oxcart Town and reported to Captain Westmore.

"Were you successful?" he asked. Nomad nodded. "Very well, I will inform His Highness. Will you be returning to your camp?"

"Yes, the prince can send for us there when he's ready."

"Very well," said Westmore, setting out toward the castle.

It started raining as Khaldun and Nomad headed to their camp. They dropped off the horses at the paddock, then Khaldun went to see Mira. The rain had increased to a downpour by the time he'd reached her tent. Khaldun poked his head inside and found Nareen sitting alone.

"I'm sorry to disturb you," he said. "I was looking for Mira."

"She's up at the castle," Nareen told him with a grin.

"The castle? Why?"

"A summons from the prince, but I'm not sure what he wants with her."

Khaldun headed back to his own tent, worried now. Why did Bichon summon Mira? But he ran into her on his way there.

"You're back!" she said, grabbing him and kissing him passionately.

"Mm, it's nice to see you, too," he said with a grin. "But let's get inside—we're getting soaked!"

They ducked inside his tent and sat down on the bedrolls. Mira kissed him again. "Tell me—how did it go?"

Khaldun recounted the entire story for her.

"How terrifying!" she said when he was done. "A portal to the spirit realm... I cannot imagine Tristan would have any idea how to control such a thing!"

"No, certainly not," Khaldun agreed. "So what did Bichon want with you?"

"I'm not sure—it was the strangest thing. His guard escorted me into the great hall again, but this time, nobody else was there—it was only the prince and I. He sat me down and... I guess you could say he interviewed me."

"He interviewed you? About what?"

"Oh, everything—where I'm from, who my father is, loads of questions about his holding and Blacksand... And he asked me about my training as a mage."

"What did you tell him?"

"That I'm not very good—I didn't get into the details."

"He was probably assessing your fitness to become the Princess of Oxcart," Khaldun suggested, his insides twisting.

"Whatever would give you that idea?"

"Well, his son could hardly keep his eyes off of you."

"Do I detect a note of jealousy in your voice?" Mira asked with a sly grin. Khaldun shrugged. "You're being silly. I have nothing to offer—I come from a holding on the other side of the continent, and not one that I stand to inherit."

"Would you inherit it if your father didn't have a son?"

"Yes, but then a union with a prince would be out of the question!"

"Why?"

"Highborn daughters retain control of their holdings so long as they marry someone of lesser station. I would have to marry a landless son of a minor lord—then our son would carry on the Grisham name and come into his lands and titles once we'd passed on."

"But if you were to marry a prince..?"

"In this case, with Prince Phillip being so far away, my family would lose everything. Our holding would pass to some other lord in Blacksand."

"What about someone closer to home?"

"Well, if I were to marry a firstborn son of a neighboring holding, then ownership of my lands would pass to him, the Girsham line would come to an end, and our son would inherit both estates."

Khaldun chuckled. "I'll never understand the highborn and their rules."

Mira shook her head and sighed. "It's all moot, anyway. I think the prince was more interested in taking me on as a court mage. But I'm afraid I'd be nearly useless in that role."

"That reminds me, I asked Nomad about your oddities on our trip," said Khaldun.

"My *oddities*? Hah. Well, what did he say?"

Khaldun told her what he'd found out; Mira considered it for a few moments, her brow furrowed. "A null. Yes, that does sound right. And that explains how Gunthar knew what I was right away."

"Indeed," Khaldun agreed. "Thank the stars Oscar was able to rescue you—can you imagine what would have happened if Henry had acquired you?"

"Not much, I'm sure—null or not, I'm not very powerful. I can cancel individual spells, but I'm nowhere near strong enough to override mages across an entire battlefield!"

"Perhaps not now, but your power will grow, just like any mage's," said Khaldun.

"I guess that's true. Well, either way, I'm also glad Oscar saved me from that fate!"

Nomad showed up a few minutes later. "We've received a summons from Prince Bichon," he told them. "He has requested that the three of us and Badru report to the great hall tomorrow morning."

"Have you spoken to Badru?" Khaldun asked.

"Yes. But he refuses to listen to reason. He insists that we must uphold our end of the bargain."

"This isn't going to go well," Khaldun said with a sigh.

Nomad gave him a grim smile before leaving the tent again.

"What was that about?" asked Mira. "What did Nomad speak to Badru about?"

"Refusing to let Bichon have the artifact," Khaldun told her.

"Ah. Yes, that probably would have been wiser. But Badru did give his word."

The next morning, Captain Westmore came to collect Badru, Nomad, Mira, and Khaldun and escort them to the castle. Inside, they found that the doors to the great hall were open; Khaldun peered inside. The furniture was arranged the same way it had been last time, with one long table at the far end of the space. Two soldiers stood guard by the rear entry. Prince Bichon and Tristan were nowhere to be seen, but Prince Phillip and the prince's adviser, Catherine, were there, along with about a dozen other people Khaldun didn't recognize. They were standing in groups of two or three, chatting noisily.

"Who are all these people?" Badru asked Westmore.

"The prince has invited members of his court to observe Tristan's demonstration."

"This hardly seems wise," said Nomad. "It could become dangerous."

"You'll have to take it up with His Highness," Westmore told him. "If you'll excuse me?" He bowed, turning and departing.

Khaldun moved into the great hall with the others. Only a few minutes later, a herald announced the arrival of Prince Bichon and his mage. The room quieted and everyone turned their attention to the head table. Phillip moved to the rear entry and greeted his father.

Bichon and Phillip took their seats behind the table, Tristan right behind them. Khaldun thought that the mage looked terrified. Catherine took her place behind the table as well.

"My fine lords and ladies, thank you for joining us this morning," Bichon called out to the group. "Our honored guests, please come forward." The wayfarers moved toward the table. "I understand your mission was a success?" Nomad nodded. "Well, let's have the report."

Nomad recounted the events of their journey, starting with their arrival at Castle Stanbridge.

"Very well, let's see this artifact, then."

Nomad held out one hand, and the black pyramid materialized in his palm. He set it down on the table directly in front of the prince.

"Doesn't look like much," the prince muttered, eyeing it skeptically. "Just an old antique."

"Your Highness, I respectfully suggest that it would be unsafe to test this device," Nomad told him. "It is a portal to the spirit realm, undoubtedly used by an ancient necromancer to summon his demons. I have sealed it; we must deliver it to the university as quickly as possible."

"Nonsense," the prince replied. "I have every confidence in the skill of my mage. Please, unseal it."

Nomad shot Badru a glance, but he nodded furtively. With a sigh, the sorcerer waved his hand. Immediately, it felt like the temperature had dropped; Khaldun felt a chill run down his spine. The torches on the walls sputtered in their sconces and went out. The prince gazed around the hall with a worried expression, but turned to Tristan and said, "Proceed."

Getting to his feet, the wizard reached out and repositioned the pyramid directly in front of him on the table. Raising his wand, he recited an incantation and spoke the word of command.

At first, nothing happened. Everyone in the room seemed to be holding their breath. But suddenly, Khaldun felt the ground trembling as if there were an earthquake. A moment later, an enormous shadow grew out of the stone floor, looming over the head table. Khaldun could see eyes burning like hot coals through its transparent form. The demon stared down at Tristan and emitted a thunderous growl; Tristan screamed, cowering away from the monster, but suddenly it disappeared.

"What happened—where did that thing go?" Bichon demanded, getting to his feet and scanning the room in alarm.

But suddenly, Tristan howled, and Khaldun noticed that his eyes were glowing red. The wizard threw out one hand and shot a fireball at one of the court members. It slammed into him, knocking him across the room. He hit the floor screaming as fire consumed him. The rest of the group fled the hall, screaming in panic.

Tristan turned his attention to Prince Bichon; Khaldun noted his neglected wand lying on the table.

"Guards! Protect your prince!" Phillip shouted, jumping to his feet and drawing his sword.

Tristan gazed upon him and laughed, but the voice was not human; Khaldun thought it sounded feral. The wizard advanced on the prince; Phillip stabbed him in the stomach but this didn't have any effect. The guards grabbed him from behind but he hurled them off of him, throwing them into the wall, and continuing his advance on the prince.

But at that moment, he spotted Catherine. Shoving the prince aside, he lunged at her instead, reaching out and grabbing her by the arm. Catherine screamed; Tristan ripped the top of her dress open.

"Sorcerer—do something!" Bichon shouted. "Seal that portal!"

Nomad looked to Badru, and he yelled, "Do it!" Nomad waved his hand again. Khaldun knew he must have closed the portal, but it had no effect. Tristan had pushed Catherine onto the table and was trying to remove the rest of her dress. Catherine screamed again, struggling to get away.

"Leave her!" Nomad commanded, his deep voice resonating through the hall.

Tristan froze, gazing at the sorcerer for a moment, but then turned his attention back to Catherine. Nomad held out one hand, and suddenly Tristan rose into the air, howling in anger. He hurled a fireball at Nomad; it exploded against him but did no damage. Instead, Tristan reached out to Catherine with one hand, magically throwing her across the room. Catherine screamed, but then her body slammed into the far wall with a crunching sound before falling to the floor.

"Get it out of him!" Bichon shouted. "Expel the demon!"

"I'm sorry, Your Highness," said Nomad. "I don't know how."

Bichon looked from the sorcerer to his mage for a moment, but then Tristan hurled a fireball at the roof, setting it ablaze.

"Kill him, then!" the prince yelled.

Nomad nodded, his expression grim. He focused on Tristan, his brow furrowed, and the wizard burst into flame; Nomad was incinerating him from the inside. The wizard screamed in pain, but the voice was still not his own. Moments later, it was over; the body turned to ash and blew across the hall.

A moaning sound filled the room, and Khaldun felt a cold presence swoop around them. The moan grew louder, turning into an anguished howl.

"The demon remains," Bichon said, fear in his eyes.

But slowly the noise faded and the presence vanished. The torches burst back to life on the walls. With a wave, Nomad extinguished the fire on the roof.

"I am sorry, Your Highness," Nomad said with a sigh, "but I did try to warn you."

Bichon stared at him in shock for a moment before collapsing into his chair. Phillip ran across the room to Catherine, dropping to his knee beside her and taking her hand in his.

"Will she live?" Bichon asked.

Phillip regained his feet, shaking his head. "She is already dead."

Bichon gazed around the hall in horror as his son returned to his side. Several guards burst into the hall, stopping short and taking in the scene around them.

"Your Highness, we must deliver the artifact to the university," Nomad told him. "It must be destroyed."

Bichon fixed him with a steely gaze. "Destroy it here. Immediately. I realize now that attempting this thing was folly, but I also see that transporting it could prove disastrous. Unlike my mage, Dredmort surely does possess the skills to use it. If he were to acquire it, the results could be catastrophic. We cannot risk that."

"I do not believe I possess sufficient power," Nomad told him, staring at the pyramid. "But I will try." He raised the artifact from the table and set it down on the stone floor. Standing back a few feet, he held out both hands and called fire. A white-hot blaze erupted around the object; Khaldun had to shield his eyes and move away from the heat.

Nomad kept it up for more than a minute, finally dropping his arms. When the flames dispersed, Khaldun could see that the floor was glowing—Nomad's fire had started melting the stone. But the artifact appeared completely unaffected.

"Guards!" Bichon shouted. "Someone fetch a hammer from the smithy."

One of the men bowed and hurried out of the hall.

"It won't be any use," Nomad told him. "We must take it to the university. The governors have in their possession spells that can be used to demolish objects such as this. There is no other way."

Bichon ignored him. The guard returned a few minutes later, the blacksmith right behind him with a giant hammer in hand.

"Your Highness?" the blacksmith asked, sounding confused.

"Destroy that thing," the prince commanded, pointing at the artifact.

The man nodded, stepping forward, but then seemed to notice the heat emanating from the floor and backed away. "Begging your pardon, Your Highness," he said pleadingly. "I dare not approach it."

Nomad held out one hand, and the artifact flew into his open palm.

"Nomad!" Badru yelled, his voice full of concern.

"It is quite cool," the sorcerer told him, setting it down at the blacksmith's feet. "You may proceed."

The man shot Nomad a puzzled glance, then focused on the pyramid. Grasping his hammer with both hands, he reached back and took a giant swing. The impact produced an earsplitting crack, but the artifact remained whole. The blacksmith stared at it for a moment, then tried again. This time his hammer shattered, the pieces flying across the hall. The blacksmith stood there for a moment, looking perplexed.

"My apologies, Your Highness…"

Nobody spoke or moved for a minute. Finally Bichon got to his feet. Clearing his throat, he said, "It seems we are left with no choice. We must transport this cursed object to the university. I will send a platoon—they can depart with it today."

"I should accompany them," Nomad said to Badru.

"Out of the question," Badru told him. "I will not leave the troupe unprotected."

"If word gets out that we brought the artifact here, Henry will send his army," said Nomad. "And when they raze the castle, they will learn that the prince sent it to the university. What chance will those men have then?"

Badru opened his mouth to argue, but at that moment, a messenger stormed into the hall, Captain Westmore on his heels.

"Your Highness," the messenger said, struggling to catch his breath. "I apologize for the intrusion... but I come from the southern border. Fosland's army is marching for the castle... they're coming *here*!"

CHAPTER EIGHT
THE BATTLE OF OXCART

e knows," Bichon muttered. "Henry found out that you brought the artifact here."

"But that's impossible," Nomad replied. "We encountered no one at Castle Stanbridge."

"Someone must have seen you," said Bichon.

"No. We were invisible the entire time."

Khaldun gasped. "Allister."

Nomad fixed him with a stare. "Yes. That's the only explanation."

"Who in the hell is Allister?" Bichon demanded.

"He was an adviser to Prince Edward," Nomad explained. "We met him on our way to Stanbridge. He'd escaped the castle, but was injured, so we sent him here with one of your guards."

"He's here, Your Highness," said Westmore. "Our healer saw to his wound and then we provided him lodging."

"Somehow he must have sent word to Henry," Nomad suggested.

Bichon shook his head. "Sent word to Henry about what, exactly? Meeting a couple of mages in the forest? Henry wouldn't send his army here unless he knew that we had the artifact."

"Why else would a sorcerer be traveling to Stanbridge, Your Highness?" asked Mira.

Bichon stared at her for a moment, a look of comprehension dawning on his face.

"Begging your pardon, Your Highness," said Badru, "but it hardly matters *how* Henry found out. His army is headed this way and our people are sitting ducks outside your castle walls! We need to move!"

"Yes," Bichon said with a nod. "Westmore—send someone to apprehend this Allister character and move him to the dungeons. And dispatch messengers to our forces on the other borders to return here immediately to defend the castle against this invasion."

"Yes, sir," Westmore replied.

"Once you've done that, move all the men we have here and in town inside the castle. We must prepare for a siege."

"Yes, sir," Westmore repeated with a bow, then hurried out of the hall.

"What about our people, Your Highness?" Badru demanded.

"Yes, yes—get them into the courtyard. But be quick about it! We need to close the gates before this army arrives."

"Sir, Khaldun and I should aid in the defense of the castle," Nomad said to Badru.

Badru nodded. "Do it. I'll get the troupe inside," he replied before running out of the hall.

"I can help, too," Mira said to Nomad.

"Yes," Nomad agreed. "Your Highness, could you direct us to your tallest tower?"

"How far are you willing to go in this fight?" the prince asked. "Will you use your powers against the attackers? Or do your vows to the university require you to use defensive spells only?"

"The university is committed to neutrality, but I do not represent them in this conflict," Nomad replied. "I made my oath to Badru; it is my sworn duty to protect our people by any means necessary. They will be within your castle walls, so I will employ my full power to repel this enemy."

"Excellent," Bichon said. "Phillip, see to the sorcerer's needs. Provide him with whatever he requires to carry out his duty. I will direct our forces, and you shall coordinate the mages' efforts with our own."

"Yes, Father," Phillip said with a bow.

"But before you go, what do we do with that?" Bichon asked Nomad, pointing to the pyramid.

Nomad waved one hand, and the artifact vanished with a pop; Khaldun knew he'd tucked it into oblivion. "They won't be able to find it," Nomad said to the prince.

"Very well," Bichon replied with a nod.

"If you'll come with me?" Phillip said.

Khaldun and Mira followed Nomad and Phillip out of the hall through the rear entrance. They made their way through the keep and up a set of stairs. Phillip led them out onto the battlements. Khaldun could see Oxcart's soldiers hurrying about in the courtyard below and their archers lining up along the wall preparing to defend the castle. At the far end of the battlement, Phillip led them inside the tower and up the spiral staircase to the roof.

"This is it," he said to Nomad. They had a clear view of the courtyard inside the walls, as well as the castle grounds and the surrounding area outside. "Henry's army will have to come up the south road, and around the bend there to reach our gate."

Khaldun gazed around at the surrounding countryside. The front of the castle faced west; an enormous field and the approach from the road lay in that direction. He could see much of the town to the north, and the wayfarers breaking down their camp outside the castle wall. There was a group of small buildings far behind the castle, but otherwise, it was surrounded by forest to the south and east.

"Could they come in through the woods?" he asked.

"Perhaps," Phillip said with a shrug. "But I doubt they would try it. The ground is rough and uneven out there. They might send some snipers in that way to pick our men off the battlements, but their main force is sure to come at us from the road. But either way, you'll have a bird's eye view of their progress from here."

Nomad took in the landscape for a minute. "I'm going to work from here," he said to Khaldun and Mira. "And I'll take care of offense. Khaldun, you will remain here with me, and make yourself invisible. We know they'll have Nineve with them, but I doubt she'll be their only mage. They will do their best to cancel my spells; I want you to concentrate on harassing them. You will lack the power to have much of an effect on them directly, but using environmental weapons, you should be able to keep them busy.

"Mira, I'm going to station you on the battlements directly above the portcullis. With Allister's intelligence report, they'll know about Khaldun and me, but there's a good chance they won't be aware of your presence here. I want you to concentrate on defense. Cancel any spells they throw at the castle itself. I'll make you invisible, but do your best to stay out of view anyway, in case one of their mages cancels the spell."

"You can't make me invisible," Mira pointed out. "Magic doesn't work on me."

"The incantation doesn't need to act on you directly," Nomad explained. "Invisibility spells essentially create a bubble—anyone outside the bubble can't see anything inside of it that you've included in the spell. Watch." Nomad raised his hand and Mira disappeared from view.

"Yep, you're invisible, now," Khaldun said with a grin.

Nomad lifted the spell. "Position yourself at one of the arrow slits, and you should be able to see their entire army," he said to Mira. "Nineve will most likely be at the head of the column, but they'll probably have their other mages on their flanks. Chances are that they'll be invisible, but you'll be able to sense it when they cast spells.

"Any questions?"

"No," said Mira; Khaldun shook his head.

"Very well. Let's get into position."

"Just a moment," said Phillip. "Could you explain precisely what your 'offense' will consist of?"

Nomad regarded him for a moment. "You'll see."

Phillip looked like he wanted to argue, but seemed to wilt under Nomad's gaze. With a nod, he escorted Mira down to the barbican while Khaldun remained with Nomad on the tower roof. The area grew noisy as the wayfarers began filing over the drawbridge across the moat and through the gate into the castle. Khaldun had thought the courtyard looked enormous before, but it seemed quite a bit smaller now as their people filled the space. He began to wonder if they could fit the entire troupe inside, but in the end, there was enough room for the animals, too.

Once everyone was inside, Bichon's men closed the gate and raised the drawbridge. A few minutes later, the prince emerged from the tower wearing full plate armor, and took his position at the center of the barbican, flanked by two of his guards.

Despite the mass of bodies packed into the courtyard, an eerie quiet descended upon the castle. Bichon's archers stood ready along the battlements; the guards from the town and castle grounds were gathered just inside the portcullis, ready for a sortie should it become necessary. Khaldun hoped that it wouldn't—there were only about a hundred men assembled there; surely they were far too few to have much impact on an entire army.

"How many men are in Henry's army?" Khaldun asked quietly.

"Based on the encampment we saw outside Castle Stanbridge, I'd guess roughly two thousand," Nomad replied.

Khaldun felt his pulse quicken. How could they hope to overcome such a force? Even if they could hold them off long enough for Bichon's men to return from the borders, it wouldn't be enough. They would still be severely outnumbered. Then again, he'd never been involved in a siege before.

The minutes dragged by, the occasional clinking of swords or neighing of horses the only sounds. The tension in the air seemed palpable as they awaited their fate. But finally, Khaldun heard the din of marching footsteps in the distance. He made himself invisible; moments later, the head of the army came into view, turning off the road and heading toward the castle.

Khaldun spotted a woman on horseback riding out front with the banners, her flaming red hair identifying her as the witch, Nineve. He didn't see anyone else obviously a mage, but knew there had to be at least a couple more out there somewhere.

The enemy soldiers poured onto the castle grounds, forming ranks as they arrived. Before long, Khaldun was staring out at a sea of men filling the entire field in front of the castle. They'd kept their distance, the closest ones positioned roughly a hundred yards away. Finally, Nineve rode forward with one of their bannermen.

"Prince Bichon," she called out as she reached the moat, "on behalf of High Prince Henry of Fosland, I implore you to surrender. You have stolen an ancient artifact from Stanbridge; it does not belong to you. Hand it over, and surely we can achieve a peaceful outcome to our current situation."

"It does not belong to Henry, either," Bichon called out in response. "You have orchestrated an unlawful invasion of two sovereign lands, and slaughtered the rightful rulers of Stanbridge. Take your army and vacate our princedom immediately and we will let you live."

Nineve laughed out loud, looking around at their forces. "You have overestimated your position, Bichon," she told him. Holding out her staff, she shot a fireball at him, but Mira was ready; the spell fizzled out before it had covered half the distance to the prince. Nineve nodded to herself; Khaldun knew she'd only meant to gauge their magical defenses.

One of the prince's archers fired at the witch. But Nineve called fire, incinerating the arrow midflight. She and the bannerman turned and galloped back to their front lines.

Moments later, a phalanx of men charged forward, shields overhead, carrying something between them. They headed directly toward the gate.

"Fire!" yelled Prince Bichon.

His archers shot their arrows at the soldiers, but they bounced harmlessly off their shields. Nomad held out one hand, and Khaldun saw fire consume the soldiers from within. They screamed briefly before turning to ash. As their shields hit the ground, he realized what they'd been carrying: a bridge to cross the moat.

More soldiers hurried forward to replace their dead comrades. Khaldun could feel the power of Nomad's spell, but this time nothing happened—one of Fosland's mages had blocked his magic. The men managed to get the bridge across the moat.

Fosland's army sent up an ear-piercing battle cry, and the lead formations charged forward. Khaldun realized that several groups were carrying ladders. Two more phalanxes rushed ahead, each carrying a bridge to either side of the first.

Nomad went to work, calling fire over and over again as the Foslanders swarmed across the bridges. Half of his spells found their targets, and the men shrieked in agony as fire consumed them from the inside out. But an enemy mage managed to cancel much of his magic. Finally, Khaldun found him, but not by sight; the mage was invisible, but he could sense his incantations. Khaldun raised his staff and called earth, knocking a group of soldiers into the mage's position by the army's right flank.

Next, he recited the spell to cancel invisibility and spoke the word of command. It worked—he spotted an older wizard getting to his feet and recovering his wand from the ground. The man pointed his wand at Nomad, trying to cancel another of his spells. Khaldun called fire, trying to incinerate him, but it didn't work—the mage was too strong for him to affect that way. Instead, he ignited the grass around the wizard's feet to distract him.

A few of the Foslanders managed to get their ladders into position against the battlements. Soldiers began scurrying up the ladders but Bichon's archers showered them with arrows as others shoved the ladders away from the walls.

But suddenly, a wall of fire erupted along the top of the battlements. Bichon's men shied away from the heat, and the Foslanders got a few more ladders into position. But then Mira went to work, canceling the flames, and Oxcart's soldiers rallied, repelling their assailants again.

Nomad focused on the ladders, calling fire to ignite them. But someone on the field was cancelling his spells before they could do much damage. Khaldun checked on the old wizard; he'd managed to extinguish the grassfire, and was pointing his wand at the ladders. Khaldun called air, hurling a fallen Foslander soldier at him, and knocking the man to the ground. He tried to spot a discarded sword or spear he could throw at him, but at that moment something hit the tower; one of the merlons exploded, spraying Nomad and Khaldun with shrapnel. Khaldun spotted Nineve in the middle of the field, standing in her stirrups and holding out her staff; he canceled her next spell before it could hit them. Using the magical force, he created an illusion of a tiger directly in front of Nineve's horse. It spooked the animal, and he reared before turning and galloping away.

"Well done," Nomad said with a grin, before returning his attention to the field.

Khaldun felt immense power radiating from the sorcerer, and he stopped to see what he was going to do next. Suddenly, he felt the tower shaking, and worried that Nineve or the wizard had done something to damage it. But a moment later, he realized that it wasn't only the tower. The ground below was rippling like the surface of a lake—was this an earthquake?

The men in the field had noticed it too, as well as Bichon's soldiers on the walls. Very quickly the entire battle stilled as everyone looked around in fear. Screams went up from Fosland's army; Khaldun realized that a fissure was opening in the field, and Henry's soldiers were falling into it. Staring at Nomad, his mouth agape, Khaldun sensed another wave of power emanating from him and realized that he was causing this. The fissure spread across the ground, widening as it went, swallowing entire companies of Fosland's army. Flames erupted through the opening, and Khaldun wondered if Nomad had opened a pit to hell.

About a third of Fosland's soldiers were trapped between the castle and the fissure; Bichon's archers hit them with a storm of arrows. The men on the other side of the gap began to flee, but suddenly an enormous shadow burst out of the road, quickly growing a hundred feet high. It took the shape of a man, with hot coals for eyes and a body of smoke. The shadow bellowed, hurling fire at the retreating soldiers.

Madness seemed to take the Foslanders as they ran screaming from the demon only to plummet to their deaths in the fissure. Khaldun spotted Nineve riding among her forces, hollering at the men to form ranks. But it was no use; terror had consumed them.

Bichon ordered his men to open the front gate; the soldiers inside the castle charged out onto the field to finish off the men trapped on the near side of the breach. The giant demon faded to smoke, but beyond that Khaldun spotted soldiers riding toward them carrying Oxcart's colors. He knew these must be Bichon's men returning from the borders. The remaining Foslanders realized that the demon had disappeared, and turned to flee again. The incoming soldiers engaged them, and the field devolved into chaos.

The ground shook again and Khaldun realized that Nomad was closing the chasm. He tried to find Nineve, but couldn't see her anywhere; the old wizard had disappeared, too.

"We did it!" Khaldun said to Nomad. "We won!"

But at that moment, the sorcerer collapsed, grasping a merlon to hold himself up.

"Nomad!" Khaldun shouted, dropping his staff and rushing to his side. "Are you all right?"

"I will be," he said, his voice weak, as he sat with his back against the wall.

"What happened?"

"I'm just drained," Nomad told him. "That spell took more power than I realized."

"I never knew you could open a fissure like that," Khaldun said with a grin. "Or summon a demon for that matter!"

"No, that was only an illusion," Nomad replied, smiling weakly. "But the chasm was real."

"I need to practice," Khaldun said. "I couldn't have conjured anything that large—or so convincing."

"The only thing you're lacking is confidence," Nomad told him. "Your illusions are plenty strong. Give me a hand getting up—we should regroup with the others."

Khaldun helped his mentor to his feet, then retrieved his staff. They headed down the stairs, running into Mira partway down. The three of them checked in with Badru in the courtyard. Khaldun was happy to learn that their people had suffered no injuries.

Bichon and Phillip strode into the courtyard and approached them.

"Never in my life have I seen such a display of power," the prince said to Nomad. "We owe you a debt of gratitude."

Nomad gave him a bow.

"The witch, Nineve, and that old wizard have gotten away," the prince told them, "but I've sent my men to hunt down the remaining Foslanders. Now, if you'll join me in the great hall, we have one more thing that requires our attention."

Khaldun, Mira, Nomad, and Badru followed Bichon and his son into the keep. Inside the great hall, Bichon and Phillip took their seats behind the head table. Moments later, Captain Westmore and one of the guards arrived, escorting a man in chains and shackles into the prince's presence. It was Allister, former adviser to Prince Edward of Stanbridge.

"Kneel," the guard commanded, kicking the man in the back of the leg. Allister fell to his knees, crying in pain.

"Allister of Stanbridge, you are hereby charged with treason," said Phillip. "You knowingly aided and abetted High Prince Henry of Fosland in his efforts to invade Stanbridge and slaughter the royal family. You then proceeded to alert the high prince to the presence of two mages heading into Stanbridge from Oxcart."

"I did no such thing!" Allister insisted. "For thirty years, I was Prince Edward's loyal adviser. Never would I betray him as you accuse!"

"Then explain how the Foslanders knew we had the artifact here," said Nomad.

"What artifact?" Allister asked. "I'm sure I don't know what you're talking about."

Nomad held out his hand and the pyramid materialized in his palm. "Using this, Henry's chief mage, Dredmort, would command power not seen in Anoria for centuries. This is the reason Henry invaded Stanbridge."

"I've never seen that before," Allister told him.

"No, of course you haven't," Nomad replied. "But after thirty years of service, you would have known of its existence."

"Well, I, uh… that is to say… I mean, of course, I'd *heard* about it…" Allister stammered.

"How long have you been working for High Prince Henry?" Nomad asked.

"But I *don't* work for him!"

Nomad pointed a finger at him, and a tongue of fire appeared in front of Allister's face. "How long?"

Allister stared at the flame, trying to back away, but the guard held him in place. Nomad inched the fire closer to the man. Allister whimpered, turning his face away from the flame. The guard grabbed his head, forcing him to face it again.

"How long?" Nomad repeated. The flame grew larger.

"All right, I confess!" Allister shouted. "Henry sent an envoy a couple of months ago. He told the prince that Dredmort had discovered a cache of records in Fosland's library, including a document that referred to an ancient magical device hidden in Stanbridge. The envoy wanted to negotiate a trade.

"Prince Edward denied any knowledge of the artifact, but I knew he was lying. We'd all heard about this heirloom, even if we didn't know its location. Only Byron knew where it was hidden.

"But the envoy came to me late that night. He told me that Henry was prepared to send an army to retrieve the artifact. There would be a reward if I cooperated, otherwise he had orders to kill me! He held a knife to my throat—what else was I supposed to do?"

"Honor your oath to your prince, perhaps?" Bichon suggested.

"How?" Allister demanded. "I'm no soldier—that man was an assassin. He would have killed me on the spot if I'd refused to aid him. So, I simply confirmed what they already knew—I told him that the prince did possess the artifact he was seeking. And he paid me with a bag of gold..."

"Did you warn your prince?" Phillip demanded.

Allister did not reply, whimpering again instead.

"You coward," said Bichon. "You sold out your prince. Edward's death is on your head."

"There was nothing I could do! Henry already knew about the artifact. There was no point in denying it—he would have invaded anyway, and *I'd be dead*!"

"And so when they sacked the castle, they *let* you escape," said Nomad. "Why? What further purpose did you serve?"

"What?" said Allister.

Nomad moved the flame closer to the man's face again.

"All right! They sent me to watch the forest trail! Nineve believed the university would send someone to recover the artifact!"

"You alerted them when you encountered us heading toward Stanbridge," said Nomad.

"Yes… but you sent me with the soldier. I couldn't risk contacting them in his presence. So I waited until I arrived here—until I was alone. They were so angry that I'd delayed—I was terrified that they would kill me!"

"How did you communicate with her?" asked Nomad.

"Mirrors," said Allister. "Nineve gave me a mirror. Dredmort has its twin."

"Dredmort?" asked Nomad. "You were in contact with Dredmort?"

"Y-yes," Allister replied, shaking now. "He relayed my message to Nineve."

"Where is the mirror now?" asked Nomad.

"In my chambers. Inside my pack."

"I've heard enough," said Bichon. "Return him to the dungeons. We'll execute him at dawn."

"What? No!" Allister screamed as the guard dragged him to his feet, hauling him out of the hall.

"Westmore, find that mirror and bring it here," Bichon commanded.

"Yes, sir," said the captain, hurrying off.

"Communicating that way, Nineve has probably already notified Henry of his defeat here," Bichon noted.

"Yes, Your Highness," Nomad confirmed.

"Where would they have acquired such a thing?" asked Phillip.

"Many such items are scattered throughout the Five Kingdoms," Nomad explained. "Only a sorcerer can imbue an object with magical properties, but Henry and his mages could have collected a few between Fosland and the other princedoms he's conquered. They're often passed down as family heirlooms—much like the artifact."

Westmore returned a few minutes later, a small pocket mirror in hand. He approached the head table with it.

"Your Highness, it could be dangerous," Nomad warned him. "It's possible Dredmort could use it for more than just communication. Allow me."

"Very well," Bichon agreed.

Westmore handed the mirror to Nomad. Khaldun and Mira moved in closer to him to get a look. It fit in Nomad's hand, and had a metal cover on a hinge. Nomad opened it. At first, it showed only the expected reflection. But an instant later, that faded into the background, and an image of a man's face superseded it.

"Dredmort," said Nomad.

The wizard had a stern face, with a bald head and a long, black goatee. His piercing blue eyes were dead cold.

"Ah, Nomad. You've found our spy, then. Well, I daresay he'd outlived his usefulness, anyway."

"You've failed, Dredmort," Nomad told him. "We routed your army."

"Yes, Nineve mentioned as much, but it's only a setback. Don't worry, we will acquire the artifact before you get it to the university."

Nomad held his other hand over the mirror and Dredmort's face abruptly disappeared. He strode to the head table and handed the mirror to Bichon. The prince examined it, a puzzled expression on his face.

"Where did Dredmort go?"

"I removed the spell," Nomad told him. "It's just a normal mirror now."

"How did he know we'd take the artifact to the university?" asked Phillip.

"It's the obvious course of action at this point," Mira told him. "None of us possess the knowledge to use it or destroy it. Taking it to the university is the only option that remains if we want to prevent Henry from acquiring it."

"But how can he possibly know that we don't know how to use it?" asked Phillip. "That demon that the sorcerer conjured on the battlefield would seem to suggest otherwise."

Nomad shook his head. "That was only an illusion. It fooled Henry's soldiers, but Nineve would have recognized it for the ruse that it was. Dredmort already knew that we lacked the knowledge, but the fact that we *didn't* use the artifact in today's battle will confirm that fact for him."

"I see," Phillip said pensively. "Well, then we'd better decide how we're getting it there. We are in danger of another Foslander attack as long as it remains here."

"I have sent scouts to conduct reconnaissance of the routes heading north," said Bichon, getting to his feet. "They should return by dawn, and then we can reconvene and weigh our options. But tonight, we shall hold a feast in honor of these mages who saved our princedom!"

CHAPTER NINE
PROPOSAL

haldun headed out of the great hall with Badru, Nomad, and Mira, but Phillip held Mira back and asked to speak with her alone. Khaldun raised his eyebrows at Mira, but she only shrugged before taking Phillip's arm and walking away.

Outside, they found the rest of the wayfarers filing back out of the castle and setting up their camp on the grounds again. Khaldun realized only then that he hadn't given any thought to his own tent before the battle. He was about to ask Nomad about this, but then Oscar came over to them, carrying two packs.

"You two were busy, so I asked Oscar to pack up your things," Badru told them.

"I'm not sure that I did this right, but here you go," he said, handing over the packs.

"Thank you," said Khaldun. Oscar was covered in dirt and blood. "You're injured," he noted as they made their way toward the gate.

"Not my blood," he replied with a grin, wiping his forehead on his sleeve.

"You were involved in the fighting, then?" asked Nomad.

"Aye. Had to make myself useful somehow. Those Foslanders were well trained, but they had no chance against your sorcery. Haven't ever seen a mage summon a demon or open a chasm in the earth before. Certainly am glad you're on our side!"

"The demon wasn't real," Nomad told him. "That was only an illusion, and well within the ability of many common mages. But only a sorcerer could command the power it took to create that fissure."

They crossed the drawbridge and followed the crowd onto the grounds. Nomad and Badru went off to assist with the organizational efforts, while Khaldun and Oscar found their spots and set up their tents.

"Where did Lady Mira go?" Oscar asked.

"Prince Phillip wanted to speak with her privately," Khaldun replied with a scowl.

"Ah. I heard his father interviewed her. They do seem to be taking quite an interest in her."

"Yes, they do," Khaldun muttered. "Mira thinks they want her to serve as a mage, but I'm not convinced."

"You believe Phillip wants her to marry him?" Khaldun shrugged. "Well, you've got nothing to worry about. Mira will refuse him."

"How can you be so sure?"

"She's turned down far more attractive offers."

"But none of those would have made her a princess," Khaldun pointed out.

"True. But it won't make any difference. Trust me."

Khaldun didn't understand how he could be so sure. They finished setting up their tents in silence.

"Ah, there's Lady Mira now," said Oscar, heading away.

Khaldun followed him over to Nareen's tent; they arrived only moments after Mira.

"Where were you?" Nareen demanded, taking Mira's face in her hands. "You had me so worried!"

"I helped with the battle, Mother," she said, but in response to Nareen's terrified expression quickly added, "But I was perfectly safe—they had me up on the battlements. I was protected behind the wall the entire time!"

"I forbid you from doing that again! Next time, you will remain by my side and let the others do the fighting!"

"What did Phillip want?" Khaldun asked.

"Oh, well… he invited me to attend tonight's feast as his personal guest," she said with a grin that looked more like a grimace.

Khaldun felt his insides squirm. "But that's silly—Bichon is holding the dinner in *our* honor—you would have been attending anyway."

"Yes, of course, but now I'll need to wear a nicer dress," Mira said, rolling her eyes. "One does not accompany a prince wearing homespun," she added, pulling at her plain, gray skirts.

"I knew it," said Khaldun. "He's going to ask you to marry him."

"Aye, let's hope so, lad," Nareen said with a grin.

"Oh, please," Mira replied, rolling her eyes. "He can't."

"Oh, and why not?" Nareen demanded, looking crestfallen.

"I'm a wayfarer, Mother—I have nothing to bring to such a marriage, particularly to a prince. He'll be required to marry someone who adds to his family's power or property in some way. And I can do neither."

"I beg to differ, my lady," said Oscar. "You're a mage. That alone makes you a good candidate."

"And you're highborn," Nareen added. "Don't you forget it. Your father would provide a dowry—he's already said so."

"Well, we'll see soon enough," Mira said, shaking her head, but smiling in spite of herself. "But if you boys will excuse me, I need to get ready for the feast," she added, ducking into their tent.

"This is so exciting," Nareen said to Khaldun and Oscar before following her daughter inside.

Khaldun heaved a heavy sigh before heading back to his own tent.

"Don't worry, mate," said Oscar, following in his wake. "She'll say no."

The two of them hung around for a few hours, talking about the battle and other things. Oscar told him he'd never taken part in such a large conflict before. He explained that he'd been involved only in a couple of minor border disputes.

Nomad came to fetch Khaldun before too much longer. Khaldun bade farewell to Oscar and headed off toward the castle with the sorcerer.

"What about Mira?" he asked as they passed her tent.

"She's already there," Nomad told him. "Phillip sent one of his guards to escort her there a few minutes ago."

"Of course, he did," Khaldun muttered.

They met Badru by the gate and headed inside. There was a lot of noise coming from the great hall this time—many chattering voices and music. Walking into the room, Khaldun noted that they'd set up all the tables for this event. They were covered with white tablecloths, fine china, and silverware. People were milling about the room, engrossed in lively conversation, wearing their best finery. A group of musicians in the back corner of the room was playing a lively tune.

Prince Bichon was nowhere to be seen, but Khaldun spotted Mira, arm-in-arm with Phillip, gathered with two other couples by the head table. Mira threw her head back, laughing at something Phillip had said. She looked beautiful in her fancy pink dress and golden jewelry, her hair hanging in loose curls; she hardly looked like a wayfarer at all.

Khaldun couldn't help feeling jealous; he wished he were holding her arm instead of Phillip. Mira's sudden return to his life had rekindled his feelings for her. There was no denying he was in love—in a way he'd never been with the other women he'd known romantically. Certainly, none of them had ever made him feel jealous.

But Mira was special. He'd felt a connection to her when they were younger that he'd never shared with anyone else. A closeness; an understanding. As a boy, he'd believed they'd always be together. And though he'd slowly forgotten about it during her absence, her arrival had revived that connection stronger than ever.

Surely Mira felt the same. She'd said as much, hadn't she? Told him that she'd never forgotten their promise, and still wanted to marry him? Yet how could she choose him over a life as a *princess*? She could live in luxury, her every need and desire satisfied by her husband's riches. How could Khaldun, the poor wayfarer, hope to compete with that?

The herald entered the room, playing a few notes on his trumpet and snapping Khaldun out of his reverie. "Ladies and gentlemen," the herald announced, "Their Highnesses, Alexander and Desdemona Bichon."

The room erupted in cheers and applause as Bichon and his wife took their places behind the head table. A man in black robes walked in behind them, and as he took his place beside the prince, the room grew quiet. Khaldun realized he was a priest. He knew most of the people of Anoria believed in the "One True God," but most of the wayfarers weren't religious, so he had very little experience with this sort of thing. There had been an old woman in the troupe when Khaldun was younger who believed in the old gods, but she'd passed away many years ago. Khaldun knew that her religion had mostly died out centuries earlier, so he didn't know much about that either.

The priest said a prayer, giving thanks for their victory and their bounty.

"Please, take your seats, everyone," Bichon called out when he was done. "Let's eat!"

Khaldun sat down with Badru and Nomad at the far end of the room. He spotted Mira sitting down next to Phillip at the head table. Servants came out carrying platters of food and flagons of wine, setting them down on the tables. Khaldun filled his plate as one of the servants poured wine into his glass.

The food was delicious, as one would expect at a prince's feast— venison and quail, potatoes and vegetables. Nomad and Badru chatted amicably with the men and women sitting across from them.

One couple was a lord and lady from a nearby holding; the other was a local merchant and his wife. But Khaldun ate in silence, unable to get his mind off of Mira and Phillip. He drank several glasses of wine to wash down the food, and soon found the alcohol going to his head.

When the meal was finished, Bichon got to his feet and asked the wayfarers to stand. He thanked them for their aid in defending the castle, and raised his glass, giving a toast to the three mages. The rest of the guests raised their glasses and drank in their honor. Then the prince ordered the tables cleared away to make room for dancing. Khaldun got up to leave, but at that moment, Phillip and Mira approached, arm-in-arm again.

"Noble sir," Phillip said, addressing Badru. Khaldun had to stifle a chuckle at the surprised expression on Badru's face; he was pretty sure no prince had ever addressed him that way before. "Given the absence of Mira's father, Lord Girsham, the vast distance to his keep, and the fact that the lady now resides in your care, I have determined that you are the one to whom I must make my request."

"All right," Badru said, shooting Nomad and Khaldun a glance, struggling to keep a straight face, "and what would that be?"

"I would be forever in your debt if you would grant the Lady Mira's hand in marriage, my lord," Phillip said, bowing slightly.

Mira blushed; Khaldun didn't think he'd ever seen her so embarrassed.

"Your Highness," Badru replied, clearing his throat. "I am no lord, for one thing, and while I appreciate the consideration, we wayfarers are a free folk. Mira is not my property, and her hand is not mine to grant, in marriage or in any other capacity, for that matter."

Phillip nodded, turning instead to Mira. "My lady, would you do me the honor of becoming my wife and princess?"

Mira stared at him in disbelief for a moment; Khaldun was on tenterhooks waiting for her reply, more so even than Phillip, who was beaming expectantly at Mira.

"Your Highness, I am flattered," she said finally. "But this is so sudden… Could I perhaps have a little time to consider the offer?"

Phillip's smile faded and he seemed to deflate. His expression changed quickly from confusion to disappointment, and then to anger and annoyance. "Yes, of course, my lady." He bowed slightly to Badru before turning on his heel and striding back toward the head table. Mira looked at each of them pleadingly before hurrying off after him.

"Well, that was unexpected," Badru said with a grin.

"Indeed," Nomad agreed. "She believed they would ask her to replace their mage."

Khaldun had had enough. He walked directly out of the great hall, his head ringing—whether from the alcohol or his anger, he couldn't tell. Why hadn't Mira simply refused the prince's offer right then and there? If she truly wanted to be with Khaldun, then why string the prince along? Returning to his tent, he found Oscar sitting outside, a bottle in hand.

"You're back early," Oscar noted.

"Yes," Khaldun agreed, sitting down next to him. "Highborn functions make me uncomfortable."

Oscar nodded. "This mead is delicious. Care for some?"

"Sure."

Oscar handed him a bottle. Khaldun uncorked it and took a long drink.

"My friend, Arman, brewed this," he said; he'd recognize his recipe anywhere.

"Aye," Oscar replied. "Met a chap named Riyan earlier. Told me about what happened to Arman in the attack. A shame, that. But I guess he left his equipment to Riyan? He's got his recipes and plans to keep brewing the stuff."

Khaldun nodded, a tear coming to his eye. "Arman was a good friend," he said. "I knew he'd been teaching Riyan to brew for a while before his death. I'm glad someone's carrying on the tradition."

"To Arman," said Oscar holding up his bottle; Khaldun clinked his own against it.

"To Arman," he agreed, taking another swig. "Sure enough, the prince proposed to Mira."

"No surprise there," Oscar said with a chuckle.

"She didn't say 'no.'"

"Well, of course she didn't. Can't go offending a prince in his own hall in front of all those people. She didn't say 'yes,' either though, did she?"

Khaldun shook his head. "She asked for time to think about it. But he didn't propose in front of the entire hall—it was only Badru, Nomad, and me."

"Don't worry, my friend. By now, she will have turned him down in private. Have to protect the fragile royal ego, you know."

"If you say so," Khaldun replied, finishing his drink in one swig, but he wasn't so sure. Turning down a lord was one thing. But a *prince*?

He sat up late with Oscar, and downed several more bottles of mead, keeping an eye out for Mira's return the entire time. But there was still no sign of her by the time he went to bed. Too drunk to stand, he had to crawl into his tent. He lay flat on his back, and it felt like the world was spinning slowly around him. Wondering what Mira was doing, he drifted off to sleep.

Nomad woke him up in the morning; Khaldun opened his eyes and realized that he had a splitting headache. Sitting up, he felt nauseated. He ran behind the tent and vomited.

"Rough night?" Nomad said, shooting him an understanding grin.

"You could say that," he replied.

"Bichon sent a messenger. His scouts have returned; he's summoned us to the great hall."

Khaldun nodded and headed toward the castle with him. They met Badru by the gate and went inside. Mira was already there with

Phillip and his father, still wearing her dress from the night before. Khaldun's heart sank.

"Good morning," said Bichon, taking his seat behind the table. Phillip joined him, but Mira stayed with the wayfarers. "Our scouts have returned. They report that the road north is clear from southwestern Fosland into southeastern Ulster. Our soldiers will depart this morning to bring the artifact to the university."

"They have to travel through *Fosland*?" said Mira.

"Only for a short distance," Bichon replied. "They could take the west road into Stoutwall, then move into Ulster from there, but it would add at least a day to the journey. But fear not, our scouts saw no troops in the area."

Nomad held out one hand and the pyramid appeared on the head table in front of the prince.

"Your mages have been a great help to us, Badru," said Bichon. "But I must make one more request."

"Yes?" Badru replied warily.

"Send the sorcerer with my men. Under his protection, they would be able to repel any attack. This would give the mission its greatest chance to succeed."

"Out of the question," said Badru, shaking his head.

"We would, of course, extend our protection to your people once again during his absence."

"With all due respect, Your Highness, Henry's army would have defeated you with ease were it not for Nomad. And Henry *will* send a force here to find the artifact. I'm sorry, but our involvement in this situation ends here."

"Sir, you and the prince are both correct," said Nomad. "Henry *will* come for the artifact, and my presence *will* ensure the artifact makes it safely to the university."

"No. We've done our part. This is out of our hands now. We will head into Stoutwall as discussed—and we should depart immediately.

With any luck, we will be well within their borders before any more Foslanders arrive here."

"Could the sorcerer hide the artifact for the journey?" asked Phillip. "As he has done here repeatedly? The mages at the university should be able to bring it back once they arrive there, correct?"

"It doesn't work that way," said Nomad. "When I tuck it into the void, I can tether it to its current location, or to me. There is no way to send it with anyone else that way."

"Would you be willing to send your wizard?" asked Bichon. "He may not be as powerful as the sorcerer, but his help would be invaluable in fending off any attack."

"I'm afraid not," said Badru. "We have already done far more than we should have. It's time for us to be on our way."

"Sir, I should go with them," said Khaldun. "He's right—I could help resist an attack, especially if Henry sends a mage."

"Khaldun, no," said Nomad. "Your progress has been impressive, but you are still no match for the likes of Nineve."

"I agree," Badru added. "I refuse to put your life in such danger."

"It's my choice," said Khaldun. "Unlike Nomad, I've sworn no oath to you. We're a free people, aren't we?" It hurt Khaldun to say these words to him; Badru had been nearly as much a father to him as Nomad. "If Henry gets that pyramid, there will be nowhere safe for us to travel—for anyone. I can help prevent that. How can I walk away from this knowing that I could help?"

Badru regarded him for a moment in silence, then shrugged and nodded. "You're right. I have no authority to stop you."

"I'll go with you, too," said Mira. "Two mages are better than one, right?"

Khaldun's heart jumped; he noted that Phillip stared down at the table at her words, saying nothing.

"Mira, no," Badru pleaded. "Think of your mother! Putting yourself in harm's way like this would torture her."

"I journeyed halfway across the continent to get here, and managed to arrive safely, didn't I?"

"You didn't have Henry hunting you then," Nomad pointed out.

"No, but we encountered his men anyway, both on the road, and in the very midst of our camp. We won't be truly safe whether we join the prince's men or not! And if Henry acquires the artifact, we'll never be safe again. I'm going to help. And I'm sure Oscar will accompany us as well."

Badru nodded. "Fine. Go. But *you're* going to have to explain this to Nareen," he said, pointing a finger at her. "Not me." He turned on his heel and strode out of the hall. Nomad gave Khaldun a look before following him out.

"Very well," said Bichon, getting to his feet. "We will send someone to fetch you both as soon as our men are ready."

Khaldun and Mira bowed, then headed out of the castle together.

CHAPTER TEN
JOURNEY

'm glad you're going with me," Khaldun said as they crossed the drawbridge. "But you *would* be safer staying with the troupe."

"Where you go, I go," she replied, shooting him a grin.

Her words heartened him, but he couldn't help still having misgivings about her involvement with Phillip. "I waited up for you last night," he said. "You never returned to the camp."

"Oh, no. I sat up late with Phillip, and dozed off in his bed. He was preparing to go down to the great hall when I awoke, so it was easier to meet you there."

Khaldun stopped in his tracks. "You *slept* with him?!"

"Sleep being the operative word," she replied, frowning at him and halting herself. "Nothing happened, of course."

"I find that a little difficult to believe," he said, resuming his course toward the camp.

"Why?" Mira demanded, hurrying after him. "I've saved myself for you this long. What makes you think I would sleep with Phillip?"

"Uh, let's see. He's a *prince*, he proposed to you, and then you spent the entire night with him. What else should I think?"

Mira tutted at him. "Oh, please. I politely *declined* his proposal after the feast—in private. But we got to talking, and he's actually quite nice. He was very interested in the history of our people, so…"

"And why didn't you refuse him immediately when he proposed to you?" Khaldun demanded. "If you've been saving yourself for me, then why did you require any time at all to consider it?"

"Khaldun! I *didn't* need any time—that wasn't the point at all. There was never any question that I would refuse him, but as you've pointed out, he's a *prince*! I'm not sure there's another highborn lady in all of Anoria who would turn down such an offer, so at the very least, I needed to do so in *private*."

"And why is that?"

"To allow him to save face, of course! The only thing worse than being rejected like that would be having it done in public!"

"Which begs the question, why would a prince be interested in a wayfarer bastard in the first place?"

Mira stopped this time, staring at Khaldun as if he'd slapped her.

"I'm sorry," he said, "that was out of line."

"Yes, it sure was," she replied, glaring at him and striding away. Khaldun hurried after her. "And for your information, he's interested in me because I'm an intelligent, beautiful, and single highborn lady. *He* doesn't pass judgement on me simply because my parents never married."

"Well it's just that it's a little unusual, isn't it? Don't highborn lords usually seek marriages that provide some sort of advantage? Land or power or *something*?"

"He's not a lord, he's a prince," Mira pointed out. "So his family already has plenty of land and power. And besides, I would provide them with something very few highborn ladies ever could." Khaldun stared blankly at her. "*Magic*. You may have noticed that they no longer have a mage. And on top of that, our kind of power runs in families, and they've never had a mage in theirs. But there's a good chance that any child I might produce with Phillip would be a witch or wizard."

"But mages are forbidden from ruling a princedom, aren't they?"

"Sorcerers are, of course, but not normal mages. I mean, it's frowned upon, but it does happen from time to time. And a ruling prince who's also a mage would help increase Oxcart's power in the region. Bichon seemed less than thrilled about my joining the family, but I think that was what clinched it for him."

They reached the camp, and walked past Badru's tent; Khaldun looked for him, but didn't see him anywhere. They reached Mira's tent and found Nareen outside waiting for her.

"So, my darling, can we call you *Princess* Mira yet? You were at the castle all night, so I assume there must have been a formal proposal, no?"

"Oh, there was," Mira said, heaving a sigh, "but I'm afraid I turned it down."

"*What*?"

"Mother, I am not interested in becoming Princess Bichon of Oxcart, I'm sorry."

"Why ever not? This is what I have always dreamed for you! A *princess*—Mira, are you crazy? Why would you refuse this?"

Mira shook her head. "I didn't return to our people, risking life and limb in the process, only to turn around and marry the first highborn who proposes!"

"But—"

"Please, forget it, would you? And besides, Mother, I need to talk to you... I'm going to be joining the mission to bring the artifact I told you about to the university—"

"*WHAT*?! Mira, no—I will not allow it!"

"You can't stop me, Mother, I'm an adult now. And I won't let Khaldun do this alone."

"You're going with *this one*?" Nareen demanded. "This is all your fault," she shouted, rounding on Khaldun now. "You've cast some sort of spell on her! That's the only reason she's refusing to become a *princess*!"

"Mother, don't be ridiculous! Khaldun has no more say in whom I choose to marry than you do!"

Mira ducked inside the tent in a huff.

"We'll discuss this more later, boy," Nareen told Khaldun, poking him in the chest, before following Mira inside.

"What's going on?"

Khaldun turned to see Oscar running over.

"I heard shouting. Is everything all right?"

"Not really," Khaldun told him with a grin. "Mira's just told her mother that she's turned down a marriage proposal from the prince—*and* that she's joining the team bringing the artifact to the university."

"She did? And she is?"

"Yes and yes," Khaldun said, heading off toward his own tent. "Come on."

"Why in the world is she going to the university with them?"

"Because I am, too, and Badru won't let Nomad go."

"Ah. That explains it. Well, I'll be joining you too, then."

"Yes, she figured as much."

Khaldun found Nomad waiting for him, but their tent was lying flat on the ground.

"You'll need this," Nomad said, nodding toward the tent.

"No, I can't—what will you use?"

"I'll be staying with Badru while you're gone. Also, I prepared this for you," Nomad said, holding something out to him. Khaldun took it and realized it was a small mirror. "It works exactly like the one we found on Allister. I've got the other one, so we'll be able to communicate while you're away."

"That's great, thank you," said Khaldun.

"Be careful out there," Nomad told him. "And practice your illusions—they could be quite useful if you get into any trouble."

Khaldun nodded and found that his eyes were watering. This would be his first time away from Nomad ever since he'd taken him in as a child. He grabbed the sorcerer in a hug.

"I will. Thank you."

Nomad helped Khaldun pack up the tent and the rest of his things, and once Oscar had finished with his own gear, they headed off to check on Mira. They found her arguing with Nareen, but she had changed into her traveling clothes, and had her pack slung over her shoulder.

"I'm ready, let's go!" she said, turning her back on Nareen, who was still yelling at her.

"Goodbye, Nareen," Khaldun said, bowing to the woman.

"Don't you talk to me in that tone, boy! You'll live to regret this day, taking my precious daughter off on some—"

"Goodbye, Mother!" Mira said, shouting over her. "Come on," she added to Khaldun and Oscar, hurrying off. "Sorry about her."

Heading out of the camp, they found Badru outside his tent, coffee mug in hand. "Are you two sure I can't talk you out of this?" he asked, taking a drink. "We've already spilled enough wayfarer blood for this cause."

"I'm sorry, Badru," said Khaldun. "I spoke harshly in front of the prince. This is something I have to do. But I want you to know how much I appreciate everything you do for us. I know you don't have an easy job."

"I understand," he said with a nod. "Your father would be proud, I can tell you that much."

Khaldun had only vague memories of his parents; he hadn't been old enough to get to know them before they died. But his father had been a mage, too, and Khaldun had grown up hearing stories about how brave he was. This quest did feel like the type of thing he would have done.

A messenger arrived from the castle, notifying them that the Oxcart soldiers were ready to get underway. Badru gave Khaldun and Mira each a one-armed hug. "Safe travels, both of you. We'll be waiting for you in Stoutwall."

Khaldun, Mira, and Oscar headed off to the paddock to collect their horses. Once they'd secured their packs and swung into their saddles, they rode to the front of the castle. They found a dozen mounted soldiers waiting for them there.

"Greetings," said the leader; Khaldun recognized him from the southern border. "I'm Lieutenant Stancil. You must be the Lady Mira?"

"Yes, and this is Khaldun, and my guard, Oscar. Do you have the artifact?"

"Aye, my lady," he said, reaching behind him and pulling it out of his pack. "But I was hoping you might be willing to take it. The thing has an unwholesome feeling to it, if you take my meaning. And as a mage, you'd be better suited to protect it, I should think."

"All right," she said, taking it from him and securing it in one of her saddlebags.

"We'll be heading north on the main road, moving straight into Fosland," Stancil told them. "We'll pass through there as quickly as we can, and then we should be fairly safe in Ulster. The scouts report the way is clear straight into Roses."

"Very well," Mira replied. "I'd like Oscar to ride point with you. Khaldun and I will stay in the middle of the pack. This should maximize our protection of the artifact."

"Yes, ma'am," said Stancil, riding to the front of the line with Oscar.

"Yes ma'am," Khaldun repeated with a grin. Mira reached over and punched him in the arm.

Stancil and Oscar led them toward the road, and Khaldun and Mira fell into line midway back. They reached the road and turned north, riding through the town at a trot.

"Well, I certainly didn't expect another long journey so soon after reaching the troupe," Mira said with a sigh as they cleared the north end of the village.

"Let's hope it's uneventful," said Khaldun. "Badru said my father would be proud, but I'm not as brave as he was. I have to confess I'm feeling a little trepidation about this journey."

"Oh, nonsense," Mira said, shooting him a smile. "Bravery is only possible in the presence of fear. You're still going, aren't you?"

"Yes, I guess that's true."

They rode for a few hours, stopping only once to eat lunch and stretch their legs. At midafternoon, they reached the border with Fosland. Oxcart's soldiers had reestablished their roadblock here after the battle at the castle. Lieutenant Stancil checked in with the captain, and then the men opened the barricade for them. Khaldun felt his anxiety increase as they crossed the border.

But were it not for Oxcart's military presence, Khaldun wouldn't have known that they'd entered Fosland. There was rolling farmland for many miles in either direction and larger hills in the distance. Henry didn't have any soldiers posted here. Only an hour later they crossed into Ulster.

"Ulster's prince won't take exception to armed soldiers from a foreign princedom passing through his territory?" Khaldun asked.

"They'll have travel treaties in place to cover this sort of thing," said Mira. "Typically they allow a prince or lord to send an armed guard of no more than two dozen to protect dignitaries or merchandise traveling through neighboring territories. Moving an entire army is forbidden, but we shouldn't have any trouble. At least, that's how it works in my father's area."

"That makes sense," Khaldun said with a nod. "The troupe has free passage through all the princedoms in Maeda and Dorshire, but of course, we don't carry weapons."

They rode for a few hours, then found a clearing by the side of the road and made camp. Oscar set up his tent right next to Khaldun's, but Mira announced that she'd be staying with Khaldun.

"I assumed as much, my lady," he said with a grin.

The Oxcart soldiers gave them some space, setting up their own camp a little farther away. Oscar gathered some firewood and they lit a fire in their area.

"So tell me something," Mira said to Khaldun as the three of them sat down around the campfire. "I understand how elemental spells work, but what about the magical force? That's what you use to cast illusions and go invisible and things like that, right?"

"Yes," Khaldun confirmed with a nod.

"How does it work? I mean, when you call fire, you're literally creating flames or heat. But what precisely are you doing when you use the magical force?"

Khaldun considered it for a moment. "Well, in a way, it's the most fundamental of the elements. I guess you could say it's the force of will. For example, if you lift your arm or move your legs to walk, you're using your mind to make your body move. And when you call the elemental forces, you're extending your will into the world beyond your body, channeling that thought through your wand or staff.

"When you use the magical force, you're essentially doing something directly with your will. Instead of calling earth or air to act on an external object, your will itself operates on it. With illusion, for example, you're simply using your will to project the image that you want to create."

"And that demon that showed up in the battle was an illusion, right?" asked Oscar. "It wasn't real?"

"That's correct," Khaldun confirmed.

"And can *you* do that?"

"I can create simple illusions—static ones primarily. Casting something enormous like that demon that can move and makes sounds on its own is beyond my abilities, I'm sorry to say. But I'm working on it."

"Well, let's see something, then," Oscar suggested.

"All right," said Khaldun, getting to his feet. Holding out his staff, he cast an illusion. Suddenly, Nomad appeared across the fire from them, staring down at them, his hood thrown over his head.

"That's impressive," said Oscar, standing up and moving over to the simulacrum. He poked it in the shoulder. "Feels solid." He lifted the sleeve of the robe, and it fell back into place when he let go. "Seems real enough. But you can't make him move?"

Khaldun focused, trying to make the illusion walk around the campfire; it did move where he wanted, but glided across the ground without moving its legs. Oscar laughed out loud. Khaldun adjusted the spell, and suddenly Nomad's voice said, "What's so funny?" but his lips didn't move.

"Yeah, that's not quite right," Oscar said, retaking his seat. "Still remarkable, though."

"And you can see it, Mira?" Khaldun asked.

"Of course, I can."

"Well, magic doesn't work on you, so I wasn't sure."

"But the illusion isn't acting on me in any way, right?"

"That's true," Khaldun conceded. "And you can cancel it?"

Mira held out her wand and the phony Nomad vanished.

"Sure can," she said with a grin. "You've got Nomad down perfectly, though, except for the lack of walking and talking. What else can you cast?"

"Anything, really."

Khaldun held out his staff again, and a human-sized version of Nomad's demon appeared.

"Not nearly as scary as the one in the battle," Oscar told him.

Khaldun focused, changing the demon into a giant hand giving Oscar a rude gesture.

"Oh, now that would be useful in a battle," Oscar said with a chuckle. Khaldun moved the illusion to make it hit Oscar on the head. "Hey!"

Mira held out her wand and canceled it again. "It *would* be helpful if you could get your illusions to move. I've heard that the magical force is the hardest one to call. Most mages can't do it."

"It comes easier to me than the elemental forces," said Khaldun. "Despite my inability to add movement."

They sat up a little while longer while Khaldun cast more illusions to amuse them. But finally they grew tired and retreated to their tents for the night. Mira retrieved her saddlebag containing the artifact and brought it into the tent with them. She lay facing Khaldun at first, and they kissed passionately. But then she turned over and fell asleep within minutes. Khaldun held her with one arm, but having her body pressed against his like this was arousing him, making it difficult to fall asleep. Finally, he lay on his back, and dozed off before too much longer.

Khaldun woke to an empty tent. Sitting up and peering out through the flaps, he found Oscar and Mira sitting around a fire again; Oscar was cooking breakfast for them. Once the three of them had eaten, they broke camp and continued their northward journey with the soldiers.

They passed through the villages of a couple of small holdings, with vast tracts of farmland surrounding each. Between them the land was mostly wooded, and they crossed a couple of small rivers. One had a bridge, but they had to ford the other.

They encountered few people—just townspeople in the villages, and a few farmers carting their produce to market on the road. But late that morning, Khaldun heard sounds coming from somewhere up ahead—clanking metal and shouting.

"Do you hear that?" Mira asked.

Khaldun nodded. They moved to the front of the line to confer with Oscar and Stancil.

"Sounds like a battle, my lady," said Oscar. "Still far off, but we'll want to proceed cautiously."

"We're well within Ulster's borders here," noted Stancil. "I'm not sure who would be doing the fighting."

"Could be a border dispute between two lords," Mira suggested.

Khaldun and Mira returned to the middle of the line. The sounds of battle grew louder as they went. After a while, they reached a long, gentle incline in the road. At the top of the hill, they reached a clear field, and found the source of the noise.

There was a sea of chaos before them, two armies in open battle. The forces had long since broken formation; the fighting had devolved into small knots of combat, with groups of men vying against each other—Ulster soldiers and men in Foslander uniforms.

"Retreat!" Stancil shouted from up ahead, drawing his sword and trying to get their group back down the hill.

But it was no use; the nearest Foslander unit attacked them next. Oscar and Stancil headed them off before they could reach the others, but in no time, they were surrounded, and being drawn farther into the conflict.

The rest of the Oxcart men formed a ring around Khaldun and Mira, and before long, the Foslanders were attacking them from all sides. Khaldun called fire over and over again, incinerating any soldiers who made it past their defenders. One of the Oxcarters fell, and then another; Khaldun began to worry that they would be overwhelmed. Taking a quick look across the field, it appeared the main battle had moved beyond them, and they'd fallen into the enemy ranks.

For every Foslander they killed, it seemed that two more moved in to take their place. Khaldun called a giant wall of fire, trying to cut them off from the rest of the force. Nobody canceled his spell—thankfully, it didn't seem like the Foslanders had a mage on the field. But two more soldiers broke through the Oxcarters; Khaldun called fire, but this diverted his focus and his wall of flame disappeared.

Finally, a group of Ulster soldiers showed up, driving their attackers back. The Oxcarters tightened their ring, and the battle seemed to move beyond them as the Ulster forces pressed their advantage. Within a few minutes, Khaldun's group found themselves alone on the field, only the dead and wounded scattered around them.

"That was too close for comfort," said Mira. "I thought we were finished."

Four of the Oxcart soldiers had died in the fight. Two of the others were injured, one with a gut wound; Khaldun knew that one wouldn't make it. Luckily, Oscar and Stancil had escaped unscathed.

"Looks like a Fosland invasion," Stancil noted. "Henry's trying to add another princedom to his territories."

"Aye, and we're caught in the middle of it," said Oscar. "Seems like the Ulster force has driven them back east for now. But the Foslanders could rally—we should hurry north before we get caught up in it again."

But they'd moved only a hundred yards before a company of Ulster soldiers approached from the north. Stancil called a halt.

"Oxcarters, you're in Ulster territory here," their leader called out when they reached them. "State your business in our lands."

"We're escorting two mages to the university on urgent business," Stancil told them. "We claim right of passage as guaranteed by treaty."

"Our prince has suspended the treaty, as authorized during time of war," the soldier responded. "You might have noticed that Fosland's invaded."

"Our group stumbled upon your battle and took heavy losses. We have no desire for any further involvement in the conflict. If you'll let us pass, we'll be on our way, and should make it into Roses by nightfall."

"I'm afraid not," the soldier replied. "I've got orders to bring any trespassers directly to the prince. Wait here. Keep an eye on them," he added to one of his men.

Khaldun moved his mount up to the front, turning his back on the watching soldier. "Now what?" he said quietly to Stancil and Oscar.

"We could fight our way through them," Stancil murmured, keeping his head down. "With your fire and our swords, we might win."

"That's a whole company," said Oscar. "Magic or no, we'd be hard-pressed. And if even a single man escapes to alert a superior, we'd have their whole army looking for us."

"Let's wait," Stancil suggested. "I doubt they're going to divert an entire company to escort us to the capital."

Just then, the soldier returned with one of his men. "This is Lieutenant Conway. I've given him orders to take a squad and escort your group to the prince. Your men will need to surrender their weapons—and your mages their staves," he added, nodding to Khaldun.

"Sir, our business with the university cannot wait," Khaldun told him. "If our mission fails, Henry could end up conquering the entire continent. Surely you don't want to be the one who allows that to happen? I'd imagine your prince wouldn't be too happy with your decision here today should that come to pass."

"I have my orders," the soldier said, "and now you have yours." He rode back to the company.

"You heard the captain," Conway called out. "Now turn over your weapons and we can get underway."

Stancil and Oscar looked to Khaldun for guidance; he nodded. Conway sent a couple of his men to collect their swords, Khaldun's staff, and Mira's wand. The larger company resumed their course to the south, and then once they'd passed, Conway led their group north. They reached another road at the far end of the field and turned west.

Khaldun tried to talk Conway into letting them go on their way, but it was no use. The man refused to hear his arguments, and insisted apologetically that he was only following orders.

"We'd better hope that Ulster manages to drive Henry's forces back," Mira said to Khaldun. "Even if we convince the prince to let us continue north, it'll be for nothing if Henry sacks his castle."

Khaldun nodded, trying to think of a way out of this. But minutes later, there was a sound of many hoofbeats coming up behind them. Turning in his saddle, Khaldun spotted what looked like an entire company of Foslanders headed directly for them. Conway commanded a halt, moving his men to the rear guard. Khaldun rode over to Conway.

"Give our people back their weapons—and me my staff!"

"No! Now get back!"

"Fool—you cannot possibly defeat that many men with a single squad! They'll slaughter you! I'm a mage, dammit—let me help!"

Conway eyed him for a second longer, then ordered one of his men to return their belongings. He handed Khaldun his staff only moments before the Foslanders arrived. Holding it in front of him, Khaldun raised a ring of fire around the enemy soldiers. They reined in their mounts, many of them rearing and neighing loudly.

Khaldun began incinerating the Foslanders one at a time. Realizing what was happening, several of them managed to urge their horses through the wall of flames, charging the Ulster soldiers. Man-to-man combat ensued, the Oxcart soldiers rushing in to help.

The wall of flames diminished as Khaldun focused more fully on eliminating individual soldiers. Some of the Foslanders charged back the way they'd come. Together, the Ulster and Oxcart soldiers managed to cut down the rest. Within minutes, it was over.

"That's it, now," said Conway, turning back to Khaldun and his group. "We thank you for your assistance—reckon we wouldn't have made it through that alive without you. But it's time to surrender your weapons again."

"I was afraid you would say that," said Khaldun, calling a finger of fire in front of Conway's face. "But I agree that you would be dead now, were it not for us. And to repay that debt, I would suggest that you let us go, so we can resume our course to the university without any further delay."

"I'm sorry, but I cannot do that. I have my orders."

"Think about it, man," said Khaldun, growing the flame a little larger. "There are ten of you, and ten of us—but you haven't got any mages. We're going to resume our mission whether you allow it or not. So you can stand aside and give us your blessing, and live to tell your superiors that we escaped in the chaos of the battle. Or you can die here. Your choice."

Oscar and Stancil moved their horses next to Khaldun's, swords drawn. Conway looked back at his own squad, then eyed Khaldun's fire again.

"You win," he said with a nod.

"You're a scholar and a gentleman," Mira told him with a smile.

Stancil ordered Conway to lead his men back the way they'd come. They moved out and Khaldun's group followed. Once they'd reached the north-south road, Stancil told Conway to ride south. They waited till they'd moved out of view, then they took off to the north.

"Let's hope we don't run into any more Ulster soldiers before we get to Roses," said Mira.

"Or Foslander ones, for that matter," Khaldun replied.

CHAPTER ELEVEN
THE TEMPLE OF MANESH

hey continued north for the rest of the day and well into the evening, trying to put as much distance as they could between them and anyone else's army. Finally, before it grew fully dark, they found a clearing in the woods not far from the road and made camp there. Once again, Khaldun and Oscar set up their tents a little away from the others'. They didn't risk a fire, and Khaldun made the entire camp invisible.

After having a bite to eat, Khaldun called a small flame to provide some light and spent some time practicing his illusions again. He focused on creating an image of Nomad, this time concentrating on getting the movement of his walking correct. Khaldun knew that to cast any illusion, he had to visualize whatever he wanted to cast. He'd seen Nomad walking with the wayfarer caravan more times than he could count, so he imagined that.

And it worked—his moving illusion of Nomad was highly accurate. But he'd also and unintentionally included a horse and rider and a wagon alongside the sorcerer.

"That's much improved," Oscar said with a chuckle, "except that your wagon just moved through a tree…"

Mira giggled.

"Yes, well," Khaldun replied, clearing his throat, "I didn't mean to include the wagon at all. So let me try again."

Khaldun cast the illusion several more times, successfully eliminating the unwanted elements, while still focusing on Nomad's movements. But suddenly, the third time he produced the illusion exactly how he'd intended, it disappeared unexpectedly. He tried again and again, but it kept vanishing only a second or two after he'd cast it.

"I don't understand," he muttered in frustration. But suddenly he noticed that Mira was giggling. "You canceled it!"

She tried to feign surprise and ignorance, but Khaldun could see right through it. And he noticed that she'd hidden her wand up her sleeve.

"That's it—hand over your wand," he said, striding over to her.

"What? Why? I didn't do anything," she insisted, but then broke down in a fit of giggles.

"Come on, let's have it!"

He tried grabbing it from her sleeve, but she rolled away. Khaldun managed to catch her by one ankle and dragged her back to him. Before he knew it, they were both on the ground wrestling each other for control of her wand. But he finally managed to grab it.

"Hey!" Mira shouted. "Give that back!"

"I will," he promised, regaining his feet and pocketing her wand. "As soon as I'm done."

"Hmph," she said, standing up and dusting herself off. "Fine."

Khaldun cast his illusion again, but before the Nomad doppelganger had taken more than three steps he disappeared again. He checked to see if Mira had somehow taken her wand back, but it was still in his pocket.

"What on Earth…"

Mira giggled again.

"*You* did that?"

"Who, me?" she said, doing her best to look innocent. "But the big bad wizard confiscated my wand. I'm just a powerless wayfarer girl."

"No, seriously—did you do that?"

"Maybe," she said, shooting him a sly grin.

"But that's astonishing—only sorcerers can do magic without an instrument!"

Mira shrugged.

"Have you ever done that before? Actively canceled a spell without your wand before?"

"I don't think so…"

"Well, try something else," said Khaldun, calling fire and creating a pillar of flame. "See if you can cancel that."

Mira focused for a moment, brow furrowed, and then the inferno disappeared.

"Astounding," said Khaldun. "How about this?" He called air, lifting Oscar off the ground.

"Whoa—hey—I don't like this," he shouted, looking around frantically.

But Mira stared at him for a moment and he returned to the earth.

"Well, this is quite something," said Khaldun, handing her back her wand. "But I would strongly urge you not to let anyone else see you do that."

"Why?" asked Mira. "It'll be pretty convenient if you ask me."

"Yes, but we already know Henry wishes to acquire you. If he gets word of this, it will only increase that desire."

Mira frowned at this. "I'm not sure why that would be. It's fairly common for mage children to do magic without any instrument in the beginning, isn't it? That's usually how their parents discover their ability."

"Yes, but it's never anything they can control—it happens accidentally. And their powers never develop unless they train with a wand or staff. For any witch or wizard to cancel spells at will without an instrument is unheard of."

"All right," Mira said with a shrug. "I'll keep using the wand then."

They decided to keep watch, and Khaldun took the first shift. A few hours later, Oscar relieved him. Khaldun knew there was a way to keep his invisibility spell intact after falling asleep, but he hadn't learned how to do that yet. But so far, no one had gone by on the road. Khaldun crawled into his tent next to Mira and went to sleep. They woke at first light, broke camp, and resumed their course along the north road.

"We should make it to Roses by nightfall tomorrow," Stancil told them.

They rode all day, taking only a few brief rests. The forest grew thinner as they traveled north. Before long, they found themselves moving through farmlands again.

"It's strange—we haven't encountered a single soul today," Mira commented late in the afternoon. "That didn't happen once on the journey from father's keep."

"It is odd," Khaldun agreed. "Feels like the very land is holding its breath to see what happens with the conflict between Ulster and Fosland."

Not long after, they passed a grove of trees surrounding a castle. But there were no guards posted anywhere around the structure, and no signs of life inside.

"Could it be abandoned?" Mira asked.

"Perhaps," said Khaldun. "Let's take a look."

He rode up to Stancil and asked him to order a brief rest. Then he and Mira dismounted and walked over to the castle. It was smaller than Prince Bichon's. There were towers at each of the four corners, and giant wooden doors where the portcullis would normally be.

"The building looks well-maintained," said Khaldun as they approach the doors. "What is this?" There was an eye carved into the middle of the doors, with a sunburst extending from its bottom.

"It's the symbol of Ohlam," said Mira, running her hand over the carving.

"Ohlam?"

"It was an ancient religion that died out in the early days of the Pythan Empire," she explained. "This must be a temple."

"Then I would guess that the religion hasn't actually died out," said Khaldun. "It may be a temple now, but this was certainly built as a castle. Someone must have converted it—and it doesn't seem old enough to predate the Pythan Empire."

"No," Mira agreed. "And it doesn't feel like it's been abandoned, although I don't get the sense that anyone is here at the moment. But it does seem a little creepy," she added with a little shiver.

Now that he thought about it, Khaldun did get a strange feeling from the place—not magic exactly, but some sort of energy. "Yeah. I agree. Well, let's get back to the others. We still have more ground to travel today."

They rode for another hour or so, but dusk began to gather, and they started looking for somewhere to camp for the night.

"I don't like it," said Oscar, dropping back to Khaldun and Mira. "It's all flat and open as far as the eye can see. Nowhere to take cover."

Khaldun gazed up and down the road, trying to find anyplace they might be able to hide from view, but Oscar was right. He would make them invisible, of course, but the open ground made him nervous, and his invisibility spell would only last while he was awake.

Suddenly, he spotted what looked a giant dust cloud far to the north, in the same direction as the road. "What's going on up there?" he asked, pointing it out to Oscar and Mira.

"Oh, shit," said Oscar. "Only an army could kick up that much dust. We've got to get off the road."

"And go where?" asked Khaldun. "I don't see anywhere we could hide."

"We should go back to that temple," Mira suggested.

"That's not a bad idea," said Khaldun, growing more apprehensive by the second. "Even if nobody's there, we could break the door down."

"Or at least take cover behind the building," Mira replied. "It was large enough to hide our little group."

Khaldun went to talk to Stancil. He gazed north for a minute, then agreed that backtracking to the temple would be best, despite the time they would lose. They turned around and headed south.

It had grown fully dark by the time they reached their destination, the moons providing the only light. This time, the entire group rode their horses right up to the building. Khaldun dismounted and pounded on the door. Listening intently, he didn't hear any sound within. He knocked again, louder this time. Suddenly a rectangular spyhole opened just above the carving of the eye.

"Hello?" Khaldun called out. There was no reply and the spyhole closed again. "Well, there's someone in there," he said, turning to Mira and the others. "There's an army coming down the north road, and we're looking for shelter," he called out, facing the door again. "We're heading to the university on urgent business, and just need to hide until the army passes. Can we come inside?"

There was no answer. Khaldun was about to pound on the door again, but suddenly, it started opening very slowly. He backed away, and saw a short man standing inside, holding a torch. He wore brown robes like a wizard, but carried no wand or staff. His head was cleanshaven. The man looked around at their group, holding up his torch to see them better.

"Who are you?" he asked, his voice raspy.

"My name is Khaldun—I'm a mage, and this is Lady Mira of Blacksand. These soldiers hail from Oxcart; Prince Bichon has sent them to escort us to the university."

The man nodded, opening the door wider for them, and standing aside. "My name is Peter. You may shelter with us; it is unlikely the army will bother you here."

"Thank you, sir," said Khaldun, bowing to him. He took his horse by the reins and led him inside, Mira, Oscar, and the others right behind him. Once they'd all moved into the central courtyard, Peter closed and barred the door behind them. The others dismounted; Khaldun called fire and extinguished the man's torch. He started in surprise.

"Sorry," said Khaldun. "But we'd prefer if the army doesn't see any light in here."

"Forgive me," Mira said to Peter, "but this is an Ohlam temple, isn't it? And you're a monk?"

"Yes, my lady," he said, bowing slightly. "You have entered the Temple of Manesh."

"Manesh?" she repeated, sounding surprised. "But he's the chief deity, isn't he? I thought the temples were all devoted to the lesser gods?"

"They were in the old days," the monk replied. "Before the fall."

"It was my understanding that Ohlam had died out centuries ago," said Mira. "Clearly I was mistaken."

"We nearly did, my lady, but a few hangers-on preserved the faith through the dark times. They handed down the teachings secretly from one generation to the next."

"Are there many temples now?"

"Sadly, no. We are one of the few. But there were none a century ago. We are making a slow comeback."

"My lady," said Oscar from the doorway, "the army approaches."

Mira joined him, staring through the spyhole. Khaldun could hear the din of the passing forces. "Oh, no—a couple of soldiers are coming this way!" Mira whispered, closing the spyhole.

"Stay silent!" Khaldun quietly urged the others.

"Tellin' ya, Aramis, the place looks deserted," a voice said from outside the door. "No lights or anything. Probably abandoned."

"Maybe, but our orders are to investigate, and it ain't up to you to question the orders."

There was a pounding on the door. Mira locked eyes with Khaldun, grimacing; Khaldun held his breath, his heart hammering in his chest.

"Open up in the name of High Prince Henry of Fosland," the first voice shouted.

"Hold on, what is that on the door?"

"Don't rightly know. Looks like an eye of some sort."

"Yes. The eye of Ohlam. This is no castle, it's a monastery. Come on—we're wasting our time here."

Khaldun held his breath a few moments longer, then exhaled, and opened the spyhole. The men were gone. He could see the army progressing down the road—it extended as far as he could see in both directions, though he couldn't see very far through the small opening. The minutes dragged by, but finally the rest of the horde went by, and they didn't send anyone else to the monastery. Khaldun heaved a heavy sigh of relief. Turning to the others, he realized with surprise that twenty more monks had appeared, all wearing brown robes—their approach had been silent.

"They've passed," he reported to the others.

"I didn't think they would trouble us here," Peter said. "We were about to sit down for dinner when you arrived. Would you like to join us?"

"We appreciate the offer," said Stancil, "but we'd better be going. It's late and we still need to find somewhere hidden from the road to camp."

"You are welcome to camp here, in our courtyard," Peter told him. "We keep the entries barred at all times, so you will be quite safe here."

Stancil looked to Khaldun and Mira. Khaldun's stomach was rumbling, and this place *would* provide excellent cover from the road. He nodded to Mira.

"We accept," she said to the monk. "Thank you so much!"

Stancil left one of the soldiers to guard their horses and gear. The others followed the monks inside the building, into the area that must have once been the keep. One large table sat in the middle, with only enough seats for the monks.

"We were not expecting guests," Peter told them, "so I'm afraid we did not prepare enough food. But please, sit down, and we will make more."

"Oh, no, please—you and your brothers should eat first," said Mira. "We can wait."

But Peter insisted, so Mira, Khaldun, and the soldiers all sat down. There were three enormous bowls of stew on the table. They passed these around and served themselves. A couple of monks disappeared into the kitchen to prepare more food, while the others stood around the edges of the room, watching them eat with their arms crossed inside the large sleeves of their robes.

"So, their religion is polytheistic, right?" Khaldun asked between mouthfuls of stew. "There was a woman in the troupe when we were little who always used to talk about the old gods."

Mira nodded. "Yes, they have six lesser gods and goddesses—three of each, with Manesh presiding over the lot."

"And was Manesh male or female?"

"Neither," said Mira. "Or both... I never fully understood that part."

"I've heard that Ohlam was quite popular in ancient times," said Khaldun. "How did it die out?"

"It was the dominant religion on the continent for centuries," Mira confirmed. "But Nyro had the temples destroyed and the priests and monks slaughtered soon after she murdered the emperor and took his place."

"Nyro... She was the great necromancer, wasn't she?"

"Yes. And she's the reason they outlawed necromancy. Her reign of terror lasted hundreds of years before the princedoms finally enlisted the help of the elves from across the sea and overthrew her. They killed her and all of her other necromancers, and then the university proceeded to destroy every book and scroll about necromancy that they could find in all of the major libraries."

"And why did Nyro wipe out Ohlam?"

"I don't know," said Mira. "Unfortunately, the university became a little overzealous in its purge, and destroyed many historical texts in the process. The mere mention of Nyro's name was often enough to get a book burned. And without those records, scholars today are not sure what motivated Nyro's actions.

"But the rest is history. Religion was outlawed during Nyro's reign. And once the Pythan Empire fell, Unitarianism emerged as the dominant religion on the continent."

Khaldun nodded. "The 'One True God' won out in the end."

Once they'd finished eating, they rose from the table, and the monks took their places. Mira and Khaldun led the soldiers out to the courtyard to begin setting up their camp. But they found one of the monks arguing with the soldier they'd left to stand guard.

"What's going on here?" Mira demanded. Khaldun realized that they were standing by Mira's horse.

"I'm sorry, my lady," the soldier said with a bow. "This monk was trying to get into your saddle bag."

"Why?" Mira asked the monk.

"What is it that you carry in there?" the monk asked.

"That's none of your business," Mira told him, moving to position herself between the monk and her horse. "My belongings are my own, and no concern of yours!"

"You have brought an object of great evil into our midst," said a deep voice from behind them. Turning, Khaldun spotted a man standing there; his robes were like the others' but white instead of brown. "And that makes it our concern."

"And who are you?" Mira demanded, as Oscar drew his sword.

"My name is Turin. I am the high priest here. You carry something that is emanating great power—what is it?"

Khaldun found this odd; he hadn't been able to sense the artifact at all since Nomad sealed the portal. He didn't understand how the priest could.

"It is nothing," Mira told him. "A family heirloom from Stanbridge that we are transporting to the university."

"Might I see it?" the priest asked.

"No, as I told your monk, it's none of your concern," said Mira.

"Then I'm afraid I must ask you and your people to leave our sanctuary," the priest replied.

"Show him," said Khaldun. "What harm could it do?"

Mira shot him a glance, then nodded. Opening the saddlebag, she pulled out the artifact and held it in her open palm. The priest reached out with one hand, but Mira backed away, and Oscar stepped between them.

"A portal," said Turin. "I suspected as much."

"The sorcerer, Nomad, sealed it before we set out on our journey," Khaldun told him. "Nothing can come through it, I assure you. We're taking it to the university to make sure that High Prince Henry cannot acquire it."

Turin considered him for a moment before turning his gaze back to the pyramid. Mira returned it to her saddle bag.

"Very well. You may camp here for the night. But you—and that thing—must be on your way at first light."

He turned and strode away, the monk following in his wake.

"That was odd," Mira said once they'd moved out of earshot. "How did they know I was carrying anything like this?"

"I'm not sure," Khaldun replied, shaking his head. "I have sensed nothing from it since Nomad sealed it."

They turned in for the night, and Mira brought the saddlebag into the tent with them. Khaldun realized how tired he was when he hit his bedroll; he fell asleep within minutes. But he woke early to find Mira rummaging through the bag.

"What's wrong?" he asked.

She stopped what she was doing and stared at him for a moment. "It's gone."

"The artifact?"

"Yes," she muttered, now emptying the bag's contents onto her bedroll. "They must have taken it. I don't understand how they could have done it without waking us."

Khaldun sat up, peering out through the flaps.

"It's not even dawn yet. Well, let's go confront them."

Khaldun took his staff and Mira her wand. They woke Oscar; he donned his sword belt, and then they headed into the temple. But the monks were nowhere to be seen. They searched the entire ground floor—the kitchen and pantry, great hall, and library—as well as the sleeping quarters upstairs, but the building was empty. But as they descended the steps again, Khaldun sensed something.

"I'm feeling some sort of presence here," he told the others, gazing around the great hall. "It's similar to what I felt when we found the pyramid…"

"Is it the artifact?" asked Mira.

"Yes—well, not the pyramid itself. But something that's probably come through it."

"What, like a demon?" asked Mira. "But I thought Nomad sealed it? Could it have opened the portal from the other side?"

"Nomad told me that wasn't possible. But this means the artifact must be here *somewhere*."

The three of them searched the ground floor again, but still found nothing.

"Hang on," Oscar said as they returned to the great hall. "Do you hear that?"

Khaldun and Mira listened for a moment.

"I don't hear anything," Khaldun whispered.

"I do," said Mira. "It sounds like… chanting."

"Where's it coming from?" Khaldun asked.

"This way," Mira replied, leading them back into the library.

They stopped and listened again. This time, Khaldun could hear a faint humming noise.

"Could there be a hidden chamber somewhere?" asked Oscar.

"Perhaps," said Khaldun.

They walked slowly around the room, trying to locate the source of the sound. It seemed to grow louder by a bookshelf on the far side of the room. Khaldun examined the area more closely, and felt a faint breeze coming from the gap between two uprights. He whistled quietly to the other two.

"What is it?" Mira asked when they reached his side.

"There's something behind this bookshelf," he told them.

Grabbing onto one of the shelves, Khaldun pulled; the entire section opened like a door. Behind it was a steep staircase delving deep into the earth.

"I'll be damned," said Oscar.

It was dark down there, other than a faint flickering, as if from torchlight. And the chanting was louder now.

"I'm going to go ask Stancil to get his men ready and pack up all the gear," Mira whispered. "We may need to get out of here in a hurry. Wait for me before you go down there."

Khaldun nodded; Mira hurried off. Once she'd returned, Khaldun led the way down the steps, staff held before him, ready to cast a spell. He heard Oscar unsheathing his sword behind him. At the bottom, they came to a long, narrow tunnel leading under the building. As they followed that, the chanting grew louder; Khaldun could discern individual words now, but they were in an unfamiliar language. They reached the tunnel's end; to the left an archway formed the entry to a cavernous chamber. Inside, the monks were standing in a circle around a stone altar, their eyes closed; the artifact was sitting in the center of the altar. Khaldun spotted their priest, Turin, at the far end of the chamber.

There was some sort of presence here with the monks; Khaldun was certain of it. He didn't think it was the same as the one he'd sensed in Stanbridge, though. It felt vastly more powerful.

"What are you doing?" Mira called out. "You will return the artifact to me immediately!"

The monks ceased their chanting, noticing Mira and her comrades for the first time. They moved between Mira and the altar, forming a human barricade.

"You must permit us to continue," Turin implored her.

"What have you done?" Khaldun demanded. "You reopened the portal!"

"No—we don't know how. We only summoned Manesh; he opened it from the other side. But we must continue our ritual to guide him back from his dungeon!"

"But Manesh is a god," said Oscar. "Who put a god in a dungeon?"

"Nyro cast the gods out of heaven when she rose to power," said Turin. "We have searched for centuries to find a way to bring them back. And you have brought us the answer! I did not realize the true nature of this artifact at first, but now, we must keep it!"

"I'm afraid not," said Khaldun, holding out his staff. He called fire, shouting the word of command. A pillar of flame appeared, spreading from him to the altar. He split it into two, driving the monks back, and forming an alleyway between them.

But at that moment, something extinguished the flames, and lifted Khaldun off his feet, pinning him to the wall. There was a low rumbling sound, and the monks looked around in fear. Suddenly, Khaldun realized it was a voice, speaking long, slow words.

"What the hell?" he shouted.

Mira pointed her wand at him, canceling whatever spell was holding him aloft. Khaldun hit the floor and Mira darted to the altar, grabbing the artifact.

"Stop!" Turin yelled, blocking her way back to the tunnel. "That's the only way we have to bring back our gods!"

Khaldun held out his staff and called earth; something invisible slammed into Turin's back, knocking him to the floor. Mira ran past him and back into the tunnel. Khaldun followed at a run, Oscar taking up the rear.

"What the hell happened down there?" Oscar said once they'd returned to the library. "Who cast those spells against you—was one of the monks a mage?"

"No, it wasn't the monks," Khaldun replied, following Mira out into the courtyard. "It was whatever they were trying to bring through the portal."

"Their god?" Oscar asked.

"I don't know," said Khaldun. "Whatever it was, it was immensely powerful. Let's be glad we got there before they'd completed their ritual!"

The camp was gone—the tents, the men, and the horses. For a moment, Khaldun began to panic, wondering how they were going to continue their journey. But then he realized that the outer doors were open; Stancil and his men were waiting for them out by the road. Khaldun, Mira, and Oscar hurried outside as the monks ran into the courtyard.

"Wait!" Turin yelled. "Come back!"

But they ignored him, mounting their horses and heading north as the sun cracked the horizon.

CHAPTER TWELVE
ROSES

hat do we do now?" asked Mira. "Can you seal the portal again?"

"I don't know how, and after what happened with Tristan back in Bichon's castle, I'm not willing to try."

"But can that thing still use the artifact to enter our world?" asked Mira.

"I don't think so," said Khaldun. "And I no longer feel its presence. I do not think it was a god—it used a spell against me, which would seem to indicate that it was a mage."

"Not a demon?" asked Mira.

"It did not feel like the one Tristan summoned—that had no corporeal form. Whatever the monks were trying to bring through the portal was not purely spirit. I could sense something—or someone—solid behind it."

"So Manesh could have been a *person*?" Mira asked. "A powerful mage rather than a god?"

Khaldun shrugged. "I don't know. I'm not convinced that was Manesh."

Mira considered this for a moment. "Will any mages we meet on the road be able to sense the artifact now that the portal is open again?"

"I don't think it's possible for a normal mage to sense the artifact itself," Khaldun replied pensively. "When we found it, I felt *something*, but I believe it was a spirit or demon that had passed through the portal. If that happens again, then yes, I do believe any mage we encounter would detect that."

"The monks sensed it somehow even though the portal was closed," Mira observed.

"Yes. But I don't know how. They're not mages, but their rituals must tap into some form of magical power—whether they know it or not. I can offer no other explanation."

"Well, let's hope we don't encounter any hostile mages between here and the university," Mira said with a sigh.

"We should cross the border into Roses later today," Khaldun told her. "That's friendly territory, so we should be safe there."

They rode in silence for a while. Later that morning, they gave the animals a rest by a lake and ate some food. Soon after resuming their course, they crossed the border into Roses. A few hours later, they spotted Rosetown in the distance. But as they drew closer, Stancil ordered a stop. Khaldun and Mira rode to the front of the line.

"What is it?" Khaldun asked.

"Trouble," said Oscar. "The flag on the keep is wrong."

Khaldun looked closer—Oscar was right. "Fosland's colors."

"Aye, and note that huge encampment outside of town," Oscar told him. "Looks like an army to me."

"Henry's sacked Roses?" asked Mira.

"It looks that way," said Stancil. "Would've been a straight shot north from Rosetown to the university, but we can't go that way now."

"Can we just go around the town?" asked Mira.

"We could," Stancil replied. "But I'm betting Henry will have men guarding the entry to the university's territory."

"We'll have to cut through the country to the northwest, find the road into Perrin, and approach the university from the west," Khaldun suggested.

"I'm afraid so," Stancil agreed. "It'll add another day to the journey, but I don't see any other way. There was a trail leading into the forest a little ways back—we should take that."

They backtracked down the road, then took the path into the woods. It was narrow, and they had to ride single-file. The going was slow, but a couple of hours later, they came to a road.

"This should be the road to Perrin," Stancil told them as they reformed their line and headed north. But only a few minutes later, they rounded a curve and came upon a company of soldiers headed straight for them.

"Retreat!" Stancil yelled, standing in his stirrups. "Ride south!"

They managed to get the horses turned around and headed the other way, but the chaos made Khaldun's mount nervous; he reared as the others took off, nearly throwing Khaldun from his back. But finally, they charged off right beside Stancil.

"Halt or we'll shoot," a voice cried out from behind them.

Turning in his saddle, Khaldun spotted a squad of soldiers giving chase. Flattening himself against his horse's neck, he urged him to go faster. But suddenly Stancil yelped, straightening in his saddle. There was an arrow protruding from his chest; he slumped over and fell to the road.

Reining in his horse, Khaldun turned, calling fire on the approaching soldiers. But it was no use—someone canceled his spell. Khaldun spotted their wizard riding at the back of the group and holding out his staff.

"Shit," he muttered, charging off again.

Not far ahead, he found Oscar and the remaining Oxcart soldiers making their stand. They'd stopped in the road, facing north with their swords drawn. Mira was behind them, wand at the ready; Khaldun rode to her side.

"They've got a mage," Khaldun announced to the group. "And he's strong—he blocked my fire spell like it was child's play."

"Wonderful," Oscar muttered.

"I'll try to take out their wizard," Khaldun said to Mira. "You work defense."

She nodded. The enemy squad reached them moments later.

"In the name of High Prince Henry of Fosland, drop your weapons and surrender!" their leader called out.

"We are not in Fosland," Oscar retorted. "Our passage through Roses is protected under treaty. Stand aside and let us pass!"

"Final warning," the enemy captain shouted as two of the other men nocked their bows.

Khaldun called fire again, muttering the incantation under his breath and focusing on their mage. He spoke the words of command and held out his staff, but again, their wizard canceled his spell. He held out his own rod, and Khaldun sensed his counter-spell hit them, but nothing happened.

"Wait," their wizard called out, moving to the front of their group.

"What is it, Lane?" the leader demanded.

"They have the two mages from the warrant."

"I see only the boy," the leader countered with an annoyed tone.

"The girl at the rear is impervious to my spell," Lane told him. "She must be the one."

"Come forward, my lady, and identify yourself," the leader called out.

Mira rode forward; Khaldun flanked her. "I am Lady Mira of Blacksand. We are en route to the university; treaty dictates that—"

"Ah, now I can see your wand," the leader said with a smirk. "You're the ones who destroyed Gunthar's staff, eh? Or your sorcerer did, I guess, but he don't seem to be around to save you this time. And you're with a bunch of Oxfuckers. Must be transporting that family heirloom Dredmort wants so badly. Very well—surrender your wand and staff. You're coming with us."

"NOW!" Oscar shouted.

Several things happened at once. Oscar and the Oxcart soldiers charged forward, brandishing their swords; the Foslander mage called fire, but Mira canceled his spell; and Khaldun called fire again, managing only to ignite the wizard's robes.

A melee broke out as the Oxcart men crashed into the Foslanders. Khaldun tried using several spells against the Foslanders but their wizard blocked his every attempt. Lane also attempted to use magic against the Oxcart soldiers, but Mira managed to neutralize him.

Men screamed and horses whinnied as the soldiers clashed and steel met flesh. Before long the battle surged toward them and Khaldun found himself in the midst of the soldiers. One of the Foslanders bore down on him, raising his sword. Using his staff like a spear, Khaldun hit him in the chest, knocking him from his horse.

Khaldun tried to get clear of the chaos, moving his mount off the road and into the trees. But his heart froze when he got an open view of the battle. Only Oscar and one of the Oxcart men remained, while half of the Foslanders had survived—and they had Mira. One of the men had dragged her from her horse; he had her in a chokehold, her wand in his other hand. Quietly muttering the incantation, Khaldun made himself and his horse invisible.

"Enough!" the Foslander captain shouted. His men disengaged Oscar and the Oxcart man. "It's over—drop your swords!"

Oscar gazed around at the scene for a moment, before turning his horse and yelling, "Ride!"

He charged down the road, the Oxcart soldier right behind him. The Foslander archers fired; one of their arrows hit the Oxcarter and he fell from his horse. Oscar rode out of view.

"Stop him—and find their mage!" the leader ordered.

Two of the soldiers galloped down the road after Oscar. Their wizard moved along the road a little, gazing around the area, trying to locate Khaldun. He was no sorcerer, so he shouldn't be able to detect his invisibility spell. As long as Khaldun could stay quiet, he should be able to escape his notice; the wizard could only cancel his spell and make him visible if he could locate him.

Khaldun held his breath as the wizard's gaze swept past his position, but he didn't see him. Instead, he moved farther up the road and kept looking. Khaldun let out a quiet sigh. If the wizard moved out of view, he could call fire to eliminate the remaining soldiers, and then rescue Mira. But it was no use—the mage had already given up his search. He gazed down the road to the south and lifted his staff, then turned and did the same to the north, before returning to the soldiers.

"Their mage has fled, or else he's nearby and invisible," he reported to the captain. "But he's not on the road—I've cast spells that would have rendered him visible if he were."

"Very well," the leader replied. "We'll take the girl back to camp. But stay alert—the boy might attempt a rescue. And you men, search their gear—they must have that heirloom somewhere."

The wizard stood guard while the soldiers went through all the packs and saddlebags. Sure enough, one of them found the artifact in Mira's bag and handed it over to the captain. The two soldiers they'd sent after Oscar returned a few minutes later and reported that they'd lost him. The leader cursed at them but ordered his men to ride. They had Mira back on her horse; one of the soldiers led her mount by the reins.

Khaldun waited till they'd moved out, then ventured deeper into the woods. He found a trail that paralleled the road, and headed north. Before long, he caught up to the squad as they rejoined the larger company. There had to be a hundred men down there—what was he supposed to do now?

Before he could think of anything, he heard someone approaching on the trail. Moving into the trees, he held his staff at the ready. But it was Oscar who rode into view.

"Oscar!" Khaldun hissed.

"Who's there?" Oscar shouted, drawing his sword and gazing around frantically.

Khaldun made himself visible.

"It's me—keep your voice down!"

Oscar heaved a sigh of relief, sheathing his sword.

"I damn near jumped out of my skin."

"Sorry," Khaldun said with a grin. "They've got Mira and the artifact."

"Aye. How do we get her back?"

"We can't now—there are too many of them."

Oscar stared down at the road, his brow furrowed in concentration. But moments later, the company began moving to the south—except for one squad of ten men who'd separated from the company to ride north.

"Look," said Oscar. "They must be taking Mira to the castle or to that encampment we saw. Let's go!"

"Hold on," said Khaldun, grabbing his arm. "Their mage is with them and he's sure to be looking out for me. They'll kill you and capture me if we try anything."

"We can't let them take Mira! Can't you incinerate the whole lot of them?"

"I tried before and their wizard canceled my spell. If I try again now, he'll know I'm nearby."

Oscar sighed in frustration. "Then what do you propose we do now?"

"Let's follow them and see where they take her," Khaldun suggested. "But we should stay hidden—I'll make us both invisible. We know that Henry wants the artifact *and* Mira, so at some point they're going to move her to the Darkhold. That should give us an opportunity to rescue her. And with a little luck, we'll be able to retrieve the artifact, too."

"What's the Darkhold?" asked Oscar.

"Henry's castle."

Oscar nodded. "Well, that might work, but if they've got a mage with them for that journey, which I'm sure they will, then we're back in the same situation we're in now."

"True. But that's a long trip. It'll take a couple of days, so they're going to have to camp overnight. They'll set a watch, but their mage will have to sleep at some point. And that's when we make our move."

Oscar mulled it over for a minute, then finally relented. "All right. I guess that's our best chance."

"Good. I'm going to make us invisible—remember, the spell doesn't block sound, nor does it hide dust kicked up from the road. So we'll still need to be careful."

"Aye, understood," Oscar replied.

Khaldun rendered them invisible and then they set out. They stuck to the path at first, but that diverged from the road after a couple of miles. But they'd crested a hill near the castle, and it provided them with a great vantage point of the land below, so they held their position and watched. Sure enough, the enemy company moved into the encampment to the east of the castle.

They made their way down to the road, rode a little north, and then found a path leading eastward into the forest. Following that for a quarter of a mile or so, they finally reached another hilltop that gave them a clear view of the encampment and the Fosland road below.

"This should do," Khaldun said, dismounting his horse. "That's the route they'll have to take to the Darkhold, so we'll see them when they move out."

"Aye," Oscar agreed, dropping to the ground. "Here we wait."

Khaldun tied the horses to a nearby tree, and then they sat down and waited. The hours dragged by without any sign of Mira. There was a lot of activity inside the encampment, and a few individual riders came and went along the road, but no large groups. They had a bite to eat just before sunset, but didn't set up their tents or risk a fire.

"Why don't you get some sleep?" Khaldun suggested. "I'll take the first watch."

Oscar curled up on the ground. Khaldun sat against a tree and kept his eyes on the encampment. But by the end of his watch, nothing had happened. He woke Oscar.

"We'll be visible once I fall asleep," he told him. "But I don't think it'll make any difference—there have been no patrols in the area."

"Understood," Oscar said through a yawn, sitting down against the same tree Khaldun had used.

Khaldun lay down and closed his eyes, but sleep eluded him. He couldn't help imagining what Mira must be enduring. From what Khaldun had seen, the Foslander army deserved its reputation for cruelty. He'd heard stories of them torturing and raping women in the towns they'd taken. He tried to convince himself that it would be different for Mira. She was a mage, and as a magical null, a valuable one. He had to hope that Henry would want her unmolested.

By the time Oscar roused him a little after dawn, Khaldun had dozed for a couple of hours. But he hardly felt refreshed. They sat on the ground and ate some breakfast.

A few hours went by without anyone entering or leaving the camp. But finally, a little before noon, Khaldun spotted a group of soldiers gathering by the southern entrance. Minutes later, Mira rode into view with the same wizard from the previous day. They joined the group and headed out along the Fosland road.

"That's it," said Khaldun. "Let's go."

They mounted their horses; Khaldun made them invisible and they set out along the trail.

"Only one mage," Oscar noted. "If we hit them while he's asleep, this might just work."

"Let's hope so," Khaldun agreed.

For the first couple of hours, the trail followed roughly the same course as the road. It strayed farther into the woods at some points, and they lost sight of the Foslanders. But each time, the trail wound its way back to the road and they found them again. But the trail ended at a village and they had no choice but to move down to the road.

The soldiers rode straight through the town. But there were people about, and riding through them while invisible could create confusion that would alert the Foslanders to their presence. So Khaldun took them around the outskirts of the village, through a field, and finally back to the road again. They'd fallen behind, but could still see the soldiers in the distance. The shoulders were grassy, so they kept their mounts in that area to avoid kicking up dirt.

A few hours later, the soldiers took a rest. Khaldun and Oscar kept their distance and ate some lunch. They set out again before too much longer.

The hours dragged by and they managed to avoid detection. Finally, a little before sunset, the Foslanders made camp by the side of the road. They weren't bothering with tents, instead laying out their bedrolls on the ground, forming a ring with Mira in the middle. A couple of the men built a fire. Still invisible, Khaldun and Oscar moved into the adjacent field, just in case the enemy mage cast any spells up the road to detect hidden pursuers. The Foslander camp grew quiet. Khaldun spotted their wizard taking the first watch—he sat down by the road with his back against a tree.

"Well, we should have a shot at rescuing Mira," said Oscar, "but I don't think we're going to retake the artifact. We don't know which one of them has the thing, and searching every pack is sure to wake someone."

"I'm willing to bet the mage has it," Khaldun replied. "We should get Mira first, but we could snatch his pack on the way out."

"That works."

"You should get some sleep," Khaldun told Oscar. "I'll take the watch. Once they relieve the mage, I'll wake you."

Oscar nodded, lying down on the ground.

Khaldun took a seat, keeping an eye on the enemy wizard. Periodically, he would get up and walk around the camp, then return to his position by the road and sit against the tree. The night wore on, but no one came to relieve the mage. Khaldun began to worry that he'd stand watch the entire night, eliminating any opportunity for them to rescue Mira.

But finally, one of the soldiers rose from his bedroll and walked over to the mage. He sat down beside him and several minutes passed without either of them moving. But in the end, the wizard got to his feet and headed to the camp—Khaldun only knew it was him and not the soldier because of his staff. The mage lay down by the rest of the soldiers.

Khaldun woke Oscar; he sat up and stretched. "One of the soldiers just took the watch. We should give it a little while to make sure the wizard is out, but we don't have a lot of time. I think it's only a couple of hours before dawn."

"What's our plan, then?"

"We'll have to take out the watchman as quietly as possible," said Khaldun.

"If we sneak up on him, I could slit his throat. That shouldn't make too much noise."

"Risky. If he hears us, we're done for."

"Aye, well if you incinerate him, he'll scream."

"I know a spell that will evacuate the air around him," said Khaldun. "He'll suffocate and won't be able to shout."

"That could work. What if he runs to the camp?"

"We'll get in closer first—stab him if he moves," said Khaldun. "They set up their bedrolls in a ring with Mira in the middle. I'll creep past them and wake her—you stand guard. Then we grab the mage's pack, return here to the horses, and get out as quickly and quietly as possible."

"It's going to be tough getting to Mira without waking anyone," said Oscar. "Any reason you couldn't just incinerate the lot of them?"

"Their wizard is much stronger than I am," Khaldun replied, shaking his head. "It's unlikely my spell would have any effect on him."

Oscar nodded. "Stealth it is, then. Well, we'll still be invisible, right?"

"Yes," Khaldun confirmed.

"All right. Let's do it."

They moved out to the road and walked toward the enemy camp, careful not to make any noise. Oscar had his sword drawn. Once they'd come within fifty feet of the guard, Khaldun raised his staff, and cast his spell, keeping his voice to a whisper.

As the guard struggled to take his next breath, Khaldun and Oscar hurried to his position. The soldier got to his feet, stumbling about aimlessly at first, as if trying to find a place with air. But then he charged toward the camp. Oscar lunged in, impaling him with his blade before he'd taken more than a couple of steps. The guard fell face first on the ground.

Khaldun held his breath for a moment, eyes on the camp to see if anyone had heard the ruckus. Their fire was still burning; Khaldun knew that the wizard must have augmented it magically to keep it going this long. But there was no activity there.

The two of them creeped closer to the camp. When they reached the horses, Khaldun nodded to Oscar. He returned the gesture and held his position, sword at the ready. Khaldun proceeded to the ring of sleeping soldiers, his heart hammering in his chest. But as he stepped through the gap between two of the bedrolls, a voice called out from behind him.

"Who goes there?"

Khaldun turned—it was the wizard. He felt his spell hitting him, removing their invisibility.

"I figured it would be you," the mage said with a sneer, before shouting, "Intruder! Rise, Foslanders!"

Oscar charged the wizard, sword raised for a swing; but the mage turned to face him at the last moment. Oscar's blade hit his forearm, knocking his staff out of his grasp. But the wizard dove after it before Oscar could strike again, rolling out of the way and vanishing as he retrieved the instrument. Khaldun hastily restored their own spell of invisibility, but it was too late—the soldiers were awake, getting to their feet and drawing their swords.

Mira had awakened, too, but the guards were forming a ring around her. Khaldun called fire, incinerating the nearest one, but the others tightened their circle to close the gap as his corpse hit the ground. Khaldun tried the spell against the next one, but nothing happened. He couldn't see the wizard, but knew he must have canceled his spell.

Khaldun darted out of the way a moment before the wizard shouted the spell to cancel his invisibility. At the same time, Oscar rushed the soldiers. He decapitated one, spun around and stabbed the next one in the heart.

"Mira, run!" Oscar shouted, as the remaining soldiers tried to retaliate against their invisible foe.

But an instant later, the wizard canceled Oscar's invisibility. One of the others stabbed Oscar in the back; he looked down in surprise at the blade protruding from his chest, and the blood spurting from the wound.

"OSCAR!" Mira screamed, struggling to get past her remaining guards to him. But it was no use—they held her back as Oscar's corpse hit the earth.

The wizard appeared only feet from Oscar, calling out to Khaldun. "You've failed, boy. Surrender now and I'll petition the high prince to grant you mercy. Who knows, he may decide to recruit you. But if you run, we will hunt you down."

Khaldun's heart jumped into his throat—for a moment, he thought the wizard had found him and made him visible; he seemed to be staring right at him. But then he shifted his gaze, scanning the area for any sign of him.

This situation was so frustrating—Mira was *right there*. She was sobbing in her grief for Oscar; the sound was heartbreaking. If only Khaldun could think of some way to get her away from these men. Knowing it would likely be futile, he raised his staff and called fire, trying to incinerate the mage. Sure enough, the wizard canceled his spell. Khaldun sprinted out of the way as he fired off his own spell at Khaldun's previous position.

"Khaldun run!" Mira cried out.

An idea occurred to him. Holding out his staff, he called the magical force, creating an illusion of himself directly in front of one of the soldiers. The man lunged, stabbing the simulacrum in the chest. Khaldun cast the same spell over and over, creating half a dozen more doppelgangers of himself. And as the soldiers cut them down, he creeped close enough to Mira to extend his invisibility spell around her.

"It's me," he hissed, grabbing her by one arm. "We're invisible— let's go!"

"Fools!" the wizard shouted, holding out his staff and shouting multiple spells.

Khaldun's illusions vanished, and he knew they'd become visible—the soldiers turned their attention to him and Mira.

"Look out!" Mira shouted at him, her eyes wide in terror.

Khaldun spotted the soldier slicing at him from behind in the nick of time; he lunged out of the way, but the blade caught him in the back of the leg. Two of the others grabbed Mira, pulling her away from him. Khaldun made himself invisible again, hobbling out of the way before the wizard could cancel his spell.

"It's over, boy," the mage shouted, hurling spells indiscriminately now. "Time to visit the Darkhold!"

Khaldun limped away from the camp, hurrying toward the trees. One of the mage's spells just missed him but he managed to take cover in the woods, his invisibility intact. Once he'd reached a safe distance, he hunkered down by a large tree to see what was happening.

It was nearly dawn now. The soldiers were breaking camp, two of them guarding Mira with their swords drawn. The wizard was prowling about the area, keeping an eye out for Khaldun. There was nothing more he could do.

Khaldun found his way back to the horses and watched as the Foslanders set out on the road again. He struggled to think of what else he could do, but came up empty. Striking while the mage slept had been their one good opportunity to save Mira. But they'd blown it and now Oscar was dead.

Fear threatened to overwhelm him. He was alone now, in the middle of hostile territory. His attempt to rescue Mira and retrieve the artifact had failed, and now he'd be lucky to get out of this alive. He remembered stories he'd heard about his father's brave deeds. Nomad had told him once about the two of them rescuing a young wayfarer woman from a warlord in Telbana. The prince had seen her perform, and wanted to make her his wife. She refused, so he sent soldiers to kidnap her. Together, Nomad and Raja managed to take her back before they got her to the castle. But this only made Khaldun feel worse: he was clearly not his father.

Heart heavy with despair, Khaldun remembered his mirror. Rummaging through his pack, he found it at the bottom. Pulling it out, he sat down on the ground and stared at himself in the glass.

"Nomad! I need you!"

CHAPTER THIRTEEN
HUNTED

or several seconds, nothing happened, and Khaldun continued staring at his reflection. He was about to give up when finally, his own image grew dim and Nomad appeared in the foreground.

"Khaldun," he said with a grin. "I wondered when I might hear from you." But then his expression became grim. "What's wrong? You look terrible."

Khaldun told him everything that had happened.

"I'm sorry we made you go through this. I wish I could have gone in your stead."

"Nobody forced me to go—I volunteered, remember? But I'm afraid I don't know what to do now. I've failed. Henry has taken the artifact *and* Mira."

"You should try to get to the university anyway," Nomad suggested. "Given the situation in Roses, going through Perrin and approaching from the west would indeed be your best move. Alert them to the situation that has developed."

"But they won't get involved, will they? Don't they have to remain neutral?"

"Things have become dire. With Henry's acquisition and his army encroaching on their southern border, it is possible they will choose to act. But there are also agents in the field who do not represent them in any official capacity, but do what they can to resist Henry. If they can alert some of those people, they may be able to do something."

"All right. I should get moving, then," said Khaldun. "Is there anyone in particular I should notify?"

"Find Enigma. He was my mentor when I was there, and he's one of the governors. He'll know what to do."

Khaldun nodded.

"Good hunting," said Nomad. "And… be safe."

"Thank you."

Getting to his feet, Khaldun felt a stab of pain in his left calf; he'd almost forgotten about his wound. He packed the mirror, and then sat down again to get a closer look at the injury. The cut was deep and still bleeding. Retrieving his water canteen, he cleaned it out the best he could. Next, he pulled a clean shirt out of his pack and ripped off a strip to use as a bandage. Examining his work, he knew he hadn't done a great job, but it would have to do.

Khaldun mounted his horse and set out, leading Oscar's mount alongside his own. Returning to the road, he headed north, making sure he and the horses were invisible, and keeping to the grassy area on the shoulder.

When he reached the village, he led the horses out into the field again to avoid making contact with any of the townspeople. North of the village, he moved into the woods and found the trail they'd taken on the way south.

Khaldun took a rest at lunchtime to eat and check his wound. The bandage was saturated with blood. Removing that, he ripped off two more strips from his shirt. One he tied around his leg above the wound as a tourniquet; the second he used as a bandage. The blood loss was worrisome, but he didn't know what else to do to stop it. He finished the water in his canteen, and drank some from Oscar's.

He'd need more water before long. They'd seen a small river to the east of the road the previous day; he'd have to find that. So he found a path and led the horses back down to the road. He kept to the shoulder again to avoid kicking up any dirt.

A few miles later, he spotted the river out to the east. He led the animals across a field and filled both canteens. The sun was getting lower in the sky—he was hoping to get back to the hill overlooking Rosetown before dark, but his progress had been much slower today. He mounted his horse again, but felt a sudden head rush, and had to sit still for a moment as his vision started going black. It passed after a minute; he took one more swig from his canteen and then headed back across the field.

But before he could reach the road, he was overcome with wooziness. Looking down at his calf, he realized that the wound had saturated the bandages again, and blood was oozing from it. He was going to have to find a healer somewhere.

Fearing he'd pass out and fall off his horse, he dismounted, sitting down on the ground for a minute. He drank more water, hoping the wooziness would pass. But it grew worse and his vision started going black again. Before long, the darkness took him, and he knew no more.

Khaldun heard a dripping sound. Something cool and damp pressed against his forehead. He was lying under a blanket on something soft—much softer than his bedroll. Struggling to open his eyes, he found he was in a dimly lit room. The light was flickering as if from a candle. He tried to sit up, but couldn't manage it.

"You need to rest," a quiet voice said.

Finally opening his eyes all the way, he saw a girl standing next to him, maybe thirteen or fourteen years old. "Who are you?" he asked, his voice raspy. "Where am I?"

"I'm Janelle. My father found you out in our fields—you collapsed. You lost a lot of blood and your wound was getting infected, but we took care of you."

"You did?" Khaldun realized his calf was throbbing.

"My mother trained with a healer when she was young, and she's been teaching me. You needed stiches; Mama says you probably would've died if we hadn't found you."

"Well, thank you, Janelle," Khaldun said with a smile. "It was kind of your family to take me in like this."

Janelle nodded, returning the smile. "Wait here. Father will want to know that you're awake."

She stepped out of the room, closing the door behind her. Khaldun gazed around the chamber; it was small, with only enough space for the bed, a nightstand, and a chest of drawers. The candle was sitting on the nightstand; his robes were hanging from one of the bedposts, his staff propped up in the corner. He had a suspicion this was probably Janelle's room. The girl returned a minute later with her father.

"Your color's improved," the man said. "You were pale as death when we got you here. Ava—that's my wife—she was afraid you weren't going to make it. I'm Stanford Brown, by the way."

"Khaldun," he replied. "It's a pleasure to meet you—and thank you for taking care of me."

"We've stabled your horses, too, but I daresay they're in better shape than you were. You're not from around here—mind if I ask what brings you to these parts?"

Khaldun took a deep breath. "I'm a wayfarer. I was headed to the university on urgent business when we were attacked by a squad of Foslander soldiers. They slaughtered our armed escort and abducted my companion."

"I'm sorry to hear that," said Stanford. "Those Foslanders are bad news. Sacked the castle about a week ago and murdered our prince and his family. My brother's farm is right outside Rosetown—bunch of their soldiers raped his daughter and left her for dead in his barn. We don't let Janelle go outside no more..."

"That's terrible, but I'm sad to say I'm not surprised. Roses makes four princedoms he's sacked now, and from what I hear, it's the same everywhere."

"Four?" said Stanford, looking confused. "I know about Smithtown and York, of course, and now Roses—but what's the fourth?"

"Ulster," Khaldun replied. "Well, I guess I don't know for sure that he's sacked it, but we got caught up in a battle there, and then passed an entire Foslander army moving into the princedom before we left." Stanford frowned.

"Yep, I'm sure he's sacked it by now, then. These are dark times, I'm afraid. Thinking about taking the family and moving out west to Dorshire somewhere. Anyway, the wife's cooked a stew—I'll have Janelle bring you a bowl."

"Thank you," said Khaldun. "I'll be on my way after that; I don't want to impose any more than I already have."

"Nonsense," Stanford replied. "You're in no shape to travel, and in any event, it's already dark out. Spend the night here, and we'll see how you're faring in the morning."

"No, truly, I don't want to be a burden. This must be Janelle's room, I'm guessing? She should sleep in her own bed—I can camp in my tent."

"It's all right," said Janelle. "I've already set up a bedroll by the fireplace. I'll be fine there."

Khaldun opened his mouth to argue more, but Stanford wouldn't hear it. Khaldun finally relented. He had to admit, a night in a feather bed would be a welcome luxury. They left him alone for a few minutes, but then Janelle returned with a bowl of stew and a loaf of fresh bread. Khaldun sat up in bed and ate his fill.

"So, Father says you're a wizard?" asked Janelle. "He found your staff lying next to you on the ground."

"Yes, that's right," he confirmed.

"I've always wanted to be a witch," Janelle told him. "But Father refuses to let me go to the university. Says he needs me to take over the farm when he gets old and decrepit," she added, rolling her eyes.

"Well, not everyone can do magic," said Khaldun. "It runs in families. If you haven't inherited it, then I'm afraid you're out of luck."

"But I can already do magic," she replied. "Can I use your staff? I'll show you."

"You're welcome to try," he said with a grin. "But it won't work for just anyone."

Janelle grabbed his staff and held it out in front of her. She recited a fire spell and spoke the word of command; a small flame appeared in her other hand.

"I'll be damned," said Khaldun. "You must have mage blood in you after all."

"My aunt is a witch," Janelle confirmed. "She's taught me a few spells, but I don't have my own wand or staff to practice."

"Well, your father's still young. You could complete your training at the university and return here in plenty of time to take over the farm for him."

"Try telling Father that," Janelle replied with a sigh. "But I'm not too keen on running the farm anyway. What I'd really like to do is become a sorcerer and teach at the university."

"People can't choose to be a sorcerer. Either you are one or you're not."

"But people aren't *born* sorcerers, are they? My aunt told me that they change sometime after puberty. Is that right?"

"Yes, that's my understanding as well."

"So, it's still possible that I could become one!"

Khaldun chuckled. "I suppose that's true."

"It would have been good if our prince had a sorcerer when Fosland attacked," Janelle said with a sigh. "They could have beaten them that way. But the Foslanders were too strong. Their witch overpowered the court mage and used her magic to force the drawbridge and gate open. The Foslanders walked right into the castle after that."

"You saw it?" Khaldun asked.

"Father and I watched the whole thing. We were in town bringing our grain to market. I think the witch lives in the castle now—you can see her on the battlements sometimes. She doesn't wear robes like most mages I've seen—she always dresses in skin-tight leather. Between that and her flaming red hair, that one's hard to miss."

"Flaming red hair?" said Khaldun. "That's Nineve. She's one of Henry's strongest mages after Dredmort. We fought her at Oxcart."

"You did?! And she didn't kill you?"

"We had a sorcerer with us—my teacher, Nomad."

"Ah," Janelle said with a knowing smile. "That explains it."

Khaldun suddenly felt drowsy, opening his mouth in a big yawn.

"I'm sorry, I should let you rest," Janelle said, collecting his bowl and spoon.

"Yes, thank you," Khaldun replied. "I am feeling a little woozy again."

"Well, goodnight, then," she said with a smile, leaving the room and closing the door behind her.

Khaldun blew out the candle on the nightstand and rolled over onto his side. He was growing sleepy, and the bed was quite comfortable, but his thoughts drifted to Mira, and he lay awake for a long time. She must have arrived at the Darkhold by now. What would they be doing to her? Dredmort would probably take over her training to help her strengthen her powers. Khaldun was sure Henry would try to force her into his service. But how? Would they torture her?

One way or another, Khaldun had to find a way to rescue her. Hopefully the university would help, otherwise he'd be on his own...

He dozed off eventually, but woke suddenly after what seemed like only minutes. Someone was in his room. "Who's there?" he asked, sitting up. It was still dark out, and there was no light in the house. But someone was standing over him.

"Sorry to startle you, it's only me," a voice said. It was Stanford. "But I'm afraid we've got a problem."

"What is it?" Khaldun asked groggily.

"Neighbor's boy just turned up here. Soldiers showed up at his farm—torched the place and killed his parents."

"*What*?!" Khaldun said, suddenly more alert. "Why?"

"They said they're looking for a wizard."

Khaldun gaped at him in silence for a moment. "Shit. I need to leave immediately—I've put you and your family in grave danger."

"We're in danger regardless," said Stanford. "We'll go with you."

"Yes, good idea," Khaldun agreed, easing out of the bed and donning his robes. He still felt a little woozy. "We should go."

Khaldun grabbed his staff and followed Stanford out of the room. They found Ava and Janelle in the kitchen waiting for them.

"What about the neighbor's boy?" Khaldun asked.

"He ran off to warn the other neighbors," Stanford told him.

"All right, then. Come on!" He hurried out the door and into the night. The land was awash in pale moonlight.

"We'll have to go on foot," said Stanford. "Haven't got any horses."

"I've got two," said Khaldun. "You and your wife take one, and Janelle can ride with me."

They hurried over to the stables. Khaldun found the horses in adjacent stalls, the saddles and bridles hanging over the wall between them. He started tacking up one of the animals while Stanford took care of the other. Once they'd finished, Janelle climbed up behind Khaldun on one horse, while her parents mounted the other.

"There's a trail through the woods on the other side of the road," Khaldun said as they rode out of the barn. "We should make for that."

174

"I know it well," Stanford replied.

"I'm going to make us invisible," Khaldun told them. "But bear in mind, the spell doesn't block sound, nor will it mask other evidence of our passage—kicking up dirt from the road, for example."

"All right," said Stanford.

"Will we be able to see each other?" asked Ava.

"Yes, as long as we're all inside the spell. But we need to stay close—it won't extend very far."

They set out across the Brown's fields, stopping when they reached the road. Khaldun looked both ways—he could see a burning structure in the distance, but didn't see or hear any riders approaching. Stanford led the way up the road and eventually across it, and onto the trail in the woods that Khaldun had been following the previous day.

"Before we encountered the Foslanders, we were trying to get into Perrin so we could approach the university from the west," Khaldun told the others. "I do still need to go there. Do you folks have somewhere safe you can go?"

"I reckon there's nowhere safe in Roses anymore," said Stanford. "As I said last night, we've been thinking of heading out west; seems this would be a good time to act on that notion. We could accompany you as far as Perrin for sure."

They followed the trail west, passing over the hill with the clear view of Rosetown below. The castle was all lit up and there was more activity in the camp than Khaldun would normally expect in the middle of the night. They paused only briefly, then pressed ahead through the forest.

Not much later, they came to the Ulster road. There was another farm in flames only a little to the south, but no sign of any soldiers approaching. They made it across the road, but as they moved into the woods on the other side, one of the horses nickered at the other. Suddenly a voice cried out, "Who goes there?"

Khaldun reined in his horse, signaling Stanford to stop, too. He spotted a couple of soldiers climbing out of the ravine on the other side of the road—he hadn't seen them before, but it was dark and they were wearing black. Khaldun's heart leapt into his throat as one of the men lit a torch and stared into the woods only a few dozen feet away.

"Don't see nuthin'," one of the soldiers said. "Musta been an animal."

"Aye, I heard an animal all right," the other replied. "Sounded like a horse!"

Khaldun held his breath as the soldiers reached the spot where they'd left the road; for a moment, the soldier with the torch seemed to be staring straight at him. But his spell held, and they saw nothing.

"Whatever it was is gone now," the soldier said. "But we'd better report it."

"Report what, exactly? We ain't seen *nuthin'*!"

"You heard Nineve—we're looking for a bloomin' wizard. Could be invisible, right? Let's go."

The two of them headed up the road, toward the burning farm. Once they'd moved well out of earshot, Khaldun led his group farther into the woods.

"That was close," said Stanford.

"We're not out of trouble yet," Khaldun told him. "Their mage will be able to track our progress, invisible or not."

"How?!"

"Using magic. There are spells that would eliminate any evidence of our passage, but unfortunately, I haven't learned them. We need to hurry."

Khaldun urged his horse faster, but it was difficult to find the trail in the darkness. They crested a hill, and found the trees to be thinner on the other side. The path was easier to see, so they risked a quick gallop. But as they climbed the next hill, Khaldun heard shouting in the distance behind them.

"They're coming for us," Khaldun warned the others. "Remember, stay close. Their mage will find our trail, but pinpointing our location will still be difficult while we're invisible."

Khaldun glanced behind them as they reached the top of the next hill. He could see flickering lights through the trees, now—they were gaining on them. They did their best to go faster along the winding trail. But suddenly, a flaming arrow hit a tree several yards behind them. Another slammed into a trunk just ahead of them to the right.

Stanford's horse reared, neighing loudly. He tried to calm it, but a third arrow hit a tree to their left. His animal charged down the path into the valley below; Ava screamed.

"Shit," Khaldun muttered. They would be visible now.

He was about to take off after them, then he heard horses galloping up behind them. Instead, he moved into the trees, away from the path. He stopped about twenty feet from the trail. Janelle whimpered softly behind him.

"*Silence*," he whispered.

Stanford's horse had reached the opposite hill, still at a full gallop. The first Foslander rider reached the hilltop right in front of Khaldun; he called fire as the rider nocked an arrow. Flames engulfed the man and he fell screaming from his mount. But another rider nocked an arrow and fired; it arced across the valley and hit Ava in the back. She screamed and toppled from her horse.

"AVA!" Stanford screamed.

A third rider fired another arrow, this one hitting Stanford. He fell to the dirt as the horse continued its charge over the next hill. Janelle was holding Khaldun tight and he could feel the silent sobs wracking her body. Khaldun called fire again, trying to incinerate the other two Foslanders, but nothing happened.

"I know you're out here, boy," a voice called out.

A witch with flaming red hair had arrived with two more riders: Nineve. Staring into the trees across the path from them, she held out her staff and shouted an incantation, before turning slowly and repeating it over and over again—she was trying to cancel Khaldun's invisibility spell.

The first two riders rode into the valley. Each grabbing one of Janelle's parents by the hair, they dragged them back up the hill to Nineve. The witch turned her attention to them.

"Where is he?" she demanded.

"Who?" Stanford asked, whimpering.

"Do you think I'm stupid?" Nineve shouted, calling a flame directly in front of the man's face. "The wizard boy you were traveling with!"

"Ain't seen no wizard! My wife and I fled when we heard you all were burning down farms!"

"Liar!" Nineve yelled, igniting the man's shirt.

Stanford rolled around on the ground screaming as he tried to put out the flames. Whispering the incantation as quietly as possible, Khaldun extinguished the fire; the witch didn't seem to notice.

"What about you?" Nineve said to Ava. "Care to tell me the truth?"

Ava sobbed, gasping for breath as blood foamed out of her mouth. Khaldun knew they must have punctured her lung with the arrow. Janelle tightened her grip around Khaldun's midsection.

"Useless peasants!" Nineve shouted, incinerating Ava and Stanford from within. "You can't escape, boy!" she added, gazing into the trees to Khaldun's right, and speaking the incantation to cancel invisibility again.

Khaldun's heart pounded in his chest; it would only be a matter of moments before she found him and Janelle. He could ride down the path now, but Nineve would hit him with her spell long before they'd be clear of the archers. Suddenly, Khaldun had another idea—but before he could act on it, a fireball exploded against a nearby tree, knocking one of the Foslanders to the ground.

Nineve screamed; another fireball arced toward them. The witch tried to cancel it but it was too late—it slammed into one of the riders, hurling him from his horse. Khaldun had no idea who was behind the attack, but it was coming from the hill up ahead. Nineve moved that way, holding out her staff and shouting multiple spells. But another fireball hit her in the chest, knocking her to the ground.

Now was the time—Khaldun urged his horse into motion, doing his best to ride right over the witch, and galloping down the path and up the next hill. Despite their invisibility, Khaldun knew the enemy would hear their hoofbeats. Sure enough, flaming arrows hit the path and the trees around them but none found their mark. Khaldun crested the hill and kept moving.

But suddenly, someone appeared on the path in front of them—it was another witch. She was waving a wand; Khaldun felt her spell hit them and knew they were visible now. Khaldun was about to try running her down, but suddenly Janelle shouted, "Aunt Sophia!"

Khaldun reined in his horse, pulling up right in front of the woman.

"Come with me if you want to live, boy," she said. "I'll make us all invisible—but stay quiet!"

CHAPTER FOURTEEN
SOPHIA

"ou're Aunt Sophia, I take it?" Khaldun asked with a grin.

"Great, we've got a wiseass," she muttered, covering her head with her hood. "Let's go."

Sophia hurried up the path on foot, lighting their way with her wand, Khaldun and Janelle right behind her on the horse. After only a few minutes, she led them into the woods to the south. There was no clear path here and the going was slow. Sophia stopped after a minute and cast some sort of spell along their backtrail. There was a sudden breeze blowing sparks through the trees.

"You eliminated the evidence of our passage," Khaldun said quietly. "I've seen Nomad do that."

"Aye, we both learned it at the same time," Sophia replied.

"Where was that?"

"The university—where else?"

"You attended the university with Nomad? But you're—I mean, you must have been there way before his time—"

"You implying that I'm *old*, boy?" Sophia demanded.

"I... uh... no..."

"It's all right, I *am* old. But Nomad is the same age." Khaldun stared blankly at her; he'd always thought of Nomad as being only five or ten years older than himself, though he knew that couldn't be true. "Doesn't look it, I'm sure, but sorcerers age slower than the rest of us. But that's enough yammering. Come on."

They resumed their course through the woods. Every few minutes, Sophia would stop them and repeat her spell. Finally, as the sky began to lighten, they came to a cave in the base of a ridge.

"In we go," said Sophia, standing by the entrance.

"What is this place?" Khaldun asked, imagining what sort of creature might have made a den for itself inside.

"What does it look like?" Sophia said sardonically. "It's a cave. Closest thing to a home I have out here in the wild. I've spent years building up the enchantments around the area to prevent anyone from finding me here. So come on, get in."

The horse balked at going inside the cave. Khaldun and Janelle dismounted, and he was able to coax the animal in after a minute. Sophia entered last, turning and casting spells at the entry.

"What are you doing?" asked Khaldun.

"Hiding us," she replied, continuing with her incantations. When she was done, she added, "Now Nineve herself could be standing right outside and she would see nothing but a wall of solid rock."

"Will she hear us?" asked Janelle.

"Unlikely. But keep your voices down just in case."

"Do you think maybe you could teach me those spells?" asked Khaldun.

"Aye, we'll be spending some time together, I think, so it would be best you learn them."

Janelle grabbed Sophia in a hug, sobbing into her chest.

"There, there, child," Sophia muttered, patting her on the back.

"I'm sorry, but how did you know we were out here?" asked Khaldun.

"We've got a spy in the Darkhold. He got word out to some of us that Henry was seeking a wayfarer wizard in this area trying to get to the university."

"You say 'we'—are you one of the mages working against Henry?"

"That I am."

"Nomad told me about you—well, not you specifically, but he said there were mages in the wild working to forestall Henry."

"Aye, not enough of us to make much of a difference, sad to say, but we do what we can."

Just then, there were noises coming from outside. Khaldun heard shouting and footsteps coming very close. Sophia turned to face the cave entry, pointing her wand and pushing Janelle behind her. Khaldun joined her, staff at the ready.

Suddenly two Fosland soldiers came into view just outside the cave. Right behind them was Nineve, now sporting a bloody gash on her forehead. Khaldun held his breath.

"You fools—how could you have lost them?" Nineve demanded. "There's no sign of them anywhere. I'm down for a few minutes and the whole thing goes to shit. Worthless…" Her voice trailed off as they moved away from the cave. Khaldun breathed a heavy sigh of relief.

"So," said Sophia, sitting down on a rock. "What's your story?"

Khaldun and Janelle each sat down facing her. Khaldun told her about his journey north with Mira, Oscar, and the Oxcart soldiers, and their failed rescue attempt. He didn't mention the artifact, saying only that they had "urgent business" at the university. Sophia sat quietly, listening patiently.

"And what is this 'urgent business?'"

Khaldun took a deep breath. "I'd prefer not to say."

Sophia nodded. "It's wise to withhold trust. Never know if you're dealing with an enemy agent. But if this business, as you call it, has anything to do with Henry, then I need to know."

Khaldun considered this for a moment. Nomad *had* told him that there were mages like her in the wild working against the high prince. And Janelle had already corroborated her identity. But it was possible that this was an agent of Henry masquerading as Sophia.

Getting to his feet, Khaldun held out his staff, casting a spell.

"Hey, now!" said Sophia, standing up and pointing her wand at him. "What the hell do you think you're doing?"

"Sorry," Khaldun said with a sheepish grin, retaking his seat. "I had to make sure you weren't an imposter—but you're not."

"How do you know?" asked Janelle, looking newly suspicious herself.

"I cast a spell to cancel any illusion. But there was nothing to cancel—she is who she appears to be."

"Good thinking," Sophia muttered, sitting down again. "So, now you gonna tell me what takes you to the university?"

Khaldun nodded. He told her about the artifact.

Sophia gave a low whistle when he was done. "Well, that sure ain't good. Woulda been better if your leader had allowed the sorcerer to transport it—I shudder to think what Dredmort will be able to do with that thing. But what's done is done."

"Do you think the university will send someone to get it back?" asked Khaldun.

Sophia scoffed. "The university won't lift a finger—not overtly, anyway. They'll do whatever they must to maintain their guise of neutrality. Won't be able to keep that up much longer with Henry threatening their very borders, but that's a conversation for another day.

"It'll fall to me or one of the others to retrieve the thing. But the university will have to provide some sort of assistance. It'd be a suicide mission otherwise."

"I'll go, too," said Khaldun.

"You don't understand what you'd be getting yourself into."

"They've got Mira. I have to go."

Sophia eyed him for a moment then nodded. "Well, we need to get you to the university first—and as soon as possible. They do need to know about this."

"What about me?" asked Janelle. "I'm scared to go back to the farm—those soldiers might come back for me!"

"No, child, we can't send you back there," Sophia agreed. "I'm afraid they've probably burned the farmhouse to the ground by now."

"Then what do I do?" Janelle asked, tears welling up in her eyes. "Can I live with you now?"

"No, wandering around in the wild is no life for a young girl. Getting you enrolled at the university would be for the best. I'll vouch for ya—you'll be a shoe-in."

The girl's face brightened a bit at this. "Yes, I'd like that," she said with a nod.

"But we should stay here for the rest of the day," Sophia replied. "The Foslanders will be canvassing this entire area looking for this one," she added, pointing to Khaldun. "We'll stay put while they do that. Then we can travel under cover of darkness. So get some rest now, both of you; you're gonna need it."

Khaldun slept poorly. The ground was hard and damp, and little stones kept jabbing him through his clothing, no matter how he positioned himself. He did manage to sleep for a while, but when he woke, it was still light outside.

Sophia was standing by the cave entry, gazing outside. Janelle was lying nearby, still sound asleep.

"Any sign of pursuit?" Khaldun asked quietly, standing next to the witch.

"They've got search parties hunting for us. But none of them have come too close. Anyway, we've got several hours before nightfall. Why don't we teach you some new spells?"

Khaldun nodded.

"Your invisibility spell is good. Erasing your trail will add to that and make it impossible for anyone to track you. When you traverse a path, you leave traces that others can follow—footprints, broken twigs on the ground, that sort of thing.

"But as a mage, your passage leaves other signs that a powerful witch or wizard can find. The spell I'm going to teach you eliminates all evidence of your movements, magical or mundane. But its range is limited, so you've got to repeat it periodically like I did last night."

Sophia taught him the incantation, and Khaldun committed it to memory. She had him practice in the cave—he walked from the front to the back, then cast the spell to remove any evidence of his passage. It took a few tries to get it right, but once he did, he was able to repeat it several times in a row.

She also taught him a spell to mask sounds. "Unfortunately, this one won't follow you, so it's not much use when you're on the move. You'd have to keep casting it every few feet. But when you're camped for the night, it'll keep any passersby from hearing you. Use this along with your invisibility spell, and it'll be very hard indeed for anyone to find you."

Once again, it didn't take long for Khaldun to master the incantation. He cast the spell around himself, then shouted on the top of his lungs, and Sophia couldn't hear him.

"What about illusions?" Khaldun asked once he'd canceled the spell. "I've been working on them, and I'm getting better, but I could use some help with moving ones."

"Well, I've never been able to master illusions myself," she told him. "Don't seem to have the knack for them. But let me see what you've got, and maybe I can offer some pointers."

Khaldun cast an illusion of Nomad, and made him walk around the cave and talk. The witch helped him fine-tune his control; Khaldun felt his confidence growing with this skill. Janelle woke up an hour before sunset, so they called it quits for the day and sat down for a quick meal.

They hadn't seen or heard anyone outside the cave the entire time they were practicing. Once night had fallen, they left their hideout and ventured out into the woods again. Khaldun and Janelle rode the horse again, and Sophia led the way on foot, calling a small flame to light their way.

The path they took this time was different from before; judging by the stars, Khaldun knew they were headed east. He asked Sophia about this.

"Aye, we'll be hooking around Rosetown and then up toward the river to cross into Perrin."

Sophia masked their trail every so often, and stopped to listen for any sounds of pursuit. But they continued through the night without encountering anyone else.

"At this point, I'm guessing they've given up the search," Sophia told them when the sky began to brighten. "As long as we stick to the forest, we should be safe until we reach the border. But I'm guessing they'll be guarding all the exits from the princedom."

There were no caves nearby this time, but they found shelter in a ravine by the bank of a stream. They filled their canteens and settled in for the day. Sophia took the first watch, and Khaldun and Janelle lay on the ground to get some sleep.

Khaldun slept like a rock this time. The witch woke him up at midday to relieve her. "Ain't seen nor heard a soul so far," she told him. "Let me see you mask our sounds."

Khaldun cast the spell she'd taught him the day before, and Sophia nodded her satisfaction.

"I'll need to cast my own invisibility spell, too, won't I?"

"No need—I already know you're proficient with that one."

"But yours will fade when you fall asleep."

"Will not. There's a modification you can make to that one that keeps it intact whether you're conscious or not. That way, you can keep yourself invisible continuously when there's any risk of encountering enemies. Here, I'll teach you."

Sophia taught him the variation on the incantation. He practiced it a few times, then once she was satisfied with his progress, she lay down to go to sleep.

Khaldun sat by the stream as the other two slept. A couple of times he thought he heard someone approaching, but it turned out to be animals. Sophia and Janelle woke a little before sunset. They ate, then resumed their journey as night fell.

A few hours later, their path reached the road where it met a small river. There was a bridge over the water, but several Foslander soldiers stood guard.

"As I suspected," Sophia said quietly, "the route out of Roses is closed."

Khaldun gazed down at the water. The river wasn't very wide, but the banks were steep and rocky; getting down there to cross it without using the bridge would be hazardous.

"Is there any other way across nearby?" he asked. "Another bridge or a ford, perhaps?"

"Aye, there are other bridges, but they're sure to be held against us, too," Sophia replied. "And the banks are like this for at least twenty miles in either direction; getting down them would be treacherous, and then we'd have to find a way to climb back up the other side. We'll need to cross here. But they don't have a mage, so this shouldn't be too difficult."

"What have you got in mind?" asked Khaldun.

"I want you to use that illusion of Nomad you've been working on. Put him on a horse coming up from the Perrin side, galloping toward the bridge. Think maybe you could add about a dozen soldiers on horseback behind him?"

"Eh…"

"Right, just the sorcerer, then. I'll take care of the rest. You ready?" Khaldun nodded. "All right, go ahead and cast your spell."

Khaldun focused for a moment, visualizing the exact apparition he hoped to create. Then he held out his staff and called the magical force.

Sure enough, Nomad appeared about fifty yards away, charging toward the bridge on horseback. Khaldun could hear the horse's hoofbeats loud and clear. Sophia raised her wand and began muttering incantations of her own.

"Hey, who the hell is that?" one of the soldiers shouted from below.

"Lone rider, it looks like," replied another.

But suddenly an earsplitting cry emanated from the illusion— Khaldun hadn't done this, and knew it must have been Sophia. Jets of fire shot up from the sides of the road as Nomad passed, and the earth shook. The soldiers mounted their horses and drew their swords, forming a blockade on the near side of the bridge.

"Oh, shit," one of the soldiers yelled as Nomad drew nearer. "That's a bleedin' sorcerer!"

"Halt! The border is closed by order of High Prince Henry!" their leader cried out.

Sophia's jets of fire crossed the bridge just ahead of Nomad. The sorcerer thundered across moments later.

"Let's get out of here!" one of the soldiers shouted. He turned his mount around and galloped down the road; the others followed close behind.

"Come on, let's move!" said Sophia, hurrying down the last stretch of the path. Khaldun and Janelle followed on horseback. "Keep your illusion going till we get across!" she added as they approached the bridge. Khaldun looked up the road, focusing on Nomad chasing the soldiers; he held out his staff and recited the spell again to reinforce it.

Sophia led them across the bridge. She turned to look up the road once they'd reached the opposite side. "We should be safe now," she told them. "I doubt Henry's authorized his forces to cross into Perrin yet." Khaldun nodded, letting his illusion dissipate. "We'll stick to the road now. It's only about ten miles to the route leading to the university's western border."

But only moments later, they heard hoofbeats approaching from behind. Turning in his saddle, Khaldun spotted the Foslanders charging toward them.

"You're sure they won't cross the bridge?" he asked.

"More or less," Sophia replied. "But they could still reach us with arrows—let's put some more distance behind us."

The witch broke into a run, and Khaldun urged the horse into a trot. But as they moved, he heard the sound of hoofbeats hitting the bridge. Reining in his horse, he turned to see the soldiers reach the end of the bridge—and continue into Perrin.

"Sophia!"

The witch had already seen them. Raising her wand, she shot a dozen fireballs at the soldiers. Several of them found their mark, knocking riders from their horses and igniting their uniforms. The others reined in their mounts and beat a hasty retreat back across the bridge. Sophia hurled fireballs at their backs, hitting two more of them. The fallen soldiers rolled around in the dirt to extinguish the flames, then got up and ran back into Roses.

"That should be the last we see of them," Sophia said as she resumed their course. "But we should keep an eye out behind us just in case they try again."

But by the time they reached the university road a few hours later, they hadn't seen any further sign of pursuit. They headed east and rode for a couple more hours. But finally, they reached a pair of abandoned guard towers, one on either side of the road, and Sophia ordered a halt.

"Why are we stopping?" asked Khaldun.

"We're here," Sophia replied. "This is the western border of the university's lands. We'll need to cross the barrier here."

"What barrier?" Khaldun asked, puzzled. Gazing up the road ahead of them, he could see nothing but wooded countryside.

Sophia picked up a stone and threw it out in front of them. It struck something with a sound like a bell before falling straight down; for a few moments, a shimmering plane appeared around the area of impact, its surface crackling with energy, before becoming completely transparent again.

"That barrier," said Sophia. "They used to keep guards posted in these towers around the clock, but about a hundred years ago, one of the governors devised a set of spells to create this dome of pure energy; it protects the entire university from invaders."

"Great," Khaldun replied, "so how do we get through?"

"Like this." Sophia raised her wand and recited an incantation. The barrier became visible where it intersected the road, and suddenly an archway opened in its surface. Sophia led them through it, closing it again behind them.

"Welcome to the university," she told them with a grin.

"So, wait," said Khaldun. "Does this mean Dredmort could show up with an army and open a portal for them? They could sack the university..."

"No, no," Sophia replied. "The governors modify the dome spells from time to time to keep out mages they don't like."

"How?"

"Don't rightly know," she said with a shrug. "Only sorcerers can manipulate that kind of magic. My understanding is that every mage has a kind of signature or fingerprint to their spell work, and sorcerers can recognize that. My guess would be that they weave the forbidden signatures into the thing somehow."

"So Dredmort wouldn't be able to open a portal like that?" asked Khaldun.

"That's right," Sophia confirmed. "But that's enough chitchat; let's get moving."

CHAPTER FIFTEEN
ENIGMA

"here's nothing here," Khaldun observed as they got underway again, gazing around the area.

"The university owns as much land as a small princedom," Sophia told him. "And the school itself is over on the eastern side of that. We've still got a ways to go."

They continued up the road. The sun rose, and still they pushed ahead; Khaldun felt exhausted, but sleep would have to wait. Finally, a few hours after dawn, they reached the university. There was a row of tall brownstone buildings; as they moved closer, Khaldun could see that they formed the front of a quad, with more structures and a courtyard behind them. Students hustled about the grounds moving between classes.

"I'll go inside and get this one enrolled," Sophia said when they reached one of the administrative buildings. "You wait here. Once I'm done with that, you and I will go find Enigma."

Khaldun and Janelle dismounted, and the girl headed up the steps to the entry with Sophia. Khaldun took a minute to stretch sore legs. Moments later, an old wizard emerged through the doors and trotted down the steps. He stopped in his tracks and did a double-take when he saw the wayfarer.

"Hello," Khaldun said with a smile.

The wizard shook his head and scowled at him before hurrying off. Several more people came and went while Khaldun waited, each shooting him dirty looks. Khaldun knew that the university refused to admit wayfarers, but felt surprised and irritated by the level of prejudice he saw here. Finally, Sophia returned with Janelle and a young witch.

"They accepted me," Janelle reported with a grin.

"That's terrific," Khaldun replied. "Congratulations!"

"So, I guess this is goodbye," said Janelle. "Thank you for everything you've done for me," she added, hugging Khaldun.

"And thank *you* for taking me in and nursing me back to health," he replied, patting her on the back.

Janelle hugged her aunt, then bounded away with the witch.

"Well, that's that," said Sophia, watching them depart. Khaldun thought he saw her wipe away a tear. "That woman will show her to the dorm and set her up with a new wardrobe and school supplies... Let's find Enigma, shall we?"

"Do you know where he's likely to be?" Khaldun asked, following her around the building and into the courtyard, leading his horse by the reins.

"At this hour? Teaching, probably."

She led him to a building at the far end of the quad. Khaldun tied his horse to a post and followed her up the steps and through the front doors. Moving through a short hallway, they came to the long central corridor. Sophia led him to the right end of the hall and through a set of double doors. Inside they found an enormous classroom that spanned the entire end of the building.

Several rows of desks and chairs hosted dozens of students. Large blackboards filled with arcane symbols and sloppy writing covered the front wall. The professor was a sorcerer, wearing black mage's robes. Like Nomad, his skin was golden in color, and the irises of his eyes red. His head was bald, and he had what appeared to be tattoos on his scalp and face. The man glanced at the new arrivals, but continued his lecture.

"That's him," Sophia whispered to Khaldun. "Let's sit down—we'll have to wait till he's done."

They took seats in the back row. Enigma was teaching a lesson about the theory behind moving objects into the void. Khaldun tried to follow, but found he was in way over his head. At the end of the lesson, the students got up and filed out of the room. Sophia and Khaldun approached the sorcerer. Up close, Khaldun realized that the sorcerer's tattoos seemed to change and move about his skin; he didn't see the transformation take place, but each time he focused on the markings, they were different.

"Sophia," said Enigma, bowing slightly. "What brings you back to the nest?"

"Grave news, I'm afraid," she said. "This is Khaldun, from the wayfarer troupe."

"Ah, yes," Enigma replied, shaking his hand. "I've heard a lot about you."

"You have?" Khaldun asked, surprised.

"Indeed. I petitioned the governors to consider your matriculation on Nomad's behalf. But alas, the old prejudice runs deep. Their loss; from what Nomad tells me, you're a gifted mage."

"Oh, thank you," Khaldun replied.

"Well, have a seat. Tell me what brings you here," he said, leaning against the front of his desk and folding his arms.

Sophia and Khaldun each took a seat. Khaldun told him about the artifact, losing it to the Foslanders, and Mira's abduction—and her strange powers. Enigma's expression grew steadily grimmer as Khaldun continued.

"Grave news indeed," he said with a sigh when he was done.

"There's more," Sophia told him. "Henry's sacked Roses and Ulster. That brings him right up to the university's southern border."

"Yes, we know," said Enigma. "He's got troops stationed along the barrier; the south road is no longer passable."

"Will you act?" asked Sophia.

Enigma shook his head. "Unless they attack, we cannot. The university must maintain its neutrality—you know this. Any action we take that favors one princedom over another would threaten our mandate."

"What mandate?" asked Khaldun.

"The university possesses sole jurisdiction over the governance of the continent's mages. We educate them, decide their assignments, and settle disputes between them. If a mage commits a crime, we are the ones who investigate and hold their trial. Every princedom has honored this arrangement for centuries. But that would end if we were to take sides in any conflict between them."

"It will also end if the high prince overruns your lands with his army, which he seems poised to do," Sophia pointed out.

Enigma nodded. "It's ironic in a way. The princedoms around the university were kept small by design after the fall of the Pythan Empire."

"I've noticed that," said Khaldun. "The ones farther out, and those in Dorshire in particular, are much larger."

"Yes. The thinking was that this would make it less likely for any of them to ever grow powerful enough to threaten us. Yet as it turns out, this isn't the first time that one of them has done so. But if Henry does attack, we will protect ourselves—our neutrality does not prevent us from defending against direct aggression."

"But Henry's got the artifact," said Khaldun. "Dredmort could use that to help him take over the entire continent!"

"Yes, he could," Enigma agreed.

"And he's got Mira! We have to rescue her!" said Khaldun.

"It would be for the best if *someone* could retrieve the artifact—*and* the girl," said Enigma, staring pointedly at Sophia. "But the university *cannot* interfere. I'm sorry."

"So you're just going to leave it to fate?" Khaldun demanded. "And hope that some random person intercedes—"

"Don't worry, boy," said Sophia, returning Enigma's gaze. "Someone *will* get the girl and the stone back. But it's going to be you and me."

Khaldun scoffed. "Without any help from the university? How? We're just going to walk into the Darkhold and take them, are we?"

"I suppose so," said Sophia.

"But you're mad—that's the most heavily fortified castle on the entire continent. Henry's sure to have an entire army protecting it."

"Aye, that's probably true."

"So how are we supposed to get inside?"

"That's where I may be able to help," said Enigma. "The university has in its possession detailed schematics for every major structure in Anoria."

"What?" asked Khaldun. "You've got the plans for the Darkhold?"

"We do. And if memory serves, there is more than one secret passage leading into it. Come with me," he said, striding toward the exit.

Sophia and Khaldun got to their feet and hurried in his wake.

"But how?" asked Khaldun. "Why would Henry allow anyone to have something like that?"

"Henry didn't. But the Darkhold is ancient—and has only been held by Henry's family for the last five or six generations. In olden times, it was the custom for all the great builders and architects to submit a record of their works to the university."

"And they included *secret* entrances in those records?" Khaldun asked skeptically as they left the building and headed back across the quad.

"Not explicitly," said Enigma. "But they're not too hard to find if one knows what to look for—which I do."

"But how can you help us like this?" asked Khaldun. "Doesn't this violate the university's neutrality?"

"Not at all," Enigma replied with a grin. "The library is open to all mages; I'll only be showing you something you could have discovered on your own."

He led them to the front of the quad, and into the largest building. Moving through the foyer, they entered an enormous space that appeared to occupy nearly the entire building. The center of the area was open, providing a view up several levels to the vaulted ceiling. It was only dimly lit, but Khaldun could see that books lined all four walls on every floor. And in the central opening stood a separate structure, rising as high as the building itself and hosting row upon row of bookshelves on every level.

"This must be the library," Khaldun said quietly.

"Genius material here," Sophia said sardonically.

Enigma led them to the rear corner of the building and down two flights of steps.

"Some of the oldest archives are in the basement," he explained.

The area grew darker as they descended; Enigma held up one hand and emitted a golden glow to light their way. They stepped into a cavernous chamber with vaulted stone ceilings; Enigma's light did not reach far enough to illuminate the other side. Like the upper levels, this area was full of bookshelves that rose from the floor nearly to the ceiling.

Enigma led them to the side wall, and strode far down the aisle. Before long, he slowed down and began checking the labels posted on the shelves.

"Ah, here we are," he said finally by a section that hosted dozens of scrolls. But after searching for a few moments, he added, "This is strange."

"What is it?" asked Sophia.

"The plans for the Darkhold are gone. Along with those for the castles in York, Smithtown, Roses, Ulster, Perrin, and several other princedoms in the area."

"How can that be?" asked Khaldun. "Where did they go?"

"Someone may have borrowed them for research purposes," Enigma suggested.

"You mean someone from Fosland for the purpose of sacking castles," Sophia retorted.

"Perhaps," Enigma conceded. "No matter. Come with me."

"No matter?" Khaldun asked incredulously as they followed him back up the aisle. "How are we supposed to get inside the Darkhold without those plans?"

"It so happens that I examined them myself not so long ago."

"You did?" asked Khaldun.

"Must've been you who helped our spy gain access," Sophia suggested.

"Yes," Enigma confirmed, leading them to the opposite wall. "And I believe I still remember the key information."

"Who's the spy?" asked Khaldun. "Will they help us once we get inside?"

"I'm afraid I cannot divulge their identity," said Enigma. "They are there covertly, of course, and I will not risk exposing them. But like Sophia, they are acting of their own free will, operating independently of the university."

"Yes, of course," Khaldun replied with a grin.

Enigma stopped halfway down the aisle and browsed through some scrolls. Finally he pulled one off the shelf and brought it to a table in a nearby alcove. When he unrolled the scroll on the table, Khaldun realized that it was a map.

"This is Fosland," Enigma told them. "The Darkhold is here, at the top of this ridge overlooking the city," he said, pointing to the castle. "If you approach from the north, you can access a path here that leads down to the rocky plain behind the building."

"What good will that do us?" asked Sophia. "I've been back there—that ridge must be a hundred feet high. And the castle walls rise another fifty feet above that."

"Yes, but there is a cave at the base of the ridge, to the south of the castle," Enigma explained. "And deep inside that cave is a gate to a secret tunnel that runs directly beneath the building. There is a series of long, narrow stairways that lead into the storage cellars."

"But Henry must know about this," said Khaldun. "Won't he have sealed it off by now?"

"It's possible," Enigma replied with a shrug. "But secret passages like these are meant to provide emergency escape routes for the royal families. There's a good chance Henry would want to keep them in place. In any event, it isn't common knowledge that we house plans to the ancient castles here. He may not have any reason to fear an intruder using them."

"I'm not so sure about that," said Sophia. "It's probably his people who took the missing plans."

"Well, this is how the spy got inside. But if you do find it blocked, there is another tunnel that can be accessed from the basement of the old temple in the heart of the city. You're more likely to be seen there, so I would try the rear entry first."

Enigma rolled up the map and returned it to its place on the shelf. Then they headed back up to the main level and out the front doors.

"I have another class in a few minutes," Enigma told them, "but I wish you both the best of luck."

He bade them farewell before striding away.

"Well, I don't know about you, but I'm starving," said Sophia. "Let's find some food and then we can make our plans."

Sophia led him to the refectory. It wasn't lunchtime yet, so there weren't too many people here, but she explained that they served food throughout the day. They each filled a plate at the buffet in the back of the hall, then sat down at a table in the corner. Khaldun hadn't realized how hungry he was; he wolfed down his food.

"I think we'll camp here tonight," said Sophia once she'd finished her meal. "Leave at first light."

"And travel by day?" Khaldun asked.

"They won't have any reason to be looking for us where we're going," said Sophia. "I think we'll leave the university by the east road, and cross the River Mayne. Henry's stayed this side of the river so far, so we should be able to travel through Strom without opposition. Then we can go back across into Fosland. Staying invisible and covering our trail, we shouldn't have too much trouble making it to the Darkhold."

"And what do we do once we get inside?" asked Khaldun, his anxiety rising at the thought.

"Find the artifact and the girl and get the hell out of there," Sophia replied with a shrug.

"You make it sound so simple…"

"Simple, yes. Easy, no. But we're both mages. We'll find a way."

"But the Darkhold is crawling with Henry's wizards and witches, isn't it? That kind of neutralizes our advantage."

"Dredmort will be there for sure. But Henry's got most of his people in the field. Getting stretched pretty thin, occupying all these other princedoms, I think. That's probably the main reason he keeps adding more mages to his collection. But don't worry—we'll be all right."

"I'm not sure how you can be so confident. We won't even know our way around in there."

"Yes, we will."

"How?"

Sophia took a deep breath, letting it out in a sigh.

"I used to serve there."

"*What*? You worked for Henry?"

"I worked for his father for many years. But I left soon after Henry came into power. Don't worry, I know the inside of that castle like the back of my hand."

"You didn't know about the secret passages," Khaldun pointed out.

"Of course not. That knowledge was kept to the royal family and their closest advisers. Dredmort was the chief mage, so he was probably aware of them, but I was lower down the food chain."

Khaldun nodded. "What will Henry do to us if he catches us in the castle?"

"Kill us, probably," said Sophia. "Or compel us into service, which might be worse."

Khaldun shivered. "I'm scared."

Sophia regarded him in silence for a moment. "I can go in alone if you'd prefer. Might even be less risky that way. One less person to make a mistake and alert them to our presence."

"No," said Khaldun, taking a deep breath. "They've got Mira. I have to help get her out."

"You've never been with a woman before, have you, boy?" she asked with a grin. "Before this Mira girl, I mean."

"That's not true at all. I've been with several women, if you must know—and I *haven't* been with Mira. Not that way."

"Then why put yourself in harm's way for her? What makes her so special?"

"She's the first woman I've loved," he said with a sigh.

"If you're not careful, love will get you killed one day."

"Well, what about you?" asked Khaldun. "Why are you willing to fly into danger like this?"

"Told you. I served in Fosland. I've seen firsthand what Henry is capable of doing; I'm not willing to just stand by and watch while he takes over the entire continent."

"What did he do? What did you see?"

Sophia looked him in the eye for a moment, but then lowered her gaze, shaking her head.

"Come on, tell me—what happened?"

"It was a long time ago…"

"What was?"

Sophia opened her mouth to reply, but then closed it, shaking her head again. "I haven't ever told anyone about this before."

Khaldun desperately wanted to know her story now, but said nothing; it seemed like she was on the verge of telling him.

"They assigned me to Fosland straight out of the university. Henry was only a boy back then; his father, Euclid, was the ruling prince in those days. Euclid was a good man. A just ruler. He had his faults, but he was no warmonger.

"But Henry was different, even as a young lad. Sneaky. Manipulative. Used to pull nasty pranks on his older brother, Godfrey, but always managed to pass the blame to someone else. A servant or stable boy or someone like that—anyone he considered inferior."

"Wait—Henry has an older brother? Why didn't *he* inherit the throne?"

"Why do you think?"

"He died?"

Sophia nodded.

"Did Henry kill him?"

"Nobody knows for sure. Euclid toured the princedom once a year to check in on his vassals. Most princes don't do that so often, especially in the larger princedoms, but that was Euclid's way. He was getting on in years, so he took Godfrey with him one year when he reached manhood. The vassals had met him before, but he was only a boy then. Now they were meeting him as their ruler's adult heir.

"Well, Euclid and Godfrey both died on that trip and Henry ascended to the throne."

"What happened?"

Sophia shrugged. "The official story is that one of the horses pulling the royal carriage got spooked. They were riding through a mountain pass, and when the horse reared, they went over the cliff. And that was that."

"You don't believe that story, though."

"Oh, the story's true enough—there were a dozen witnesses."

"Was it a plot—were they all in on it?"

Sophia shook her head. "No, not a chance. I was... uh... *involved* with the commander of the prince's guard. Drake was his name. He was right there when it happened; saw the whole thing. And he told me that the horse reared for no reason at all. But it took the prince and his heir right over the cliff with it."

"So it was just an accident, then."

Sophia shook her head. "Dredmort was on that trip. He'd only entered the prince's service a couple of years before that."

"They expelled him from the university for experimenting with necromancy, didn't they?" said Khaldun.

"Aye. But Euclid was looking to take on another mage and requested Dredmort. I'm not sure how he'd heard of him, but the university sanctioned it. I'm sure they figured that by going to a small, peaceful princedom, far enough from the university to deprive him of its resources, but close enough that they could rein him in if necessary, that he wouldn't get into any trouble. But they didn't know about Henry.

"Well, I think Dredmort saw in that boy an opportunity. When they returned from that fatal trip, Henry summoned them all to the throne room. Dredmort made a big production of pinning the whole thing on Euclid's chief mage, Melnor. He said he saw the old wizard raise his wand to cast some sort of spell right before that horse reared.

"Of course, nobody else saw anything of the kind. And Commander Drake refuted Dredmort's claim in his sworn testimony.

But then Dredmort produced another witness. A servant girl who claimed she overheard Drake plotting with Melnor to assassinate Henry and take the throne for himself." Tears came to Sophia's eyes, and Khaldun was pretty sure he knew what must have happened next. "Henry had Dredmort confiscate Melnor's staff on the spot. And the next day, he had Drake and the wizard executed. They beheaded them both right in the middle of the courtyard for everyone to see."

"I'm sorry," said Khaldun. "That must have been terrible to witness." He thought he understood the witch's dedication to opposing Henry a little better now. "But why did Dredmort accuse them of such a conspiracy? Henry would have inherited regardless— he could have let everyone believe it was an accident."

"Melnor and Drake were Euclid's staunchest supporters; they needed them out of the way. Dredmort has enabled Henry's lust for power and his cruelest inclinations, and in turn, Henry has given Dredmort free rein to continue his experiments. If Melnor and Drake had lived to witness any of this, they would have tried to put a stop to it."

"And they probably would have realized that Dredmort was the one responsible for killing the old prince and his heir," added Khaldun, nodding his understanding.

"Aye, indeed they would have," Sophia agreed, clearing her throat. "Well. That's enough reminiscing for today. Let's find somewhere to camp for the night, and we'll get underway first thing in the morning."

CHAPTER SIXTEEN
FOSLAND

hey left the refectory and went back to get Khaldun's horse. But when they reached the post where Khaldun had tied him, they found that the animal was gone. "Someone stole my horse?" Khaldun exclaimed. "Here?"

"The beast was tired and hungry," someone said with a scratchy voice. Turning, Khaldun spotted an old man approaching them. "So I brought him to the stables for some food and water."

"Terrance, how are you?" said Sophia, grabbing the man in a hug.

"Old and arthritic," the man replied with a grin. "How about you, old friend?"

"Headed in the same direction. This is Khaldun; he's a mage from the wayfarer tribe."

Terrance nodded to him. "We don't see too many wayfarers here."

"No, I wouldn't expect so," Khaldun muttered, feeling irritated. *Of course, you don't,* he wanted to say, but held his tongue.

"Well, follow me and I'll show you to the stables."

Terrance led them out behind the quad and across a field, chatting with Sophia the whole way. Khaldun followed a few paces behind; he was annoyed with the man for taking his horse, and with himself for not taking better care of the animal. Sophia chose one of the university's mares for herself, and then they bade Terrance farewell.

They set out on foot, leading the horses by the reins as Sophia took them eastward across the university's land. After passing through a grove of trees, they reached the road and continued east. After only another mile or so, they reached a meadow, and Sophia suggested that they camp there for the night.

"We're still within the boundary, so we should be safe here. No need to keep watch."

"Perfect," said Khaldun, retrieving his pack from the horse's back. "I could use a good night's sleep." He started setting up his tent.

"What are you doing that for?" asked Sophia.

"Oh—you're welcome to share it with me, if you'd like," he said, realizing that the witch didn't have any gear with her. "I just figured it would be nice to have a proper camp for once."

"Suit yourself," she replied, looking at him askance. "I much prefer falling asleep under the stars. As long as there's no rain, that is, and there ain't a cloud in the sky."

Khaldun finished setting up his tent, and laid out his bedroll inside. Then he sat up chatting with Sophia until nightfall, despite his exhaustion. He figured it would be best to stay awake as long as he could to try and get himself back into a normal sleep cycle.

But as he lay in his tent, he found he was too restless to sleep. His thoughts turned to Mira, and wondering what Henry and Dredmort might be doing to her. And despite Sophia's confidence, he still felt anxious about trying to break into the Darkhold unnoticed. Perhaps he should abandon this mission and let Sophia proceed alone. Khaldun was only a lowly wayfarer boy; what did he know about daring rescues and glorious deeds? He felt like he'd gotten himself in way over his head.

But they had Mira. He wouldn't be able to live with himself if he didn't do everything he could to help.

Khaldun managed to doze off eventually, but woke with a start to find that it was light out. And someone was out there—he could hear Sophia talking to at least two others.

Poking his head out the flaps, he realized it was just a couple of university students making their way toward campus. He wondered what had brought them out here at this hour—it was only a little after dawn. But by the time he'd gotten dressed and stepped out of the tent, they'd moved on.

"Those were students?" Khaldun asked.

"Aye. Returning from a little holiday in Arthos. Ah, I remember those days like they were yesterday…"

"I've heard of Arthos—that's the free city, right?"

Sophia nodded. "Independent of any princedom. Has a bit of a reputation as a party city—well earned, too. I spent more than a couple of holidays there back in my day. Anyway, we should get moving."

Khaldun packed up his gear, then they mounted the horses and set out. Only minutes later, they reached the two guard towers that marked the edge of the university's territory. As on the western end, they were unmanned. Sophia opened a portal in the barrier, and they passed through it. They crested a hill, and Khaldun could see a massive metal-framed bridge spanning the River Mayne.

"That thing is huge," he commented.

"Aye. The university commissioned it many years ago. Used to be a rickety wooden thing that had to be rebuilt every time the river flooded. That's Strom on the other side; the prince refused to pay for a new bridge, so the university footed the bill. Worth it, I reckon, for all the traffic they have coming from this direction."

They crossed the bridge and then turned onto the south road. The landscape became more barren and rocky with every mile they traversed. The road more or less followed the river, straying inland only a few times to cut out great loops in its course. They passed a few farmers and merchants transporting their goods to market, but didn't run into any trouble. A little before sunset, they found a place to camp for the night.

"Henry's kept his forces on the other side of the Mayne so far," said Sophia as Khaldun set up his tent. "But just in case, we should keep a watch tonight."

"All right," Khaldun agreed. "I'll take the first shift if you'd like."

"Aye. And if you don't mind, I'll make use of your tent—it's looking like rain tonight."

Sophia was right; there were storm clouds moving in from the west. She climbed inside, and minutes later, the skies opened up, drenching Khaldun. He retrieved a tarp from his pack and covered himself with that, but he was already wet.

The rain tapered off to a drizzle after a while. Khaldun thought he heard approaching footsteps a few times, but calling fire to cast some light on the area didn't reveal any intruders. Just to be safe, he tried canceling invisibility, too, but there was nobody there. He figured there must have been small rodents crawling around in the rocks.

The temperature dropped, and still damp from the rain, Khaldun found himself shivering by the time his shift ended. He woke Sophia, and she called air to dry him off with a warm breeze. Khaldun slept for a few hours, then awoke at dawn and broke camp.

"That's still Roses across the river, isn't it?' Khaldun asked as they mounted their horses and set out.

"Aye. We should reach the Fosland border around midday. I'm planning to wait till we're as close as possible to the capital before crossing over. Hopefully that works out."

"Why wouldn't it?"

"We'll see," was all she would say.

As they traveled, the banks of the Mayne rose higher, and before long the river was flowing through a gorge far below. They reached a wooden bridge, and there were soldiers stationed on the other side by a shack. Their horses were tied to a hitching post beyond the building.

"I figured as much," said Sophia. "Henry's not one to leave a border crossing unguarded."

"I count only six men," Khaldun replied. "We shouldn't have any trouble getting past them."

Sophia didn't reply; they continued southward.

A couple of hours later, they spotted a tower on the other side of the river.

"That marks the border with Fosland," she told him. "The bridge we need to cross is coming up soon. With any luck, that won't be any harder to cross than the last one."

The bridge came into view when they crested the next hill; it was three times as wide as the last one. Camped on the near side of the river was an entire company of soldiers, flying Strom's colors. And on the other side was an even larger Foslander encampment.

"This is what I feared," said Sophia.

"We're not getting through here," Khaldun replied.

"No, we are not. We'll have to go back and take the Roses bridge."

They reversed direction and rode until their destination came into view.

"Let's rest here until sunset," Sophia suggested. "We'll have an easier time getting across at night." Khaldun nodded. "And I'll make us invisible, just to make sure they're not expecting any trouble."

They dismounted, and Sophia cast the spell to hide them from view. Khaldun tended to the horses, then they sat down, leaning against a boulder until darkness fell.

When the time came, they climbed onto their horses and moved closer to the bridge. The noise of the river flowing through the gorge drowned out any sound of their passage. Khaldun could see four soldiers sitting around a campfire outside the shack on the other side of the bridge.

"Let's give it some more time," said Sophia. "Most of them boys will retire into the shack before long. Then we'll make our move."

They dismounted again and waited. Before long, two more guards emerged from the building, and sat down with the others. But a couple of hours later, four of them moved inside, leaving the last two outside.

"That's probably the best it's going to get," said Sophia. "Those two will be keeping first watch. We'll stay invisible and the river should stop them from hearing us."

"What do we do if they notice us?"

"You leave that to me," Sophia told him. "Even if these two discover us, we still have to be careful not to wake the others. Just be ready to ride hard if I give the word." Khaldun nodded. "All right, let's go."

They made their way to the bridge; Sophia started across, keeping her horse to a walk, and Khaldun followed close behind. As they neared the other side, Khaldun could hear the two soldiers chatting, but couldn't make out their words over the rushing water below. He also spotted them taking swigs from a couple of bottles, and noticed a pile of empty ones by the shack, and realized they'd been drinking.

The men were sitting on the ground between their shack and the north side of the bridge; Khaldun and Sophia stayed as close to the southern side as possible, although the structure wasn't very wide. But just before they reached the opposite bank, one of the soldiers stood up, staring in their direction.

"Who's there?" he called out, swaying unsteadily.

Sophia reined in her horse; Khaldun stopped right behind her. The soldier moved to the very end of the bridge, only a few feet from Sophia's mount; Khaldun held his breath, his heart hammering in his chest. But after gazing across the structure for a moment, the soldier returned to the campfire and sat down.

Khaldun quietly breathed a sigh of relief. Sophia continued forward, but as her animal's hooves hit the dirt beyond the bridge, both soldiers jumped to their feet, drawing their swords.

"Show yourself!" the first man called out. "We saw the dirt you kicked up—we know you're there!"

Sophia charged forward, rounding on the men and drawing her wand. She called earth and something invisible slammed into one of the soldiers, knocking him over the edge and into the gorge. Next, she called air, and a gale blew the second man after his comrade; Khaldun could hear him screaming all the way down.

"Let's go," Sophia hissed, returning to Khaldun. "Quietly!"

She guided her horse up the road, keeping him to a walk; Khaldun followed. But as they passed the shack, one of the other soldiers emerged.

"What the hell is going on?" he demanded, rubbing sleep from his eyes. But he became more alert as he realized the two watchmen were nowhere to be seen. "Butch? Hackney? Where are you guys?"

Sophia called air again, hurling him into the gorge. He howled on the way down; Khaldun thought for sure that the other soldiers would wake up. But they waited a few minutes, and nobody else emerged from the shack.

"The other three are sure to raise the alarm when they wake up," Khaldun said quietly. "We should call fire and burn the shack to the ground."

"No," Sophia replied. "Right now, there's no sign of a struggle. Those men were drunk—there's a good chance their friends will think they fell into the river trying to take a piss. We burn the shack down, then whoever comes to relieve them will know for sure that they've got enemy mages in their territory."

Khaldun considered this for a moment, then nodded in agreement.

Finally, they continued up the road. Once they'd put some distance behind them, they urged their horses to a gallop for a while. They stopped again and moved off the road, waiting a few more minutes to see if there was any pursuit, but none came. They rode for another hour, then Sophia brought them to a halt.

"Let's get off the road and find somewhere to get a little sleep. We'll set out again at dawn, and then we should reach the Darkhold by nightfall."

The land was barren and rocky, so there were no trees or grass. They found a sandy area fifty yards from the road and decided that would have to do. Sophia took the first watch, and Khaldun curled up on the ground, falling asleep almost immediately. It seemed like no time had passed at all when the witch awakened him. But he got to his feet, taking his turn on guard duty so Sophia could sleep. He woke her up at dawn; they mounted their horses and continued westward.

They passed several squads of soldiers that morning. Sophia kept them invisible, and they moved off the road as soon as they spotted anyone approaching. But around noon, they reached a fork in the road.

"The main branch leads to Fosland City, looping around to the north of the castle," Sophia explained. "We'll turn off here and take the road onto the plain to the east of the city."

Khaldun nodded, and they headed south. The road was little more than a path through the desert; it didn't seem like anyone traveled this way very often. As the afternoon wore on, the Darkhold came into view far in the distance. Its walls were black, as if made from obsidian. It sat upon a high ridge, its back end overlooking the wasteland below. Khaldun couldn't help but feel like there were eyes looking down on them from the high towers, and felt thankful that they were invisible.

As they drew close to the castle, an eerie dusk fell about them. The sun hadn't set on the city yet, but was no longer visible from this vantage point. It had grown dark by the time they reached the ridge. Staring up, Khaldun could see the castle high above them, appearing to grow out of the sheer rock beneath it. They rode for a while longer, then found the cave exactly where Sophia expected it to be, its entrance hidden behind a giant outcropping of the main ridge.

"This is it," said the witch, getting off her horse. "We'll need to leave the animals here."

Khaldun dismounted, looking around for something they could use as a hitching post.

"There's nowhere to tie their reins," he concluded.

Sophia pointed her wand and called earth.

"There. Now the reins are heavy enough to hold them here till we return."

Khaldun tested his, and found he could barely move them.

"Huh. I never thought of that."

"Let's go, boy genius," Sophia muttered, heading into the cave.

CHAPTER SEVENTEEN
THE DARKHOLD

haldun followed her into the cave. It was utterly dark here; the witch called fire, creating a small flame to light their way. The space was only wide enough for them to walk single file, and barely high enough for Khaldun to stand straight. But it grew smaller as they went, and before long, he had to crouch.

Finally, they came to a metal door embedded in the rock. Sophia tried the handle, but it wouldn't budge.

"Now what?" asked Khaldun.

Sophia raised her wand and recited a spell that Khaldun didn't recognize. Then she tried the handle again, and the door creaked open. "These types of exits are always sealed magically," she explained, leading the way inside.

Khaldun moved in behind her, closing the door behind them as quietly as he could.

"I won't bother resealing it," Sophia whispered. "In case we need a quick exit."

"You should teach me that spell," Khaldun suggested. "In case we get separated and I run into any more locked doors."

"Good thinking," the witch agreed.

She taught him the incantation, and Khaldun spent a few minutes magically sealing and unsealing the door.

"I think I've got it," he said finally, and they moved on.

They were in a tunnel large enough to stand straight and walk side by side. But Sophia's wand provided the only light. They walked for several minutes, finally reaching a narrow stone staircase. Sophia led the way up the steps, and they climbed for what felt like an hour; Khaldun's legs ached by the time they reached a landing. But turning, he saw that another set of steps led farther up.

In the end there were six sets of steps, arranged in switchbacks, leading up to the castle cellar. They reached the top to find another metal door sealed magically. Sophia lifted the spell, and cautiously pushed it open. Peering through the crack, Khaldun could see that there was a storage room inside. They moved into the area, closing the door again behind them. The room was only dimly lit, but it was enough to illuminate their way, so Sophia put out her flame. The walls were stone, and looked like they'd been carved out of the ridge.

"Let's find the girl first," Sophia whispered. "They'll have her in the dungeons—you'll have to let me know when you spot her. Then we can look for the artifact."

Sophia reinforced their invisibility spell, then led the way across the room. They came to a doorway and moved into a long corridor. Khaldun followed her to the far end, and around the corner into another passage. Barred cells lined each side of this area.

Every cell was occupied by at least one man or woman, all wearing nothing more than loincloths. Most of these people looked weak and emaciated; they were dirty, and they smelled awful; Khaldun guessed that they had been here for a very long time.

But there were several prisoners who looked far healthier; one man was fat and looked like he'd bathed recently. Khaldun figured that he must have lived a lavish lifestyle before being imprisoned here. A woman in another cell seemed to hear them passing; she covered her breasts with her hands, backing into the rear corner. Her expression was defiant; she had the air of someone used to commanding authority. Khaldun suspected that these last two might have been mages.

But they reached the end of the row without finding Mira. Where could they be holding her if not here? He shot Sophia a questioning look, but she only shrugged. They moved back out to the main corridor.

"Now what?" Khaldun whispered.

Sophia considered their situation for a moment. "The old wizard, Melnor, had his workshop down here," she said. "Dredmort's probably taken that for his own, and that may be where he's keeping the artifact."

"What about Mira?"

Sophia took a deep breath. "I don't have any more ideas, lad. Let's see about the artifact, and then we can search the upper levels for her."

She led the way to the opposite end of the corridor. There was another stone passage here, but it was much shorter. Khaldun followed her down that to a wooden door; it had been left slightly ajar. Sophia pushed it open and they walked inside.

They found themselves in a large room, cluttered with desks and tables. Many were piled with books or scrolls; a crystal ball sat on a stand in the far corner. A large globe occupied another corner, and one wall was lined with wooden cabinets; glass vials and jars filled their shelves, containing potions of many different colors. At least a dozen candles were positioned around the chamber, filling it with a flickering light.

But suddenly, Khaldun heard a voice; his heart jumped into his throat as he frantically scanned the area for its source. But finally, Sophia pointed toward another wooden door at the far end of the room that was wide open.

The two of them crept across the chamber, moving as close to the far door as they dared. Inside, Khaldun could see a tall wizard standing with his back toward them. His head was bald and he wore long, red robes. He held his staff in front of him with his right hand, shouting an incantation. This was Dredmort.

Looking beyond the mage, Khaldun spotted a naked man lying on his back on a long table, his head closest to the wizard. The man appeared to be unconscious, and Khaldun realized that his body was blackened as if by fire.

Suddenly the wizard raised a silver dagger in his left hand and plunged it into the man's chest. Khaldun had to stifle a gasp; the victim screamed, but still seemed unconscious. The man's scream ended abruptly and Khaldun was pretty sure he must have died. The wizard placed a staff on top of the corpse, hurried around to the foot of the table, and recited a long string of incantations. Suddenly blue flames erupted from the victim's body; if he were still alive, surely, he would have cried out again, but he made no sound. The staff vanished in the fire.

And in that moment, Khaldun realized that there was a black pyramid sitting on the table, just to the front of the dead man's head: the artifact. Faint tendrils of dark smoke emanated from it, swirling around the small chamber. Khaldun was about to point this out to Sophia, but she edged closer to the door, inadvertently bumping a stack of books with her elbow. They fell to the floor, making thumping noises as they hit the stone.

"Who's there?" the wizard demanded, rushing toward the door.

Sophia shot Khaldun a fearful look; he froze in terror.

"Make yourself invisible!" she hissed. "And go back to the corridor!"

"What? We are—"

"*Now!*" she said, shoving him away from her.

Khaldun hurried out of the chamber, murmuring the incantation to make himself invisible. Passing into the corridor, he turned to see the wizard burst into the room, holding out his staff and canceling

Sophia's spell; she would be fully visible now. Khaldun realized that she'd sacrificed herself to save him—had she run, too, Dredmort would have pursued them to discover who was there. This way, he'd found only Sophia. Dredmort's features registered surprise for just a moment when he spotted the witch, but then a grin spread across his face.

"My, oh, my," he said, "the great Sophia. Never again did I expect you to grace this castle with your presence."

Khaldun thought about trying to get into the back room to grab the artifact, but Dredmort was in the way. He had to hope that Sophia could somehow maneuver the wizard out of his path.

Sophia glared at Dredmort, then raised her wand and called fire, trying to incinerate him from within. But he canceled her spell with a flick of his staff.

"Now, now, that isn't polite," Dredmort told her, shaking his head. "Tell me, what brings you to our humble abode?"

Sophia said nothing, but her eyes darted behind him to the dead man. Dredmort turned briefly, following her gaze.

"Ah, of course. You came to retrieve the artifact. I should have known they'd send you—who else could find their way around the Darkhold?"

"Nobody sent me, Dredmort. I'm here on my own mission."

"I'm sure," he drawled. "Well, there's someone I'd love for you to meet."

A chill ran down Khaldun's spine and he felt a sense of dread wash over him. He and Sophia both looked around the room, as if someone else had been hiding there, invisible. But suddenly Sophia let out a little scream.

Khaldun snapped his eyes back to her, but saw that she was staring into the smaller room again. Looking through the door himself, he realized with a start that the table was empty. An instant later, the dead man shuffled through the doorway, stopping when he reached Dredmort.

"What have you done..?" asked Sophia, staring at the figure in terror.

"Oh, don't you recognize him?" Dredmort said with a tone of mock surprise. "I'm sure you two have met before—yes, I'm certain I recall a time when he came to visit us here at the Darkhold. But it was so long ago, perhaps your memory is failing you in your old age?"

Sophia stared at the figure, her brow furrowed, but there was only confusion in her face.

"Why, this is Byron!" Dredmort told her. "Stanbridge's chief mage!"

"*What*?" said Sophia, with a look of dawning recognition. "No—what did you do?"

"It's an ancient ritual," Dredmort said matter-of-factly. "Dreadfully tricky to master—you see, it involves killing and *resurrecting* a mage. I'm afraid my first few experiments failed miserably. But my success rate has improved of late.

"Show her what you can do, Byron."

The figure raised its hand, and suddenly a tongue of fire appeared right in front of Sophia's face. The witch backed away, her expression a mixture of fascination and horror: the monster wielded no wand or staff.

"But… that's impossible," Sophia whispered, shaking her head in disbelief.

"Do you doubt your own eyes?" asked Dredmort, flashing his smile. "All the power of a sorcerer, but no free will of his own."

Sophia raised her wand and called fire. A towering inferno engulfed the monster; Dredmort backed away, shielding his face with one arm. But the flames subsided, having had no effect on the figure. Sophia called air, creating a vacuum around the creature in an attempt to suffocate it, but it just stood there, staring at her. Finally, she called earth; Khaldun knew her spell should have knocked it back into the smaller chamber, but it didn't move. Sophia stared at Dredmort in horror.

The wizard chuckled quietly. "He's a wraith, Sophia. Impervious to magic. Impossible to kill. And they possess unwavering loyalty to *me*."

"They?" Sophia said with a gasp. "How... how many are there?"

Dredmort smiled at her. "We should pay the high prince a visit, I think. He'll be thrilled to see you."

Sophia turned to run; Dredmort was ready for this. He held out his staff, shouting a word of command. A glowing sheet of energy formed in the air directly in front of Sophia; she ran right into it, and it wrapped around her like a blanket. Her wand clattered to the floor; Dredmort squatted down to retrieve it with his free hand.

Straightening up, the wizard turned and spoke a word of command. The door to his private chamber slammed shut, glowing faintly red for a moment, magically sealing the artifact inside. The wizard held out his staff, and Sophia floated across the room in front of him. Khaldun retreated down the corridor, pressing himself into the corner. As they passed, he realized that Dredmort's staff was shaped like a naked woman, impossibly elongated; a shiver ran down his spine. The wraith followed them through the corridor, leaving the workshop empty.

He waited until their footsteps faded, then hurried back to the chamber. Dredmort had left the outer door open; Khaldun ran inside and turned his attention to the sealed inner door. Holding out his staff, he tried to cancel Dredmort's spell, but it was no use. The door would not open; the wizard must not have used the same incantation Sophia had taught him.

"Shit," he muttered out loud. What was he supposed to do now?

Khaldun had no idea where to find Mira, and no way to get to the artifact. Without Sophia, he was lost. Freeing her was his only chance. Hurrying into the corridor, he reached the corner just in time to see Dredmort vanishing into a stairway. Khaldun crept along as quietly as he could, then followed them up the steps.

Dredmort moved up to the main level of the castle, escorting Sophia and the wraith into the great hall. Khaldun slipped into the room behind them, just before the two guards closed the enormous wooden doors behind them. Khaldun waited at the back of the room as Dredmort made his way to the front.

There was a huge marble throne on a dais, and sitting there was High Prince Henry. Khaldun thought he must be nearly as tall as Dredmort, but he was fat. On his head he wore a metal crown with a black horn protruding from each side, making him look like some sort of animal. He was holding an enormous stein in one hand, resting it on the arm of the throne.

Several other people were gathered around the high prince—Khaldun recognized the witch, Nineve, and the wizard, Lane, who had abducted Mira. There was a third mage—a dark skinned witch with heavy makeup on her face, wearing only a loin cloth and bandeau, her wand clutched tight by her side. He also spotted a military commander, and two other advisers of unknown roles, both older men. Lastly, farthest from the throne, was a servant boy, about the same age as Khaldun, wearing only a loincloth.

"Dredmort!" Henry called out with a hearty laugh. "What do we have here?"

"This was Byron," Dredmort told him, indicating the wraith. "The ritual has worked—"

"Yes, yes, very well—I meant *her!*" said the prince, pointing to Sophia, and taking a great swig from his stein.

"The mage, Sophia. Perhaps you remember—"

"Sophia!" Henry shouted, getting to his feet, and stepping down from his dais to examine her. "I'll be damned," he muttered, walking slowly around her as she hovered in midair. On his feet, Henry seemed much larger than Dredmort, despite being a couple of inches shorter. "What in the hell is she doing here?"

"I believe the university sent her to retrieve the artifact, Your Highness."

"Yes, they would do that, wouldn't they," the prince grumbled, returning to his throne. "Well, *they can't bloody have it!*" he screamed at Sophia. "Release her, dammit," he added to Dredmort.

The wizard called out the word of command and Sophia fell to the floor, scrambling to regain her feet. She looked around wildly for a moment, as if searching for an escape route, but there was none—all the doors were closed and guarded.

Henry laughed quietly. "There's no way out of here, you old loon. But would you care to explain how you got *into* my castle?"

"I served here for years—I know all the secret passages."

"Bullshit. I didn't even know all of them until my spy stole the plans from the university. Tell me the truth!"

Sophia said nothing. Henry nodded to Dredmort; he produced a tongue of fire right in front of her face. Sophia backed away, but the wraith grabbed her from behind, holding her by both arms. The flame moved within an inch of her nose; she turned her head away from it, but it followed her.

"How did you get in my castle?!"

"The postern gate—from the cave down on the plain!"

Henry stared at her for a moment. "Servant—more ale!" he shouted.

The boy ran over to the throne, took Henry's stein, and scurried away. He returned a few moments later, carefully handing it to the prince, then retaking his position beyond the advisers. Henry gulped down half the mug, then wiped his mouth on his sleeve.

"How did you know about the postern gate?"

Sophia remained silent. The flame touched her nose and she screamed, but still didn't answer him.

"Enough!" Henry bellowed; Dredmort canceled the fire. "It hardly matters—one of those university fuckers must have memorized the secret tunnels before we stole the plans." He stared at Sophia for a minute, brow furrowed. "But we stole the plans ages ago—way before we learned about the artifact. So why did they memorize *my* tunnels?"

Sophia remained silent, returning Henry's stare.

"*They've got a spy in my castle!*" the prince screamed. "Dredmort! Root out the fiend and bring him to me!"

"Yes, Your Highness."

Suddenly, Sophia tore herself free of the wraith's grasp, lunging at Dredmort. He raised his staff, but she was going for her wand, still in his left hand. Taking it from him, she rounded on Henry, shouting an incantation and hurling a fireball at him.

The dark-skinned witch was ready for her; she lunged in front of the prince, shielding him with her own body, and canceling Sophia's spell at the same time. And in that moment, Khaldun realized who she was: Mira.

"No!" he shouted, his heart dropping into his stomach.

Nineve and Lane both charged in front of their prince, but it was Mira who canceled Khaldun's invisibility. The guards by the main doors grabbed him, taking away his staff and dragging him up to the prince. The wraith took hold of Sophia again and Dredmort snatched her wand away.

"And who in the hell are *you*?" Henry demanded when Khaldun reached the dais.

Khaldun didn't answer, clamping his jaw shut and giving Henry a defiant stare.

"His name is Khaldun," Mira told the prince, staring at Khaldun without so much as flinching. "He's a wayfarer; their sorcerer has been teaching him magic."

Khaldun stared at her in utter disbelief; what the hell was happening? Mira was working for Henry—of her own free will? And she'd turned on him without hesitation. Had she been in Henry's service all along? No, that was impossible. He *knew* her; this had to be some sort of ruse. Khaldun felt certain in his heart that Mira would not betray him this way.

"Why are you here, boy? Did you come with this crazy bitch?" Henry asked, indicating Sophia.

"He's probably here to rescue *me*, Your Highness," said Mira.

Henry considered this for a moment, taking another swig of ale. "A hero and a harlot, then," he said with a chuckle. "Guards—get them out of my sight! I'll deal with them later. Right now, I want to hear more about Dredmort's latest experiment."

Two guards grabbed them, dragging them out of the hall.

"Lane—go with them!" Henry shouted. "Make sure there's no more trouble!"

"Yes, Your Highness," the wizard said, bowing slightly and following them out.

As they pulled him through the doors, Khaldun glanced back to get one more look at Mira. But she had returned her attention to Henry.

CHAPTER EIGHTEEN
RUSE

ira stole a glance at Khaldun as the guard dragged him across the hall, but returned her gaze to Henry immediately. Her ruse depended on her ability to play her role convincingly, and staring longingly after Khaldun could be her undoing. The look of pain on his face when she betrayed him had ripped her heart out; hiding her own emotions had been excruciatingly difficult. But she had to do it, especially now that they had Khaldun.

"Guards—fetch some robes for this thing," Henry shouted, getting to his feet. "I told you, Dredmort, I don't want them parading around naked like this. Useful though they are, I don't need to see their shriveled cocks."

"Apologies, Your Highness," Dredmort said with a slight bow. "In my haste to bring the intruder to you, it slipped my mind."

Henry approached the wraith, drawing his dagger. "You are a frightful-looking beast, aren't you," he said, poking it in the chest with the blade. The wraith didn't even flinch. "Amazing, aren't they?" he said enthusiastically, looking around at his advisers; they smiled in agreement, but Mira thought their expressions looked more like grimaces. "No free will of its own, it feels no pain, and yet it can do magic without any kind of instrument—just like a sorcerer! But they don't like sunlight, eh, Dredmort? Have you had any luck with that?"

"I'm afraid not, Your Highness. Although I don't understand it, their aversion to the sun seems to override all other concerns."

"Yes, well that's their one shortcoming, I suppose. Make it do something!"

Dredmort nodded, then muttered something to the wraith. It held out one hand, forming a tongue of flame in its palm.

"Hah! Superb, Dredmort, simply superb. With an army of these things, we'll reclaim the kingdom in no time!" Since her arrival, Mira had witnessed the high prince receive at least a half dozen wraiths—though she knew there were more—demanding a demonstration every time, yet losing none of his ardor. "Nineve—try lighting it on fire!"

"Yes, Your Highness," said the witch. She held out her staff and called fire; a towering inferno erupted, completely engulfing the wraith. Nineve kept it up for a full minute before putting out the flames. Yet the creature was unscathed.

"He's already burnt to a crisp, though, isn't he?" said Henry. "Try something else."

Nineve called earth; nothing happened.

"What was that?" Henry demanded. "What did you do?"

"A spell that should have hurled it across the hall," Nineve told him with a sigh. Mira could tell that unlike the prince, she had grown bored with these demonstrations.

Just then the guard returned with robes for the wraith.

"Ah, excellent," said Henry, returning to his throne and picking up his stein. "Empty," he grumbled. "Boy—more ale! And Nineve, clothe the thing, would you?" The servant boy hurried over for the stein and ran off to fill it again.

"Yes, Your Highness," the witch said with a scowl, handing her staff to one of the advisers. She took the robes from the guard and set about her task with a look of disgust on her face.

"How many is this now, Dredmort?" asked Henry. "Eight? Nine?"

"This one is the eleventh," Dredmort replied.

"Fantastic," the prince muttered. The servant returned with his stein; Henry took a giant gulp from it, then set it down on the arm of the throne again. "Convert that bitch, Sophia, next. Just reward for her treason. And that wayfarer boy."

Mira felt ice running down her spine at these words.

"Yes, Your Highness," Dredmort said with a bow.

"Forgive me, Your Highness," said Mira, "but the boy is not yet a full mage—his skills are rudimentary at best. From what I've heard here, only the strongest mages are suitable for the ritual."

"Perhaps you have feelings for the boy?" Nineve asked with a smirk. She'd finished robing the wraith and retook her staff from the adviser. "Was he your lover while you were with the troupe?"

"I hardly knew him," Mira lied dismissively. "But I saw him training with the sorcerer. He's weak."

"Your Highness, the girl is right," said Dredmort. "Only a full mage would retain their power after the transformation. He would be useless to us."

"Mm, very well," said Henry, drinking more ale. "But I want the witch for sure—do her tonight."

"Your Highness, the hour is late," Dredmort replied. "But I will attend to her in the morning—"

"*Do it tonight!*" yelled Henry. "I don't want that madwoman in my castle any longer than necessary!"

"Yes, Your Highness," Dredmort said with a bow. "My apologies. I will require a little time to prepare—"

"Fine, fine," Henry said, waving him off. "Do what you must, but don't take a minute longer than you need."

Dredmort bowed.

"We'll keep the wayfarer boy for ourselves," said Henry. "Train him up, Dredmort. Our mages are spread pretty thin—we could use another wizard in the field. Especially while we're waiting for Gunthar to regain his power."

"Yes, Your Highness."

"Very well," said Henry. "Out of my sight, all of you."

Mira stepped away from the dais; she knew Dredmort would escort her up to her room now. But Henry said, "Not you, girl." Mira stopped in her tracks. "Come here a moment."

The advisers had already hurried out of the hall, Nineve close behind, but the witch stopped when she heard Henry hold Mira back. Mira approached the throne. Henry grabbed her by the wrist and pulled her into his lap. Mira felt panic-stricken but did her best to project calm.

"What do you say you join me in my chambers tonight, eh?" he said, running his hand up her thigh.

Mira felt revolted, but kept her face blank. She didn't know what to do—the prince had made sexual comments to her before, and had grabbed her breasts and buttocks more than once, but this was the first time he'd made such an invitation. How could she refuse him without incurring his wrath? She felt herself casting about for some sort of response as the seconds dragged out—how could she get out of this?

"Your Highness!" Nineve strode back to the throne. "I hardly think we can trust this girl to be alone with you!"

It was an open secret in the castle that Nineve and Henry were lovers. Mira knew she was probably acting in her own self-interest rather than looking out for the prince's safety. But she sped her a silent *thank you* regardless.

"Jealous, Nineve?" Henry said with a leer. "You're welcome to join us if you'd like."

"Your Highness knows that I would if it were someone trustworthy," she replied, glaring at Mira. "But this girl has yet to prove her loyalty."

"She fended off that witch's attack faster than you did, Nineve," Henry pointed out. "And she didn't hesitate to identify that wayfarer boy."

"Forgive me, Your Highness, but it could all be a ruse. She's a clever girl, I'll grant her that—she's doing what she must to earn your trust. But she could just be plotting her escape or even her revenge—"

"Argh, all right already," said Henry, pushing Mira out of his lap. "You've made your case, you stubborn wench. But I'm drunk and I want to fuck. Fetch that servant girl from last time and meet me in my chambers."

"Yes, Your Highness," Nineve said with a bow. Shooting Mira one last sneer, she turned and strode from the hall.

"After you, my lady," Dredmort said with a grin.

Mira walked out of the hall as quickly as she could without making it *look* like she was hurrying, Dredmort and his wraith right behind her. She climbed the grand staircase to the second floor, and headed to her chamber at the end of the hall. The door was sealed shut.

Turning to face Dredmort, she found him holding out this hand; Mira turned over her wand. He held out his staff and unsealed the door.

"Sleep well," the wizard said with a leer.

Mira stepped inside the room, closing the door behind her. She knew Dredmort would seal it shut again, but the spell made no sound. Once his footsteps had faded down the corridor, she tried the door on the off chance that he'd forgotten to secure it, but had no such luck.

Mira collapsed in her bed with a sigh. Keeping up her act was trying at the best of times, but tonight had nearly broken her. Between betraying Khaldun, and enduring Henry's sexual aggression, she didn't know which was harder. Thank the stars Nineve had intervened; Mira still couldn't imagine how she would have gotten out of that.

From the moment Lane and the soldiers had captured her, she'd started fabricating her story. And by the time they'd arrived at the Darkhold, she was ready. They brought her directly to an audience with the high prince, as she'd expected. He had been sitting on his throne in the great hall. Dredmort, Lane, and Nineve were there, along with several guards, advisers, and servants. Gunthar had told Henry all about her peculiar abilities, and he had demanded a demonstration.

Lane had already confiscated her wand, so she would have been defenseless as a normal mage. But when he called fire against her, the flames didn't touch her. Henry commanded him to cast several more spells, delighted every time when the magic failed to work against her. Finally, he ordered Lane to give her back her wand. Lane and Nineve cast a dozen more spells, from illusions to invisibility, walls of fire to gusts of wind, and Mira was able to cancel them all.

At that point, they knew that magic wouldn't work on her, whether she had her wand or not. And they knew that she could use her wand to cancel spells not directed at her. But they did *not* know that she could perform the latter task *without* her wand—and keeping that secret would be paramount to her success.

"You've got a choice, girl," Henry had told her once he was satisfied. "You can join my court as a mage, or you can rot in my dungeon."

"Your Highness," Mira had replied, taking a deep breath. This was the moment of truth; if she could play the role she'd designed for herself convincingly, then she had a fighting chance. "It would be an honor to join your court."

"Why should we trust you?" Nineve asked. "You acted against us by helping that rabble bring the artifact to the university."

"It was my only choice. My father, the Lord of Graystone in the far western princedom of Blacksand, banished me from his estate to go live with my mother's people—the wayfarers. He sent armed guards to escort me on the journey and transfer me to their keeping.

"But I wanted nothing to do with the wayfarers. When I heard they were going to the university, I volunteered to join them. I was planning to enroll there when we arrived. It still wasn't the life I had always desired, but it would have been better than perpetually wandering around the continent."

"I don't believe you," Nineve replied, giving her a sly smile. "The university won't accept wayfarers. Surely you must have known that?"

"Yes. But I had to try. I'm only half wayfarer—my father is a highborn lord. But serving as a court mage is much more to my liking. I very much want to live in a castle again."

"Satisfied?" Henry asked Nineve.

The witch regarded Mira with her cold stare for a moment longer. "For now. But she should prove herself before we hand her the keys to the realm, so to speak."

"Very well," said Henry. "Your status for the present shall be that of a servant. Boy—fetch the Lady Mira the appropriate garb for a servant girl."

His servant, clothed only in a loincloth, bowed and hurried from the hall. Mira shivered slightly; the servants she'd seen so far paraded around half-naked. But she did her best to hide her reaction. The servant returned, handing her a bundle of cloth.

"You will wear those," Henry told her.

"Yes, Your Highness," she said.

"Now."

"I... but... in front of all these people?"

"Your Highness," said Lane, "if she is going to join the court eventually, then we should spare her the indignity—"

"*Now!*" Henry screamed.

Mortified, Mira stripped out of her clothes. She caught Dredmort looking her up and down, and quickly donned the loincloth and bandeau the servant had given her. The boy picked up her clothes and hurried off.

"You will train with Dredmort during the day," Henry told her, "and attend court when I require you. We will allow you your wand during those times. But you are confined to your chamber at night, and you will turn over your wand before you retire every evening.

"If you behave and demonstrate loyalty to me and my princedom, then we will make you a court mage. But if you step out of line, the consequences will be severe. Understand, girl?"

"Yes, Your Highness," she said, bowing low.

"Very well. Now get out of my sight."

Nineve eyed her suspiciously as she left the great hall, and the witch's doubts had not diminished at all since that first night. But Mira knew Henry was the one she had to convince. Dredmort had escorted her to her chamber after that, magically sealing her inside. Once she was sure he'd left, she collapsed on the bed and cried her eyes out.

Mira knew that she could unseal the door without her wand, but it was critical that her captors not discover that particular ability. She'd have to take extreme care to keep that a secret.

This ruse was going to be difficult and dangerous. But if she could gain Henry's trust, then in time, she'd felt confident she would be able to find the artifact and escape with it. The only trouble was that it might well be too late.

The very next day, Dredmort had presented Henry with his first wraith. Mira had never seen or heard of such a creature before, but it was dreadful. From their conversation, Mira was able to glean that Dredmort had discovered a hidden cache of ancient texts buried in the Darkhold's library. These had included the ritual he used to create the wraith. And though Dredmort had attempted the rite numerous times before, he'd been unable to successfully complete it—and ended up murdering each mage he tried it on.

The trouble was that he'd lacked the power necessary to perform the ritual in the way he was attempting; apparently, that would have required a sorcerer or necromancer. But Dredmort had also found a reference to an ancient artifact in some old mage's journal—an object he could use to augment his own power by tapping into the spirit realm. And the artifact was reportedly an heirloom of the ruling family in Stanbridge.

Dredmort had continued experimenting with the rite, adapting it to his purposes, while Henry sent a spy to infiltrate Stanbridge's court. Once they'd confirmed the presence of the artifact, they sent an army to retrieve it. And now that they finally had it, Dredmort had wasted no time in putting it to use.

But Mira still had to try to take it away from them; there was no telling what else Dredmort could do with it. Yet to accomplish that, she'd have to figure out where he was keeping it, and the only way to do that was to earn their trust and become a court mage. This was going to be a long game.

However, that very first night, something happened that made her question her plan. She'd fallen asleep after a couple of hours, but awakened to a soft rapping at her door. Startled, she sat up in bed and held her breath, waiting to hear if it happened again; it did. She slipped out of bed and moved to the door, her heart pounding now.

"Who is it?" she asked.

"Lady Mira?"

"Yes; who are you?"

"I am Cassius, but nobody else here knows me by that name—so if you report my visit, it won't matter."

"What do you want?"

"That depends."

"On what?"

"Where your loyalty truly lies."

Mira stifled a gasp; this was a trap. It had to be. "I am loyal to the high prince."

There was no reply for a moment.

"Hello? Are you still there?" Mira asked.

"I don't believe you. I heard some of the soldiers talking about the way you canceled Gunthar's magic like it was child's play the night they attacked the wayfarer camp. If you wanted to become Henry's court mage, you could have gone with Gunthar that night. But you chose to stay with the wayfarers."

"What do you want?" Mira repeated.

"I want to take that artifact away from them before they can create any more of those wraiths. What do you want, Lady Mira?"

Mira said nothing. She wanted the same thing, but there was no way she could admit that to this person.

"I know where they're keeping it. But I'm no mage—I can't get in there. You can."

Mira wanted to believe this, but knew it had to be a trap. Nineve had sent someone to test her loyalty; she wasn't going to fall for this. "I have no intention of helping you. And I *will* report your visit tonight."

"Tell me why you fought Gunthar that night. Why did you stay with the wayfarers?"

"I… I didn't know who he was. I didn't want to be with the wayfarers, but we were under attack—all of us, myself included. I defended myself, as I would have done no matter the attacker."

"You're lying. Every highborn lord on the continent knows who Henry's chief mages are—they're all nervous that he's going to restore the old kingdom."

"Well, after it was over, I found out who it was. But I'd never seen Gunthar before—how was I supposed to know?"

There was no answer.

"Are you there?"

"You think this is a trap, don't you?"

Mira didn't reply.

"I'm guessing you believe that Nineve sent me to try to trick you into revealing your true intentions. But I swear, that's not the case. I'm with the resistance. My father served Henry's father as an adviser. But after Henry had the old prince killed and ascended to the throne, he murdered my father, along with everyone else who was loyal to the old prince.

"I managed to escape. I was only a boy, but one of Euclid's mages found a way to get me and some of the others out of Fosland. He brought us to the university and they trained us—I became a spy."

"They don't train non-mages," said Mira.

"Not openly, no. They have to maintain their appearance of neutrality, but they run a secret program to develop and place spies in key locations.

"But now that Dredmort's got that artifact... I have to find a way to get it. And you're the only hope I have of getting through the wizard's spells. I need you, Lady Mira."

Mira took a deep breath. She desperately wanted to believe this. With his knowledge and her skills, they could actually take the artifact and get it to the university. But it was too great a risk. If she agreed to this, and it was a trap, then they'd kill her for sure.

"I'm sorry. I can't help you. Now go away—I need to get some sleep."

There was only silence for a few more moments, but then she heard footsteps receding down the corridor. Mira went to bed, but lay awake for a long time that night. She felt like she might have let a huge opportunity slip right through her fingers. But the risk was far too great. She would have to play her long game, and in time, she would be able to discover the artifact's location for herself.

The next day, Dredmort arrived soon after dawn. He'd brought a servant girl with him; he instructed Mira to sit down on her bed while the girl applied heavy make-up to her face.

"The high prince likes the women in his service to be pleasing to his eye," the wizard explained with a smirk. Mira had to fight to suppress a shiver.

Once the girl was done, Dredmort brought Mira to the dining hall for some breakfast, and then down to his workshop in the cellar.

She spent hours training with him; he tried to help her cast spells, but it was futile. So instead, he helped her improve her skills in countering magic.

And the entire time, Mira paid attention to her surroundings. The room was cluttered, and she figured he probably had the artifact here somewhere. But she couldn't find it. There was a door at the far end of the room; it was closed the whole time, but maybe the artifact was in there. Mira was sure he'd keep it magically sealed if that were the case, but she could get through that protection. She realized that he might be keeping the thing tucked into the void, and didn't know if her powers could bring it back—was that a spell she could cancel? She'd never tried. Mira decided she'd have to cross that bridge when she came to it.

That afternoon, Henry summoned her to the great hall. She took her place with Nineve and Lane, standing by the prince's side while he held court. That evening, Dredmort had brought Henry the first wraith.

The next day, Mira spent her entire time at court. She wondered why Dredmort hadn't brought her to his workshop for more training, but had her answer that evening when he showed up in the great hall with *five* more wraiths. Dredmort had been busy.

But the day after that, the wizard came to fetch her, and brought her down to his workshop for more training. And this time, Dredmort had left the inner door open. Mira tried to get a look inside when the wizard wasn't looking. There was a table in there—empty, unlike all the surfaces in the main room. But there were also shelves on the walls, and these were cluttered with all manner of magical trinkets—crystal balls, telescopes, vials of potion. She couldn't see the pyramid, but neither did she have a clear view of the room. There was a good chance it was in there.

"We'll have to wrap this up here," Dredmort said after a few hours. "But the high prince is not holding court today. If you'd like, you can stay and assist me with a special project."

Mira's eyes went wide. "You're going to make another wraith?" Dredmort nodded with a wide grin. His twisted enthusiasm was revolting, but this was her chance; she knew this must be what he was using that empty table in the inner room for. "Yes, I'd like to stay," she said, trying to sound eager.

"Very well, come with me."

Mira followed him to the dungeon. He moved to a cell halfway down the corridor, and addressed the old witch inside.

"Today's your lucky day, Miranda," he said with a grin.

"No, you sick bastard—I know what you're going to do to me!" she cried, covering her breasts with her hands and trying to shrink into the far corner.

"It is an honor to serve your prince in a way that only a select few will ever be chosen to do."

"Honor, my ass," she said, spitting at him. "You're going to turn me into one of those monsters! If it's such an honor, why don't *you* do it?"

Dredmort held out his staff and a glowing sheet of energy appeared inside the cell. Miranda tried to avoid it, but it wrapped itself around her, rendering her immobile. Dredmort unsealed the door, and led them back to his workshop, the woman hovering along in front of them. He moved her into the back room and lay her flat on her back on the table.

Mira was about to look around for the artifact, but there was no need. Dredmort removed it from the top shelf and placed it on the table above the witch's head.

"Ready?" he asked Mira.

"Y-yes," she stammered. "What do you need me to do?"

"Just watch," Dredmort replied.

Mira observed in terror as the wizard conducted the ritual. Miranda screamed as he began his incantation and the flames engulfed her, burning away her loincloth. Mira felt like she was going to vomit by the time Dredmort drove the dagger into the woman's heart. When he was done, the woman rose from the table, now another of Henry's wraiths. Mira felt overcome with dread.

Dredmort created two more that day, bringing them all to the great hall the next morning for Henry to examine. The entire affair had sickened Mira. But it was worth it: now she knew where to find the artifact. Dredmort kept the door to the inner chamber sealed, but she would have no trouble with that when the time came.

And now the only thing she needed was a way out of the castle. Walking out the front doors would not be a possibility—they were guarded at all times. But having grown up in a castle herself, she knew these buildings always had secret exits. She'd decided that she would turn her attention to finding one, and when she did, she would act.

But now they had Khaldun—and he'd *entered* the castle using one of the secret passages. The time for Mira to act had come. She waited, lying awake in her bed until the third bell after midnight. Then she canceled the spell sealing the door, cautiously opened it to make sure there was no one standing guard, and set off for the dungeons.

CBAPTER NINETEEN
ESCAPE

he guard threw Khaldun roughly into the cell. He tripped, bashing his knee on the stone floor and hitting his head against the wall. Jumping to his feet, he tried to rush the cell door before the guard could close it, but it was too late; Lane had already sealed it shut. They'd thrown Sophia into the cell next to his.

"Let us out of here!" Khaldun shouted to Lane's retreating back. But he departed with the guards without any reply. "Now what?" he asked Sophia.

The witch tried her cell door, but it wouldn't budge. She examined the lock for a moment, but then threw her hands up in frustration.

"Now what is nothing. Unless you're actually a sorcerer, and can cancel Lane's spell without your staff."

"I wish," he muttered. "We'll just have to wait—Mira will find a way to get us out of here."

"She was the half-naked one up there by Henry?"

"Yes."

Sophia chuckled derisively. "Wouldn't hold my breath waiting for that. She's working for the enemy, now!"

"No, that's impossible. I know her—it's got to be a ruse."

"You saw her! She blocked my spell and told them who you were!"

"Well, yes," Khaldun admitted. "But if I were in her shoes, I'd be doing everything I could to get them to trust me."

Sophia shook her head. "Don't be so naïve; nobody's that good an actor. She moved *fast* to protect the high prince—and she gave you up without even flinching. Somehow, they turned her."

"No. I can't believe it—I won't. You don't know her," Khaldun insisted. "She plotted her return to the wayfarers—to me—for *years*, without letting her father catch on. I bet she started planning her escape the moment they got her here. Get them to start trusting her, give her a little freedom, and then she could make her move. Find a way to grab the artifact and get out of here."

Sophia still didn't seem convinced. "Maybe you're right, maybe not. But you'll forgive me if I don't feel like counting on it. I think our only move is to fight next time they open one of our cells. Dredmort's probably got your staff and my wand in his workshop. So if one of us can get in there and grab them, we can release the other."

"Wouldn't he keep his rooms sealed shut when he's not there?"

Sophia sighed. "Aye. That he probably would. Worth a shot, though."

Khaldun sat down on the floor, leaning against the wall with his head in his hands. He couldn't believe it had come to this. To be trapped in Henry's dungeon after traveling so far—this was not how he thought this would go. He thought of using his mirror to contact Nomad, but that was in his pack, which he'd left on his horse.

At some point, Khaldun dozed off. But he awoke to the clanging of metal. Opening his eyes, he realized that Dredmort was here. He had encased Sophia in a sheet of energy and was guiding her out of her cell.

"Hey! What are you doing with her?" Dredmort moved the witch down the corridor without answering, but Khaldun thought he knew exactly what was about to happen. "*NO! Don't do it! Please!*"

"Shut up, you idiot!" hissed an old man form the cell opposite his. "You keep makin' that racket, he'll come back and torture all of us!"

"Grow a spine, Vance," said the woman in the next cell; Khaldun recognized her as the woman with the air of authority they'd seen when they first arrived. "If we don't resist then we might as well curl up and die. They'll torture us either way."

"You shut up, too!"

Khaldun ignored them. He tried his cell door again, but it wouldn't budge. Hurling himself against it, the only thing he accomplished was bruising his shoulder.

"Ain't no use, boy," Vance told him.

Khaldun opened his mouth to retort, but at that moment, he heard a blood-curdling scream. It was Sophia. Khaldun held his breath, listening for any more sounds, but he could hear nothing more for several minutes. But then there was another scream, this one ending abruptly. Khaldun recalled Dredmort plunging the dagger into Byron's chest, and a shiver ran down his spine.

He stood at his cell door for what felt like hours, gripping the bars so tight his hands went numb, but there was nothing else to hear. He feared the worst, but waited to see if Dredmort would bring Sophia back to her cell. Finally, he heard footsteps. Dredmort moved into view, a hooded figure in black robes close behind.

"Ah, good—you're still awake," he said to Khaldun with a smirk. "How do you like what we've done with your friend?"

Dredmort stepped aside, and the hooded figure moved up to Khaldun's cell, turning to face him. It threw back its hood, and sure enough, it was Sophia. Her skin was blackened, and her gaze was blank; she was staring straight at Khaldun, but there was no light of recognition in her eyes.

"*NO!*" Khaldun screamed, tears streaming down his face.

Sophia—no, she wasn't Sophia anymore; the wraith pulled its hood over its head and shuffled back down the corridor. Khaldun sank to the floor, sobbing, as Dredmort disappeared from view. Khaldun sat there crying for several minutes, unable to get Sophia's screams out of his mind.

"Could be worse," Vance told him. "At least they didn't turn *you* into one of them creatures."

A shiver ran down Khaldun's spine; he figured he would be next. And being turned into a wraith seemed a fate worse than death. He sat awake trying to think of some way out of this. The dungeon had grown quiet, but before long, he heard Vance snoring. Eventually, Khaldun's exhaustion won out over his terror, and sleep stole him away.

But he woke to find someone shaking him by the arm. Opening his eyes, he saw Mira squatting down next to him. She cupped her hand over his mouth before he could speak.

"I don't want to wake any of the other prisoners," she whispered. "Let's go."

Khaldun got to his feet, letting her lead him by the hand out through the open cell door. His head was foggy with sleep, and it was difficult to piece things together; but the fact that Mira was rescuing him made his heart soar. He had been right.

He realized that Mira had led him to Dredmort's workshop. The door was closed, and didn't budge when Mira tried it. She pressed her palm against the lock for a moment, and then it lurched open; Khaldun knew she must have canceled the spell sealing it shut. They crept inside, closing the door behind them. Dredmort had kept a couple of candles lit, providing a little light.

"You saved me!" Khaldun whispered.

"Of course, I did," she replied, grabbing his head in both hands and kissing him passionately. "You didn't think I was going to let you rot down here, did you?"

"Well, I didn't want to believe it, but the thought *had* crossed my mind… Everything you did with Henry—that was just an act?"

"Did you doubt it?"

"Well… I…"

Mira kissed him again. "Let's talk later—we need to get the artifact!"

"I think he's keeping it in that back room," Khaldun told her.

"Yes, I saw it in there," she said, heading to the door.

"But he seals it with a spell I don't recognize," said Khaldun.

"Doesn't matter," she replied, pressing her palm against the lock; it creaked open. Khaldun cringed at the noise, but Mira slipped inside, returning moments later with the black pyramid in her hand. "I was worried he would keep it tucked into the void—and I'm not sure I could have brought it back."

"At least a few of Henry's other mages must know void magic," Khaldun pointed out. "But I bet he devised his own spell to seal that door—nobody but him would be able to get through that."

"Except me, and I was very careful to hide the fact that I don't need a wand to cancel magic," Mira replied. "Now we have to find a way out of this castle!"

"We can use the secret tunnel I took when we came here, but hold on," Khaldun replied, spotting his staff in the far corner of the main room. He hurried over to grab it. "What about your wand? I don't see it…"

"Forget it—I don't need it! I only used it to fool them!"

"Yes, but it would be best to keep up that part of your ruse."

They spent a few moments searching for it, and finally found her wand on one of the tables.

"You'll need clothes, too," Khaldun said, eyeing her head to foot.

"We're running for our lives and you're worried about my modesty?"

"If we want to make it to the university, we need to avoid attracting notice—and that's going to be impossible with you dressed like this!"

"Ugh," Mira said.

They hunted around the room some more, and found a bundle underneath a desk. Mira held it up and shook it out—the fabric was covered with dust, but they were witch's robes. She threw them on over her clothing. They were a little small, coming down only to midcalf.

"It'll have to do," Khaldun said.

He led the way out of the room, staff at the ready. They crept through the corridor and into the storage room. The door to the secret tunnel was sealed but Mira canceled the spell. But once they'd passed through it, they stopped short at the sight before them. Someone had blasted the ceiling and walls of the stairway, blocking the way with an enormous pile of rubble.

"Uh-oh," said Mira.

"Hold on," Khaldun replied, moving up close to the debris. Holding out his staff, he called fire, creating a small flame at the top of the rubble. Standing on his tip-toes, he peered down the shaft, but it was blocked as far down as he could see. "It's no good—the whole thing is obstructed. Even if I call air to remove this rubble, there are five more stairways beyond—they've probably blocked them all."

"We'll have to try getting out the front doors," Mira suggested, her tone not remotely confident.

"There's at least one more secret tunnel," Khaldun told her. "I know one of them comes out in the basement of a temple somewhere out in the city, but they didn't tell me where the access point is *inside* the castle."

"It could be down here somewhere," Mira suggested. But they looked around the storage room and back in the corridor, and couldn't find any other doors or passageways. "Well, make us invisible, and let's see what the front entry looks like."

Khaldun nodded. Holding out his staff, he cast the spell to hide them from view. "Come on."

They headed up to the main level and moved as quietly as possible across the central atrium. But it was no good—there were guards stationed at both ends of the entry hall and the doors were closed. Khaldun thought of trying the spell to suffocate the guard, but these men were all awake and alert and he could only take out one at a time that way.

Mira grabbed him by the arm, leading him back across the atrium to one of the side corridors. But at that moment, a wraith moved into view at the opposite end of the hall. Khaldun backpedaled, pulling Mira along with him and searching for somewhere to hide. But it was too late—the wraith was emerging from the corridor. They pressed themselves flat against the wall. Dredmort had claimed these creatures were as powerful as sorcerers—did that mean they could detect magic as well? If this one sensed their invisibility spell...

The wraith was walking past them; Khaldun held his breath. But suddenly the creature stopped, turning its head toward them, and then sweeping its gaze across the atrium. Khaldun realized that it was smelling the air as if it had caught their scent.

Slowly it moved closer to them, swaying slowly side to side, sniffing as it went. Mira squeezed his hand, her grip like a vise. Holding up his staff, Khaldun mouthed the incantation for an illusion. Suddenly a cat appeared by the entry hall, meowing loudly. The wraith snapped its head around, turning its attention to the animal. Khaldun and Mira edged silently along the wall, putting more distance between them and the creature. He focused on the cat, moving it quickly toward the wraith. His spell work was horrible—the cat's gait didn't match its movement; he hoped the wraith wouldn't notice. As the cat reached the monster, it threw out its hand. Something invisible hit the illusion, knocking it across the floor toward the entry hall.

Khaldun and Mira froze; they were huddled in the far corner of the room now. The wraith sniffed the air again, then continued its progress across the atrium and into the opposite corridor. Khaldun breathed a quiet sigh of relief; apparently, the wraiths could *not* sense magic like a sorcerer.

Mira led him into the hallway where they'd first seen the wraith. At the far end they came to the kitchens. They searched the area, but found no hidden passages. They moved back out to the atrium and then into the great hall. Together, they checked behind the tapestries and paintings hanging from the walls, as well as the area behind the dais, but still couldn't find another way out.

"This is useless," Mira whispered with a sigh. "There's nothing here."

"Somewhere in this castle is at least one more secret exit," said Khaldun. "And we've got to find it before someone discovers us. Where else could it be?"

But suddenly, Khaldun realized that someone had entered the chamber. It was Henry's servant boy, standing by the doors.

"Lady Mira?" he asked in a loud whisper. "Is that you?"

Mira gasped, grabbing Khaldun's arm; he was sure the noise was loud enough for the boy to hear. They stood perfectly still as the servant moved across the room toward them.

"I found the door to your chamber ajar," the boy whispered. "I know you're out here somewhere. I want to help you—*I'm Cassius.* Please, talk to me and allow me to assist you!"

"I'm here!" Mira whispered.

Khaldun cupped her mouth with one hand. "*What are you doing*?!" he hissed into her ear.

But Mira pulled his hand away from her mouth. "Make us visible! He's with the resistance! But be ready with your staff in case this is a trap!"

Khaldun stared at her for a moment, reluctant to trust this boy. But before he could act, Mira stomped her foot in frustration, then held out her hand and canceled his spell. The boy's eyes went wide as he caught sight of them.

"Cassius!" Mira whispered, hurrying over to him. Khaldun followed her, staff at the ready. "I had no idea it was you! We've got the artifact—but we have to get out of here. They've sealed off the tunnel leading out through the storage room and we can't find another way. Can you help us?"

"Yes, I can," he said. "Follow me!"

"Wait," said Khaldun. "Why should we trust him?" he asked Mira. "How do you know he's with the resistance?"

"I don't," Mira replied. "I'm taking a leap of faith. If he leads us astray then go ahead and roast him!"

The boy stared at her and gulped.

"All right," said Khaldun. "We don't seem to have any other option. I'll make us invisible—stay close together."

He cast the spell, and Cassius led them out of the great hall. They moved up to the second level and into the library at the end of the corridor. Cassius strode to the far end of the room, grabbed a section of the bookcase, and slid it away from the wall. Behind was an opening just big enough for a man to pass. Khaldun and Mira followed him into it, and the boy shut the bookcase behind them. It was utterly dark here; Khaldun called a flame to provide some light, and spotted a narrow stone stairway leading down.

"These steps will take you to an underground tunnel," Cassius told them. "Follow that all the way to the end and you'll come out in the cellar of the temple in the middle of the city. There shouldn't be anyone in there at this hour, so you should be able to get out with no problem."

"Thank you," said Mira. "Will you come with us?"

"No, my lady, my duty is here. Will you take the artifact to the university?"

"Yes, definitely," said Mira; Khaldun nodded in agreement.

"I must ask if you can make but one stop on your way out of the city," said Cassius. "I have vital information to report to my university liaison, but it is days yet before our next supply run, and if I am found to be missing, they would execute me upon my return."

"What is it?" asked Mira.

"Henry is plotting an invasion of Oxcart. I only found out this past evening, but their army will be moving out *tomorrow*. My handler has a mirror that is paired with one in Enigma's possession—he can get word to him immediately."

"But the university won't interfere," said Khaldun. "They didn't even attempt to prevent the takeover of Roses, and that lies on their southern border."

"Perhaps not directly, but Enigma can send an independent operative to the region," Cassius replied. "But if you carry the news to him yourself, it will be too late."

"We should split up," Mira said to Khaldun. "You go directly to Oxcart and warn them—assist them in the battle. I'll take the artifact to the university."

"What? But why—Oxcart isn't that important in the grand scheme of things. Surely getting the artifact to the university is more urgent. And I do not intend to send you off into the wild alone. We should go together!"

"Oxcart matters more than you know," Cassius told them. "Henry's coffers are empty; he's overextended himself occupying the princedoms he's taken so far. He needs them to fund his military."

"But I don't understand," said Khaldun. "Oxcart possesses no wealth; Bichon's castle is no bigger than most minor holdings."

"It makes no sense to me, either," Cassius replied. "But that's what Henry told his advisers. Perhaps he knows something that we don't?"

"Yes, he does—I'll explain later," Mira added to Khaldun. "Somehow we have to get the artifact to Enigma *and* warn Oxcart."

"Talk to my liaison," Cassius suggested. "Perhaps he could take care of the artifact, freeing the two of you to assist Oxcart."

Mira nodded. "That would work. Where do we find him?"

"His name is Isaac, but he works undercover as a baker named Salisbury. His shop is only a couple blocks from the temple, to the south. He lives on the top floor of the building."

"Perfect," said Mira. "Thank you, Cassius."

The boy nodded. "Good luck, both of you."

Slowly opening the bookcase again, he peered through the opening before slipping back into the library, closing the door behind him.

"Shall we?" said Mira, nodding toward the steps.

"Yes, but tell me how you knew about Cassius."

They started out down the stairs, Khaldun first to light their way. Mira explained how the boy had come to her door late at night and related his story.

"I would have guessed that to be a trap as well," Khaldun said when she was done. "But Enigma did tell me they had a spy here."

"I'm a little surprised they haven't blocked this tunnel, too," said Mira.

"Even Henry would want to leave at least one emergency exit," Khaldun replied. "But we need to be wary—they may have guards posted down here. Now, tell me how conquering Oxcart is going to help finance Henry's military."

"Oh," said Mira. "Do you remember that night when I stayed at the castle with the prince's son, Phillip?"

"How could I forget?" Khaldun muttered.

"Yes, well, I wasn't entirely truthful when I told you about that. Phillip gave me a tour of the castle. But they're hiding a big secret there. Khaldun, they've got an entire gold mine underneath the building. Bichon's father started an excavation to build an addition on the rear section and discovered a massive gold-bearing quartz vein in the underlying rock. Over the years, they've uncovered dozens of veins. There's enough gold down there to fund their entire princedom for generations!"

"You're joking! Their castle is plain and his army is small, their equipment basic. If Bichon possesses so much wealth, then what is he doing with it?"

"Hoarding it, primarily," said Mira. "Phillip told me that his father insists on keeping it a secret to avoid making themselves an attractive target for someone like Henry. They use some of it to purchase iron ore from a princedom in Shifar. Then they use the iron to trade with their neighbors in Maeda. That way, the other princedoms don't know about their gold, and if anyone ever catches wind of their mining operation, they'll assume it's the iron ore they're pulling out of the ground."

"And if Henry does sack their princedom, then he'll gain access to that gold."

"Precisely. And there's more than enough there to finance his takeover of the entire kingdom. We've got to do everything we can to prevent him from getting control of it!"

"But how did Henry find out about it if they're keeping it so secret?" asked Khaldun.

"That's a good question; I'm afraid I don't know," Mira replied. "They could have planted a spy there. And they have people working in the mines; Phillip told me that they live in a separate settlement and aren't allowed to interact with the villagers, but who knows. Any one of them could have let something slip somewhere."

Khaldun considered this for a moment. "Well, this explains why Phillip was willing to marry a landless wayfarer girl. They already possess all the wealth in the world; what more could they need?"

"Yes, exactly," Mira agreed.

They continued in silence. Several minutes later, they came to the bottom of the steps and proceeded through a narrow tunnel. The floor was dirt, and they found several piles of animal remains. Something had been hunting rodents and eating them down here. Khaldun was thankful they did not meet the predator.

Finally the end of the tunnel came into view. Khaldun reinforced their invisibility spell, and prepared to call fire if they encountered any guards, but the way was clear. There was a wooden door; Khaldun tried opening it, but it was sealed. Mira canceled the spell, and they pushed it open slightly, peering through the crack.

There was only a cellar beyond, cluttered with junk. Khaldun pushed the door wide; it creaked on its hinges. And as they walked into the cellar, a voice cried out, "Who's there? Show yourselves!"

CHAPTER TWENTY
FUGITIVES

haldun spotted two guards who had been hidden from view by the clutter. The one who spoke had just stepped out from behind an armoire; he was brandishing his sword, nervously looking toward the door to see who had opened it. Another was across the room by the steps. The one by the steps turned to run up to the main level. Khaldun called fire, incinerating him from within; the man screamed for a moment until the flames consumed him and his charred corpse toppled to the cellar floor.

The other soldier lunged toward Khaldun, stabbing blindly with his sword. Mira grabbed Khaldun and yanked him out of the way in the nick of time. Khaldun recovered his balance, then called fire again, killing the second soldier.

"Thanks for that," he told Mira with a grin.

They hurried across the cellar and rushed up the steps, slowing as they neared the top. Taking in their surroundings, Khaldun saw that they were in a long corridor. Mira followed him into the nave; thankfully, there was no one within. There were vaulted ceilings and stained-glass windows, a large altar at the front, and rows of benches facing that. They hurried to the main doors at the rear of the chamber, but peering through the windows to the street, they saw at least a dozen more soldiers stationed outside.

"Shit, now what?" asked Khaldun.

"There must be a rear exit," said Mira. "Come on!"

They hurried back across the nave, and into the rear corridor. Sure enough, they found a service entrance leading to a back alley. They stepped outside, moving up toward the street. But peering around the corner, Khaldun saw that there were quite a few more soldiers moving about here.

"We've got to get across the road if we want to go south," he whispered to Mira. "But doing it here would be dangerous—if someone bumps into us, we're in trouble."

"What's our alternative?"

Khaldun scanned the area behind her; it ended at a fence. "Come on," he said, running to the end of the alley.

Khaldun climbed the fence. From the top, he had a clear view of the Darkhold, several blocks away at the top of the hill. The front of the next building was three stories high, but the rear section was only a single floor. They could reach that from the fence.

"We can cut across to the next alley from up here," he said to Mira.

She climbed up behind him, and they clambered onto the adjacent rooftop. Hurrying across that, they skidded to a halt just before its end. But at that moment, a trumpet blast emanated from the Darkhold.

Staring up at the castle, Khaldun watched as they lowered the drawbridge over the moat and opened the gate. The trumpet blared again, but this was quickly drowned out by a shrieking noise that sent a chill down Khaldun's spine. He watched in terror as Dredmort, Nineve, and Lane crossed the drawbridge, followed by half a dozen wraiths, all on horseback.

"We've got to hurry," said Mira, sitting down with her legs dangling over the edge. Turning, she grasped the roof with both hands and lowered herself down, dangling by her fingertips for a moment before dropping to the alley below.

Khaldun followed her down, and they crept up to the main road; he led the way across and they ducked into the closest alley. Gazing back up the road, he didn't see any sign that the soldiers had noticed their passage. But looking the other way, he spotted Dredmort and two of the wraiths approaching their position. The wizard was casting spells into every alley they passed to cancel invisibility.

"We've got a problem," said Khaldun.

"We sure do," Mira agreed, following his gaze.

They hurried to the far end of the alley; there was a gate, but that was locked. Khaldun realized there was a gap between the fence and the building. He guided Mira through that, then turned and cast the spell to cover their trail. A light breeze blew sparks up the alley as Khaldun slipped through the gap. Peering back through the opening, he saw Dredmort ride past with his wraiths, casting his spell up the alley they'd just vacated.

"That was close," he whispered, gazing around the area. They were behind the building now, and there was a space between it and the adjacent structure barely wide enough for them to pass. They shuffled along until they reached the next alley. "Come on!"

Khaldun led them over to the next street. He could see Nineve—she was already farther down this road. They crossed two more blocks this way, finally reaching a road with a bakery. There was a sign hanging over the door that read "Salisbury Bread."

"That's it," Khaldun said, pointing it out to Mira.

There wasn't anyone on this road. They hurried over to the bakery, but the door was locked. Khaldun tried knocking, but there didn't appear to be anyone inside.

"We have to move!" said Mira.

Looking up the street, he spotted Lane moving into view with two wraiths. Like Dredmort, he was casting cancelation spells up every alley he passed.

"Crap, now what?" said Khaldun.

"Into the alley," Mira told him. "There should be a rear entry."

They hurried around the corner, and sure enough, there was an entry on the side of the building. But this was locked too. Khaldun pounded on the door, but there was no answer.

"Forget it, let's go!" said Mira, heading toward the end of the alley. But there was a brick wall here instead of a fence, and it rose two stories high. They could find no way to climb it. "Shit!"

But suddenly, the side door opened. An old man poked his head out, looking both ways, but seeing nothing, was about to close the door again.

"Wait!" hissed Khaldun.

The old man poked his head out again; Khaldun and Mira ran over to him.

"We have urgent business with Isaac—is he here?" Mira asked.

"Quick, get inside," the old man said, his eyes not quite meeting their invisible ones.

Khaldun and Mira ducked inside and the man quickly closed the door behind them. Through the front window, Khaldun could see Lane and his wraiths moving past the edge of the building.

"Now, who are you?" the old man said, pointing a wand at them and canceling their invisibility.

"I am the Lady Mira Grisham of Graystone in the princedom of Blacksand and this is Khaldun of the wayfarer troupe. Are you Isaac?"

"Nobody in this city knows me by that name. How did you find me?"

"Cassius told us about you," Mira told him. "He said you can contact Enigma?"

"Maybe I can, but one does not disturb a sorcerer without good reason."

Mira told him about the artifact and what they'd learned from Cassius. But suddenly the old man looked beyond her, his eyes opening wide in fear, and there was a scream somewhere outside.

"You've got to hide," he told them. "Quickly, this way."

He opened a door, and Khaldun saw steps leading down.

"In the basement?" he asked skeptically.

"No," Isaac replied, reaching in and sliding open a section of the wall alongside the steps. "In there."

There was a small gap in the wall, not large enough to call a closet. Khaldun climbed in, Mira right behind them, and the wizard slid the door shut again. The basement door slammed shut, and the next instant, there was a pounding on the front door.

"Make yourselves invisible again!" the wizard hissed before shuffling off.

Khaldun was pressed tight between the walls on three sides and Mira's body on the fourth, but his staff was firmly in his grasp. He whispered the incantation to hide them from view.

Moments later, Khaldun heard the front door opening.

"Yes, how can I help you, master wizard, sir?" Isaac's voice said.

"You're Salisbury?" It sounded like Dredmort.

"Yes, that would be me."

Isaac made a grunting noise and Khaldun heard heavy footsteps walking on the floor.

"We're searching for a couple of young wayfarers—a man and a woman. The man may be carrying a staff. We have ah, reports of them passing along this street; have you seen them?"

"Ain't seen no one yet today," Isaac said with a cough. "Don't open for business for another couple of hours. My apprentice ain't even arrived yet."

"I'm sure you won't mind if we have a look around?"

Dredmort's footfalls continued before the old man had replied.

"Be my guest, sir."

Dredmort walked past the basement entry and continued into the rear of the bakery. Khaldun heard him recite the spell to cancel invisibility, then heard the rear door opening. Dredmort's footfalls returned, and then the basement door opened. Khaldun held his breath as he listened to Dredmort descend the steps into the cellar. He called out the spell to remove invisibility again before climbing back up the steps.

"If you do see a couple of wayfarers passing this way, you will make sure to notify us, won't you?" Dredmort said. "Otherwise it would be a shame if we had to close down this establishment."

"Yes, of course, master wizard, sir. Any wayfarers come around, I'll report to the guards right away, sir."

Khaldun heard more footfalls, then the sound of the front door slamming shut. But just to be sure, they stayed put until Isaac came and slid open the sliding door again.

"All right, the coast is clear. Come on out, and make yourselves visible—I hate talking to empty air."

They stepped out of the hiding space, and back into the bakery.

"Wait here a moment. I need to run upstairs."

The wizard disappeared into a rear hallway, and they heard his footsteps moving up a set of steps, and then across the ceiling above them. He returned a minute later holding a small mirror, similar to the one Khaldun used to communicate with Nomad.

"Enigma, are you there?" Isaac said, staring into the glass. "This is Isaac—I have urgent news."

A few moments later, the sorcerer's face appeared in the mirror. "Isaac. I wasn't expecting to hear from you for a few more days yet."

"I'm sorry to disturb you, sir, but this couldn't wait." He gave the sorcerer the information Cassius had provided. Enigma took a deep breath, considering the situation for a moment. "Nobody I can send would get there in time."

"Sir, this is Khaldun," he said; Isaac handed him the mirror. "Sophia and I managed to get inside the Darkhold. They took us prisoner... Dredmort was using the artifact to create wraiths... and he turned Sophia into one."

Enigma closed his eyes, letting out a long sigh. "I am sorry to hear it. Go on."

"Mira got me out of the dungeon, and we've got the artifact. We want to bring it to you straightaway, but we also need to warn Bichon and assist him in the battle…"

"If I leave now, I could beat Henry's army to Oxcart," said Isaac.

"I'm reluctant to expose your true identity," Enigma replied. "And without you, we have no liaison for Cassius."

"Mira and I can go to Oxcart," said Khaldun. "Isaac is stronger than either of us, but I can speak to Nomad. He may be able to join us."

"If Badru approves," Enigma replied with a nod. "Isaac, can you bring the artifact here?"

"Aye," the wizard said. "I'll have my apprentice run the shop while I'm gone. He can tell anyone who inquires after me that I've gone to see my ailing mother in Stiles."

"Very well," said Enigma. "Safe journeys, all of you." The sorcerer vanished from the mirror.

"All right, come with me," said the wizard.

Isaac led them into the basement. Waving his wand, he cast a spell to cancel illusion, and suddenly a steel door appeared in the rear wall. He spoke another incantation, unsealing it, and then opening it wide. "You two wait for me in here. I'll join you as soon as my apprentice gets here."

Khaldun and Mira walked through the door to find themselves standing in a sewer tunnel. Isaac closed the door behind them. There was a channel in the ground, with water flowing through it; they were standing on a stone walkway that ran alongside it. Only a few minutes later, the door opened again, and Isaac stepped through it.

"Off we go, then," he said setting out along the walkway. "We'll come out beyond the city wall, just to the north of the castle. You two would be best served to loop around to the east, and travel along the plain below the city to avoid going through it. Gonna be a long walk for all three of us, but with them searching for you, we can't risk stopping at the stables."

"Sophia and I left our horses outside the postern gate on our way into the castle," Khaldun told him. "If they're still there, you're welcome to take one."

"Aye, we can check," Isaac replied. "Sure would make things easier."

They continued along in silence for several minutes. Isaac led them along a winding course beneath the city, finally reaching a gate, with a view of the countryside to the north. The gate was locked, but Isaac produced a key and opened it for them, closing and locking it again once they'd gone through.

Isaac made the three of them invisible, and they continued on foot up to the road, then headed east. Before long, they reached a fork and took the branch leading down to the plain. And as they approached the outcropping with the hidden cave, Khaldun spotted the horses right where they'd left them. They whinnied as the humans approached.

"They're going to need food and water," Khaldun noted, canceling the spell holding their reins to the ground. "But they seem to be all right."

"There's a stream by the south end of the city," Isaac told them. "Fill your canteens and water your animal there. Once you get beyond that, the country grows less arid. You'll find some grass for him before long."

Mira produced the artifact and handed it to the wizard. He held it in one palm, using his other hand to wave his wand and push the pyramid into the void.

"Isaac, there's a young girl who just enrolled at the university," Khaldun told him. "Her name is Janelle and, well… Sophia was her aunt, and the only family she had left in the world. Could you find her while you're there and give her the news?"

Isaac nodded. "I'll do my best."

"Thank you," said Khaldun. "It would mean a lot to me."

"All right, then," he said, shaking their hands in turn. "Good luck."

"You, too," Mira told him as he mounted his horse and headed back up toward the main road. He and his horse disappeared from view as his invisibility spell moved beyond Khaldun and Mira. Khaldun cast his own spell to hide them from view again. He climbed onto their horse, Mira right behind him, and they rode south, the Darkhold towering ominously above them.

They reached the stream a little south of the city as the sun cracked the eastern horizon. Khaldun filled their canteens and Mira brought their horse to the water to drink. The country did indeed grow less arid as they progressed southward and before long they found a grassy field. They dismounted and let the horse graze for a while. Khaldun dug the mirror out of his pack and contacted Nomad, updating him on everything that had happened.

"Mira and I are heading to Oxcart to warn the prince," he concluded. "And we were hoping that maybe you could go, too, and help in the battle against Fosland. I'm not too confident that the two of us can repel those wraiths."

"I'll speak to Badru," he told him. "He won't like it, but we've reached a holding in Stoutwall. The troupe should be safe here; I may be able to persuade him."

Khaldun and Mira continued southward, reaching the Oxcart road before too much longer. There wasn't much traffic, but Khaldun kept their invisibility spell in place and they kept to the grassy shoulder to avoid kicking up any dust.

A little after nightfall, they found a meadow set back from the road and made camp. Khaldun tethered the horse to a tree and set up the tent. They didn't risk a fire; Khaldun's spell would hide the flames from view, but someone could still spot the smoke against the sky as it rose above his protection. They lay on the ground for a while, holding hands and gazing up at the stars.

"You had me so worried," Khaldun told her. "I thought for a moment that you'd turned when you were working for Henry. I was devastated."

"Never. I told you I've made my choice, and the troupe is where I want to be. With you."

Mira propped herself up on one elbow and kissed him. After a while, she crawled into the tent to get some sleep while Khaldun kept the first watch. He woke her a few hours later, and she relieved him. Khaldun fell asleep the moment he hit the bedroll.

For the next two days, they rode from dawn to dusk without any trouble. But Khaldun woke the third morning to Mira shaking him frantically.

"Huh? What's wrong?" he said, sitting up with a start.

"Come and see!" she whispered.

Khaldun climbed out of the tent with her, getting to his feet and gazing up the road. His heart almost stopped at the sight before him. An entire army was moving into view, Dredmort, Nineve, and several wraiths at its head.

"They must have marched overnight," said Khaldun.

"Must be—it's the only way they can take their wraiths with them," Mira replied.

"What? Why?"

"I heard Henry say that they hate the sun. It's nearly dawn, so they'll have to go into hiding somewhere soon."

"That's good to know," said Khaldun. "But we've got to get moving!"

"But they can't see us, can they?"

"No but if they get past us, we'll have a tough time getting around them and beating them to Oxcart."

Khaldun hurriedly packed up their gear. They mounted the horse and took off, sticking to the grassy shoulder, only a hundred yards ahead of the army. Thankfully, that many men didn't move very fast, so once they'd increased their lead, they risked a gallop for several minutes. Slowing down and gazing behind them, it became apparent that the Foslanders had halted and were setting up camp for the day.

"That was much too close for comfort," said Mira.

"Agreed. But we've got to hurry. That army is now within a day's march of Oxcart."

CHAPTER TWENTY-ONE
BRACING FOR THE STORM

haldun and Mira reached the border a few hours later. There was a company of Oxcart soldiers stationed on the other side of the line, and they'd barricaded the road. Khaldun had urged their horse to a gallop when they'd spotted the boundary, and their guards must have seen the dirt the animal was kicking up from the road. Though they were still invisible, the soldiers cried out an order to halt as they approached. Khaldun reined in the horse, removing their spell of invisibility.

"Who are you and what is your business in Oxcart?" one of the guards demanded.

"I am Khaldun of the wayfarer troupe, and this is Lady Mira of Blacksand. We have urgent business with Prince Bichon—please allow us to pass!"

"I'm afraid not," the soldier replied. "We have strict orders not to allow anyone through but our own citizens."

"You don't understand—Henry is sending an army to invade and conquer your princedom!" Khaldun told him. "They'll be here *today*—we must warn your prince!"

Another soldier came over to see what was going on. Khaldun recognized him as Captain Westmore. "What's the problem, soldier?" he asked.

The guard started to reply, but Khaldun spoke over him. "There's a Foslander army on its way here to sack your princedom! We have to get word to Bichon!"

"Very well," Westmore replied. "I'll send a rider to the castle immediately."

"Will you let us accompany him?" asked Khaldun.

"Can't do it. We have strict orders not to let anyone cross the border," Westmore told him apologetically.

"Sir, I'm afraid you're not comprehending your peril," Mira told him. "Henry has sent Dredmort and Nineve with his army, along with at least half a dozen wraiths. Your prince no longer has his wizard; we're both mages. You must let us through to assist in the defense—it's the only chance you have to survive!"

Westmore considered her words for a moment. "Very well," he said finally. "Let them through."

"But sir," the soldier objected. "Our orders—"

"I'll escort them to the castle myself and take full responsibility for the decision," Westmore told him. "Now let them pass!"

The soldiers cleared the barricades, moving them back in place once Khaldun and Mira had passed. Westmore hurried into their camp, returning moments later with his horse. He mounted and said, "Follow me!"

They rode as fast as they could, but it took several hours to reach Oxcart Town. The villagers hurried out of their way as they made their way down the road. They reached the castle to find the drawbridge raised. Westmore called out to the guards on duty and they lowered the bridge and raised the gate. They followed him into the courtyard. Leaving their horses with a stable boy, they ran into the keep.

The guards stationed at the doors allowed them to enter the great hall, but there was nobody inside. Westmore sent one of them to find the prince. Only minutes later, Bichon and Phillip arrived, taking seats behind the head table.

"What is going on here, Westmore?" the prince demanded, eyeing Khaldun and Mira. "And why have you allowed these two to enter our land? Were my orders not clear?"

"I apologize, Your Highness," Westmore said with a bow. "But they came here to warn us that there is a Foslander army on its way here to attempt a takeover of our princedom!"

Phillip looked alarmed at this news, but Bichon remained calm. "You could have relayed this news yourself," he noted.

"Yes, Your Highness, but—"

"Prince Bichon, Nineve and Dredmort himself ride at the head of the invading force," Mira told him. "And they bring at least half a dozen wraiths! You no longer have a wizard, so Khaldun and I came here to help you defend against the Foslanders!"

"*Wraiths*?" said Bichon, narrowing his eyes suspiciously.

"They are creatures of necromancy, with no free will of their own," Mira told him. "Henry was collecting so many mages only so Dredmort could turn them into wraiths. They can cast spells without a wand or staff, and are impervious to magic."

"How has he come to be in the possession of such monsters?"

"He captured me and the artifact on our way to the university," Mira told him.

Bichon cried out in dismay. "How could you let this happen?" he demanded.

"We have since managed to retake the dreaded object and send it to be destroyed," Mira said, "And when we learned of the threat to your princedom, we rode straight here to warn you and assist!"

"But why would Henry have any interest in Oxcart?" said Bichon. "We have no strategic value!"

"He has overstretched his resources occupying the other princedoms," Mira told him. "But with Oxcart in the fold, he will be able to fund his military indefinitely." Bichon seemed taken aback, opening his mouth to say something, but then closing it again. "Your

Highness, we know about your gold, and Henry must have found out as well."

"What?" Bichon cried, getting to his feet. "How do you know about that?"

Mira turned her gaze to Phillip; Bichon noticed and rounded on his son. "What have you done? You revealed our secret to this *wayfarer girl*?"

Phillip seemed to wither under his father's gaze, unable to look him in the eye.

"Your Highness, he was merely attempting to impress me to make his marriage offer more attractive," Mira told him.

"And you betrayed our secret to Henry?!"

"No, Your Highness! I most certainly did not! I don't know how he found out, but I assure you, it was not from me!"

"*Whom else did you tell?*" Bichon demanded of his son.

Phillip squirmed in his chair for a moment. "I showed Lady Wanda the mines," he admitted finally. "But I can't believe she would have betrayed—"

"You fool! If the Foslanders conquer us today, it's on your head!"

"Who's Lady Wanda?" Khaldun said quietly to Mira, but the prince heard him.

"She is the daughter of the Lord Watson of the Meadowlands," Bichon said.

"The Meadowlands?" Mira replied incredulously. "But that's a holding in southern Fosland!"

"Indeed it is," said Bichon. "They visited here not too long ago to negotiate a trade agreement on Henry's behalf. And it seems my idiot son all but gave them the keys to the princedom. Were you trying to use our wealth to woo Wanda as well?" he asked Phillip.

"I... uh... Apologies, Father..."

"Westmore," Bichon said, shaking his head. "Send messengers— recall our forces from the borders. Immediately!"

"Yes, my prince," the captain said, bowing before turning and hurrying out of the great hall.

"Your Highness, Henry stole plans from the university for all of the castles in the region," Khaldun told him. "Including this one. And those plans show the secret passages leading into the building. You should have those sealed off before the Foslanders arrive."

"*What?*" the prince demanded. "The university had plans to *my castle?*"

"It is my understanding that the original builders would have submitted them to their library—"

"Very well," Bichon said, throwing his arms up in frustration. "Phillip, do something useful and arrange for those entries to be demolished."

"Yes, Father, but our engineers are with the company on the southern border—we'll have to wait until they arrive."

"We can help," Khaldun told him. "There's no need to wait."

Phillip nodded.

"Do you know what the timing of the Foslanders' invasion will be?" Bichon asked.

"When we encountered them, they were setting up camp within a day's march from here," Mira told him.

Bichon nodded. "And how large is their force?"

"Roughly the same size as the one that marched here from Stanbridge," said Mira. "Perhaps a little larger."

"A little over two thousand men, then; our numbers will be equal. We will take up position north of the town and meet them on the field."

"But Your Highness," said Mira. "With their mages and wraiths, they're sure to overwhelm you. It would be better to retreat within the castle walls—"

"Will the two of you assist us against their mages?" asked Bichon.

"Yes, that's why we're here," Mira replied. "But that's *Dredmort* they've got with them, in addition to Nineve. Khaldun and I are no match for them, never mind their wraiths. But fighting from the castle walls, we'll have far better odds—"

"No. I will not sacrifice the villagers to them so easily. We will stand and fight in the field. Seal off those entries and then prepare for battle."

Bichon turned and strode out of the great hall. Phillip led Khaldun and Mira into the keep. "Well, I sure do feel stupid," he confided.

"As well you should, I'm sorry to say," Mira replied.

"Wanda told me they hated Henry and that her father wanted to secede from his princedom. I suggested that we could make them part of Oxcart; I thought I could trust her!" Phillip told them. "Anyway, I've never understood the point of possessing so much wealth if we're not going to use it! We could have raised an army ten times larger to protect against Henry's aggression!"

"And doing so would likely have made you an attractive target long before now," Mira told him. "No use crying over spilt milk at this point."

Phillip led them to the rear of the keep, and down a long stairway into the cellar. Opening a wooden door at the rear of that area, he revealed a tunnel leading farther down.

"This used to be nothing more than the escape tunnel," Phillip told them as they headed into it. At its end they found an open pit with several more passages branching out from it. "Those four lead to the active mining areas. This last one goes to the settlement out behind the castle grounds where the miners live; it was the original hidden exit. Let's make sure there aren't any stragglers out there."

Khaldun and Mira followed him through the passage. It ended at a steel gate in the side of a low ridge. Beyond that, they found a group of shabby wooden structures. Phillip checked them all, but there was nobody here. They moved back inside to the open pit. Calling earth, Khaldun collapsed the tunnel at several points along its length, making it impassable.

Phillip led them back inside the keep, and up to the prince's suite on the top floor. In the back of a closet was a section of wall that overlapped with another, a small gap between them. Moving through that space, they reached a narrow staircase leading downward quite steeply. Khaldun and Mira followed Phillip to the bottom of that where they found a dark tunnel. Khaldun called fire, creating a small flame to illuminate the area.

"This passes beneath the castle and leads into a hidden subbasement beneath the tavern in town," Phillip told them.

"We shouldn't collapse this area," Khaldun told him. "It could damage the castle."

Phillip nodded, leading them far into the passage until they reached a ninety-degree turn. "We're beyond the castle walls here," he told them.

Khaldun rounded the corner, moving another fifty paces along the tunnel, then he went to work. He called earth, demolishing the ceiling and walls at several different spots as he retreated toward the others. When he was done, the tunnel beyond the castle was completely blocked.

"Where else?" Khaldun asked.

"Those are the only two escape passages," Phillip replied.

"Are you sure?" asked Mira. "Most castles have more than that."

"The building is small," Phillip replied with a shrug. "We don't know of any others."

"That's the best we can do, then," said Khaldun. "Let's hope there isn't a third in the plans Henry stole from the university."

They returned to the prince's chambers, and back down to the main level. Exiting into the courtyard, they found soldiers busily preparing for the coming battle.

"Let me go don my armor, then I'll meet you back here and escort you to the front lines," Phillip told them before hurrying back inside.

"We should check in with Nomad while we're waiting," Khaldun said to Mira.

They found their horse in the stables, and Khaldun dug through his pack until he found his mirror. He was about to call out to Nomad, when he found him staring back at him through the glass.

"There you are," the sorcerer said. "I'm afraid Badru is not willing to send me. The two of you are on your own."

"Damn," Khaldun replied with a long sigh.

"I'll keep working on him, but I wouldn't count on me at this point."

"Understood," said Khaldun.

"Do the same thing we did last time—if you and Mira station yourselves on the ramparts, you should have a clear view of the attack. Make yourselves invisible and have Mira cancel anything they throw at you."

"We would, but Bichon is determined to meet Henry's army head-on," Khaldun told him. "They'll have to pass through the town to reach the castle, and he's not willing to sacrifice his people."

Nomad nodded. "Look for an elevated position, then, and employ the same tactics."

"We will," said Khaldun. "But how do we deal with the wraiths? They can cast spells without any instrument, and they are impervious to magic."

"I'm afraid I don't have any advice," Nomad said with a sigh. "Such creatures have not been seen in Anoria for centuries; I know of them only from legend."

"They didn't teach you about them at the university?" Mira asked.

"Unfortunately not; they fall under the purview of necromancy. But according to the stories I've heard, the only way to destroy them is to behead them, then burn their corpses to ash."

"Easier said than done, no doubt," Khaldun muttered.

"But I thought fire couldn't touch them?" Mira asked.

"No, *magic* can't touch them, but they will burn in a normal fire. It's just got to be extremely hot."

"Well, we'll put our heads together," said Khaldun. "I'm sure we'll think of something."

"Good luck to both of you."

Khaldun stowed his mirror and they returned to the courtyard, leading the horse by the reins. Phillip showed up a few minutes later wearing full plate armor, several members of the prince's guard right behind him. The stable boys brought them their horses. Once they'd mounted, Phillip led them out of the castle.

They rode through the village, and about a half mile farther south found the Oxcart army forming ranks. Their force spanned the road, spreading out across the adjacent fields. Khaldun spotted Bichon at the front of the lines conferring with his commanders.

"We're stationing our archers on that hilltop," Phillip told them, pointing to the army's left flank. "Do you want to work from there?"

"No, I don't think so," Khaldun replied. "They're sure to concentrate some of their force on those men. It would be better for us to take an isolated position, away from anyplace there's likely to be heavy fighting. What about that next hilltop?"

Phillip nodded. He assigned two of the prince's guards to accompany them. They wished the prince luck and parted ways. Khaldun and Mira reached the hill with the two soldiers minutes later.

"I'm going to make us invisible now," Khaldun told them. "Stick close to us," he added to the soldiers. "I'm sure Henry's got scouts monitoring our preparations, but this way, they won't see us setting up here."

The soldiers nodded. They climbed the hill on horseback, dismounting at the tree line and securing the animals' reins to the lowest branches. Taking position nearby, Khaldun scanned the area. This vantage point would provide them with a clear view of the entire battlefield.

"This is perfect," said Mira, gazing out across the countryside. "Now, we wait."

CHAPTER TWENTY-TWO
THE SECOND BATTLE OF OXCART

'm worried about the wraiths," said Khaldun. "Despite what I said to Nomad, I have no idea how to fight them."

"Well, magic doesn't affect them *directly*, but physical objects should," Mira pointed out.

"So, maybe we let the soldiers handle them?" Khaldun suggested. "They're the ones with the weapons."

"Which will work great as long as they don't discover us."

"What have you got in mind, then?"

Mira furrowed her brow in concentration for a moment. "You've got to do something to physically hinder their movement. I mean, if you were to drop a house on one of them, then it should be stuck there, right?"

"Nomad might be able to cast an air spell powerful enough to lift a house off the ground, but I'm not," Khaldun said with a sigh.

"All right... what about a tree? Could you rip one out of the ground and use it to pin a wraith to the ground?"

"A smaller one, perhaps," he replied, gazing into the woods behind them. "But I'm afraid I would lack the precision it would take to drop one on a target. I could call earth to make their robes super heavy and pin them to the ground—*they're* impervious to magic, but their clothing shouldn't be. But it would be good to have something else ready to go, too."

"Hmm. What about opening a fissure in the ground like Nomad did?"

"That spell drained him of all his energy," said Khaldun. "And I'm nowhere near that powerful."

"But it wouldn't need to be so large," Mira told him. "If you could open a hole just big enough for a wraith right beneath its feet, then close it again when it falls in, that would work!"

"Maybe, but it would just dig itself back out again."

"Sure, but that would take time. And the soldiers could decapitate them as they emerge."

"True," Khaldun conceded. "Let me see what I can do." He chose a spot nearby and called earth. The ground shook a bit but nothing else happened. Adapting the spell a bit, he tried again, and managed to open a small pit in the earth.

"That's great!" said Mira, moving over to it and peering inside. "Can you make it a little larger?"

Khaldun nodded. "Watch out—I don't want *you* falling in!"

Mira backed away and Khaldun tried the spell again. The pit opened wider, more than large enough to accommodate one of the creatures. He called earth again, sealing the opening shut. For the next half hour, he practiced the spells, improving each time.

"I feel more confident with this now," he said finally. "This will be our best tactic to use against them, I think." Mira nodded. "But I have a question… Are you able to cancel a wraith's magic?"

"Why wouldn't I be?"

"I'm not sure, but we don't fully understand your powers, and we know next to nothing about the wraiths. Are their spells the same as a mage's?"

"I don't know… you're making me nervous now…"

"Did Henry have you try canceling their magic when you were in captivity?"

"No—I was there when Dredmort demonstrated their abilities, but I was only a witness. And they didn't have Nineve try to cancel their spells either."

"Well, I guess we'll find out soon enough..."

Khaldun spoke to their guards, and let them know what he was planning to do against the wraiths. He instructed them to do their best to behead the monsters once he'd used magic to immobilize them.

"Even that won't completely eliminate them," he told them, "but it should remove them from the field for a while, at least."

"Decapitating them wouldn't end them?" one of the soldiers asked in disbelief.

"Not from what I've been told. We'd have to burn them to ash to accomplish that, and I don't imagine we'll have the time to do that in the heat of the battle."

Khaldun and Mira sat down, watching the Oxcart army finish their preparations for the onslaught. But before long everyone was ready, and there was nothing more to do but wait. The afternoon dragged by with no sign of the enemy. But finally, with the sunset came drum beats in the distance.

"That must be their army," said Khaldun, getting to his feet and peering into the distance. Mira stood by his side. He put his arm around her and could feel her shivering.

"Are you cold?"

"No," she said, taking a deep breath. "Scared."

Khaldun knew how she felt. The first thing they could see was a giant cloud of dust rising up from the road. Within minutes, the Foslander army moved into view. Khaldun spotted Dredmort riding at its head, but didn't see Nineve anywhere—or the wraiths.

But suddenly, there was a cry in the distance, joined moments later by several others. Khaldun felt a chill run down his spine. The wraiths were out there somewhere. Perhaps Nineve was hanging back with them.

The enemy forces formed ranks less than a quarter mile away. But darkness fell and they held their position. One by one, torches sprang to life amidst both armies.

"What are they waiting for?" Mira asked. "They're not setting up camp or anything..."

"No, they're ready to attack. It won't be much longer now."

Suddenly, a sense of cold dread overcame Khaldun, as if the wraiths were climbing their hill. But looking around, he didn't see them anywhere. Nervous that perhaps they were moving under the cover of invisibility, he held out his staff and fired off cancellation spells in a circle around them, but there was nobody there.

"What is it?" Mira asked.

"Nothing, apparently," he replied with a frown. "But I thought I sensed the wraiths approaching."

"I felt it, too..."

Time went on, Khaldun's apprehension steadily increasing. The enemy drumbeat continued, and Dredmort began parading back and forth on his horse, out in front of their lines. Bichon rode in front of his own men, calling on them to be brave and cut down the enemy. Khaldun's heart beat in time to the Foslander drums but still they did not attack.

"I wish they'd get on with it already," he commented. "The tension alone is going to wear me down."

"That's the point, I think," Mira replied. "Just breathe. They'll be here before you know it."

Just then, Foslander horns blared, and their army advanced.

"This is it," Khaldun whispered. "Be ready for anything."

The Oxcart archers fired a volley but Dredmort called fire, incinerating their arrows before they could find their targets. Mira had held out her hand to cancel his spell, but she was too late.

"Damn," she hissed.

Dredmort hurled a fireball at the archers, but Mira canceled it. They fired another volley, and this time Mira acted in time to prevent Dredmort from stopping them. Several of the leading Foslanders fell.

The archers managed two more volleys before the armies engaged. But then the battlefield quickly devolved into chaos as the lines clashed and the soldiers cut each other down with their blades.

Khaldun called various spells against Dredmort—trying to ignite him from within, raise a gale to blow him off the field, and even casting an illusion of a mountain lion he'd seen once to scare the wizard off, but Dredmort was too strong for the first two to have any effect, and he didn't fall for the third. Dredmort kept calling fire against the Oxcart soldiers, but Mira was able to neutralize him every time. Khaldun didn't open a pit beneath the wizard; he wanted to save that for the wraiths, and had no wish to tip his hand.

Mira continued blocking Dredmort's every spell. Khaldun went to work against the enemy soldiers instead. He raised a wall of fire in the midst of their ranks, preventing fresh soldiers from replacing the fallen at the front line. But Dredmort canceled this before too long.

Khaldun started incinerating individual soldiers from within instead. He chose them at random, and worked too quickly for Dredmort to stop him. Dredmort tried the same tactic against the Oxcart men; with a direct view of the wizard, Mira had an easier time canceling his spells. But then Dredmort made himself invisible, and Mira could no longer stop his individual spells. She tried canceling his invisibility, but he'd moved, and she couldn't find him again.

"Shit!" she shouted as one after another, random Oxcart soldiers went up in flames.

"I wonder why he didn't hide himself sooner," said Khaldun.

"Intimidation," Mira told him. "Everyone knows about him— his mere presence down there must strike fear into those soldiers' hearts."

"Aye, my lady," one of their guards agreed. "That's exactly right."

"But now that they know he's here, he's more effective hiding himself from me," Mira added.

The Oxcart soldiers repelled the invaders for a while. Khaldun spotted Phillip on the battlefield, darting among his men with a handful of knights from the prince's guard, shoring up their defenses wherever they seemed weakest. But eventually the Foslanders started gaining ground. Then Bichon himself headed a cavalry charge, leading twenty knights right through the heart of the enemy force, cutting down men as they rode.

A cheer went up from the Oxcart soldiers, and they rallied, pushing the enemy back. Bichon led his group through the enemy army, then around their flank and back behind his own lines. Dredmort tried casting spells against him as he moved, but Mira managed to block them all.

But suddenly, a wall of fire erupted in the middle of the Oxcart ranks, blocking the men in the rear lines from reaching the front. Mira canceled the spell, but another formed nearby. For the next several minutes, Dredmort kept calling fire, driving back the Oxcarters, and burning several alive each time before Mira could cancel the spell. And then a cry went up from the Foslanders as they pressed their advantage, driving the Oxcart soldiers ever closer to the village.

But then Khaldun felt a chill run down his spine. Turning, he expected to see wraiths storming their hill—the monsters had not yet made an appearance in this battle. But then he heard their cry and realized they'd made it around behind the Oxcart lines.

Fires began springing up behind them. The main Foslander army was driving their opponents toward the wraiths and their magic.

"Mira!" Khaldun shouted. But she'd seen this, too, and went to work canceling the wraiths' spells. Much to their relief, this worked. But with her attention diverted to their rear, Dredmort had free rein to wreak havoc to their front. Khaldun focused on the wizard, canceling as many of his spells as he could.

But suddenly, he spotted a group of Foslanders moving toward their hill. For a moment, he worried that Dredmort had found them and eliminated their invisibility. But when he tried reforming the spell, he found it was still intact. Then he realized that the approaching men were archers; they were going to take the hill to fire on the Oxcarters below.

"Mira—we have to move!" Khaldun told her, pointing out the approaching men.

Khaldun tried calling fire against the archers but it was no use; Dredmort was prepared for this, and negated his spells.

They mounted their horses and hurried down the other side of the hill, their guards right behind them. Moving around the rear lines, Khaldun went to work on the wraiths. He raised his staff and called earth, opening up a pit beneath the nearest one. The creature fell into it and Khaldun closed the hole. He eliminated two more this way, but suddenly three others charged directly toward them.

And with a start, Khaldun realized that they were visible—that was the only way the wraiths could have located them. Glancing over his shoulder, he spotted Dredmort standing upon the hill they'd vacated—he must have been firing random cancelation spells and hit them by chance.

A ring of fire erupted around them. Mira canceled the flames and Khaldun restored their invisibility spell. The three wraiths continued their advance; Khaldun opened fissures beneath them, one at a time, then closed the pits once they'd fallen in.

Dredmort managed to make them visible again and tried to incinerate them, but Mira canceled his spell. Khaldun hid them from view once more, and they charged away before Dredmort could find them again.

But the wraiths he'd buried started climbing out of the ground. As instructed, their guards attacked them, trying to cut off their heads with their swords. But the monsters' flesh was tougher than thick leather; the blades barely made a dent. The wraiths broke free, freezing men's hearts with their shrieks as they cut through their lines, felling soldiers with their spells. Mira did her best to cancel their magic. Khaldun weighed down one of the creature's robes, pinning it to the ground. Their guards went to work hacking it with their swords, but the wraith managed to shed its clothing and rejoin the fray.

Khaldun took a moment to check in on the rest of the battle. His heart sank in dismay; it was clear this was turning into a rout. Everywhere he looked, Henry's forces were running down the Oxcarters.

Finally, Bichon ordered his men to sound the horns, signaling their retreat. Mira and Khaldun provided cover from Dredmort and his wraiths as the Oxcart commanders did their best to organize their soldiers in a tactical withdrawal.

As they moved through the town, some of the Foslanders broke off to torch the buildings. Khaldun and Mira attempted to put out the fires, but it was overwhelming trying to protect the army and save the village at the same time. Before long, an inferno engulfed the buildings as their occupants ran screaming into the woods.

Khaldun kept working on the wraiths, but every time he buried one, another broke free and rejoined the fight. He tried his spell against Dredmort one time, creating a fissure directly below the wizard's feet. And it worked—Dredmort fell into the pit. But he was ready—he called air, launching himself out of the ground again before Khaldun could close the hole.

As they approached the castle, Khaldun realized that the archers had already made it back and started providing covering fire as the rest of the army crossed the drawbridge and moved into the castle.

Flaming arrows started felling the Foslanders. Khaldun focused his attention on the soldiers now, too, calling fire over and over again, igniting them from within.

Finally, the Foslanders broke off their pursuit, reforming their lines just beyond the reach of the archers. Khaldun and Mira hurried inside the castle with the last of the Oxcarters; Bichon, Phillip, and the remaining members of the prince's guard rode in at the very end. And as Bichon ordered the gate closed and the drawbridge raised, Khaldun wondered again why Nineve had not yet entered the battle.

CHAPTER TWENTY-THREE
DEFEAT

ichon removed his helmet, shouting orders to his commanders. Then he ran up the steps to the battlements, Phillip and the prince's guard right behind him. Khaldun and Mira jumped off their horse, then followed them up, gazing out across the grounds. The Foslander front lines maintained ranks, their torches burning bright, but behind them, the army was setting up camp. Bichon stormed off the ramparts again moments later. Phillip left a couple of guards to keep watch, then followed his father down the steps.

"What are they waiting for?" Khaldun asked, staring out at the enemy camp.

"They'll probably let their soldiers rest tonight then attack again at dawn," Mira told him. "Or at least, that's what they want Bichon to believe. There's always a chance they'll try to catch them flatfooted by striking at night—especially considering they can't use the wraiths in daylight."

They stayed there for several more minutes, but it didn't seem like anything was happening out there. Their mages and wraiths were nowhere to be seen, and Khaldun could see cookfires springing to life in the camp. He realized he was famished himself, so they headed down the steps. Once he'd stabled their horse, they continued into the keep to the great hall. The staff was serving food, but everyone had grown still and silent—Bichon and Phillip were standing in the middle of the room, hollering at each other.

"This is on *your* head!" Bichon shouted, pointing a finger at his son. "That son of a bitch sent them here to spy on us and you played right into their hand! We lost nearly a thousand men tonight—and you might as well have driven a sword into their hearts yourself!"

"You are the one who insisted on hoarding our gold instead of using it to strengthen our princedom! We could have raised an army ten times larger, hired an entire team of mages, and fortified our castle to make it impregnable!"

"And in so doing put a target on our backs. Henry sits across our northern border. He would have attacked long before now if he'd suspected we possessed that kind of wealth."

"And we could have repelled him! Fosland is strapped, their forces spread thin occupying all the territories they've conquered. We could have built the strongest military on the entire continent with all this gold, but *you* have always been too meek to put your wealth to use!"

"*This never would have happened if you'd kept our secret!*" Bichon yelled, spittle flying from his mouth.

"Oh, bullshit. We've got two dozen people working in the mine. It was only a matter of time before someone slipped and word got to Henry."

"Try as hard as you want, you cannot escape responsibility for this disaster!" the prince shouted.

"No, father—*you* are the ruling prince. It is your poor judgement that has created this debacle."

Bichon stared daggers at his son for a moment before shoving him into one of the tables and storming out of the hall. Phillip regained his balance and followed him out. Slowly the room grew louder as the soldiers returned their attention to their meals, but the mood remained somber.

Khaldun and Mira grabbed a quick bite to eat then headed out to the stable. Khaldun fetched his mirror and tried contacting Nomad, but there was no response, so they returned to the battlements. Nothing had changed; the Foslander camp remained quiet.

"I don't see how Bichon can turn this around," Mira observed. "It's only a matter of time before they breach the walls, and then..."

Khaldun felt cold dread seeping through his veins. "We are going to die here tonight."

"No, love," Mira said, smiling and stroking his cheek. "You and I are too valuable to them as mages. Their men will have orders to capture us and return us to the Darkhold."

"We've failed, though. They're going to take this castle and Henry will have the resources to overrun the entire continent."

Mira sighed. "We'll fight them until the bitter end. Maybe with a little luck..." She averted her eyes. Khaldun knew she didn't see a path to victory any more than he did.

They sat quietly, keeping an eye on the enemy camp. There was no movement out there, but Khaldun started hearing strange noises floating across the field. It sounded like a low rumble, coupled with a squeaking sound. There was also a murmuring sound, as if a vast number of people were speaking in hushed tones. Khaldun kept scanning the area but couldn't figure out what was making the noise.

But then, slowly at first, he felt a sense of dread coming over him. And there was a ghastly shriek somewhere out behind the Foslander camp. Mira shot him a worried look; she'd heard it too.

"Wraiths," Khaldun muttered. And suddenly a terrible thought occurred to him. "Mira, can you reach out and cancel any illusions they might have cast over their camp?"

Mira looked confused, but nodded. She concentrated for a moment, holding out one arm in a sweeping motion. Sure enough, the sleeping camp had been a ruse. The Foslanders had formed ranks—the entirety of their remaining force stood ready to attack.

And they'd wheeled siege engines into place—Khaldun spotted a giant battering ram and three towers, with teams of armored oxen to move them, and there were wraiths standing by the equipment.

"Alert the prince!" Khaldun shouted at one of the guards. "Fosland attacks!"

The guard stared out at the field for a moment longer, a look of dismay on his face, before hurrying down the steps to find Bichon.

Khaldun raised his staff, making Mira and himself invisible, then called fire, trying to ignite one of the siege towers. But it was no use— they'd stationed the wraiths there specifically to cancel any spells they might cast against the equipment.

The Foslanders must have realized that their illusion was gone. Horns sounded and they started beating their drums again. Dredmort appeared out of nowhere at the front of their lines, giving the order to march.

All hell broke loose. The Foslander infantry charged, their oxen moving the equipment toward the castle. Bichon and Phillip hurried up the steps to the battlements, dozens of soldiers behind them. The men took their places along the wall, and Bichon ordered his archers to fire. Flaming arrows hit the animals moving the siege equipment, but the wraiths extinguished the flames and the oxen kept coming. Khaldun wondered how they would get the engines across the moat, but then he realized they had bridges affixed to the fronts of them.

Khaldun called earth, opening pits beneath the two wraiths guarding the battering ram, and closing them again once they'd fallen in. But the wraiths had wised up to this tactic, calling earth themselves to re-open the fissures and leap out. Khaldun tried igniting the siege equipment, opening fissures beneath the oxen, and tipping over the engines, but the wraiths canceled his every spell.

Dredmort called earth, and something invisible slammed into the castle wall directly below their position. The battlements shook as dirt and debris sprayed everywhere; the wizard had knocked a hole in the wall. Mira was ready for him the next time he tried it, though, canceling his spell before he could do any further damage.

"He was targeting *us*," Khaldun pointed out. "He must have seen us before I made us invisible. Let's move!"

He guided her over to the northern tower, and they climbed to the top. Once he'd reinforced their invisibility spell, he went back to work. The Foslanders had moved the siege towers almost all the way to the castle. Khaldun tried again to ignite the oxen from within, but the wraiths kept canceling his spells. Instead, he created walls of fire in front of the animals to impede their progress. This worked—the oxen stopped in their tracks, refusing to move into the flames. But the wraiths put out the fires, and the animals resumed their forward motion. The Oxcart archers kept raining flaming arrows down on the oxen, but the wraiths put these out as well.

Before long, the engines reached the moat. Foslander soldiers went to work sliding the bridges up the front of the towers, and dropping their top ends onto the castle walls. Soldiers began pouring over the bridges; the archers changed targets, focusing on those men instead. Many of them fell screaming into the moat far below, but it didn't take long before the rest reached the battlements. Bichon himself led his men against them, fighting at close range with their swords.

Khaldun managed to set the battering ram ablaze, but once again Dredmort canceled the flames. The Foslanders wheeled it up to the moat, but had no way to get it across. Khaldun wondered why they'd bothered bringing it here.

Suddenly, he spotted a company of soldiers moving around to the north of the castle. He didn't understand what they hoped to do there—the moat was much wider on the other three sides. But this thought was quickly driven from his mind; Foslanders continued to stream across the tower bridges, and the fighting on the battlements was quickly moving toward their position on the tower.

"Mira, we've got to move!" Khaldun told her.

But at that moment, screams went up from the Foslanders at the rear of their lines, far across the field. Looking for the source of the commotion, Khaldun saw a raging inferno sweep across the battlefield, swallowing every man in its path.

"I don't understand—who did that?" said Mira. "There's another mage on the field?"

Just then, Khaldun spotted a rider in black, his arms outstretched and his face gleaming in the flames.

"It's Nomad!" Khaldun cried, his heart soaring. "He made it here after all!"

"Look!" said Mira, pointing down toward the ground.

Khaldun spotted the wraiths abandoning their posts, hurrying across the field to engage the sorcerer. He called fire, igniting the nearest tower. It burst into flames, the men inside of it screaming as the fire roasted them alive. Khaldun quickly set the other two towers ablaze, and a cheer went up from the Oxcart soldiers on the ramparts.

Gazing across the field, he spotted Dredmort and the wraiths bearing down on Nomad. The sorcerer had erected a ring of fire around himself to keep the wraiths away. Dredmort kept canceling sections of it, trying to provide the wraiths a pathway to the sorcerer, but Nomad restored the flames every time.

But finally, one of the wraiths made it through. Khaldun held out his staff, opening a pit beneath the monster's feet. The wraith fell into the hole, and Khaldun sealed it around him. A moment later, Nomad extinguished part of his fire wall, and when another wraith charged toward him, he duplicated Khaldun's spell, and the earth swallowed the creature whole.

Suddenly, Khaldun noticed that Dredmort had canceled his invisibility spell, exposing him and Mira. But before he could restore it, Mira screamed, "Khaldun!"

He realized that two Foslanders had made it through the castle's defenders, charging toward them with swords drawn. Khaldun called fire, igniting them from within moments before they reached Mira. She darted out of the way as the men fell to the stone. Two more soldiers made it to the tower; Khaldun called air, launching them over the wall. They fell to the moat screaming the whole way down.

Out on the field, the remaining wraiths had retreated with Dredmort. Nomad advanced on the Foslander lines, hurling fire tornadoes at them as he moved. Khaldun started to feel like they might just win this battle and save the princedom, but then he heard the screams from the courtyard below.

Looking for their source, he spotted a woman with flaming red hair leading a group of soldiers from the stables, wielding a staff in one hand. Nineve had arrived.

"Oh, no!" said Mira. "How did she get inside?"

"There must be another hidden tunnel somewhere!" Khaldun replied.

Nineve raised her staff, firing off earth and fire spells and felling one Oxcart soldier after another. The Foslanders rode through the infantrymen, cutting them down with their swords. Khaldun called fire, trying to ignite the witch's clothing, but his spell didn't get through. He tried raising a tower of flame around her instead, but this revealed the problem: Nineve had created a sphere of protection around herself and her horse. It acted as a shield, repelling Khaldun's spells.

"Shield spell," said Khaldun. "Can you cancel that?"

"I think so," Mira replied.

"All right—when I give the word, take it out, and I'll hit her with fire. Ready?" Mira nodded, holding out one hand. "Now!"

Mira eliminated Nineve's shield; an instant later, Khaldun cast his fire spell, trying to ignite the witch's clothing. But Nineve neutralized the spell and re-established her shield.

"Damn!" Mira shouted.

"Come on," he replied. "Let's get one of the archers and we'll try again with an arrow."

He spotted Bichon and Phillip rushing down the steps, their men hurrying in their wake. Khaldun took Mira by the hand, and ran across the battlements. But suddenly, a lone Foslander soldier ran across the bridge from one of the towers, his clothing ablaze, wildly swinging his sword. Khaldun grabbed Mira, pulling her out of the way; the Foslander went right over the edge, falling to the courtyard below. But Khaldun had lost his balance, and stumbled over the edge himself.

"Khaldun!" Mira screamed.

Clutching his staff, Khaldun called air, creating an updraft directly below himself. It was enough to cushion his landing; he hit the ground, rolling painfully across the dirt. But he came to rest at an enemy soldier's feet. The man swung his sword; Khaldun dodged out of the way, but the man raised his sword for another strike. But at that moment, Phillip reached them, stabbing the man in the chest. The Foslander fell down and didn't move.

"Thank you," Khaldun said, breathing a sigh of relief.

"I thought that fall was going to kill you," Phillip remarked.

Getting to his feet, Khaldun froze at the sight before him: Nineve's men had reached the gatehouse and were lowering the drawbridge. Others were raising the gate. Khaldun called fire against the men in the gatehouse and the bridge stopped moving. Phillip charged the soldiers raising the gate. But more men arrived, overwhelming Phillip and replacing their fallen comrades in the gatehouse. Khaldun called fire again, but someone canceled his spell. He tried once more, but it was no use; the Foslanders got the drawbridge down and soldiers poured across it, entering the castle.

"Nice try, boy," someone said from behind him.

Turning, Khaldun saw Nineve riding up to him, raising her staff to cast a spell. But at that moment, a fireball shattered her protective shield and slammed into her, knocking her from the horse. Glancing around, Khaldun spotted Nomad standing behind him.

"Thank the stars!" Khaldun said, grinning from ear to ear.

"Don't thank them yet—we need to get the royal family out of here! The castle is lost!"

Mira had descended the steps and came running over to them. Chaos filled the courtyard as the incoming Foslanders clashed with the remaining Oxcart soldiers. Phillip had recovered and entered the fight once more. Bichon was by the keep, cutting down enemy soldiers from his horse.

Nomad raised one hand, separating Phillip from his opponents with a wall of fire.

"Your Highness," he said, approaching the young prince, "it's time to evacuate you and your parents. The battle is lost!"

Phillip gazed around the courtyard and nodded. But at that moment, the Foslanders managed to drag Bichon off his horse. He found his footing and continued fighting, but suddenly Nineve appeared in front of him. Raising her staff, she called air, raising the prince off the ground.

"You've lost, Bichon," she cried out. "I claim this princedom in the name of High Prince Henry of Fosland!"

Bichon's armor began to glow red; Khaldun realized that Nineve had called fire, too, and was now cooking the prince alive. Bichon screamed, ripping his helmet off his head and casting it aside. Nomad reached out with one hand, canceling Nineve's spells, and Bichon dropped to the ground, struggling to remove his armor. But suddenly one of the Foslanders lunged in, stabbing him in the throat.

"NO!" Phillip screamed, trying to run to his father, but Khaldun held him back.

But someone else screamed and Khaldun spotted the princess running toward her husband; she'd been watching from the keep.

Soldiers surrounded her, but Khaldun enclosed her and her fallen husband within a ring of fire.

Nomad extended one hand, hurling another fireball at Nineve. But she was ready; she canceled it, then vanished.

Khaldun, Mira, Nomad, and Phillip ran over to the princess as the battle raged around them. Khaldun put out his flames, and Phillip dropped to his knees by his mother, coaxing her away from Bichon's corpse.

"How do we get out of here?" Khaldun asked.

Though the battle was lost, the fighting continued, particularly intense by the gate where the rest of the Foslanders were still pouring into the castle.

"Nineve entered the courtyard from the stables," Mira told them. "There must be a third tunnel over there somewhere!"

Nomad nodded. They got Phillip and his mother to their feet and escorted them through the melee. Inside the stables, Khaldun spotted a section of stone that had been pushed back into a recess behind the wall. Hurrying over to it, he gazed inside. Sure enough, there was a tunnel, large enough for a horse and rider to pass.

"This is it," he told the others.

Khaldun and Mira mounted his horse. Nomad chose another, and Phillip and his mother climbed onto a third. Nomad led the way into the passage. Phillip and the princess went next. Casting one last glance back inside the castle, Khaldun brought up the rear with Mira.

They moved along the tunnel, leaving the last of the battle behind.

CHAPTER TWENTY-FOUR
ON THE RUN

hey reached the end of the tunnel; it came out in another stable.

"We should collapse the passage to make sure no one follows us this way," Khaldun suggested.

Nomad nodded. Holding out one hand, he called earth; the tunnel walls and ceiling caved in, sending a cloud of dust into the stable.

"Where are we?" asked Mira.

"I'm not sure," said Phillip.

They followed him out of the structure. Turning, Khaldun realized that they'd emerged on a farm at the northern end of the town. The fire had burned itself out, leaving blackened shells of the village's buildings in its wake, many of them still smoldering.

"So much death and destruction," the princess said, staring across the area with tears streaming down her cheeks.

"We need to get you and your son to safety, Your Highness," said Nomad. "Do you have any suggestions as to where we could take you?"

"Stoutwall's rulers are my cousins," she suggested. "I believe they would take us in."

"The troupe's in Stoutwall, isn't it?" said Khaldun.

"Yes, camped outside the castle in Walberg, a small holding on the border," Nomad replied. "If we can get that far, then we should be safe. Stoutwall is the strongest princedom in the region; I do not believe Henry would authorize his forces to trespass there."

"The trouble is going to be making it that far," said Mira. "Coming from Stoutwall, you would have reached the Oxcart road to the south of the castle, right?"

"That's correct," Nomad confirmed.

"We're at the north end of town right now. To get to the Stoutwall road, we've got to get through the village and past the castle. And Henry's army lies between here and there."

"We can't go that way," said Phillip. "But I know a trail in the forest that loops around to the east of the castle. We can take that until we reach the south road, cross that, and then move through the woods until we reach the west road to Stoutwall."

Nomad nodded. "Lead the way. I will make us all invisible."

They set out, Nomad in the lead with Phillip. Crossing the farm, they reached the end of the open field and moved into the woods. Phillip found the trail, and they proceeded single file along it, Nomad taking the lead now. As they rounded the castle grounds to the east, Khaldun could see flames rising from the building and hear shouts and screams.

The trail crossed a small brook. Once they'd reached the other side, Khaldun turned and raised his staff, casting the spell to hide their passage. A small breeze rose, carrying sparks along the trail the way they'd come.

"I was about to do that," Nomad told him.

"Well, I've learned a few things in my travels," Khaldun replied with a grin.

They continued along the trail for another half hour, finally reaching the south road. Nomad stayed in the woods with the royal family while Khaldun and Mira ventured ahead to make sure the way was clear. Khaldun gazed north and south, but the road was empty as far as he could see in either direction.

Nomad led the prince and his mother across the road, then they moved back into the forest on the other side. They found another trail that seemed to lead in the direction they wanted to go. Only minutes later, they reached the west road, and set off along that, sticking to the shoulder to avoid kicking up dust.

But ten minutes later, Nomad called a halt. Khaldun rode up next to him to see what was wrong, but nothing was apparent.

"I smell smoke," the sorcerer whispered. "There was nobody out here when I traveled this way from Fosland."

Khaldun sniffed the air, and caught the scent, too, but it was faint. "Could just be a campfire," he suggested. "Someone traveling this way."

"Perhaps," Nomad replied skeptically. "But stay alert. I have a bad feeling about this."

They continued westward, taking their time and staying on the grass. But as they progressed, the smell of smoke grew stronger. And before long, Khaldun could hear voices in the distance, though he couldn't make out what they were saying.

Nomad called a halt again and approached Khaldun. "There's a large group up ahead. Wait here and make the group invisible—I'm going to scout ahead."

Khaldun nodded. Nomad rode ahead and he cast his spell to hide the rest of them from view. The sorcerer returned only a few minutes later.

"There's another Foslander army camped up ahead," he told them. "They're holding the Stoutwall road. Dredmort must have ordered them into position here after I reached the castle."

"They're after my son!" said the princess. "They must have realized that he'd flee to Stoutwall!"

"But I don't understand," said Khaldun. "They've taken the castle—and now the gold is theirs. What more interest would they have in your family?"

"No, she's right," said Mira. "If Phillip escapes, as the rightful prince, he could make a claim to the throne, and return one day to retake the castle."

"With what army?" Khaldun asked.

"Stoutwall's, perhaps," Mira suggested. "If they decided they didn't want Henry for a neighbor. Who knows. But the point remains—eliminating Bichon's sole heir is the only way to ensure that doesn't happen."

"So how do we get to Stoutwall?" asked Phillip. "It's a long way from here, and that road is the only route I know of."

"Well, the good news is that I do not sense any mages or wraiths with this army," Nomad told them.

"That may be, but it's an entire army," Phillip retorted. "We can try going around through the forest, but they're sure to have lookouts posted. Invisible or not, the sounds of our passage will alert them to our presence."

"We should cast an illusion of our group moving down the road, and once they spot that, have the doppelgangers turn around and flee," Khaldun suggested. "While they're busy chasing ghosts, we can slip through."

"They won't leave the road unguarded," Phillip pointed out. "Others will move in to take the place of the ones who give chase."

"I'll go back and cause a diversion," said Nomad. "Their camp is on the north side of the road, so the rest of you find a path through the woods to the south. Once you've made it past their camp, return to the road and keep heading west until you reach the border. I'll catch up with you there."

"You shouldn't go alone," said Phillip. "Even without any mages to back them up, you can't take on an entire army on your own."

"I'll be all right," Nomad told him. "Trust me."

Nomad headed back up the road again, this time fully visible and setting off at a gallop. Khaldun and Mira led Phillip and the princess into the trees to the south of the road. Before long, they found a path heading westward, and took that.

It was rough going. The moons hadn't yet risen, and Khaldun didn't dare call a flame, so they had to find their way in the dark, and the path was narrow for the horses. But they forged ahead.

The noise of the army grew louder and Khaldun knew they must have almost reached their camp on the other side of the road. Only minutes later, he saw a giant pillar of fire rise high into the sky, and heard men scream.

"That must be Nomad's diversion," Mira noted.

"Yes, that should keep their attention away from us," Khaldun agreed.

But just then, he heard a noise between them and the road. He figured it was an animal, but then spotted the silhouette of a man flitting between the trees.

"What was that?" Mira whispered.

"Wait here," he told her, jumping off the horse. Bounding into the woods, he tried to find whoever was out there. The man heard him approaching and ran toward the road. Khaldun figured it had to be a Foslander scout, but wanted to confirm this before taking any action. "Halt and identify yourself!" It was no use; the figure kept running. Khaldun called air, lifting him off his feet.

"Put me down, you wayfarer scum!" the man shouted when Khaldun reached him. He was wearing a Foslander military uniform. Khaldun held out his staff, hurling him into a tree. He hit his head on the trunk, collapsed on the ground, and didn't move.

Khaldun ran back to the others. "We've got to move," he told them, mounting his horse. "Their lookout spotted us. I knocked him out, but when he fails to report back, they'll know they've got trouble."

"We should kill him!" Phillip told him.

"It won't matter," Khaldun replied. "Whether we do or not, they'll know someone's out here. Let's go!"

They hurried up the trail, reaching the road again after about a quarter of a mile. Khaldun checked both ways but didn't see anyone nearby.

"We should set out at a gallop," he suggested. "Get to the border as quickly as we can."

"We'll kick up a lot of dirt that way," said Mira.

"There's no moon, and we're pretty far away, now," Khaldun replied. "And they're going to come looking for us regardless, so at this point, it's a risk we'll have to take."

"I agree," said Phillip.

They rode up to the road and urged their horses forward with all haste. After a couple of miles, they eased up to avoid exhausting the animals. There was no sign of pursuit, but Khaldun knew it was only a matter of time. They pressed ahead, and several hours later, finally reached the border with Stoutwall.

"We should be safe now," said Mira. "But just in case, let's get off the road. See if we can hide somewhere while we await Nomad."

They continued for another mile or so, and Khaldun spotted a farm in the distance.

"There," he said, pointing it out to Mira. "We could hide in their barn."

But moments later, Khaldun heard hoofbeats in the distance. Someone was pursuing them, and fast.

"Come on!" he said to Phillip, galloping toward the farm.

They reached the barn and Khaldun dismounted to open the doors. Once they'd moved the animals inside, he closed it again, peering through the crack. Several riders rode into view, wearing Foslander uniforms. They reined in their horses as they reached the barn.

"Shit," Khaldun muttered. "They're coming to check the building."

"How many are there?" asked Phillip.

"I count ten," Khaldun replied.

"Can you get rid of them with your magic?"

"One at a time, yes. But be ready—once I eliminate the first, the others will know for sure that we're in here. If they charge the barn, I won't be able to take care of all of them before they get here."

Phillip nodded, dismounting and drawing his sword. Khaldun peered outside again; the first soldier was halfway to the barn. Khaldun called fire, incinerating him from within. The man screamed, but the sound ended abruptly as his corpse hit the ground.

"Mage!" one of the others cried as they rushed toward the building.

Khaldun called fire against two more, but the others had dismounted their horses, their leader throwing the barn door open. Khaldun raised a wall of fire separating his party from the soldiers; Mira and the princess moved to the rear of the building.

One of the soldiers charged right through the flames, sword raised, and lunged for Phillip. An instant later, another sprang toward Khaldun. He called fire again, igniting the man from within. But his wall of fire disappeared when he shifted focus.

Phillip had managed to disarm his opponent and stab him in the chest. But the remaining soldiers moved through the entrance.

"Surrender now, and we'll take you to our camp alive," one of them said.

"You are trespassing here," Phillip told him. "Stoutwall is a sovereign princedom and you have no authority here."

"We have all the authority we need right here, boy," the soldier replied, brandishing his sword. "It's called strength in numbers. This is it, now—last chance."

But suddenly another rider came galloping into view, jumping from his horse before it had stopped. The figure raised both arms and a ring of fire sprang up around the soldiers.

"Nomad!" said Khaldun.

The sorcerer tightened the circle and the soldiers screamed. One of them jumped through the flames, but Nomad ignited them all from within.

"We have to hurry," he told them. "Dredmort and his wraiths are headed this way, and they're bringing their whole army with them."

"But we're in Stoutwall now," said Mira. "This will mean war!"

"Only if we can make it to Walberg castle before they catch us," Nomad replied. "Let's go!"

They mounted their horses and moved out of the barn. Nomad leapt onto his mount and galloped up the road, the others close behind. They reached Walberg castle twenty minutes later. The wayfarer camp was close by in an adjacent field. They dismounted their horses, and moments later, Badru came running over to them.

"Sir, we have to move the troupe inside the castle," Nomad told him. "Dredmort and his wraiths will be here any minute with an entire army."

"*What?*" said Badru, his face registering shock as he processed this news. "Come with me!"

Khaldun, Mira, Phillip, and his mother followed Badru and Nomad to the castle. The gate was open, but the guards stopped them from going inside.

"We must speak with Lord Gerald immediately!" said Badru.

"It's not even dawn yet," the guard replied. "Come back later and we'll see if we can get you an audience."

"There's no time," Nomad told him. "A Foslander army marches here as we speak!"

The guard turned to his comrade, who shrugged, his eyes wide.

"All right. Follow me."

He led them inside. This castle was not even half the size of Bichon's; there was no way they'd be able to fit the whole troupe inside. They hurried over to the keep, and the guard told them to wait there while he went to fetch Gerald. He returned with the lord a few minutes later; Gerald was in his robe, and his eyes looked sleepy. Nomad explained the situation. Lord Gerald blanched, suddenly becoming much more alert.

"But our prince is one of the most powerful in all of Maeda," he protested. "Henry wouldn't dare—"

"My lord, I assure you he would, and he has," said Nomad.

"We need to move our people inside your walls before that army arrives!" said Badru.

"No, out of the question," Gerald replied. "I'll send a messenger to the prince immediately, but until he gets here with *his* army, I need to look out for my own!"

"My lord, this is Prince Phillip of Oxcart and his mother," said Nomad. "Treaty requires you to provide them safe harbor, at the very least."

"Oh!" said Gerald, bowing to Phillip. "My apologies, Your Highness, I didn't recognize you. Yes, of course, you are welcome to ride this out in my keep. But where is Bichon?"

"Henry's soldiers murdered him when they sacked our castle," Phillip replied.

"But that's terrible... I'm so sorry."

"We should send Khaldun with the messenger to make sure he gets there safely," Nomad said to Badru. "He's a wizard," he added to Gerald.

"I'll go, too," said Mira.

"No, my lady," said Nomad. "I'm going to need you here to help me defend the troupe."

Mira met Khaldun's gaze, her inner conflict apparent in her eyes, but then nodded to Nomad.

"Very well," said Gerald.

He ordered his guard to escort Phillip and his mother into the keep. Then he called out to one of the other guards, and ordered him to ride to Stoutwall Castle and alert the prince to the impending invasion.

"We need to get our people away from here," Nomad said to Badru once Gerald had moved back into the keep. "It's that prince the Foslanders want. The farther away from here we can get them, the safer they'll be."

"You're abandoning Phillip?" asked Khaldun.

"I can return to render aid once we've moved our people to safety."

Badru nodded, and they hurried off to the camp.

"Let me fetch my horse and I'll meet you back here," the guard said to Khaldun. "Do you need one?"

"No, mine's outside."

The guard nodded and hurried off.

"I want so badly to go with you," Mira told Khaldun, taking his hands in hers. "We belong together; our last separation broke my heart. But Nomad is right—he's going to need all the help he can get."

"I know," Khaldun replied, pulling her into a hug. "It pains me to fly from danger like this and leave you behind."

"We'll be all right," she said. "Come back to me safely."

They kissed, then Mira ran off after Nomad and Badru. The guard returned on horseback a few moments later.

"Ready?" he asked. Khaldun nodded. "I'm Eric, by the way."

"Khaldun," he replied, reaching up to shake his hand.

They left the castle. Khaldun mounted his horse, and they headed up the road at a gallop, passing the wayfarer camp on the way out. They were already packing up their tents and getting ready to move out. But suddenly, Khaldun felt a cold dread run down his spine, and heard the wraiths' shrieks. Reining in his horse, he looked back and saw the torches of Henry's army in the distance. His heart ached at the thought of leaving Mira here, but he turned and galloped after the messenger.

CHAPTER TWENTY-FIVE
INVITATION

ira had run into the camp right behind Badru and Nomad. They'd hurried about, waking everyone and telling them they needed to pack up and move out immediately. But then Mira's mother had spotted her, ran over and hugged her, and proceeded to scream at her.

"Mother! Enough! We have to get out of here!"

Suddenly, a chill ran down Mira's spine. And as if to illustrate her point, ghastly shrieks pierced the night. Mira knew the wraiths were getting close now.

She helped her mother pack up her belongings, then rushed about helping as many others as she could. In the end, it took very little time for the troupe to set out up the road. Mira was surprised how quickly they'd moved, but given their constant traveling, supposed she should have expected this.

As the last of their people reached the road and headed west, Mira spotted Henry's army moving around the castle. Nomad rode over to her, watching the enemy's progress. But it quickly became apparent that the troops were not stopping at the castle.

"What's going on?" said Mira, her heart jumping into her throat. "Why are they still marching?"

"We have a problem," said Nomad, his tone grim.

Dredmort rode into view, galloping ahead of the army, several wraiths on horseback close behind. They shrieked, sending a shiver down Mira's back.

"Cancel anything they throw at us," Nomad said. "I'll be right back."

He rode off, heading up the side of the road, probably to alert Badru, shouting at their people to move faster as he went. Mira faced their pursuers, steeling herself against her fear. Sure enough, Dredmort hurled a fireball at them; Mira extinguished it long before it reached them. The wraiths rode ahead, surrounding the end of their line, hurling fire spells at anyone they could reach; Mira canceled them all. But suddenly, one of the wraiths grabbed a little wayfarer boy and rode off with him. His mother screamed, chasing after the monster; Mira rode over to her and dismounted.

"Madeline, no—they'll kill you!"

"I have to save my boy!" the woman screamed between sobs.

"He's already dead," Mira told her, though saying the words broke her heart. "Please, stay with the troupe!"

Another wraith rode by, calling fire as he went, igniting one of the wagons. Mira extinguished the flames, and one of the older women came over to coax Madeline back to the others. The wraiths kept hitting them with fire, and it was everything Mira could do to cancel the flames. But there was nothing she could do to stop them from scooping up random wayfarers and carrying them off. Finally Nomad returned, Badru right behind him.

Their leader stared in shock at the approaching army and the wraiths wreaking havoc with their people. The soldiers had been hanging back, letting the wraiths do the dirty work. But when they spotted Nomad, a group of them charged. Two of them fired arrows; Nomad incinerated them mid-flight. He called a wall of fire directly in front of the riders, and their horses reared, unwilling to run through the flames.

"I don't understand this," said Badru. "What do they want with us?"

At that moment, Dredmort appeared out of nowhere, only fifty feet away, striding toward them. The wraiths gathered behind him, flanking him on either side.

"Greetings, sorcerer," the wizard called out with a smirk. "I come to you on behalf of High Prince Henry of Fosland. He has sent me to offer you a place by his side. With your power, his armies, and Oxcart's gold, the high prince believes he could restore the old kingdom, and ultimately, the empire. What say you?"

Mira couldn't believe it. They weren't after Phillip after all. Nomad glanced at Badru; he shook his head in disbelief.

"You can tell that tyrant to go to hell," Nomad yelled back.

"Now, now, let's not be hasty," said Dredmort. "We will give you one hour to consider the offer. But you must realize that whether you do so willingly or not, you will be accompanying me to the Darkhold."

Dredmort vanished. The wraiths shrieked, spreading out around the troupe again, as if to remind Nomad what could happen if he refused.

"You should flee," Mira told the sorcerer. "Take a horse and ride to Stoutwall! It's you they want—they don't care about the troupe!"

"No, Mira," said Badru. "They will slaughter us if he leaves."

"Make sure they see him go—they'll chase him and I can defend against any magic they throw at us."

"You would be helpless against the soldiers," Nomad told her. "I cannot leave. We have to do what we can until Khaldun returns with soldiers from Stoutwall."

"Let's get our people moving again," said Badru. "We can cover a good amount of ground in an hour."

The troupe resumed its westward trek; the Foslanders followed close behind, their wraiths circling them menacingly the entire time.

"I'm going to try something," Nomad said to Mira. "It will require my full attention, so stay alert and deflect any spells they throw at us."

Mira nodded.

Nomad closed his eyes for a few moments, raising both arms to his sides. He began muttering in a language Mira didn't recognize. Suddenly, she spotted a shimmering glow forming around the troupe. It grew brighter, until she realized that he'd formed a dome of energy over them, much like what Nineve has used back in Bichon's castle, but much larger.

"That will repel their riders and deflect most of their magic," Nomad told her. "But it will require my full power to maintain, and at this size, may not be powerful enough to stop Dredmort's strongest spells. You'll need to ride patrol around the troupe and cancel anything that breaks through."

"Understood," Mira replied.

The wayfarers kept up their march, drawing ever closer to Stoutwall. But at the end of the hour, Dredmort returned. Nomad told him he had his final answer. Dredmort unleashed the full fury of Fosland's forces.

Their riders surrounded the troupe, firing arrows and throwing spears, but they bounced off Nomad's spell. The wraiths rode around the troupe like vultures, looking for any weakness in the dome. Mira rode patrol, ready to neutralize anything that made it through, but the wraiths' magic wasn't strong enough to penetrate it.

But Dredmort's was. He hurled a giant fireball at the front of their line, and it passed through Nomad's spell. Mira held out one hand, canceling it before it could do any harm. But Dredmort wasn't going to give up that easily. He circled the wayfarers like a shark, periodically hurling a powerful spell through their defenses. Mira was able to keep up, nullifying his every effort, but she knew it was only a matter of time before something slipped by her. And in the meantime, the constant threat and dread had to be fraying their people's nerves.

She checked in with Nomad, and could tell that sustaining the dome was draining him. He wouldn't be able to hold it indefinitely. Luckily, Dredmort's effort seemed to be exhausting him, too; his attempts to penetrate the dome became fewer and farther between. But after an hour of constant engagement, Mira knew they'd be in trouble soon. She could only hope that Stoutwall's forces arrived before it was too late.

CHAPTER TWENTY-SIX
THE BATTLE OF WALBERG

haldun and Eric rode for over an hour, intermittently galloping and trotting in an attempt not to kill their horses. Khaldun tried using his mirror to check in with Nomad, but found Badru staring back at him instead. He told him that Henry's army was attacking the troupe in an attempt to capture the sorcerer. But finally Castle Stoutwall loomed into view. The building sat at the top of a hill and had to be forty feet high. Khaldun guessed one could call the water surrounding it a "moat," but it was more of a lake. The siege towers Henry had used at Oxcart never would have made it across.

There were several barracks buildings out beyond the castle. It looked like they had an enormous standing army in place.

"Well, this looks impregnable, but 'Highwall' might have been a better name than 'Stoutwall,'" Khaldun said to Eric as they started across the bridge leading to the gate.

Eric chuckled.

"Well, those walls are also twenty feet thick."

"Ah, that explains it."

"They say that this castle has never been breached."

"I could believe it."

They reached the gate and Eric greeted the guard on duty.

"We need to see Prince Augustine. Fosland has invaded the princedom—they have an army in Walberg."

The guard looked stunned.

"Yes, we must alert the prince immediately, but he is not here."

"What? Where is he?"

"The royal family moved into the palace two days ago."

"What palace?" asked Khaldun, his heart sinking. If it was far, they'd never reach the prince in time.

"Follow me," said the guard, hurrying over the bridge.

Khaldun and Eric dismounted, leading their horses by the reins and following the guard back to land. He led them around behind the castle, and a second building came into view. It resembled a castle, but would have been completely indefensible. There was no moat, and there were enormous stained-glass windows within reach from the ground.

The moons had risen, and out beyond the palace, Khaldun could see an enormous lake, with the biggest waterfall he'd ever seen spilling into it.

"That's quite the view," he commented to Eric.

"That's the River Torsa," the guard told him. "It marks the ancient boundary between the kingdoms of Maeda and Dorshire."

Khaldun had crossed the Torsa a few times in his life, but not this far south. He'd never known that Castle Stoutwall sat so close to the border.

The guard led them up to the main gate. He spoke to one of the men there, who hurried off into the building.

"He's fetching the prince," the guard told them.

Five minutes later, the guard returned with Prince Augustine. He had short, salt-and-pepper hair, and a neatly trimmed beard. His eyes were a piercing blue, and he was a little taller than Khaldun.

"Tell me," was all he said to Khaldun and Eric.

Khaldun explained what had happened in Oxcart, and everything that had taken place in Walberg.

"How many men?" Augustine asked.

"I'm not sure... they had an army of two thousand in Oxcart, and this one looked to be about the same size," Khaldun replied.

"Any cavalry?"

"Maybe a dozen or so riders. All the rest are foot soldiers."

The prince wasted no time. He ordered his men to alert the barracks. "I want two dozen knights in full plate, plus another hundred cavalry. And find Shatter."

"Yes, Your Highness," the guard said with a bow before hurrying off.

"Wait here," the prince added to Khaldun and Eric. "I will ride with you."

"What's shatter?" Khaldun asked once the prince had departed.

"The court sorcerer," Eric replied.

"Oh—and why do they call him Shatter?"

"Because he can shatter a man's skull with a single punch," he said with a grin.

Khaldun frowned, sure that he had to be exaggerating.

Less than twenty minutes later, a squire arrived, leading the prince's horse. Only moments later, the prince returned, wearing full plate armor. He mounted and said, "Come with me."

Khaldun and Eric climbed onto their horses and followed him around to the front of the castle. Waiting there were twenty-four knights on horseback, another hundred light cavalry, plus the prince's sorcerer. Unlike any mage Khaldun had seen before, Shatter wore armor, with a black cape billowing behind him, but no helm. His head was shaved clean and his golden skin glinted in the moonlight. He looked twice as large as the other knights, his arms and legs twice as thick; Khaldun no longer doubted Eric's explanation of the sorcerer's name. The horse he rode must have been specially bred for him—it dwarfed the others.

"Fosland has invaded our princedom," Augustine told his men. "Their army has crossed our border, and as we speak, they attack the wayfarer troupe in an effort to take their sorcerer. I do not have to tell you how dire the situation would become if Prince Henry were to acquire such a mage. So tonight we ride not only to defend our land, but all of Maeda!"

The soldiers cheered, then the prince led the way down the hill. They set out at a gallop, thundering up the road to Walberg. Less than an hour later, they spotted the Foslander army ahead, moving slowly toward them, a translucent dome in their midst. Khaldun didn't understand what that was at first, until they drew closer and he realized that it was shielding the troupe. He'd never seen Nomad do this before, but guessed that it had to be taking all of his power to sustain it.

The surrounding soldiers kept hacking at the dome with their swords, and the wraiths hurled spells, but nothing could get through. Khaldun spotted Dredmort riding around the front of the dome, throwing a massive fireball at it; that penetrated the barrier, but faded away before hitting any of the wayfarers.

The Foslanders must have noticed the approaching Stoutwallers; they rode ahead of the troupe, quickly forming ranks. Stoutwall's forces reached the enemy, their knights plowing through their lines, cutting down soldiers on their way through. Augustine sent half of his cavalry to surround the wayfarers, providing protection for them so Nomad could join the battle.

Shatter raised both arms, and suddenly a fiery orb formed in the middle of the Foslander troops, at least thirty feet in diameter. As it faded, Khaldun realized that it had vaporized everything inside, leaving a crater in the earth.

Nomad let his shield collapse, and entered the fray. Khaldun saw him raise both arms, and suddenly a fire tornado formed in the Foslander ranks, picking up men and throwing them into the sky, flames streaming off of them like a comet.

Dredmort turned his attention to the sorcerers. He neutralized Nomad's spell first. Nomad hit him with a jet of fire, but Dredmort formed a sphere of energy to shield himself. Shatter kept dropping fire orbs on the Foslanders, vaporizing twenty men at a time; Dredmort tried canceling one of these, but it was too late—the spell did its damage the moment it formed.

The wraiths charged Shatter, forming a ring around him and hurling fireballs at him. They hit the giant sorcerer without any noticeable effect. He grabbed one of the creatures right off its horse and hurled it over the battlefield; the wraith shrieked as it flew over the melee.

Khaldun called earth, opening a pit beneath one of the other wraiths; it fell in and he collapsed the ground around it. He repeated this twice more, but then the sun cracked the eastern horizon, and the wraiths withdrew, flying off into the forest. Shatter went back to forming his fire orbs. Khaldun spotted Nomad spinning off another fire tornado; this time the twister chased Dredmort as he galloped down the road away from the battle. Khaldun wondered why the wizard wasn't canceling this one.

But the Foslanders decided they'd had enough. One of their commanders sounded the trumpets signaling their retreat. Prince Augustine ordered his knights to stay behind to protect the troupe while he pursued the Foslanders with the rest of his cavalry. They rode through the enemy ranks, cutting them down as they fled. Shatter galloped away, and Khaldun had a feeling he'd be going after Dredmort.

Khaldun regrouped with Nomad and Mira. He jumped off his horse and hugged the sorcerer, patting him on the back, then embraced Mira, kissing her passionately. But suddenly, Nomad dropped to the ground, lying flat on his back.

"Are you all right?" Khaldun asked in alarm, rushing over to him.

"Just exhausted," the sorcerer replied with a grin. "That last fire tornado put me over the edge; I've got nothing left."

"I'm surprised Dredmort didn't cancel it the way he did the first one," Khaldun observed.

"We've got Mira to thank for that," Nomad told him.

"Oh?" Khaldun asked her, raising his eyebrows.

"I realized that I could cancel Dredmort's cancellation spells," she said with a shrug.

"Good thinking," Khaldun replied, nodding appreciatively.

Badru strode over to join them, sitting down next to Nomad. "I think the three of you have earned a vacation," he said with a grin. "And I know I speak on behalf of the entire troupe when I say that you have earned our eternal gratitude."

"It is our duty to serve," Nomad replied.

"How many people did we lose?" Khaldun asked.

"Eight. The wraiths grabbed them and carried them off into the forest. I've sent a search party to see if we can recover any of them, but..." he finished with a shrug. Khaldun knew the wraiths had probably taken them to their deaths. "It would have been much worse without Nomad's shield."

"This won't be the end of it," said Nomad. "Henry will never stop until he acquires a sorcerer."

"Yes, well, I think we'll be moving into Dorshire for the foreseeable future," Badru told him. "We can't risk venturing too close to Henry's territories anymore."

Prince Augustine returned a few hours later, along with Prince Phillip and his mother. He told them that they'd chased the Foslanders back across the border into Oxcart. Dredmort had vanished and there was no sign of the wraiths. Augustine explained that he'd left most of his cavalry to monitor the border and make sure the Foslanders didn't return. He invited the wayfarers to visit Stoutwall, and Badru happily accepted. His knights escorted the troupe to the castle, and they set up camp on the grounds, between the castle and the palace, with a view of the River Torsa and the waterfall beyond.

As he erected their tent, Khaldun felt relieved to finally put their involvement with Fosland behind them. Ever since the night Mira had arrived, events had turned their life upside down. He was eager to have things return to normal—and to spend a lot more time alone with Mira.

Chapter Twenty-Seven
A Parting of the Ways

hat evening, Khaldun, Mira, and Nomad attended a feast held in their honor inside the palace, along with Badru, Nomad, and the wayfarer elders. Prince Augustine treated them like dignitaries, and gave a speech thanking them for helping defend the princedom. They sat at the head table with the prince and his family, and the palace servants waited on them hand and foot. They had an eight-course meal, and the wine flowed; there was music and dancing once they'd finished dinner.

Prince Augustine invited them to sleep in the palace for the duration of their stay. Nomad and Badru took him up on the offer, but Khaldun and Mira returned to his tent. They lay together in his bedroll, kissing passionately. Before he knew it, they'd both removed each other's clothing. Khaldun desperately wanted to make love to her, but accepted her desire to wait.

"So, when would you like to get married?" he asked. His head was spinning from the wine, and he was so full he could barely move. But he held Mira in his arms, and felt the happiest he'd ever been.

"As soon as possible," she said. "We can ask Nomad to perform the ceremony for us."

"Your mother's not going to be happy," he said with a chuckle.

"Tough luck for her. Especially after this ordeal, I've had enough of the highborn and their castles and armies. This is where I want to be. Are you sure about this, though?"

"About getting married?" She nodded. "Yes, why wouldn't I be?"

"Well, it's not our people's way..."

"It's not common, no, but it's not completely unheard of. There are a few married couples in the troupe."

Mira considered this for a moment. "And you're comfortable becoming monogamous? Because I'm not going to be willing to share you with anyone else..."

Khaldun kissed her. "I've loved you for as long as I can remember, and I've never felt this way for anyone else. Despite your absence."

The next day, they set up the giant circus tent. They held a performance that evening, and people from all over Stoutwall came to watch. The crowd cheered for the jugglers and the magician, laughed at the clowns, and oohed and aahed for the trapeze and high-wire acts. There ended up being standing room only, and they decided to hold several more shows in the coming days.

Khaldun spent most of his time with Mira, talking and laughing as they finally caught up with each other, and reminisced about their younger days together. They took long walks by the river, admiring the waterfalls up close, and slept together in Khaldun's tent every night—over Nareen's vehement objections.

Mira spoke to Nomad and he told her that he would be delighted to serve as the officiant for their wedding ceremony. Nareen didn't take the news nearly as well, and broke down in tears, but on some level seemed to accept it; at least, she didn't try to stop them. Khaldun and Mira made plans to hold the ceremony behind the palace overlooking the river.

But on the fourth morning after their arrival at Stoutwall Castle, Khaldun woke to the sound of a loud voice outside their tent. Sitting up and rubbing the sleep from his eyes, he realized they were calling out to Mira. Khaldun woke her, and she got to her feet, donning her robe to cover her nakedness. She stepped out of the tent; he stayed in his bedroll, but poked his head out of the flap to find one of the prince's guards standing there.

"Lady Mira, I'm sorry to wake you," he said. "But there is a messenger here from Graystone." She looked around in confusion for a moment—there was nobody else in sight. "Over at the castle," the guard told her.

Mira ducked back inside the tent; the two of them got dressed, then followed the soldier out of the camp and across the grounds. Out by the road, they found a half dozen armed riders waiting for them; one of them had dismounted.

"My lady," the man said, handing her a scroll, "we have traveled here with the utmost haste. We had great difficulty finding you, with the upheaval Henry has caused, so I must apologize for the delay. But your father's steward has instructed us to escort you back to Graystone as quickly as possible."

"What? Why?" Mira asked.

"It would be best for you to read the scroll, my lady."

Mira broke the seal and unrolled the parchment. Her expression registered shock as she read it, and tears streamed down her cheeks.

"What is it?" asked Khaldun.

Mira opened her mouth to reply, but sobbed instead, covering her mouth and handing him the scroll. She walked away several yards while Khaldun read it, then read it again, his heart sinking and his skin growing cold.

Dropping the parchment on the ground, he strode over to Mira and gathered her in his arms. She returned his embrace, crying into his chest.

"I'm so sorry," Khaldun whispered.

"I c-can't believe they're gone," Mira said through her sobs. "Devon was so young."

Khaldun didn't know what to say; he held her tight.

"I'm sorry to intrude, my lady," the soldier said, approaching her after a minute, "but Reginald was insistent that we take you home as quickly as possible."

"I need a little time," she replied, pulling away from Khaldun and wiping away her tears. "We'll leave by midday."

"My lady—"

"My decision is final."

"Yes, my lady," he said with a bow, backing off.

"I'd better go inform Mother," Mira said with a sigh.

"I'll go with you," Khaldun told her.

"No," she replied, taking him by both hands and kissing him on the cheek. "Let me do this alone."

Khaldun nodded and Mira headed off to the camp. Feeling lost, he wandered into the palace, and found Badru and Nomad eating breakfast in the great hall. Khaldun had lost his appetite, but didn't want to be alone. He went to sit with them.

"What's wrong?" Badru asked, taking a sip of his coffee. "You look like you just lost your best friend."

"It's Mira," he said, taking a deep breath. "She's going back to Graystone."

"*What?*" said Nomad, concern in his eyes.

"Her father and elder brother were killed in a hunting accident. She's the only heir now, so the holding passes to her."

"I'm sorry," Badru said quietly.

Nomad said nothing, but patted him on the back.

Khaldun sat with them while they ate, then returned to the camp. Mira wasn't there. But Nareen had spotted him as he headed toward his tent, and shot him a smug grin. He was pretty sure he knew where Mira would be, so he headed across the grounds, and out around the back of the palace. Sure enough, he found her sitting on a bench overlooking the river. He sat down next to her; she smiled at him, taking his hand in hers.

"I could leave the troupe and go with you to Graystone," Khaldun said.

Mira stroked his cheek with one hand, her eyes welling up with tears. "This changes everything, though," she said, choking up. "I…"

"You're going to have to be a highborn lady, now. And that means marrying a lord and producing an heir. I don't suppose a penniless wayfarer mage would fit the bill?"

Mira shook her head, sobbing and embracing him. Khaldun held her tight, gently stroking her back. She pulled away after a minute, getting to her feet and taking a deep breath.

"It would never fly. It took a long time for our people to accept *me*, and I'm only half wayfarer. But… I could abdicate."

"Give up your inheritance?" Khaldun asked; Mira nodded. "What would happen to Graystone?"

"I don't know," she said with a shrug. "It would be absorbed into the prince's estate, and he could either keep it or bequeath it to another family. His lands aren't adjacent to the holding, so it would probably pass to someone else."

"It would also mean the end of your father's line, wouldn't it?"

"Yes. I would be giving up all rights and titles along with the holding."

Mira seemed like she had more she wanted to say, so Khaldun waited quietly.

"I want to do it," she said finally, retaking her seat and holding his hand. "I want to do it so desperately," she added with a sigh. "But all those years that I spent biding my time until I could return to the troupe, I always counted on Devon inheriting Graystone and carrying on the family name. I never questioned it—I don't think I even consciously thought about it. That's just the way it was always going to be. Except now it's not."

"This is no easy decision," Khaldun said. "But I know that life isn't what you want."

"No, it's not. But it's not only about me anymore. As long as Father had Devon, I could run off and look after myself. But now I have to consider what his wishes would have been, and he never would have wanted Graystone to pass to anyone outside his family.

"But it's more than that. He was loyal to his people. Always. And they counted on him to protect them and provide for them. Father always said the people of Graystone were our family, and I don't think I can just abandon them. I grew up with those people. Who knows who they'd end up with if I abdicate."

They sat for a long time, holding each other and gazing out at the river. But eventually they headed back to camp and Mira packed up her belongings. Khaldun stayed with her, ignoring the smug looks Nareen kept giving him. Once she was ready, Mira bade her mother farewell, hugging her tight. Then Khaldun headed out toward the castle with her.

They ran into Badru and Nomad on the way. Mira hugged them each in turn, and they wished her well. Badru insisted that she take one of the troupe's horses—hers had been lost in Fosland. So Khaldun accompanied her to the stables, and helped her tack up her mount.

He walked to the castle with her, leading the horse by the reins. They found her escort waiting for her by a grove of trees. Mira let them know she was ready to depart, and they mounted their horses.

"Well, this is it," Mira said, holding Khaldun's hands. He nodded, his eyes welling up. "Promise you won't forget about me this time," she said with a grin.

"Never," he assured her. "We'll be sticking to Dorshire, so maybe we'll make it up to Graystone one day."

"We'll meet again," she said. Mira kissed him passionately.

"I'll love you as long as I live," he told her.

"Me, too."

Mira climbed onto her horse, and followed the soldiers up the road. Glancing back, she gave Khaldun a smile. He waved, then headed back to his tent. Khaldun sat alone for a long time, watching the hustle and bustle of the camp, his heart heavy with this loss. It had felt so good to have Mira back in his life; it was like a dream.

Finally he got up and strolled over to the bench he'd shared with Mira, and watched the sun setting over the waterfall. Nomad joined him, sitting beside him with a bottle in each hand. He gave one to Khaldun; they clinked them together, then Khaldun took a swig.

"Is this the last of Arman's brew?" he asked. "It's sweeter than I remember."

Nomad shook his head. "It's Riyan's. This is the first batch he started brewing with Arman." He took a deep breath. "We haven't had a chance to talk after everything that happened, but I wanted you to know I'm proud of you. And I know your father would have been, too."

Khaldun sighed. "I appreciate it, but he would have done a better job. Oscar and Sophia would still be alive if it had been him."

"You broke into the *Darkhold*, rescued Mira, and retrieved the artifact. Raja never tried anything so dangerous."

"Yeah, but I was too late. Dredmort already created the wraiths."

"And who knows how much more he would be able to do were it not for you. The entire continent is in your debt. Raja was a great wizard and a dear friend. But you have surpassed him in every way."

They sat quietly for a minute, drinking their mead and listening to the roar of the falls.

"I'm sorry about Mira," Nomad said finally. "Are you all right?"

Khaldun took a deep breath, a tear slipping down his cheek. "No. But I will be."

EPILOGUE

nigma was sitting back in his chair, fingers steepled in front of him, gazing at the black pyramid sitting on his desk. It had been days since Isaac had brought it here, meeting Enigma at a secluded location out in the forest to make the transfer. The wizard had removed the thing from the void and handed it to the sorcerer, his relief palpable. Enigma had immediately tucked it back into oblivion.

And now he had a decision to make.

He'd told none of the others. They would insist upon destroying the thing—and they were probably right. If it didn't exist, then there was no chance of Henry—or any other like him—ever acquiring it.

Enigma could destroy it right now. He was one of only a handful of mages who possessed the power and the knowledge necessary to do so. But...

She would want to know about it.

Enigma had probed the artifact, and recognized the full scope of its potential. It was a portal, yes. But not only to the spirit realm. Dredmort had used it to create his wraiths; he could have used it to summon demons, had he possessed sufficient power. He did not. Perhaps he would one day; and someone else could always come along who did. And that was the peril they had to avoid at all cost.

But there were other uses for this. And other than Enigma, she was the only one who would ever recognize it. Those monks at the temple clearly hadn't realized what had fallen into their hands—it was the one on the other side who must have alerted them to the possibilities. But thank the stars, he wasn't strong enough to break through entirely on his own and the monks didn't know how to help.

Enigma made up his mind. Getting to his feet, he tucked the artifact into the void and strode out of his office. It was the middle of the night, and nobody was afoot, but he made himself invisible anyway before leaving the building. He hurried down the steps and headed to the end of the quad. Rounding the corner, he followed the path past the rear of the buildings, and before long, reached the seven-sided tower.

The building had no doors or windows. It was ancient, and few today knew its purpose here—not even all of the governors. Raising his arms to his sides, Enigma spoke an incantation, then walked through the brick wall.

Entering this place was always unsettling. The darkness seemed to extend forever in every direction. Only the stone floor was visible. Enigma took a knee, removing the artifact from oblivion and setting it down before him. And then he waited.

Only moments later, he spotted a golden glow moving through the darkness. It was only a spark at first, but grew into the shape of a woman. As always, he could make out no features, only the outline of her form.

"What is this?"

Knowing the question was rhetorical, Enigma said nothing.

"I'll be damned... I thought they were all destroyed. You must realize what you have here, or you wouldn't have brought it to me."

Enigma made no reply; none was expected. She regarded him for several minutes, and he could sense the same indecision in her that had plagued him.

"Leave it here. I must consider this with great care."

Enigma bowed his head. The artifact vanished, as did the woman, diminishing to a spark before flitting away again. Her departure left the sorcerer alone in the endless darkness. Rising to his feet, he exited the tower.

Ken Warner

To be continued...

331

Made in the USA
Monee, IL
28 August 2022